SHADOW OF DREAMS

Eva Marie Everson and
G. W. Francis Chadwick

PROMISE
PRESS
An Imprint of Barbour Publishing

© 2001 by Eva Marie Everson and G. W. Francis Chadwick

ISBN 1-58660-143-1

Published by Promise Press, an imprint of Barbour Publishing, Inc., P.O. Box 719, Uhrichsville, Ohio 44683, www.promisepress.com

Member of the
Evangelical Christian
Publishers Association

Printed in the United States of America.

Dedication

Eva Marie dedicates this book to the
Northland Writer's Critique Group:
Carmen, Mary, Kaye, Greg, Linda,
Robert, Lee, Carole, Eileen, and Randy. . .
Thank you for pushing me forward.
. . .and to my brother.

G. W. Francis Chadwick dedicates this book to
his mother, Joyce. . .
for her love and encouragement,
and for being "The Hen."

Most of you won't stop to read this part. But for those of you who do I would like to begin by saying that a book such as this comes with a lot of research and development over an extended period of time. For example, what we knew about New York City real estate brokerage was practically nil. Our basic knowledge of hotel management began and ended with the patron's point of view. The aspects of exotic dancing, the positives and the negatives, was a subject matter neither one of us had ever explored.

Over time we lost some of the names of those who came to our rescue, and for that we truly apologize. Please take comfort in knowing that you are an intricate part of our story.

- First and foremost, thank You, Heavenly Father, for allowing all the prodigals to return to Your heart and for giving two of them this story. Thank You for our unlikely friendship. You are the Creator of chance meetings.
- A huge, huge "thank you" to Promise Press: Tim, Greg, Susan, Kelly, and staff. A southern "thanks" to Ramona Richards, who did an extraordinary job editing this work. And, of course, "thank you" to our agent, Mr. Bill Watkins.
- More "thank yous" to: America Online, Donna Ayala-Newman, Tim Bass, Janice Blunt, Lori Boyd, Brianna, Charles Cochran, Jessie "Tink" Dalton, Deneé, Ruth Erhart, Kristi Esarey, Dennis Everson, Jessica Everson, Lon Garber, Stepháne Goldberg, Kris Grantz, Donald Harris, Jennie Jimenez, Eunice Kicklighter, Craig M., Robert A. Marino, Kaye Noble, Northland, A Church Distributed of Longwood, Florida, Jeff & Mona Poynter, Betty Purvis, Preston L. Purvis, Van Purvis, Dick Reis, Laura Taylor, Melanie Van Dell, Peter Wirth, and the residents of Sylvania, Georgia. . .from whom come many fond memories.
- . . .and a final "thank you" to Lois Grayson ("WoWo") for telling us that we should.

The Prodigal Son

Jesus continued: "There was a man who had two sons. The younger one said to his father, 'Father, give me my share of the estate.' So he divided his property between them.

"Not long after that, the younger son got together all he had, set off for a distant country and there squandered his wealth in wild living. After he had spent everything, there was a severe famine in that whole country, and he began to be in need. So he went and hired himself out to a citizen of that country, who sent him to his fields to feed pigs. He longed to fill his stomach with the pods that the pigs were eating, but no one gave him anything.

"When he came to his senses, he said, 'How many of my father's hired men have food to spare, and here I am starving to death! I will set out and go back to my father and say to him: Father, I have sinned against heaven and against you. I am no longer worthy to be called your son; make me like one of your hired men.' So he got up and went to his father. "But while he was still a long way off, his father saw him and was filled with compassion for him; he ran to his son, threw his arms around him and kissed him.

"The son said to him, 'Father, I have sinned against heaven and against you. I am no longer worthy to be called your son.'

"But the father said to his servants, 'Quick! Bring the best robe and put it on him. Put a ring on his finger and sandals on his feet. Bring the fattened calf and kill it. Let's have a feast and celebrate. For this son of mine was dead and is alive again; he was lost and is found.' So they began to celebrate."

LUKE 15: 11–24 NIV

PROLOGUE
September 1975

For late September, the night was hot and muggy. A few blocks from Times Square, in a section of New York City known as Hell's Kitchen, the window of a filthy apartment living room looked out onto the inky, rain-slick street below. It shone like glass, vividly reflecting the colored neon lights that danced overhead. An occasional taxi cruised the avenue. City buses regularly made their screeching stops. A few old-model cars rambled by, spraying pothole mud and reeking of oil and gasoline. Locals gathered on dimly lit sidewalks and the storefront stoops. They spoke in hushed tones of unmentionable exploits. Occasionally, someone let out a hoot and a holler that reverberated eerily off the buildings only to be dissipated quickly by the miasmic dullness of the stale air. Overhead on the wrought iron fire escapes and balconies, men in soiled tank top undershirts were leaning aimlessly with their forearms on the railings and cigarettes hanging from their lips. Sidestream smoke shone gray and white from the lights below. The pervasive odor of cigarette smoke and alcohol hung in the air, blending with the lingering stench of street urine and the scent of inexpensive perfume that wafted from parading prostitutes. From somewhere down the street, the cheers of a craps game could be faintly detected over the sounds of the couple across the street having their nightly dispute. Music from neighboring apartments, honky-tonk bars, and street-corner dances blared and blended, stirring eighteen-year-old Katie Morgan from her drug-induced slumber.

Lying on box springs carelessly shoved into the corner of the apartment's living room, Katie moaned, twisting her trim torso with compelling gracefulness. Blinking her eyes a few times as she straightened herself out, she briefly wondered who and where she was. "Junkies have their own clock," someone had informed her. "It's called 'junk time.' When you're coming down, you just got to wait for that junk clock to stop ticking—that's the worst part." She continued to lie there, shrouded by the squalor of her inauspicious surroundings. It was always like this afterward. . .that moment of unfamiliarity, descending from "junk time." She hated it but always anticipated it. Hating it for taking away the control she so earnestly sought in her life and yet anticipating it as a predictable aftermath of her implacable escape from reality. Even amid the gauzy haze of those few seconds, she knew that if she thought about it long and hard enough, everything would come back to her. Not that she much wanted that right now. Especially right now. She was acutely aware of her blood flowing like dishwater through her veins and her brain dissolving like cotton candy. Taking a deep breath, she became conscious of a profound rumble of thunder, at first wondering if a storm was coming. She smiled ironically at her fogbound thoughts. No storm, she reminded herself. Just the repetitive "thunder" of the subway train as it rumbled beneath that part of earth called Eighth Avenue.

Within seconds, who she was came rushing back. She was Katharine Elizabeth Morgan, the daughter of Carolyn Mills Morgan and the late Stanley Morris Morgan. She had been raised in a large, antebellum home located on Main Street in the small, sleepy, southern town of Brooksboro, Georgia. *From salt-of-the-earth to scum-of-the-earth,* she thought bitterly.

And then where she was came back to her, too. She was in New York City, lying in a roach-infested apartment belonging to her friend's sister. She also recalled how she got there, though it didn't seem real anymore. In the span of four short months, her life had shifted from a dream to a nightmare. For Katie, this city, which opened its arms each year to literally millions of tourists, artistic hopefuls, and business professionals, had become both home and hell. It had only been three months since she and her new friend Abby stepped off the bus at the Port Authority Bus Terminal, but it felt like a lifetime.

She met the sixteen-year-old Abby at one of Atlanta's YWCAs. Both runaways, they gravitated to one another, needing what the other could give. Katie was the elder—and by far the smarter—but Abby was streetwise beyond her years. Her sister, Alexi, lived in New York City. A sister, Abby assured Katie, who would allow them to stay with her and who would get each of them a job. It seemed so promising for Katie: a fresh start without a mother who choked and sucked the life out of her, an adult life with an adult job. For now she would put her plans for college on hold. One day, by her own means, she would achieve her goals.

Now she lay in the corner of Alexi's cluttered and grimy living room on the makeshift bed Alexi's boyfriend put together when she and Abby had shown up three months before. For hours, she tried to sleep off the effects of the drugs and alcohol she had consumed earlier that day. Abby was working her second night at a men's club, Private Dancer, where she was employed as an exotic dancer, leaving Katie alone with Alexi and her live-in boyfriend Mark David, called M.D. The nickname had come about for two reasons. First, due to his initials, and second, he had become the self-appointed "pharmacist" in the Theater District where they lived.

If you can call this living, Katie groaned inwardly. She had been told that Hell's Kitchen was so named because of the numerous mom-and-pop restaurants that spangled the urban landscape with bright lights in dark streets at night. Later, someone informed her that it was because of a nineteenth-century beat cop's observation that it was "as hot as hell's kitchen" there. Right now, she tended to believe the latter.

Over the stores were walk-up apartments, some of them six stories high, with hallways so narrow one turned sideways in order to squeeze by another resident. Not all the apartments had bathrooms. Most of the tenants shared baths located at the end of the hallway. Luckily, Alexi's apartment was one of those with a bath, and Katie did not have to suffer the indignity of sharing a bathroom with a floorful of strangers. Though, she surmised, sharing a bathroom would make them no longer such.

Many of the residents were artistic hopefuls, and many of those hopefuls were dancers who used the studios and rehearsal halls or went on auditions by day and performed in one of the many exotic dance clubs burrowed deeply within the shadowy recesses of Hell's Kitchen by night. Katie had brushed by their willowy forms in the somber hallways, exchanging curt greetings with darting eye contact. Holed up in their lairs by day, the prostitutes, pimps, pushers, pickpockets, muggers, delinquents, and vagrants emerged at night like stealthy foxes in pursuit of prey. They lurked and skulked and prowled, doing what they knew to do to survive, like so many untamed city creatures of the night.

With a disaffected grunt, Katie shifted her hips and long legs on the old, standard-size box springs that she and Abby shared for bedding. The green army blanket underneath her body was scratchy against the smoothness of her sensitive skin, and her stomach acids churned with the long-neglected pangs of hunger. Filtered through the dusky blur of an imprecise memory, she tried to recall the last time she had eaten. Another roll of her stomach and she remembered. Earlier in the day she had eaten the cold, greasy fast-food fries she had found lying alone on the second rack of the old Frigidaire in the less-than-sanitary kitchen. Before that. . .well, she couldn't remember before that, and if she could, it would only serve to make her more nauseous than she already was.

She became aware of muffled music playing on the stereo as it drifted through the wall directly behind her head, which was where the only bedroom in the apartment was located. Alexi and M.D. had put their favorite Moody Blues album on, which typically Katie enjoyed. But tonight the bass line pounded on her brain as if it were a kettle drum. She wished she had the gall to storm into the room and demand a little peace and quiet, but she knew better than to do so. Alexi had been nice enough to allow her and Abby to stay rent-free until they could find a place of their own. M.D. scared the living daylights out of her. Sometimes when the four of them and others from the neighbor-hood sat about on the living room floor passing a joint securely held by a roach clip, she would shoot a quick glance at him. He was short but well-built and had dirty-blond hair that fell in kinky waves beyond his shoulders. His skin was bronzed from his job at a construction site, his lips full and red, and his narrow, slanting, glassy eyes a crystal shade of blue. It was with those menacing, piercing eyes that he leered at her, leaving her to wonder about his intentions. Even more disconcerting was that during those times, he never looked away, but forced her to do so, as if she were some sort of mouse that should scurry back to its hole.

Well, she now thought angrily, she was not some mouse and she did not come from some hole. She was Katharine Elizabeth Morgan of the Brooksboro Morgans. She had, until now, never been hungry, never gone more than a day without a bath or shower, nor had she been ogled by a neighbor she found disgusting. Back home she had friends who loved her, respected her, and—she was certain—missed her. She had lived a seemingly perfect life in which she had been showered with all the desires of her heart by her warm and loving father. She had dreams of going to college. She had not settled on a major yet, but she had been all set to apply for entrance. If only her mother hadn't screwed it up. If only she could have let her be. Left her alone. Stayed out of her life! Katie clenched her teeth together as she brought her tight fists up to her temples. A sound resembling a growl escaped and she shuddered.

Through the wall she could hear the song "Black Satin Blue" begin to play. Katie loved that song. It was haunting. Moving. Relaxing her tense body, she closed her eyes and allowed herself to ride it like an inner tube gliding down the dark murky waters of the Ogeechee River near her home.

Soul calls to soul
Like black calls to blue
Screams pierce the night
When I call to you. . . .

She left home in May, the night before her graduation ceremony was to take place. Eighteen. Angry. Impetuous. She arrived in Atlanta with five thousand dollars of her mother's money that she had, essentially, stolen. Six days later she was robbed of it. She couldn't bear to think now of how it had happened. She had thought about calling her mother, begging for forgiveness, but a peculiar mixture of guilt and pride kept her from doing so. So instead, she found her way to a nearby YWCA, where she met Abby. She was on her way to The Big Apple, she told Katie. She was going to live with her sister, who was an exotic dancer, and Abby was certain she could get them both a job at her club. Katie hadn't been certain of much, but she was sure she didn't want to be an exotic dancer. But with nowhere else to go and no one to turn to, she thumbed her way up the east coast with Abby.

When they arrived—tired, hungry, and haggard—Katie realized what a mistake she had made. After a shower and a meal, she looked around for pen and paper so that she could write a letter to her mother and ask for train fare home. Unable to locate either and too timid to ask, she decided to get a good night's sleep and start fresh in the morning.

But "morning" never came, and four months later she was unable to unearth exactly how things had fallen apart. She had started at the bottom and phenomenally dropped lower with each passing day. She had worked a few odd jobs as a waitress, short-order cook, front desk receptionist at a dry cleaner. But she never lasted for more than a few days. . . two weeks at the most. More than once she had scribbled a note of apology to her mother on the back of an I LOVE NY postcard. She had even stood in front of a pay phone on the street corner, white-knuckled fist wrapped tightly around the receiver, contemplating a collect call. But then she would remember their last months together. . .the last few hours. . .that horrible fight. . . .

Of course, it was more than just that. She was so ashamed of not only taking her mother's money but of allowing herself to be conned out of it. Katie reasoned that in her present state, it was better that her mother not know where she was rather than to know what she had become. She was no longer a virgin. She was a druggie. How could she possibly face her mother with the sins of her past few months?

Surround me in beauty
Beauty that surrounds

Katie opened one eye slowly and took in the room around her. Overhead, a twenty-five-watt bulb hung by a wire from the ceiling, shedding precious little light in the apartment. This was actually a good thing. This was the filthiest place Katie had ever set foot in, and yet horribly, she was now part of it. There seemed to be no fighting it. No turning back. Large throw pillows, dingy and lumpy from use, served as seats instead of chairs. Overflowing ashtrays sitting on upturned cinderblocks were scattered about the room. There were no table and chairs for eating, reading, studying, conversing. Not that they truly ate. A meal was whatever you could beg, borrow, or steal. And no one seemed to care about that either.

Just beyond the living room was an L-shaped opening that served as a kitchen. It, too, was filthy, cluttered, and disorderly. In the beginning, Katie had made several irresolute attempts to clean it, then gave up. Once she began to trip with the others, she found it bearable and acceptable.

And when the truth is heard
The world will know...

Truth? Katie closed her eyes against the pain of what she knew was truth. She wanted to go home. She simply wanted to go home. But that place was lost to her now. She could never go back. Never.

That I love you.

A tear escaped Katie's eye and slid slowly down her cheek. She wiped it away with the long, slender fingers of her too-thin hand, then took both hands and pushed her short mousy-brown hair away from her impressively majestic, almond-shaped face. *Mama,* she thought, then she closed her eyes and waited for the end of the song.

She heard the door to the apartment open with the squeaking of dry, rusty hinges, then click shut. Katie opened her eyes to see Abby, who was, in her way, a pretty girl. She just wasn't overly smart. She wore her auburn hair in a popular bobbed hairstyle. Her skin was milky-white and her eyes a sly shade of green. She was short in stature, petite in build. Katie would have given her eyeteeth to be that short, but instead had topped out at five feet, eleven inches. She knew that some women dreamed of being as tall, but to her, it was a curse.

"Hey, Katie? You awake?" Abby whispered from across the room.

Katie stirred and propped up on her elbows. "Yeah," she answered groggily.

Abby quickly crossed the room, bringing with her the smell of liquor, smoke, and vomit. Katie's nose wrinkled.

"I know I stink," Abby began. "I'll shower up in a minute. But I gotta tell ya. Ya gotta come down and meet Leo, Katie. Leo'll give you a job at the club. He told me he would. And it ain't so bad or nothin'. I mean, you don't gotta do nothin' you don't wanna do."

"You do stink, Abby," Katie responded honestly. "Why would I want to work somewhere that's going to make me come here smelling like you?"

Abby reached down the top of her tight, powder blue T-shirt with the word "Available" airbrushed across it and pulled out a wad of rolled bills. "Here's why. I made close to three hundred dollars tonight, Katie. And I ain't even full time yet. Between the two of us, we can get enough money together to get outta here. Get us our own place. A better place."

A better place. That certainly appealed to Katie. Even if she had to sell her soul to do it. "What do you have to do?" Katie whispered back.

"Just dance."

I just bet, she thought. "What do you wear?"

14

"They give you little outfits."

Katie had seen those outfits. "Little" was the operative word. She grimaced and felt herself dropping lower still. Could she really do this? Could she take off her clothes and allow strange men to watch her dance naked? Just five months ago she had been slow dancing with her boyfriend Buddy at the senior prom. She had worn a blue satin halter-top gown. The bodice fit tightly around her abdomen, the long skirt draped over her slender hips and fell in folds at the top of her feet, which were adorned with flat, white dress sandals. Their song, "Precious and Few," was playing on the sound system. Around them, other couples shuffled their feet as they clung to each other, their heads resting on each other's shoulders. The room was filled with a mixture of English Leather aftershave and Charlie cologne. The twisted ribbons of crepe paper fluttered above their heads, forming a canopy that enveloped swaying, colorful balloons.

She felt like she was too young to be indulging in bittersweet memories of this sort. Trying to cast them aside, she focused her mind on the practicalities of her meager financial situation. And now where would she be dancing? She had seen Private Dancer. It was a club sandwiched between an erotic bookstore and a laundromat. Outside, pink neon signs flashed Girls! Girls! Girls! and reflected gaudily off the black T-shirts worn by the three large men who stood outside, their muscular arms folded across their beefy chests. Inside, the main lounge was dark. A suffocating haze of cigarette smoke hung like billowy clouds, rising slowly to the black steel girders overhead. The putrid odors of beer and liquor mingled with the scent of cheap cologne, imbuing the atmosphere with an even greater sense of ugly reality. A large round stage was situated in the center of the room. Cages that hung by chains from the ceiling were placed near the four corners. Small, round mixed-and-matched tables and chairs were scattered about. Stretched against the back wall was a bar holding dirty ashtrays and small green bowls of peanuts. Behind it were shelves with rows of half-filled liquor bottles and downturned glasses of varying sizes. Overhead, in the center of the room, was a large disco ball that slowly and seductively spun on its axis.

The walls were carpeted in pink indoor/outdoor carpet. The flooring was scuffed, unpolished oak. In the back were rooms—private rooms for private dances—and the management office. Beyond was the locker room for the girls. It was dirty and rundown with gaping holes in the walls that inebriated, strung-out, or infuriated dancers had kicked or punched. Could she really be a part of all this? *Sink or swim, Katie,* she told herself. *Like Buddy used to say, sometimes ya gotta do what ya gotta do!*

"Come on, Katie," Abby pleaded. "I wanna get outta here. I mean, my sister has been real cool to let us stay here and all, but I don't really like M.D. and I dunno. . .this ain't what I had in mind, ya know?"

Katie plopped back onto the uncomfortable box spring. It was more than "not what she had in mind," Katie thought. It was, for her, a living hell. Here, like the song said, there was no night and day. No black and white. Everything was colored in a dingy gray. People, freaky people, came and went in the apartment like they owned the place. "Directionless, bohemian deadbeats," an artist friend of hers described them, apparently including himself in that scathing epithet. There was no food. The noise from the street was deafening. Car horns blew at all hours. People cursed and screamed at one another inside and out. Unattended children cried. The streets were littered with trash and lined with the semirecumbent forms of the homeless. Broken liquor bottles were scattered along the sidewalks, steps, and hallways of the residences and businesses.

Katie was frightened to think of herself ending up here. Even more frightening was the extent to which she was becoming accustomed to all this debris. Katie took a deep breath and exhaled slowly. "All right," she agreed. Her stomach churned once more as she said the words. *A foreshadowing,* she thought with a distorted smile. But she couldn't see any other way out. Her life had become a shadow of what it had once been. . .what it had promised to be. A dark, thin, groundless shadow—into which she would tumble and fall through for the next twenty-five years.

CHAPTER ONE
June 2000

Katie wanted to go home. She simply wanted to go home. And even though she had spent the last twenty-five years forcing herself not to think about the things that fondly cradled themselves in the farthest regions of her mind, she now allowed herself the luxury of freeing those memories and permitted them to wash over her. During the train ride from Virginia to Savannah, she had managed to sleep, although she wasn't sure how. Perhaps it was the gentle rocking of the car on the tracks. Perhaps just the fact that she had been so tired—not so much physically, though she was getting over a summer cold, as mentally. In truth, it had been pure mental exhaustion; and the sleep, though brief, left her feeling strangely alive and alert.

After arriving at the Savannah Amtrak station and securing her luggage, she walked out the glass doors of the small cement block building that some ill-advised person had painted chocolate brown, squinted her eyes against the blinding sunlight, and searched the parking area for a taxi. Within moments, she spotted one to her left. She walked gracefully to it and asked the driver if he was available to drive her to the nearest bus depot.

"That's what I'm here for, Ma'am," he said, with the drawl of a true southerner. While he flipped his meter so that it could calculate her fare, she opened the car's back door and slid into the coolness of the air-conditioned taxi.

"My, that feels much better," she whispered through her teeth.

"Not used to our hot summers, huh?" he asked, pulling the gearshift into drive and swinging out of the parking lot.

She licked her bottom lip. "I'd forgotten how hot it could get down here."

"It's the humidity. You from around these parts?"

"Brooksboro. I grew up there." She shifted her large suitcase over a fraction of an inch, giving herself a little more room. She was wearing a calf-length, sleeveless sundress that was sticking hopelessly to her lower legs. She discreetly pulled the hem of it over her knees, which allowed the cool air to rush up her thighs. Katie glanced at the rearview mirror to assure herself that he had not noticed her minor adjustment.

"Really? You don't sound like you grew up there."

"Oh? I'm always told I sound so southern. I find it hard to believe that I've actually lost my accent."

"Maybe not all of it," he said with a laugh, as he turned out of the Amtrak property and onto the highway. "Where ya been?"

"New York." She glanced out of her window and watched the kudzu-covered pine trees stream past her in a blur. She didn't remember the ivylike vine being as prominent as it appeared now.

"City?"

"Sort of...suburbs...sort of," she answered in a guarded tone, without turning away from the window. "I don't remember the kudzu being this thick," she remarked, changing to a safer subject. Was that honeysuckle growing out there, she wondered. She closed her eyes against the painful pleasure of the memory. How long had it been since she stood in front of a honeysuckle vine, pulling the stem out of the tiny white flowers, then holding it to her lips as the nectar oozed out?

"It's like Yankees in Florida," he called back to her.

Startled, she looked back at him. "How's that?"

"We planted a little bit of the stuff—foreign stuff—to help with erosion and to give the cattle a little somethin' to eat. It's totally taking over, choking the life out of the vegetation. Replacin' all that is rich and sweet about the South with its long fingers."

"Are we talking about kudzu or something else?" she asked lightly.

He gave her a quick glance in the rearview mirror. She saw him smile.

"Kudzu."

She smiled back and decided to go on with their conversation. "Why are we allowing it to take over?"

"It's not a matter of allowing. . .it has no natural enemies. Nothing here to stop it. You know. . .kill it."

She looked out the window again with a brief thought that he was unusually deep for a cabdriver. But he was, in fact, correct. It blanketed the ground, winding its way up the trunks of the trees and choking out the vines of the honeysuckle. It hung thick and unruly through the branches and over the treetops. The Spanish moss, which dripped from the trees like clusters of grapes, could hardly be detected.

Her eyes narrowed. "Sometimes a decision can irrevocably alter the future."

He gave her another quick glance in the rearview mirror. "You talking about kudzu or something else?"

She caught the reflection of his eyes. They were pleasant and teasing. She paused for a moment. The truth lay deeper than her willingness to disclose it, especially with a stranger. She shook her head slightly as if to free it from her thoughts. "Kudzu."

He laughed lightly. "I think I understand."

There was a moment of silence. It was not an uncomfortable silence, because it was as if they both understood the implications of what they had just said. He stared out of the windshield and she resumed her position of looking out the window. He finally broke the silence with, "How long ya been gone?"

She ran her fingertips lightly across her delicate brow as it drew together. She had been gone such a long time. She wondered if she would be recognized. With the help of her hairdresser, she changed her hair from mousy brown to chestnut. In high school she had worn it in a short shag, but now it fell in soft waves to her shoulders. She was a good twenty pounds lighter than when she left. What was once a bit of baby fat was now toned and firm. Her skin had a healthy glow from the outdoor activities she had come to enjoy: tennis, swimming, and golf.

She looked up and caught the driver giving her a questioning stare in the mirror. She shouldn't be discussing her life with anyone—not if she wanted to keep her life in New York obscure. Every move she made from now on, everything she said about her life, could endanger her. Nervous, she gently laid her hands palm down in her lap and studied her manicured nails. They were long. . .and her own, thank you very much. . .and painted blood red. Her mother would think her a harlot, but the two of them would hopefully get past all that.

"Mama used to be so critical of my choices," she whispered inaudibly. "Perhaps now she has even more reason to be."

She glanced out the window again, seeing more of the foliage that grew thick on the sides of the road. "Is that honeysuckle?"

"Yes'm. That's honeysuckle."

"Oh, my. I haven't tasted honeysuckle in—"

"A long time?"

She gave him her best smile, showing white, but slightly uneven teeth. "A very long time."

"Ya wanna stop and check it out?"

"Do you mind?"

"Lady, it's your nickel!" he exclaimed, then swung right onto the shoulder of the road and brought the taxi to a stop. She slid to the passenger's side of the car, opened the door, and got out. Turning back to the driver, she said, "Will you stay or go with me?"

"I'd better not leave my cab," he said, with a shake of his head. Disappointed, she frowned slightly, and he added, "Oh, all right. What's it gonna hurt?"

She smiled in response and waited as he turned the cab off and got out, carefully watching for oncoming traffic. Meeting her on the other side, they cautiously made their way down the slight embankment to the line of trees wrapped in the white flowering vine.

"Watch for snakes now," he instructed. He pulled his sunglasses down low on his nose and peered over the rim.

Her eyes darted from the right to the left, and she shuddered. "Oh, yeah. It's been so long, I almost forgot."

A minute later she plucked a dainty white blossom, snipped its green end with her fingernail, and pulled the stem as she brought it to her mouth. A light trickle of juice fell to her lips and she licked them slowly, closing her eyes in the moment. The perfumed nectar was as she remembered: luscious and sugar-sweet. It took her back to another time.

She was ten years old, in her mother's English-style garden, standing before the honeysuckle bush in the center. The weather was hot and the humidity high. Her fine, mousy brown hair wrapped itself around her neck in damp strands. She pushed her bangs off her forehead. She could hear the other children in the neighborhood and their squeals of delight as they played. Someone was calling her name, "Katie! Where are you? Come on! Don't be like this! Where are you?" She shook her head. She did not want to play anymore. They weren't playing fair and she wanted to be alone. She reached out her chubby little hand and took another piece of the honeysuckle and broke off the tip. Putting the flower to her lips, she sucked at it, forcing the juice into her mouth. It was thick and smooth. Like the juice from the flower, the hurt and the anger began to flow away from her. She turned, then went inside to her mama. . . .

What had once nurtured her childhood dreams now gave her cause for regret, turning her distant memories into bittersweet realities.

"Mmmmm," she moaned and inhaled deeply.

Beside her, the young cabdriver was also tasting the honeysuckle, but without emitting the same exclamation of delight. He treated the moment nonchalantly. The honeysuckle bloomed every year. Obviously, it had been a constant in his life.

Plucking one more of the flowerettes, she turned to him and

smiled. He was a nice-looking young man. In fact, he did not fit the bill as a cabdriver. At least not the ones she had known in New York. This one was no more than thirty, had slightly receding brown hair and almond-shaped brown eyes, a long face with a sturdy chin, and wore a gold hoop earring in one ear.

She spoke her thoughts. "You don't look like any cabdriver I've ever known in New York."

He responded with a smile, showing a single dimple in his left cheek. "You mean, I look American?"

She paused for a moment, squinting one eye against the afternoon sun as she continued to look at him. "Did anyone ever tell you that you look like the guy. . .what is his name. . .that actor. . ."

"All the time."

"Do you know who I'm talking about?"

"Yeah, I know. All the time." He reached over and took another flower off the vine and broke its stem. "Did anyone ever tell you that ya oughta wear sunglasses?" he asked, then brought the broken stem and flower to his lips.

Embarrassed, she laughed as she looked down. "I lost mine somewhere between New York and Virginia. I should stop and buy some."

Without missing a beat, the young cabdriver whipped off his gold-rimmed, John Lennon sunglasses and offered them to her. "Here ya go. Take mine."

She extended her hand as if she would take them, then just as casually withdrew it to the top of her head, raking her long fingernails through her chestnut hair.

"No. No. I couldn't. I mean, thank you, of course, but I. . ."

"No, really. Go ahead. My old man's an optician." He could read the disbelief in her eyes and he chuckled. "I swear! I got another pair in the cab."

Timidly, she reached for them, then slowly and with both hands placed them on her face, securing them behind her ears, then pushing them up on the bridge of her nose.

"Thanks a lot," she whispered, pursing her lips together and suddenly aware of the tears beginning to well up in her eyes. Somehow, this stranger's act of kindness softened her heart—a heart that had become somewhat distrusting.

He didn't speak for a moment. He just stared at her, then the sound of a car horn blowing came from the highway and startled him out of his reverie.

"We'd best get goin'," he said, turning toward the cab waiting on the shoulder of the highway.

She opened her eyes and cleared her throat discreetly. "Oh. Yes. I hope I did not keep you too long. . .cause you any problems."

They began to walk. "No, Ma'am. You're no problem at all."

"By the way," she began in a quiet voice, "my name is Katie."

He gave her a sharp glance. "Nice to meet 'cha, Katie. I'm Kevin." He extended his hand and she returned hers for a firm handshake, making him smile.

She felt the need to explain herself. "I just thought I should introduce myself. After all, we did just pick honeysuckle off the side of the road together." There was a new lilt in her voice.

They reached the cab, and he opened her door for her. Because the car had not been running and the air conditioner was off, a gush of hot air met them. "Whew!" he exclaimed, then added, "you ready to get to that bus depot now?"

She nodded, sliding onto the vinyl seat. This time it was scorching hot against the thin material of her summer dress. She raised herself up sharply until she could adjust to its heat. He caught her action and chuckled as he slammed the door shut. She really had been gone a long time. People here knew to wait a minute or two before jumping into a hot car.

Inside the car, Katie adjusted the skirt of the dress under her. She took in a breath of the stagnant air that enveloped her and sighed. "As ready as I'll ever be. I guess this is it."

She arrived in Brooksboro at quarter till six in the evening. She fully expected the town's sidewalks to be rolled up and the residents long gone to their respective homes for dinner and family hour. Just now mothers would be setting dinner on kitchen tables (dining rooms were kept for special dinners and guests). Fathers, having just arrived from work, would be tossing keys and small change onto trays sitting on bedroom dressers. Then they would spend quality time with their children, finding out what grade little Susie received on her school project and how little Johnny's Little League practice had gone.

She was surprised to find store doors still unlocked and people moving about as if it were the middle of the afternoon. *Progress,* she thought, as a bittersweet smile flashed across her face. Or was it regression? Had rural America fallen backward in its quest to compete with the metropolitan sprawl?

Things had changed, she noted, staring bleakly from the bus window. She had seen a McDonald's on the way in, which had been a Tastee-Freeze when she left twenty-five years ago. She also noted two large national chain grocery stores; one was sprawled proudly beside the interstate highway at State Road 250, which led into town, and another about two miles up the road from there. She wondered if the mom-and-pop grocery was still in business downtown. When Katie was a child, her mother spent one full afternoon a month at a warehouse-sized grocery in downtown Savannah, where she purchased a trunkload of staples. But she always purchased her meats from Mr. Harold's small grocery because she said they were fresher, more tender cuts.

The bus came to a stop in front of what had once been a small, dilapidated service station but was now a modern convenience store and truck stop. The bus driver called for all those getting out at Brooksboro to please step forward. She was the only one who rose from her seat, causing idle eyes to glance up at her with a look that read, "Who, in their right mind, gets off here?" Holding her purse close to her chest, she made her way down the aisle, glancing to the left, then the right, until she reached the door. She took short, shallow breaths in anticipation of getting off the bus, feeling her heart pound through her dress and onto her fingertips that clasped the purse closer still.

"You got bags?" the driver asked her. He was an older man, stocky with bushy eyebrows, wiry white hair, and large wet lips.

She looked away quickly. "Yes."

He heaved himself out of the seat and followed her down the steps and out the door. "I was afraid of that," he commented under his breath. He called to the rest of the passengers, "I'll be back in a minute," as he rapped the side of the bus with the palm of his beefy hand.

She felt, unnecessarily, like a burden. *Welcome home,* she thought, with winsome irony as a twisted smile formed on her lips. There was a deep sense of apprehension mingled with tinges of nostalgia that was starting to overwhelm her.

Minutes later, with her luggage strapped on a wheeled carrier behind her, she began to make her way up the slight incline of the road that led to Main Street. She was met by inquisitive stares and glares from passersby as she wended her way down this "memory lane" to her childhood home. Their looks signaled both frosty curiosity and a glimmer of recognition. "Stranger, who are you and where are you heading?" and "You look familiar, but I can't quite place you." When she spotted people she recognized, she spoke quietly as she passed them, giving a perfunctory nod or greeting. She would call them by name if she remembered it. There was a quick double take of surprise on their part, and she smiled with wry, almost smug, satisfaction. It was almost a game. A part of her felt a supernatural sense of control. Another felt like an intruding phantom, present and yet somehow not really belonging. And yet this was where she had grown up, played, lived for almost twenty years. The effect was otherworldly, transcending time, giving her memories a sense of unreality as if they did not really belong to her but to someone else. She was not sure how well she knew that other person. Or perhaps it was the person she had become she did not really know.

The heat had diminished with the near setting of the sun, and she pushed her new sunglasses up onto the crown of her head. The smile on her face broadened as she thought about him. On the way to the bus depot, he had told her that he wanted to be a novelist and had asked her if she wanted to share her story with him so that he could make a million dollars. Becoming immediately suspicious of his motives, her head had snapped around from lazily gazing out of the side window to staring at him in the rearview mirror.

"What do you mean?" she had asked, her eyes wide.

Catching her expression in his rearview mirror, he had quickly reiterated, "Everybody's got a story, Katie. Didn't mean to frighten you."

Her eyes softened, but the tension in her shoulders remained. Even that had not escaped him, and he had grasped for humor to ease the moment. "It was a joke. . .a kind of a joke. Okay, it was a bad joke, but it was just a joke! I'm afraid I have the natural curiosity of a writer. I wasn't trying to imply that I expected you to share anything with me." His eyebrows had risen as a quizzical expression spread across his face. "Okay?"

She had given him a Mona Lisa smile. "Okay." There was silence for a moment, until she had added, "Are you really a novelist?"

"A wanna-be."

"Ever written anything?"

"I've written plenty," he answered with a chuckle.

She had smiled then. "I mean, ever publish anything?"

"A couple of short stories in local newspapers. I'm just waiting for the right story to come along and then, move over, Michael Crichton!"

"Is he a novelist?"

She had noted a look of astonishment on his face. "Lady, he's the best! Ever hear of *Airframe*?"

She had shaken her head.

"Disclosure?"

She shook her head again.

"Jurassic Park?"

"The movie?"

"The movie was a book before it was a movie. That's what I wanna do. Write a book so great they make it into a movie."

She had tucked a strand of her hair behind her ear and smiled. "I wish you luck."

He had glanced into the rearview mirror and returned the smile with one of his own, dimpled and sincere. "And I thank you." He had looked back at the road, then had added, "How is it you know about Mr. Crichton's movie, but not his book?"

She took a moment to consider her life with her husband, Ben, his endearing overprotectiveness, his all-consuming passion for his own ideals of beauty and culture. The likes of Michael Crichton had no place in that world, a world in which she had become ever more enmeshed. Although she was certain that Mr. Crichton was excellent at his craft—he must be to have so many novels published—Ben insisted that she read the classics: Brontë, Austen, Shakespeare, Jonson. Especially Ben Jonson, one of her husband's favorite classical poets. Her husband had also taught her to appreciate the great southern authors such as Faulkner, Hemingway, and Wolfe. His ideals and aspirations had become hers in a very real way. This man driving her in his cab, as understanding as he appeared to be, could never have been made to understand that without a lot of background information. Even with a lot of time, it would have been difficult to impart what she had with Ben, their special moments of tenderness and hilarity.

But she would never make some flip remark about someone's idol. This was where she and Ben were the most alike from the start, sensitivity to others. Since then, of course, especially in matters of culture, the arts, or history, she had been like putty in his hands, a willing pupil, yet all the while remaining her own person. In fact, he had always encouraged this even while paying for art and music classes at the local university.

Oh! How she missed him. She was going home but away from the man she loved. It didn't seem right, but it was something she had to do.

"I saw it advertised. Didn't they make *Disclosure* a movie as well? I think I saw a poster about it at a shopping mall. I noticed it because. . . well, before I married. . .ah. . .I used to like Bruce Willis. *Moonlighting*.

I never missed an episode."

"Hey, me neither! Great show! And that Shepherd. . . ," he had said, then added a low whistle. "And those legs. . .although I don't have to tell you about legs!"

She had noticed a slight blush cross his face as he quickly added, "I didn't mean any offense."

She giggled. In her childhood, family and friends had commented on how tall they thought Katie would be as an adult. All the fuss made her feel special, as if she had been uniquely set apart. As an adolescent, though, her height had been her nemesis. Her classmates teased her mercilessly. After school she would dash up the staircase to her room, throw herself on her bed, and cry until there were no tears left. Neither of her parents had been aware of her plight, until one afternoon when her father had come home early from the office and she collided with him in the foyer, the tears already starting to flow.

"Kitten," he said tenderly. "What's this? Tears?"

She sobbed openly as he stroked her hair. When she was done, he tipped her chin so that she looked up into his handsome face and said, "You know, of course, that only tall women can be models. A very elite group of girls. I would suppose that your friends are jealous because they know that you can. . .oh, I don't know. . .go to New York or Hollywood and be a glamorous model. But they never will. No, no. Never in a million years. Because New York and Hollywood only use tall women."

"Really, Daddy?"

Her father raised his hand as if to take an oath. "My word as a gentleman," he said, his chest bowed out and his chin raised proudly.

From that day forward she felt differently about being statuesque; and though it didn't alter the teasing, it changed the way she felt about it. Years later, Ben told her she held a glorious power with "those legs going all the way up to your throat." How she loved him for that!

"No offense taken," she had replied to Kevin.

"I suppose you've had to deal with comments about your height before, haven't you?"

28

"Only my whole life," she had answered good-naturedly.

"I'm not being critical!" he had continued in an effort to further vindicate himself. "It was a compliment! Believe me!"

She had smiled. "I believe you!"

Now, she reached Main Street and shook thoughts of him away dismissively as she turned right and walked toward the part of town where the commercial zone ended and the residential began. There, old houses stood proudly on lush lawns. An arcade of trees sheltered the pavement that separated the orderly row of houses that bespoke tranquillity if not wearisome predictability. Large dogwoods, magnolias, and multicolored azalea bushes had been in full bloom just two months previous. Katie regretted that she had missed seeing the explosion of color that took place in her hometown during the spring of the year. Long stretches of sidewalk separated the properties from the streets. . .sidewalks where she had played hopscotch and marbles as a child, gossiped with neighborhood girlfriends as an adolescent, and sauntered lazily on with boyfriends in the cool of the evening when she came of age for dating. She was struck with the cutesy quaintness of it all; and after her life in New York, it all seemed rather oppressively tedious, in stark contrast to her fast-paced lifestyle. But it was home.

Her mother's house was no more than three blocks away. She noticed immediately that the two homes on facing corners adjacent to the original town buildings had been converted into businesses. There appeared to be a convenience store behind the house on the left. A moment of panic seized her. What if her childhood home had been converted? What if it were now a law office or a funeral parlor?

She began walking again, this time at a quicker pace. Looking around, she noted the changes with shrewd concern as well as those things that had remained the same. The Richardsons' home had been bricked. The Phillipses' home had an engraved wooden shingle hanging by a chain off the front porch ceiling that read: The Williamses. . .Sam, Becky, and Chase. She wondered where—and when—the Phillipses had moved.

She stopped when she was in front of the house that children used to call "haunted." It had been bricked and the second-story, center window had been replaced with stained glass. She and her friends would stare at that window for hours, anticipating the ghost of Old Mr. Cheevers walking past it. Legend was that Mr. Cheevers had found his young wife in a compromising situation with his best friend, grabbed a butcher knife from the kitchen, and began swinging at the couple. According to the story, the man's right index finger had been severed from his hand, and Mrs. Cheevers had accidentally been stabbed in the heart. As she lay dying, her life's blood oozing from her chest, her lover had run out of the house, screaming in panic. Mr. Cheevers calmly walked out of the bedroom, past the central upstairs window to the room across the hall. There, it was said, he hung himself.

Katie shuddered at the memory. But then she remembered the day she and her best friend Marcy had stood quietly waiting in front of the house. They had been about ten years old at the time.

"I think I saw a man without an index finger yesterday," Marcy whispered. A slight breeze had freed strands from her waist-length braid, and they gently caressed her cheek.

Katie's eyes never left the window. "Are you sure?" she whispered back.

"Well, it was hard to tell. He had gloves on, but the index finger didn't look filled out."

"Ooooh. . .you think he could be the man?"

"I asked my mama, but she said the story was nonsense."

"Mamas say things like that. They don't want us to know about bad things in the world."

"Do you believe the story is true, Katie?" she asked, brushing the strands away with her small hands, only to have them return to tickle her face.

"Would I be here if I—Wait a minute! I think I saw. . .I think I saw. . ." Katie's voice increased in intensity and pitch.

Marcy jumped up and down. "What? What?"

In reflex, Katie jumped beside her. "I saw eyes! Yellow, piercing eyes!"

Marcy's scream had been so loud that if Mr. Cheevers's ghost had been inside, it would surely have vacated the property. Katie turned and watched as her friend ran down the sidewalk toward Katie's home, and Katie was no more than six feet behind her.

Apparently, no one continued to believe the ghost story. Draperies hanging at the open windows billowed inward, and Katie could detect the faint outline of furnishings. Wondering who might be brave enough to live in a haunted house, she turned and began making her way up the sidewalk.

Before she had time to prepare herself fully, there it was. . .her home. It was a broad, white, two-story home with a massive wraparound porch and thick white columns that seemed to strain under the weight of the second-floor balcony. Before her were two narrow steps that led to the concrete walkway leading to the six wide steps up to the front porch, which was painted steel gray. The double front doors had the beveled, oval glass she had always complained about bitterly.

"It allows people to practically see into our lives," she whined, wrinkling her nose. She and her parents were standing in the foyer, observing the doors.

Her father smiled knowingly as he shifted the stem of his pipe from one side of his mouth to the other. "Now, Kitten. . . ," he began, using the endearment he bestowed upon her at birth. In fact, she never recalled him calling her anything but Kitten. She sometimes thought that she wanted Ben to call her by that name, but then decided that if used by anyone else—even Ben—it would take away the special bond that had existed between father and daughter.

Her mother immediately interjected into the conversation. "Don't pacify her, Stan." Carolyn lightly brushed her fingertips down the glass without actually touching them as she turned to Katie. "The fact of the matter is, Katharine," she began calmly, "these are the original windows on the door. Therefore, they are a part of history and should never be changed if at all possible. I know you don't understand this now, but you will one day."

Her mother had been correct. Katie had not understood then, but it was obvious to her now.

Katie felt torn between embracing her childhood with all its mingled memories and returning to the fear and uncertainty of her present plight in New York. She held her breath for a moment, then heaved the luggage up the tiny steps. She took her time going up the walkway, ever aware of the sound of her footsteps against it, followed by the rolling of the wheels of the carrier. She couldn't remember the last time she had walked in through the doors ahead of her, but she certainly recalled the last time she had walked out of them. She had been eighteen years old. Angry. Impulsive. Determined.

Her heart felt heavy. It was too much. Too, too much. . .

And then she was at the bottom of the front porch steps. She decided to leave her luggage at the base, then took one deliberate stair after another until she reached the stretch of the porch where her mother's ferns spilled from white wicker planters between the front porch rockers. Katie blinked at them. Even lined up in a tidy row, they seemed lonely and isolated. Vacant. Waiting for members of the family to come out in the cool of the evening to sit quietly and rock to and fro, to speak in quiet tones, and to allow the cares of the day to slip along the old boards of the porch, down the steps, and into the night.

Taking another deep breath, tugging slightly on her dress, then pressing the front and back of it with her palms, she considered herself ready. She moved assuredly toward the old doors, rang the doorbell, and then turned back toward the street.

"Who says you can't go home again?" she muttered to herself rhetorically and then silently answered: *Well, Thomas Wolfe, but he was referring to a quest for lost values.* She raised her eyebrows and beamed. Well, Mr. Wolfe may have had a point: You could never entirely recapture your youth. Yet, she never imagined herself again getting this close to all the associations of hers and the accompanying memories, potentially charged with such emotion. And she could never see herself being as idealistic as Wolfe. In fact, this place, these people, compared to the world she had come to know, were the embodiment of those "lost values."

Vastly different worlds, imposing their values compellingly on any and all in their midst. Was this place the idealistic world Wolfe had sought so passionately? More specifically, could it become her life again?

Within moments she heard the still familiar footsteps of her mother. She clasped her hands together and whirled around as the front doors opened simultaneously with the front porch light coming on overhead.

"Yes?" the distinguished voice inquired. When Katie examined her mother's face, it bore only a vague resemblance to the face she had known. The light brown hair that had once stylishly framed her face was now stark white and closely cropped. Furrowing the soft cheeks and pleasingly high forehead lay deep wrinkles wrought by time and travails. The dark brown eyes that had once held fire and laughter were now rather dull and sunken. Her slim, girlish figure could now best be described as frail. The pitiless, unrelenting march of time had not left her unscathed.

It had played a wicked trick.

And in that moment, her mother saw through the more than twenty years and recognized her only child, her daughter. A hand flew to her throat, clasping it in astonishment.

"Oh, my—"

Katie smiled weakly, a smile that she knew did not show in her eyes. "Hello, Mama. I'm home."

CHAPTER TWO

Returning home after being away for so many years was an eerie experience. Even surrounded by the trappings that had compelled Katie to leave, it was as if her childhood held a special charm for which she was yearning. It was only those last few years spent in the home of her youth that she tried to push from her memory. Standing in the foyer of the antebellum home, the curious sensations she felt seemed to stem from two sources. First, standing here in her childhood environment induced a stream of memories that were genuine and unaffected by adult experiences and judgments. And yet, second, she was observing this environment with a fresh eye, almost as if seeing it for the first time. The immediacy contrasted strangely with the distance she felt from those experiences. She had deliberately distanced herself physically and psychologically from her childhood. Being now confronted with those memories, made stranger still by her prolonged absence, she was also confronted with the choices she had made with her life and what it was within her that had prompted this extended separation from her mother, her home, her friends. She allowed those feelings to fill her with regret and even a longing for what she had missed. But her somber mood was momentary because she now became enraptured by the long-lost familiarity of her present surroundings. It was with a sense of awe that her eyes slowly took them in, feeling inspiration she had never before known.

Other than new carpeting and fresh coats of paint, the interior of the house was very much as she always remembered it. At the left of the foyer was a grand staircase; its mahogany banister gleamed, portions of it reflecting patches of mottled color from the shafts of refracted light that filtered through the oval stained glass window over the first landing. On the opposite wall going up the staircase was a collection of Baroque lithographs, framed in heavy gold leaf and covered with beveled glass. A small table with a mahogany base and intricately carved marble top sat against the short wall in the hallway that led to the back of the house, where the library, family room, and the large kitchen were.

To her right were closed French doors that gave into the formal parlor. To her left a matching pair of doors led to the morning room. Those doors were open, and she casually glanced into the room. The overstuffed furniture was in a Victorian pastel floral print, and the gold leaf–framed prints on the walls were of several varieties of old-fashioned roses, hung there long before the cultivated tea rose became the rage. A lit milk glass lamp sitting on one of the rose-carved tables gave the room a warm and inviting glow. She had always loved that room. She would spend hours within its sanctuary, reading one of her mother's historical books plucked from one of the library shelves or journaling in her diary that she kept well hidden behind the curio cabinet that held her mother's collection of miniature china tea sets.

She wondered if it was still there. She doubted it. She blissfully thought of the prospect of curling up on the sofa, her favorite dog-eared book in her hands, a cup of hot cinnamon tea perched on the table beside her. She would truly be home.

Glancing up the staircase, she found herself wondering if her collection of stuffed animals was still piled in the center of the yellow floral bedspread on her bed. Or if the matching Priscilla curtains still hung at the windows. She momentarily remembered the powder blue princess telephone on her bedside table and wondered if she could ever again recreate the secure feeling of being propped up in bed, mounds of pillows behind her, giggling to friends during endless phone conversations.

Katie heard the front door close behind her, bringing the moment of reflection to an end. After an uncomfortable and tight hug between mother and daughter, Katie pulled her luggage farther inside the foyer, then followed her mother to the kitchen in the back left corner of the house, where chicken had been frying in a deep pan, turnip greens were simmering, steaming corn on the cob was already placed on the small Formica kitchen table, and hot biscuits were browning in the oven. Her mother looked back at her, feeling somewhat ill at ease as they walked into the dimly lit kitchen. She then grabbed her oven mitt and pulled out the biscuits.

"You're just in time," she said softly.

"What can I do to help?"

Her mother looked around as if silently looking for the answer, then said, "Put the ice in the glasses and pour the tea. Oh, and set another place at the table."

Nothing more was said as they set about doing their tasks. She looked at the table and saw the single place setting, cringed at the loneliness it represented, then continued performing the tasks her mother had requested of her. It took a few moments for her to reacclimate herself. But after opening a few wrong cabinets, the layout of her mother's kitchen came back to her.

They moved about silently, taking food off the stove and placing it in serving dishes, then onto the table. When they finally sat, they bowed their heads for the blessing, then mechanically spooned the food onto their plates and proceeded to eat.

"I am amazed at the amount of food you cooked for yourself," Katie commented in an effort to ease the pain of their silence. Her mother made no comment. She only pressed her lips tightly together and nodded slightly.

Katie stared down at her plate, thinking that perhaps her return had been a mistake. She should have gone elsewhere. She could have spun the globe on her husband's desk and pointed out a destination, then packed her bags and left. But she had chosen to return to her mother, to the safety and tranquillity she prayed to find here. Perhaps that had only been in her imaginings. Safety and tranquillity would have to be found in another place. Tomorrow morning she would leave. This time she would say good-bye.

Through the palpable tension, her mother suddenly exclaimed, "Katharine!"

Katie jumped in her seat and looked up into her mother's face. There were tears brimming in her eyes. "Where have you been?"

Katie slowly dropped her fork onto her plate and dropped her eyes. She took a deep breath, then exhaled slowly. "New York."

"For twenty-five years?"

Katie began to chew on her bottom lip—a habit she had long since lost. Until now. "Mama, please. Let's not get into this tonight, okay? I'm so very tired. . .and hungry."

"Are you sick? You sound as though you've been ill."

"I've had a bit of a cold. I'm okay now, really." The chewing continued.

"How did you get here? To Brooksboro?"

The chewing stopped. She took another deep breath and answered, "I took the train to Savannah. Then a bus."

"Why didn't you call? I could have met you in Savannah."

Katie looked back up to her mother's face and recognized the strength that had returned there. Her mother had always been strong willed and controlling. It was what had finally come between them. Katie wondered if it might be the one factor that could bring them back together. She would need her mother's fervor for survival if she was to make it through the next few weeks or months.

"It was best this way."

"What do you mean, 'best this way'?"

Katie looked around the room to gain time before she answered. The kitchen cabinets and countertops had been replaced. The cabinets were a light oak and the countertops were tiled in white squares. The appliances and light fixtures were contemporary. There was bright, new linoleum on the floor. The wallpaper had been changed to a dusty rose

Victorian stripe with matching floral border. The kitchen table where they sat had a light oak base with tile top bordered by light oak. Katie thought the room to be an incredible blend of Victorian and modern—the past meeting the present.

The irony of it caught in her throat as she started to answer her mother, who looked resignedly at her and said, "Well, I can see I'm not going to get anything else out of you." She took another bite of food, then continued. "I suppose you took a cab to the house."

"No. I walked." She laughed lightly. "You should have seen some of the faces! They thought they knew me, but they weren't sure where from. It was as if they had seen a ghost."

Carolyn Morgan did not look amused. If anything, she looked disgusted. "I see no humor in that, Katharine. You'll have the gossips waggling their tongues by morning. I can see it now. Madelyn Simpleton: a coffee cup in one hand and a telephone in the other."

Katie had not thought of Madelyn Simpleton in years. She wasn't a real person. She was the name her mother gave to the type of woman who thrived on gossip and some false sense of social prominence or self-importance. While her mother certainly enjoyed a satisfactory social position in their little town, she never resorted to gossip. Katie took after her mother in this regard.

"I don't think anyone recognized me." She looked down to her food. *Would it be such a crime if they had?* she wondered.

"Not with those nails and that hair they didn't," her mother muttered.

There it was. She knew it would come and now there it was. Right before her. Suspended in the air between them, a juicy morsel taunting them: Which woman would take the bait? Which one would bite first? And probably choke on it. Katie determined it would not be her. She wouldn't fight her mother now. Not on their first night together. Not when she needed her so very much.

She looked into her mother's eyes. "I'm sure you're right."

Her mother looked flabbergasted. What? *No fight,* her expression seemed to say. She took a moment to think this over. Katie could almost hear her thoughts. Perhaps her daughter had grown up. Perhaps she now knew how to choose her battles.

"I never thought I'd hear you say that," she said, then smiled at her daughter.

Katie returned the smile, broad and childlike. "Neither did I!" On impulse, she extended her left hand, palm up, across the tiled tabletop. She heard her diamond engagement ring clank against it. Carolyn heard it, too. Reaching out, she took her daughter's manicured hand and squeezed it gently. Then she turned it, causing the huge diamond's Amsterdam-cut facets to sparkle with a brilliance she had never before witnessed. The effect was subduing, even for Carolyn Morgan. She brushed her thumb across the stunningly radiant solitaire, then looked at her daughter.

"You're married."

Katie withdrew her hand from her mother's and placed it in her lap. Her right hand automatically grasped her left one.

"Yes," she whispered.

Carolyn looked behind her, as if her son-in-law would now casually step into the room. She again looked at Katie. "Is he here? With you?"

Katie had a mental image of Ben sitting on his suitcase in front of the convenience store and she smiled. Her Ben, who was the epitome of culture and refinement.

"No, Mama. He's not here."

"Are you separated?" There seemed to be genuine concern in her voice.

"Only by distance."

Carolyn stared at the ring for a long moment. Her face showed her confusion, then she took a deep breath, as if setting her thoughts aside. "I have ice cream for dessert." It was said more like a question than a statement.

Katie knew her mother had called a temporary truce. She narrowed her eyes mockingly. "What kind?"

"Chocolate Chip Cookie Dough."

Katie rolled her eyes toward heaven. "Oh, my—" she moaned. *There goes my diet,* she thought. "It's my favorite! How did you know?"

Carolyn pushed back her chair and stood, made her way toward the kitchen cabinets, and took out dessert bowls. "It just so happens that it's mine, too."

Katie awoke to the sounds of birds singing their morning songs outside her bedroom window. She had slept with it open, something she had not dared to do since she had left. The sweet smell of gardenia hung in the air about her, no doubt from her mother's flower garden below. She sat straight up in her bed, gently rubbed her eyes, then brushed her hair away from her face with her nails. Her back arched in a luxurious stretch, then curved as she relaxed.

She had not studied the room last night. She had been too desperate for a hot shower and sleep. Even now, her luggage was wide open on the polished oak floor near her bed. She had pulled out lingerie, her toothbrush and toothpaste, and left the rest for later. She looked over at it. She had packed enough clothes for a week. If she stayed longer, she would have to purchase more. She moaned at the thought.

Swinging her long, tanned legs over the bed, she stood and walked to the window. The hideous bedspread and curtains had been replaced by a subtle floral from the Laura Ashley Collection. The stuffed animals were boxed and put away, succeeded by Victorian throw pillows. The antique Queen Anne cherry dresser, bedside table, and chest of drawers that matched her bed were devoid of the teenage paraphernalia she had left behind. Makeup, books, photos, bristle hairbrushes, briefly worn clothes, and candles were no longer cluttering the surfaces. Instead, her mother had placed a pair of Victorian lamps on the dresser, a framed photograph of Katie at sixteen on the chest of drawers, and a small lamp. The old princess phone was still on the bedside table.

Katie quickly made the bed. She unpacked her clothes, hanging them in the closet or folding them into the chest of drawers. She took all her toiletries to the adjoining bathroom and set them on a white wicker shelf above the toilet. She brushed her teeth and hair, which she pulled up into a pony tail high on her head. On her way out, she paused to take in the old, freestanding bathtub. Its white enameled surface had small chips in places along the rounded rim on the outer edge of the flange. The bear claw iron feet that supported it seemed to have been freshly painted. It brought back memories of evening bath times. As a small child she had been an unwilling participant, but later she came to relish the indulgence of a long, languorous soak. She momentarily wished her life could be that simple again.

Back in her bedroom, she chose a pair of jeans and a white pocket tee to wear. She rolled up the cuffs of the short-sleeved tee, then slipped her feet into simple white sandals. Before leaving the room, she grabbed her purse, left beside the bed the night before. Reaching deeply into one of the hidden, zippered pockets, she brought out an envelope and held it to her breast. Inside was a cashier's check in the amount of one hundred thousand dollars. She glanced around the room for a safe hiding place. Her shrewd eye caught the framed photograph standing on the chest of drawers. Deciding on the space between the photograph and the backing, she stepped purposefully toward it. After placing the frame face down, she carefully swiveled the retaining clips to one side and removed the cardboard backing. Surely the check would be safe cached here. About as safe as she was in this town, she thought ruefully. Replacing it carefully, she angled it as her mother had positioned it there, then walked toward the bedroom door.

When she opened it, she was met with the scent of her mother's face cream. As a child, its sweet balminess had brought her comfort. It told her that her mother was both awake and in the home. Taking a moment before heading downstairs, she walked down the hall and opened the wide door to the guest bedroom and was struck with the little things that had not changed. The semimusty smell, emanating from the massive antique furnishings, old quilts sewn by her grandmother, and lace table runners tatted by her great-grandmother, remained. She found it refreshingly reassuring. Right now she could use as much security as she could latch onto. Closing the door, she continued down the hall toward her mother's bedroom, the scent of the face cream becoming stronger still. The door was open and Katie stepped in timidly. In this room, as a child, she had all but worshiped her mother's daily rituals performed here. In the coolness of the summer mornings, Katie would sit Indian-style on the oval wool rug, her head tilted back as she watched her mother prepare to work in her garden.

Carolyn would slip out of her satin nightgown and into a pair of well-worn slacks and a camp shirt, then sit on the stool in front of the vanity to pull on her socks and sneakers. Swinging around to face the mirror, she would take the jar of face cream in hand, whip the top off with a quick turn of her wrist, then lightly brush the sweet-smelling cream across the elegant features of her face. She would then turn back to her daughter, slap her hands down onto her thighs, and say, "Well, Miss Priss, let's get you ready, shall we?" And Katie would nod as she stood and slipped her tiny hand into the softness of her mother's grasp.

Little about the room had changed. The oval rug still lay on the floor next to her mother's bed. The jar of cream still sat next to her mother's silver brush set. There wasn't any perfume on the vanity top. Her mother had never worn any and apparently continued not to. The antique Rice bed was the same, but it held a new comforter set: a woven, sage-colored jacquard with classic scroll column stripe, finished with satin rope cording. There were two matching European shams behind two standard shams. The look was finished with several matching toss pillows and a neck roll. At the base of the bed was a matching fringed throw. The two floor-to-ceiling windows in the room were devoid of draperies, but had scarf valances in the woven jacquard material of the comforter set. In front of one of the windows was a Louis XV–style tapestry chair and in front of the other a small table with a Waterford accent lamp and two old leather-bound books lying next to it. The walls had been painted creamy saffron, and the trim and brick fireplace had been painted off-white. Above the mantle was a gilded Baroque accent mirror. On the left side of the mantle were three items: a miniature hope chest and two small, framed photos. Somehow called out to by them, Katie slowly walked across the room to where they sat at angles to each other. She recognized them immediately. One was a photograph taken of Katie and her father building a sandcastle at the beach, and the other of her and her mother, down on their hands and knees in her mother's garden. Carolyn was digging a small hole, while Katie held the flowers that would be planted there. A faint smile came to her lips, and she turned and walked out of the room.

When she reached the top of the staircase, she was greeted by the rich inviting aroma of freshly brewed coffee—her passion—and she skipped down the stairs, then walked briskly into the kitchen. She thought her mother would be there, but she wasn't. Reaching into the cabinet for a coffee mug, she glanced over at the clock that hung on the wall over the stove. It was almost nine forty-five. She hadn't expected it to be so late. She prepared her coffee the way she liked it—creamy and sweet—then glanced out the window that looked out to the backyard. It, too, was pretty much as she remembered it: wholly taken up by the English garden her mother had designed and begun when they had first moved to this great, old house. She spotted her mother there, dressed in overalls and a long-sleeved cotton shirt, down on her knees in the front section of the flower garden. She appeared to be planting more flowers.

Making a decision to join her, she walked from the kitchen into the family room and out the back door. Her mother had her back to the house and didn't seem to be aware of Katie's presence until she spoke. "I see your thumb is as green as it ever was."

Carolyn neither stopped in her work, nor looked up. She replied matter-of-factly, "And I see you still sleep as late as you ever did."

Katie took a sip of the hot coffee and began to walk the brick path that wove through the garden. She felt the old tinge of annoyance at her mother's deliberate sarcasm. It didn't bother her, as it would have normally. She was back home. She felt more rested than she had in a long, long time. And it was a gorgeous day. Nothing would spoil it. Nothing! She stopped in front of the Moroccan Broom that grew up and spilled over the north wall of the high wooden fence. The leaves, which were covered with silky white hairs, gave it a silvery appearance, and the yellow blooms of its flowers permeated the air with the scent of pineapple.

"Actually, I tend to get up pretty early these days. I suppose I was just so tired. But I seem to be over my cold." She took a deep breath. "I can actually breathe again." She turned and looked at her mother, who continued to dig little holes in the rich, dark earth, then stuff flowers into them with her gloved hands. "How did you sleep?"

Carolyn patted the dirt around what Katie thought was a pansy. She had never been very good at recognizing flowers. There were, of course, those that she knew on sight. There were climbing roses growing up a trellis against the back of the house. Carolyn had chosen Climbing Ena Harkness, for its deep red color and very rich fragrance. Groupings of multicolored tea roses were planted in the sunniest part of the garden. Violet-blue Japanese Wisteria dripped along the back wall. A portion of the brick walkway was bordered with gangly daisies. Her mother used to tell her that they smiled up at her when walking past them, and therefore they were the happiest of flowers. In front of the south wall of the garden were various breeds of tropical-colored day lilies. Katie remembered that as a child she had asked her mother, "If daisies are the happiest of flowers, are day lilies the saddest?"

"Why do you think that?" her mother had inquired.

"Because they only live a day," she had answered with certainty. "If I knew I only had a day to live, I would be very sad."

Her mother had patted her head lightly and smiled. "You may be right, Katharine. I suppose I hadn't really thought of it that way. But what about butterflies? They only live a couple of days, but look how happily they flit through the air. And they are every bit as beautiful as the day lily. I would guess the Lord put them there for us to enjoy and to show us that they just are without having to labor or toil like we have to. And yet they are so absolutely beautiful."

It was one of the few moments Katie remembered having felt really connected with her mother.

Carolyn brought Katie out of her languid reminiscence by slapping her hands together to rid the gloves of the dirt that clung to them. She sat back on her upturned feet and looked at Katie squarely. "Well, I'd have to say I slept better than I have in twenty-five years, knowing where you were. Knowing you were alive."

Katie turned slightly so as to break the line of eye contact between her and her mother and found herself staring directly at the honey-suckle bush that continued to bloom in the center of the garden. She instinctively walked toward it. "Did I tell you I plucked honeysuckle from the side of the road yesterday?"

Carolyn gathered her gardening tools, then stood. She didn't answer her daughter's question. Katie was aware of her mother's silence and continued as if there had been a response. "In Savannah. I saw it and commented on it to the cabdriver. He actually stopped the cab and allowed me to pluck some." She pulled a bloom from the vine, held it to her nose, and breathed in the scent. "It tasted as wonderful as I remembered. And Kevin—the cabdriver—stood right there and did the same. But I don't think he found the moment as special as I did. And the kudzu! I just couldn't get over what was happening with the kudzu!"

Katie whirled around to face her mother and stopped short in her effusive description of yesterday's novelty. The only thing left of her mother's morning ritual was the old, green wheelbarrow. Apparently, her mother had fired the last shot of the morning. Katie took a deep breath, dropping the fragile, white flower, and began to make her way back into the house.

Around noon, Katie went into the kitchen to make lunch. She found a head of romaine lettuce and Caesar salad dressing in the refrigerator. Looking into the pantry, she found croutons. Balancing the three items in her hands, she walked to the cutting board next to the sinks and began to prepare the salad. Within moments she heard her mother walk in behind her and she peered over her right shoulder.

"I'm making a salad. Want one?"

"That'll be fine," Carolyn answered in a monotone. "I'll get the ice in the glasses and the tea."

Katie reached into a cabinet and brought out two salad bowls. As she tore fresh, deep green lettuce into each, she gazed out the window to the little flowers that her mother planted earlier. In an effort to make conversation, she commented, "Your pansies are very pretty, Mama."

"What pansies?" Carolyn asked, setting the ice-filled glasses on the kitchen table.

"The ones you planted this morning."

"Pansies don't grow in the summertime, Katharine."

Wiping her hands on a towel, Katie turned. "I thought they were pansies."

"They are impatiens. Pansies grow in the wintertime."

Katie brought the salad bowls to the table. "Oh. Do you plant pansies? I mean, will you? This winter?"

Carolyn walked to the silverware drawer and brought out two salad forks, then grabbed two paper napkins out of a wicker basket that sat close by on the countertop. Bringing them back to the table, she answered, "I always have. They bring the color of summer to the dead of winter."

Simultaneously they sat, bowed their heads for a quick blessing that Carolyn gave, then began to spear their salads with the forks. They ate in silence for a few minutes until Carolyn spoke softly. "You were always crazy about purple pansies, though I doubt you remember it."

Katie looked up. "I remember little, velvety purple flowers. I thought they were violets."

"I never planted violets in my life. I like violets, but I never planted them. But I always planted those pansies. Every year. Just for you. I suppose to remember you by. Even after you were gone, I'd plant them. Twenty-five years of pansies that you never even saw."

Katie tried to determine if her mother was being nostalgic or if she was angry. It was difficult to know. "I shall look forward to seeing them this year," she answered tenderly.

Carolyn cocked an eyebrow upward. "You'll be here?"

Katie shifted nervously. "I don't know if I will be living here, but I promise I'll come to see the pansies. No matter what."

Carolyn answered by looking at her salad and continuing to spear at it. Katie decided that the best thing to do was to change the subject. "I saw that someone moved into Old Mr. Cheevers's house. I can't imagine doing that. Someone new in town, I suppose."

Carolyn looked up and Katie saw a glint of mischief in her eyes. "You'll never believe me when I tell you who lives there."

Katie's brows drew together while her eyes narrowed playfully. "I'm game."

"Marcy and her husband bought that house."

Katie began to choke on her food. She reached for her tea glass, took a few sips, then swallowed. When she regained her composure, she said, "I know you're kidding me!"

"They moved in about ten years ago. Right after Mark was born."

Katie felt the air go still around her. She momentarily became deaf. Life had continued without her. Nothing had stayed the same. Not even Marcy. The one constant in her life, especially during her tumultuous adolescence, had been Marcy. Their parents had been neighbors forty years ago, living side by side in a duplex located on the other side of town. Carolyn Morgan and Roberta Anderson went through the joys and pains of pregnancy together. Marcy had been born just weeks before Katie. They had been more like twins, joined at the hip.

In high school, Marcy contemplated pursuing a law career. She would be a prosecuting attorney to be reckoned with, she said. She'd live in Atlanta and make lots of money. If she married, and that was a big if, he would also be a professional. They wouldn't have children, she said. Children would cramp her style. But they would have parties. Lots and lots of parties. And Katie would be invited. Katie, who didn't know what she wanted to do. . .

"Marcy has a child?"

"Marcy has children. Three of them. Michael is sixteen, Melissa is thirteen, and Mark is eleven. She's done a fine job raising those kids. They are all good students, fine kids. Michael plays with the city league ball team. Roberta, Sam, and I go to his games a lot. Someone told me he'll go to college on a scholarship."

Katie could scarcely digest one piece of information before her mother gave her another. "Who'd she marry?"

"Charlie Waters. I think he was a couple of grades ahead of you."

"Charlie Waters. . .Charlie Waters. . . I don't remember him."

"Your high school yearbooks are in the library bookcase. Maybe you can find him in there."

"Sure. I'll do that later," she said, bewildered. Katie was not only shocked, but felt somewhat betrayed. Marcy was supposed to get out. . . make something of herself. But she had settled. Settled for a life trapped in Brooksboro. Why hadn't she left, Katie asked herself. Why hadn't she become the glamorous professional with the beautiful home? Why wasn't she having parties? What about the parties?!

After the lunch dishes and kitchen had been cleaned, Carolyn told her daughter that she wanted to lie down for a few moments and rest. Katie smiled, telling her mother that she would be in the library looking at the old yearbooks. "I still can't believe this."

Katie sat on the small, worn sofa of her mother's library slowly turning page after page of her senior year high school yearbook. Her eyes periodically narrowed as she searched her memory for the names of the young boys and girls she had once called out on a daily basis. One such photo made her stop for several moments. It was of one of the "famous couples." The popular ones whose very presence at a party could make it or break it. Katie remembered wanting to be like them—she and Buddy to be like them—to be able to openly date and have their photos taken. Katie and Buddy were always trying to stay one step ahead of her mother.

"I can't remember," she now sighed heavily. Then she smiled. Wasn't that just the way? One decade you're the most popular couple on campus; two and a half decades later, your classmates can't remember your names.

But she remembered Buddy.

She turned to the senior section. "The Mighty Seniors" they had called themselves. "We're big, we're bad, and we're boss," they had chanted at football games and while walking down the halls of the school.

Katie turned another page, and another, and another until she came to the beginning of the photos. Buddy's photo was first. . .it was always first. Chad "Buddy" Akins, the caption read, then gave a list of his high school accomplishments.

Katie felt her eyes mist with tears. Why couldn't Carolyn have liked Buddy? Why couldn't she have at least tried? And if she had, what kind of life would they have had together? Would they have come back together after Katie had returned from college? Would they have married? Had children?

She closed the book. She didn't want to do this anymore. She didn't want to remember right now. There was too much pain. . .that last day. . . that last night. . .the argument she had with her mother. . .the bus ride out. . .Atlanta. . .

Katie stood and replaced the book on the shelf. "Oh, Mama," she sighed. "Why?"

"Because Buddy Akins would have never been good enough for you." Katie could still hear her mother saying it, just as she had said it that fateful night. The voice, firm and tinged with anger, reverberated in her head. "You were meant for bigger and better things. A life of domestic drudgery? Is that what you want? Tell me! What do you want, Katharine? A doomed life? How many people know this? How many people have laughed behind my back? What could be worse than this?"

Katie closed her eyes against the memory. Indeed, what could be worse? Perhaps an estranged daughter living a thousand miles away, dead to her mother. Or would it have been worse to have been estranged and living in the same town?

She was suddenly very tired. She flipped off the overhead light, walked out of the door, and made her way silently up the grand, old staircase that led to her room.

CHAPTER THREE

The wind whipped at Katie's long, chestnut hair as her gold Mercedes SL500 convertible sped along the hot asphalt of the narrow road. Endless sprawling acres of New York's finest apple groves and lush, gently rolling hills spread out before her. Katie trembled in anticipation, knowing that soon she would turn right and take the winding, oak-canopied drive that led to the stately mansion. It was an imposing abode, a red-bricked Louisiana-French style with a large front porch, which was the weekend home to her and her husband.

Glancing briefly at the watch that Ben had given her just days before, she noted that it was almost five o'clock in the afternoon. Ben would be home within the next few hours and she thrilled at the thought of showing him her day's purchases. Ben loved to lie back on their bed, sipping a glass of wine as she modeled the latest additions to her extensive wardrobe or opened boxes filled with various other items for herself. As always, a sweeping aria would pour out of the sound system, blending with the laughter between husband and wife.

Turning into their long, winding driveway, she was confronted with the menacing swirl of black storm clouds gathering ahead. She looked skyward. It would rain soon. She should hurry or take the chance of soaking the inside of the car and her packages. Pressing her foot harder against the accelerator and feeling a surge of responsive power, she could feel the wind turn cold against her face. Directly in front of her, a squirrel scurried across the road. Hurry, little squirrel, *she thought.* Hurry home before the storm comes. Don't let the storm catch you.

Moments later, her car safely nestled in the garage, she ran through the front door and into the black-and-white marble-tiled foyer. As always, she could not help but feel overwhelmed by its baronial grandeur. She had seen Ben's burgundy Jaguar parked in the semicircular drive on her way into the compound. It was only five o'clock, but perhaps he had decided to call it a day early. For once.

"Ben?" she called, taking quick steps into the living room to her left. "Ben?" she called out again, then took in the room around her. The fireplace, which by this time usually roared with a boisterous, crackling fire, was empty of all but the ashes from the night before. The heavy, tapestry drapes were pulled tightly together, shutting out all but a trace of attenuated light. Standing in a filigree silver candelabrum, a solitary ivory tapered candle flickered atop the Renaissance Revival bedroom desk near French doors that led to the rose gardens, pool, and tennis court. Its light illuminated an oil painting of an ornate goblet and a loaf of bread that Ben had purchased during their first trip to Paris together. She walked slowly toward the only light in the room, becoming increasingly aware of the stillness inside her home.

Where is Ben?

She jerked open the French doors as a bolt of lightning and crash of thunder broke the dark sky apart. Rain began to pelt the brick veranda. She felt the light mist of dampness on her face, then slammed the doors shut.

Running out of the living room and through the foyer, she began calling for the housekeeper. "Maggie? Maggie, are you here?" As she gripped the banister at the base of the staircase, she felt tightness in her chest. The room became darker. She reached over to the light switch to her right and flipped it, but the room remained dark. Looking upward toward the lights, she flipped the switch up and down a few more times as if to make sure.

She ran up the stairs and walked quickly down the hallway toward her bedroom. Her heart pounded in her chest, keeping time with the rolling thunder beyond the safety of the walls around her. She passed a guest bed-room and noticed the closed door. That was unusual. Ben had a rule about the doors being kept open. Katie was certain it had been open when she left for the city earlier in the day. Perhaps Maggie had closed it. If Maggie had cleaned in there today, why would she have closed the door? Grappling with these details at all only added to the free-floating turmoil that was escalating within her.

Inching her hand toward the doorknob, she felt a tremor race up her spine. Something was wrong in this house. Where was Ben? Where was Maggie? In all the years she had lived here, one or the other had met her when she walked through the front door. But. . .not today. No roaring fire to welcome her. No lights burning invitingly. Her eyes narrowed and her breathing became erratic, rasping deep in her throat. The cadence of the rain pounding harder against the house added to the intensity of her feelings. Her ears began to clog and her throat to constrict. Something was wrong in this house. . .something was wrong. . .something was. . . She had to know. She had to. . .

She opened the door.

Katie bolted up in her childhood bed with a sudden gasp. Her face and hair were drenched in perspiration, the hair wrapping itself around her throat. Her breathing was labored and her heartbeat rapid. Without a moment's hesitation, she grabbed the phone beside her and began to dial her home in New York, then slammed it down before she had completed the numbers. She remembered the last thing Ben had said to her before she left him.

"Remember, Katie. Tell no one who you are. Tell no one who I am. Tell no one where you've been. Do you understand me, Katie?" He distinctly made each point almost as if he were talking to a child. During the first years of their marriage, before she more fully understood his complex personality, this kind of semipatronizing speech had silently angered her, reminding her somewhat of her mother. As Katie came to realize the love behind Ben's tone, she had allowed it to be a comfort to her, much like the way her own father's calm sense of purpose and decisiveness would make her feel centered or balanced, thus offsetting her rebellious and wayward spirit. She had heard somewhere that one's relationship with the opposite sex parent was the most important to overall adult functioning. She thus felt truly blessed to have had the kind of father she had and now reasoned that both the intensity and simplicity of Ben's heartfelt intonations, beseeching her to maintain a code of silence and secrecy, had settled deeply within her subconscious, producing a dream of such vivid proportions as to truly shake her being to the core.

She had looked into his handsome, well-chiseled face through the tears that spilled down her cheeks. "Yes. Yes, I understand, Ben."

"And don't call me. No matter what, don't call me. I will contact you when it's safe, I promise."

"You promise?"

He had kissed her tenderly on the lips, then on the cheeks, and had drawn her close, with her face resting against his solid chest. "Oh, sweet Katie. I promise. This won't be forever. Go back to your mother's home. Make things right again. Bring the shadows of your past into the light and allow me to fight the demons here. Okay, Sweetheart?"

She had lightly trembled. "Okay, Ben. For you. I'll do it for you. But call me. Promise you'll call me."

"I'll call when it's safe. Not until then." She had felt him look beyond her, as if to be certain no one could hear his words, then tilted her chin so that he could gaze down into her eyes. "No one will know where you are, Katie. No one but me."

"What about Cynthia?"

"Not even my lawyer."

She had wrapped her arms around his narrow, trim waist and buried her face against his powerful chest. "Tell me something wonderful, Ben. Give me some words to live on."

Something in the moment took him back to the time he had spoken to her in a small Boston cafe of the "lure" and "allure" of riches. That was before they were married, when she had marveled at the casual, almost uncaring attitude of the wealthy. She had often spoken to him of her dislike for their self-satisfied arrogance, as if they had either forgotten what it was like to have nothing, or worse perhaps, had never experienced financial deprivation. She had been impressed with his levelheaded approach to wealth and success. . .and she still was. He never ceased to amaze her, but she had gradually realized that the feeling was totally mutual. In fact, over the years they had spurred each other to ever-greater levels of development, and since their very first meeting, he had expressed awe of her remarkable development from a frightened but streetwise young woman to the secure, genteel lady he now held in his arms.

He had straightened, then started the game, a game he had begun with her while she was attending the university for studies in literature. He would quote a famous writer, philosopher, or poet, and she was required to provide the name. If correct, she was rewarded with a kiss. If incorrect, he sent her back to her desk for more studies.

"Okay. Ready for our little game?"

Katie had understood. "Yes. I'm ready, Ben. Just please quote something that I can take with me."

He had given her a wink. "Who said: 'Prosperity is not without many fears and distastes; and adversity is not without comforts and hopes'?" He had spoken with an air of authority.

She had leaned back, cradled in his arms, and looked up adoringly. "Francis Bacon," she had answered assuredly.

"*Sir* Francis Bacon," he had gently corrected her.

"*Sir* Francis Bacon," she had repeated, her eyes never leaving his.

He had brought a hand around and touched the tip of her nose with his finger, and she felt herself glowing in the warmth of the simple caress. "Who said: 'I love you'?" he whispered.

She had smiled. "William Benjamin Webster."

"Don't ever forget it, Katie."

"May I quote you?"

"Anytime."

"I love you," she had repeated. They had stared at each other for a long moment until she had whispered, "Stay safe, Ben."

Now, sitting alone in her old bed, she placed her hand against her chest, took a deep breath, and exhaled slowly.

"He's all right, Katie," she told herself. "It was only a dream."

CHAPTER FOUR

The next morning, Katie grinned as she dressed, remembering a conversation from the night before. She had told her mother that she would probably rise early the next morning and go for a jog. Her mother had looked surprised.

"I never knew you to have an athletic bone in your body."

"I played softball in high school," Katie had argued.

"You played at softball in high school. I can still see you standing in the outfield, shoulders slumped, hip cocked to one side."

Katie had moaned, "It was so hot!"

"It's still so hot," Carolyn had noted matter-of-factly.

Katie had grinned at her mother. "That's why I'm going early in the morning."

"You? Up early in the morning? This I have to see—"

Katie had sashayed out of the room. "You'll see, Mama. You'll see."

Now it was a quarter past seven in the morning and she was tightening the laces of her running shoes. She wondered if her mother was up, then thought that she probably was. If she wasn't in the garden, she was probably having coffee and watching a morning news show. It was how she had always begun her day.

Sure enough, Katie found her, coffee cup in hand, sitting in an overstuffed chair in the family room, with her feet propped up on the matching ottoman, gazing at the *Savannah Morning News* show on the television. Carolyn glanced over at her daughter, who was dressed in form-fitting bike shorts and a matching cropped top.

"Where do you think you are going in that outfit?" she asked.

Katie began to stretch. "Running. I told you last night—"

"In that? You didn't tell me you'd be half-naked."

"Oh, Mama! This is what one wears to run. They're called bike shorts, or exercise shorts." Katie lifted her arms high over her head and stretched.

"Well, I hope no one recognizes you."

Bending down to touch her toes, Katie replied, "Because of what I'm wearing or because of who I am?" She popped back up, placed her hands on her hips, and without breaking eye contact with her mother, began to twist from side to side.

Carolyn huffed and looked back at the television. "Everyone knows who you are. I just don't want them to get any wrong ideas."

Katie laughed lightly, then turned and strolled out of the house through the front door. Pausing on the porch, she took in a deep breath and listened. The air was rather thick with humidity but surprisingly fresh and pleasant. This was her favorite time of day. Getting up this early and jogging made her feel in charge. With so much chaos in her life, a sense of control was what she needed. It was going to be a scorcher, she thought. Marvelous! A hard sweat would do her a world of good.

With the ease and grace of a gazelle, she bounded down the steps and began to jog toward the sidewalk, then turned left. Within moments Old Man Cheevers's—Marcy's house—came into view. She slowed a bit when she noticed that Marcy's mother was standing on the front porch, coffee cup in hand, gazing out at the street. Why was her mother there so early in the morning?

She hadn't changed a bit in all the years Katie had been gone. Her dark, wavy hair was still cut short, her frame still petite. The natural olive complexion of her skin gave her a youthful glow. She was wearing jeans and a tee, and Katie thought fleetingly that she never remembered Roberta Anderson dressing so young. That's when it hit her. It wasn't Marcy's mother standing on the porch. It was Marcy. Katie stopped abruptly and stared at her old friend. How could this have happened? Marcy had become her mother? Had she, Katie, also become her own mother? She didn't think so. But would she have, had she stayed?

Marcy turned slightly toward her. Shielding her eyes against the sunlight with her hand, she squinted as she tried to determine who was standing just beyond her property line. Whoever she was, she looked as if she'd just jogged off the cover of a sports magazine. She was stunning. And so tall! She'd only known one other girl that tall and she. . .

Her eyes widened. "Katie!" She walked down one of the steps from the porch.

Katie began to cross the lawn slowly. "Hi, Marcy."

Marcy quickly set the cup of coffee down on the top porch step and began to run toward her old friend, who was standing with her arms outstretched. They embraced, swaying back and forth, laughing and crying at the same time.

Marcy drew back, keeping her hands firmly on Katie's shoulders. "I can't believe this! I mean, what are you doing here? How long have you been home? Where have you been, Katie Morgan?"

"Webster. Katie Webster," Katie laughed. "Which question do you want answered first?"

Marcy released Katie's shoulders. "Oh my, oh my! Katie! Can you come in? For a cup of coffee?"

Katie glanced toward the house. "I can't believe you are living in that house."

Marcy took a few steps back. "Come on in. It's nothing to be afraid of, I promise."

Katie hesitated. "I really need to run. I haven't in days and I am feeling it. Can I come over later? We'll play catch-up. I'll fill you in on everything." *Or as much as I dare,* Katie thought.

Marcy's face showed disappointment. "Oh. Okay. Sure. What time?"

"Ten o'clock. Okay? I should be done by then. Showered and changed. . ."

"Well, thank goodness! If my sixteen year old sees you in that outfit, he'll never get over it!"

Katie chuckled as she made her way back to the sidewalk. Calling out, "Yeah! We're gonna talk about that, too! See ya in a bit!"

Katie ran strong and steady down the street that would lead her to the elementary school. She noted certain changes that had taken place, though most of the street had stayed the same. The tall, white, flat-faced building where she had taken dance classes was now a Century 21 real estate office. A small, framed house had been converted into a florist shop, a cutesy one, painted powder blue, trimmed in mauve. Along the windows she saw baskets of silk arrangements, bunnies in straw hats, bears made from quilts, and small decorative birdhouses. She smiled. There was something very quaint and precious about it.

She ran past the home of her mother's longtime friend, Dorothy Pace. Dottie, she was called. Her husband, Van, and Katie's father had worked for the same accounting firm in Savannah. She wondered if Mr. Pace still worked there. Or had he retired? Died? She hoped not. She had always liked the Paces. They were a fun-loving, happy couple, both hard-working. They had three children: a son and two daughters. Jillian, the oldest daughter, was a few years older than Katie; and the twins, Tricia and Timmy, were two years younger. Passing the home, she remembered a particular, hot summer's day when her mother and Dottie had driven to the farmer's market to buy corn while the children stayed at the Paces' home to play. Katie had been about seven at the time. After returning, the ladies made peanut butter and jelly sandwiches with potato chips for the children to eat on the back patio. Kool-Aid was served from the wide pitcher with the Kool-Aid logo proudly emblazoned on the side, the bright eyes and happy smile hinting at the good times that would be had by all just by consuming the product. Katie could almost hear the slurping sounds from drinking the cold, sweet punch too quickly.

Later, as the children continued to play in the back, Tricia had walked into the house, then returned with a disturbing announcement: Katie's mother had left without taking Katie home.

"Uh-uh!" Katie said vehemently.

"Uh-huh!" Tricia countered. "She's not with my mama anymore and her car is gone!"

Tears brimmed in Katie's eyes. Could her mother have forgotten her? She had run through the house screaming, "Mama! Mama!" then ran right into Mrs. Pace, who was standing at the kitchen sink, washing a sink full of corn on the cob.

Looking down at the child clutching her lower torso, Dottie Pace exclaimed, "Oh, my goodness!" Then she chuckled. "Looks like your mama forgot she brought you!" This naturally brought a cascade of tears from Katie. Moments later, Carolyn Morgan waltzed into the house, nearly cackling with laughter at what she had done.

"Oh, Priss-Pot," she had said, using the term of endearment she had always given to her only child, as she wrapped her arms around the thin and lanky body. "Looks like I was trying to get rid of you!"

Katie knew now that her mother had been kidding, but then she thought it to be true. It was a mere prelude to the agony that would become a part of their lives some ten years later.

On the right-hand corner, straight ahead, was Jenkins Funeral Home. The large, white, aluminum sign that swung slightly in the light morning breeze informed her that it was now known as Brooksboro Funeral Home.

The funeral home was actually an old, red brick, Victorian two-story house. Downstairs was used for the business, while the upstairs was the residential home of the family who ran it. She wondered why the Jenkinses had left and made a mental note to ask her mother when she returned home.

Funeral homes rarely held pleasant memories, and this one was no exception. She had only been inside it once, for the viewing of her high school classmate, Bobby Weaver. Bobby had been a friend and school chum since first grade. He was bright, witty, good-looking, smart, and a true confidant. He had been one of the few people to know all about her and Buddy Akins in the beginning. She remembered the advice he had given her about keeping their relationship a secret from her parents.

"Katie-Katie," he said, calling her by the nickname she allowed only him to use, "I'd keep this one under my hat if I were you. You like Buddy? Fine. You wanna date 'im? Go for it. But your mama'll bust something if she finds out, and you know it, Babe. And it'll probably be Buddy's head, if not something else."

They had been sitting on top of the trunk of his Chevy Nova in the parking lot of the Tastee-Freeze that autumn afternoon. The air around them had been crisp, the sun bright, and the sky deep azure. White, billowy clouds floated by them, and for awhile they tried to pick out pictures amid the swirling formations. Then Bobby ran up to the order window and got them a couple of root beers. They chatted heartily as they drank. Bobby was seeing Monica Carpenter, and he talked to Katie about how they were doing. She then told him she wasn't sure whether or not to let her parents know about her seeing Buddy. Up until then, they had met at various places or parties. Unrealistically, she wanted him to be able to drive up to her house and pick her up like a proper date. She did not want their relationship to remain a secret any longer. They had been seeing each other for five months, and she felt that it was now time to spill the beans.

Bobby's advice had been different. Being like a brother to her, she both accepted and acted upon his advice.

Bobby had not lived long enough to witness the outcome of his sage advice. The following summer, he died tragically when his car had spun out of control following a brief rain. He had been driving too fast, which was normal for him, and hydroplaned into the cement bridge over the Ogeechee River. The Class of 1975 had been devastated, but no one as much as Monica. Katie could still hear her cries of anguish as she stood over the opened coffin. She could still visualize Monica's father clutching her shoulders firmly as he led her to the back of the funeral home.

"Come on, Monica," he said. "Daddy wants to tell you a story."

Katie had often wondered what the story had been about, for fifteen minutes later father and daughter returned, dry-eyed and composed. There seemed to be a peace about her that had not been there before.

Katie looked down and noted the rhythm of her feet as they pounded against the pavement. She consciously tried to avoid the cracks that ran every five feet. "Step on a crack, break your mother's back," she could hear the voice of Marcy as a child, calling out as they ran and played on the sidewalk in front of her home.

Just a few more yards, she thought, and the school would come into view. The building itself had been a mammoth bulk of brick and white-washed concrete that had been erected in the early 1920s. Front and center were long, narrow concrete steps that led to the wide foyer with a high ceiling, which echoed with the voices and footsteps of the children, parents, and teachers who had walked through it. The floors throughout the school were made of long, unvarnished, dark oak planks that kept the school cool during the hot months of the school year, while unreliable radiators attempted to keep the rooms warm during the few months of cold weather. Katie remembered well the days she had worn her coat all day, trying to keep her teeth from chattering and her body from shivering.

Katie looked up, knowing the school would now be in front of her, and came to an abrupt halt.

It was gone! The entire school was gone!

Her heart was racing beneath her chest, as she took several slow, easy steps toward the block of barren land. Large oak trees that had stood for more than a hundred years offered haphazard shelter to various items from her past. There were old bike racks, cement benches, the broken, semicircular drive, dominated by the towering, flagless flagpole, swingless swing sets, and a leaning set of monkey bars. Weeds grew rampant, and broken pieces of scattered brick that once framed the imposing building lay randomly about, as if snubbing their collective nose at her past. Those hallowed halls of learning once stood with welcoming grace and charm, at once inviting and yet stately. How our memories enslave us, she thought remorsefully as she gaped at the empty lot. They hold us captive to how things used to be. They can even rob us of our future possibilities by making us fearful of change as we cling desperately to the old—even when holding on to the past does not serve us anymore.

"What have they done?" she asked aloud, stretching her arms outward in a forlorn gesture of cheerless desperation. "What have they done and why?"

CHAPTER FIVE

Returning home after her run, with thoughts of the flattened school building fresh in her mind, she found her mother's note taped to the refrigerator handle. "Katharine," it read, "Roberta and I have gone out to Mr. Jenkins's farm to pick peas." *How totally quaint,* Katie thought with a smile. It had been years since she picked vegetables, a mundane task strangely comforting to her in both its monotony and domesticity. She wasn't sure if she was happy or sad about the revelation. The last thing she needed was to get overly comfortable in Brooksboro. Her life in New York had not been made of such things as pea picking on a sweltering June morning. Perhaps the simplicity of this act brought such a frown to her face because she realized how complex and involved her life had become over the past few years. She found it disconcerting to be caught in the middle of two totally different lifestyles, both of which she was intimately acquainted with and both of which she could appreciate and enjoy. She wondered if she could ever make the transition back to this lifestyle after becoming so used to what her circle deemed more "civilized" or at least more "cultured." When she was living in New York, Georgia seemed so irrelevant. Yet, now that she was far removed from the city, with all its endless culture, even that was starting to fade into insignificance. The conflict was definitely distressing, troubling her more than she ever thought it would.

She rested for a few minutes, gulping down a large glass of tepid water from the kitchen sink. It tasted different from the water she had grown accustomed to drinking in New York. Cleaner. Fresher. She wondered why. Well water, perhaps. She'd have to remember to ask her mother about it.

After a cool shower, she wrapped herself in a large bath towel, dried her hair, and then expertly applied her makeup. She wanted to look nice today. She not only was going to visit her old best friend, but she also needed to go to the bank and deposit the check she had hidden in the picture frame. Casually, she glanced out of the bathroom and into the bedroom at the frame sitting on the chest of drawers, concealing her only asset. She wondered what kind of red tape, if any, she would have to go through in order to get it cashed. She had her driver's license, but Ben had taken all her credit cards so that she would not leave an electronic paper trail.

"I don't want you to take any chances," he had told her as she slipped the plastic cards from the flap in her brown, soft leather wallet. "And the cashier's check should be enough until I can get you back up here."

"How long do you think it will take?" She had held out the cards and he had gently taken them from her. She looked up at him and noted the look of concern on his face. Please, not long, she had thought. She wasn't sure how long she could live without him.

"It could be weeks or months, Katie." His voice had betrayed his obvious frustration. "I've gone over this with you. Don't ask me to do it again."

She had looked down forlornly. "Don't be angry with me, Ben. I just don't want to live a single day without you if I don't have to."

His look had softened then, and he had gathered her into his arms. "You will never be without me, Katie. Every breath you breathe, I will be aware of. No matter where you go, I will be there with you. And every night I will hold you in my arms until you fall asleep. Remember that. Remember that and we will be okay."

Looking back at her reflection in the bathroom mirror, she spoke softly, "I remember, Ben. I remember."

She stood resplendent in her panties staring blankly at the few clothes hanging in the closet of her youth. Absentmindedly, she chose something bright and cheery from her limited, but tasteful wardrobe. The royal blue silk culottes and matching top, set with gold buttons in the shape of oyster shells, would be nice for the visit with Marcy and her trip to the bank. Dressing quickly, she slipped her feet into a pair of gold thong sandals. She glanced into the mirror for one last look-see, fluffed her hair a bit, and then quickly walked out of her room and down the stairs.

Walking to Marcy's took only a few minutes, but it was enough time for her to reflect on her surroundings. The temperature was hot and the humidity began to stifle. Looking for any sign of a breeze, she glanced up at the trees lining the sidewalks that gave shelter to the lush lawns. Not a leaf stirred. Everything stood silent and still. Everything, that is, but time itself, and even that seemed blissfully suspended in what felt like an otherworldly, ethereal small-town existence.

Marcy's front door was open, but the screened door was latched. Before Katie could knock, she saw Marcy walking up the hallway. She was wearing a light-colored T-shirt tucked into her unbelted jeans. Katie noticed that she still possessed the same dainty, petite frame.

"Hey," Marcy called as she unlatched the screen and swung it wide to allow Katie entrance into the house. Stepping in, Katie felt the thick pile of hunter green carpet beneath her sandals. She took a quick look around as Marcy relatched the door, then shut the front door behind it.

Marcy's living room was spacious and open, painted stark white. On the far left wall was a brick fireplace, also painted white. There was a black leather sofa facing the fireplace and dividing the room. On either side of it were black, wrought iron and glass-topped end tables with matching lamps and hunter green shades. A matching cocktail table sat in front of the sofa. A glass bowl in a wrought iron stand sat in the middle of the table. Emanating from the bowl, cinnamon-scented potpourri filled the air with its subtle fragrance, reminding Katie of the aprés-ski hot cider served them at Zermatt, Saint Moritz, or Aspen. She opened her mouth to comment on this, then stopped. The Marcy she had known as a child aspired to such, but now settled for the scent of it in the potpourri-filled glass bowl.

A large Ansel Adams print framed in black lacquer hung on the wall opposite the front windows. There were no other furnishings in the room. It was totally modern and Katie liked it. It reflected the practical and straightforward personality of its owner.

"I have the air on," Marcy was saying to her, "but I opened the door so I could see you when you came up the walkway." Noting her friend's observing eye, she added, "It's my favorite room in the house. I wanted to keep it simple." She walked into the center of it and Katie followed her, clasping her hands behind her back and feeling somewhat as if she were being shown around a museum.

"Well, you certainly did that," Katie said. "I think it's wonderful what you've done with this old house; modernized. . .great atmosphere. And to think how we used to get ourselves all worked up about the ghost of Old Man Cheevers living here!"

"That might have been the reason we got it for such a good price. Everyone our age never really considered buying this place. I don't know about you, but I grew out of that fear of ghosts thing pretty quickly. Face the ghosts, and you find they never even existed," she said with a wink. "Anyway, it saved us enough to be able to furnish and remodel the place."

"Well, I think you made a very smart move. I really like it."

"Thanks. So! How does it feel being back home?"

Katie walked to the Ansel Adams print before answering. "I feel as if I am walking around in a dream, seeing home again after all this time. What was it Shakespeare said—'Life's but a walking shadow'?"

Marcy gave a little laugh. "Let me get this straight. . . . You're quoting Shakespeare?"

Katie laughed with her and walked over to the nearest end table to inspect the lamp. She lightly touched it. "I like these."

"Target," Marcy said.

"Pardon me?"

"Target. You know, the discount store."

Katie found herself at a loss. "Actually, no, I don't know. I'm afraid I've never heard of it."

"You're kidding me, right? You've never heard of Target?"

Katie smiled and shook her head. "Is there one here?"

"No. There's one in Savannah. I'll have to take you sometime. You'd love it. Want some coffee?" She began to move toward the back of the house as if she had already received her answer.

"It's my passion," Katie informed her. "And I haven't even had one cup this morning."

"Well, you've come to the right place!"

Katie followed her friend into the hallway that led to the back of the house. The living room was the only centrally located room in the house. Katie noted a door to the right leading to another room. French doors led to the hallway, from which every downstairs room could be accessed.

The second door on the left led to the large kitchen, which Marcy had painted a bright yellow. In the center of the room was an antique farmhouse kitchen table of solid oak. Looking at odds with the primitive rusticity of the table, a large, bright yellow bowl filled with gala apples sat with pristine, yet carefree, elegance on the burnished surface. Six matching ladder-back chairs were pushed up against the table. Katie noted the spongy, dark yellow cushions in each chair.

"Have a seat, have a seat," Marcy offered, and Katie pulled out one of the chairs and sat down, feeling the padding of the cushion through the thin silk of her culottes. It was soft and worn. She liked the feeling it gave her. A family lived here. They ate here. They sat around this table for meals and laughed and talked about their day here. The children most likely did their homework here. Marcy and her husband probably sat here deep into the night and talked about their lives in this little town.

"A penny for your thoughts," Marcy said, placing two candy-apple red mugs down on the table, then turning toward the coffeemaker on the counter.

Katie blushed a bit. Her friend could still read her mind, or at least knew when she was deep in thought. "I was thinking that I liked these cushions."

Marcy brought the pot over and poured the coffee. "Target, again. Cups are from Target. Coffeemaker from Target. See that clock?"

Katie looked over to the wall where Marcy pointed to a large, round, red-lacquered clock with large black numbers on its face.

"Target?" Katie asked.

"Nope! K-Mart," Marcy said, chortling at her own teasing humor. "My everyday dishes are from Target, though, and if I can convince you to come over for supper some evening, you'll get a chance to eat off them."

Katie smiled. "I'd like that. I really would. Will your whole family be here?"

Marcy replaced the coffeepot and placed a sugar bowl on the table. With good-natured folksiness, she bantered, "Where else would they be? Milk?"

Katie's smile broadened. Milk. When was the last time she had been asked that? She thought about the elegant dining hall of their country club. Small, intimate tables draped in fine linen tablecloths. Single candles flickering in the center, giving off a warm glow and adding to the ambiance. Soft music filled the room, mingling with the light conversations at each table. Katie dressed in a beaded cocktail dress and Ben in a black tux. Dark, Turkish coffee poured into bone china cups. Sterling silver spoons nestled on the matching saucers. "Will you have cream with that, Mrs. Webster?" the waiter was asking her.

"Yes, please," she was answering, waiting as he poured just the right amount into her cup, swirling into the dark liquid, making it light and creamy.

"Katie?" Marcy, standing with her hand on the refrigerator handle, was calling her name. "Earth to Katie."

Katie shook her head gently. "What? Oh, milk. Yes, please."

Marcy pulled a large plastic carton of milk out of the refrigerator and set it on the table. "My son drinks one of these a day. Can you believe that? A day!"

Katie began to prepare her coffee as Marcy pulled the silverware drawer out and rattled around for two spoons. "I still can't believe you have children, much less a son who drinks a gallon of milk a day. Whatever happened to the 'no kids' clause?"

Marcy handed her a spoon, then sat and began preparing her own coffee. "I don't know. I guess I fell in love and got married. Charlie wanted children, and I guess deep down I did, too."

"When did you start seeing Charlie? I don't recall that you two were dating before I left, right?"

Marcy took a tentative sip of the steaming coffee as she shook her head no. "I was all set for the university, remember?"

Katie nodded. Those years seemed like a lifetime ago. A dream. A story she had possibly read, but had not especially cared for.

"Anyway, I guess it was about a month after you left, I got a call one day from Terri Mills. You remember her, right?"

"Terri Mills?"

"Terri Donaldson, then. She's Terri Mills now."

Katie nodded. "Yes, I remember Terri."

"Okay. Terri wanted me to go to a softball game with her. She was dating Jim Rainey at the time, although God only knows why, and he was playing that night. She didn't want to go alone, so she asked me if I was up for it. I said yes. . .Charlie was on the team. . .he saw me, I saw him. . .he asked me out for a burger afterwards, and the rest, as they say, is history."

"You fell madly in love and got married."

"Totally. I couldn't see straight I was so in love. He was and is the light of my life. A wonderful guy if there ever was one."

Katie gave her friend a half-smile. "If it weren't for the happiness reflecting in your eyes, I might be thoroughly disgusted."

"Why's that?" Marcy rested her elbows on the table and waited for an explanation.

Katie took a deep breath and sighed. "For so many years I lived vicariously through your aspirations to become an attorney—remember that?"

Marcy nodded. "I remember."

"I often found myself wondering what you were doing to achieve your heartfelt ambition. I would imagine your apartment located on Peachtree Road in Atlanta. Modern, of course."

"Of course."

"In my daydreams I could feel your daring and determination as you argued with defense counsel in cherry-paneled courtrooms with high ceilings, gleaming chandeliers, and furnishings of highly polished mahogany."

"That's quite the imagination. Then again, you always did have an imagination."

Katie smiled back at her friend, then furrowed her brow mockingly. "Your Honor, I object!"

Marcy burst out laughing. "Sustained!"

"It would always be sustained, because you were always perfect. . .in my dreams."

"What was I wearing? Certainly not blue jeans and T-shirts."

"No. Snappy suits. St. John Knits and Coco Chanel."

"Oh, I like that! What else? What else?"

"You'd win every case."

"Of course."

"And because you won every case, you come with such a price." Katie spoke the last three words in a staccato.

The air grew silent around them as both women thought for a moment how it might have been. Finally, Katie whispered, "I'd never known anyone with such drive and determination as you. Sometimes that was all that got me through."

Marcy looked Katie in the eyes. "What do you mean?"

"Hmmm?"

"What did you mean by that last statement?"

Katie thought for a moment. What had she said? She thought she had merely thought this truth, but apparently she had spoken the words. "Nothing." She forced a smile. "Tell me more about Charlie. What does he do? For a living, I mean." Katie swallowed the last of her coffee, and Marcy slid out of her seat to refill the mug. "Oh, thanks. I could have gotten it."

"Today, you're my company. Tomorrow, you're just one of us."

Katie smiled. She liked the sound of that. Since leaving her home in New York, she did not feel as if she belonged anywhere. Certainly not at her mother's. That her mother harbored some resentment toward her seemed certain. It was unnerving, though, not knowing for sure the extent of her mother's anger. She seemed to vacillate between anger and relief; thus perhaps even her mother was not sure about her feelings at this point. Possibly in a few days things would be ironed out between them. She still wasn't sure.

Marcy continued. "He owns the farm. His dad's. His father and mother retired, gave him the farmland, and Charlie works it. His dad and mom stay on at the house out there. I wouldn't live there if you paid me. I just have to be in close to town or I'd die."

Katie couldn't help it. She burst out laughing. Marcy looked perplexed and asked, "What? What's so funny?" When the laughter did not subside, she joined her friend in the melodious peal.

Minutes later the two women, doubled over, tears spilling down their cheeks, reached across the table and gave each other an awkward hug. "Oh, Marcy," Katie began. "I can't tell you how I've missed you."

Marcy got up to refill her coffee cup. "Do you mind telling me what was so funny?"

"It's just that I. . .I live. . ." Katie could feel the laughter beginning to bubble up inside her again. She took a breath to control herself and then finished. "I live in New York City and. . ."

Marcy sat with a thud. Her eyes were wide and her lips formed a silent "O." "New York City?"

Katie sobered. She had not meant to embarrass her friend. "Yes. New York City."

Marcy looked to the back door at the far side of the long and narrow room. She was clearly shocked. "I guess you think I'm crazy then. Talking about living near town."

Katie reached over and grabbed her friend's hand. "No! No, Marcy. I think this is all wonderful. Believe me." Marcy apparently did not seem convinced. "I mean, yes, I live in New York, but look at all you have!"

Marcy pulled her hand from Katie's and walked to one of the counters, where she grabbed a yellow sponge and began to vigorously wipe it. "Like what? I'm standing here telling you all about items bought at Target and. . .well, you probably buy all your stuff from. . .I don't know. . .one of those fancy stores I only read about like Saks Fifth Avenue or Macy's or Lord and Taylor. What could I possibly have that you don't have?"

It took Katie a fraction of a second to answer the question. "Three children for one thing." *And no one who wants to kill you for another,* Katie thought, but did not say. *A husband who is totally safe and sound. A life you don't have to hide. . . .*

Marcy stopped her wiping and turned, resting her hips against the counter. "That's true. I'm sorry, Katie. I—"

"No, I'm sorry. I never meant to. . .we seem to be having some strange ups and downs in this conversation, aren't we?"

They smiled at each other, and as it had always been between them, the argument was over. "Marcy? What happened to the elementary school? I went by there this morning and. . .I mean. . .I just couldn't believe. . ."

Marcy nodded. "A sin against man!" she exclaimed. "But, that's progress. At least that's what they are calling it. They built a new one out by the old junior high, which is now a special ed school."

"Then where is the junior high school?"

"Out by the Torrington plant."

"But why?"

"I told you. Progress. Nothing stays the same, Katie. Surely, you didn't expect to return and find everything as you left it."

Katie took a sip of her coffee. In truth, she had. What a slap in the face the last few days had been. Very little had stayed the same. Even her bedroom was different. She thought that coming here would offer two forms of safety, the first being that no one in New York knew she was from Brooksboro and would think to look for her here, and the second was the safety found in the old and familiar. The warm embrace of familiarity would have been comforting and reassuring to her in her time of need. She imagined herself sinking into it, even though it would be only for a moment.

"Yes," she answered softly. "But I guess I was wrong."

A moment of stillness filled the room until Marcy walked back to the table and sat in her chair.

"Marcy? Do you ever miss it?"

"Miss what?"

"The dream?"

"No. Not at all. Don't get me wrong. It's not like I've been changing diapers and mopping floors all this time. I've taken classes at the university in Statesboro. I still read voraciously, especially crime dramas. I write a weekly column for the *Savannah Morning News*."

"You do? About what?"

"It's called 'From Where I Sit.' I write about current events from the perspective of an everyday housewife and mother. Everyone tells me it's the first thing they read every Sunday morning, but I don't believe it. Maybe the second thing. . .but not the first!"

Katie laughed. "I can't believe Mama didn't tell me. When do you do this?"

"Every day. I watch the news, read the paper, and every afternoon I sit down at my computer and scan current events. Then, one day a week I sit at that same computer and write my viewpoint. Then I zip it off in an E-mail to the paper and on Sunday morning. . .there it is!"

"I suppose you have every single issue, too."

Marcy gave a single nod. "Some of them—the ones I'm the most proud of—are framed and hung on the wall of the little corner of our bedroom where the computer is. Right next to the yearly school pictures of the children."

"Would you show me sometime?"

"I'd be proud to show you the clippings and the photos. Katie?"

"Yes?"

"Mind if I ask you a question?"

Katie felt herself stiffen. "I suppose not."

"You don't have children?" she asked softly.

Katie looked down into her coffee. She would have, had she not been such a fool so many years ago. Five years after moving to the city, while working at a club called Private Dancer, she had become involved with one of the patrons. . . .

David Franscella was a tall, powerfully built, handsome Italian. He had taken notice of her from the moment he saw her dancing in one of the cages suspended by heavy chains from the ceiling. After her set of dances, Leo, manager of the club, called her back to his office. As she stood in front of his desk, scantily clad in pink satin lingerie, he informed her that someone wanted to meet her. If she knew what was good for her, she would go along with the patron's wishes. It sounded like a veiled threat.

"What do you mean, 'if I know what's good for me'? You threatening me, Leo?"

"No, I ain't threat'nin' you," he said, removing the short, fat stogie from his clenched teeth. "I'm telling you, this man can do things for you. He's a class act. He's got connections. If he likes you, you just may amount to somethin' someday."

Katie thought she was already amounting to something. Being a stripper wasn't anything to write home about—not that she would—but she made very good money. More money than most college graduates. With the money she had been setting aside every week, she would be able to quit in a few years and pay her way through school. Possibly meet a nice man, marry, and have a couple of children. Then again, maybe this man Leo wanted her to meet would be an easier route.

"Sure, Leo," she said. "What'd you say this guy's name is?"

"David. And if he wants you to know his last name, he'll tell ya. Now, get outta here and go play nice to the man. He's the good lookin' one at table nine."

David had been everything Leo had told her he would be. Handsome, classy, connected to important underground people, and willing to spend any amount of money on Katie that she desired. They maintained a mutually understood relationship that thrived on the city. Katie worked five nights a week, stripping for men who leered lasciviously and made indecent propositions, but never really had a chance with her. At closing, David would pick her up in his shiny, new Corvette and take her out for a late dinner, then back to her apartment, for which he had begun paying the rent. Although they had been dating for some time, she had never known where he lived. He didn't offer the information and she didn't ask. She had known he was using her as much as she had been using him. If he was as involved with the underworld as she suspected, she wanted to know as little about him as possible. She was a stripper, but she wasn't stupid.

A year after meeting, she had discovered that she was pregnant. At first she was stunned, but then she entertained notions of getting married and having children. She had become so enmeshed in this dysfunctional relationship that love did not seem to matter. Even if David didn't marry her, she could raise the child on her own. Several of the girls at the club did it. She'd have to postpone her education, but that would be okay, too. However, she had not been prepared for David's angry reaction.

"Tell me this is a joke!" he stormed through clenched teeth. "Tell me now, or I'll slap your pretty little face until you do!"

She had endured years of foul words from the patrons at the club, but this had cut her to her soul. Speechless, she slumped onto the chaise lounge in her living room.

"Tell me!!" he bellowed.

"Keep your voice down, David," Katie pleaded. "The neighbors. . ."

"I don't care about your neighbors! I don't care about the whole city right now. I want you to tell me exactly. . .exactly. . .how this happened!" The veins on the sides of his neck bulged and she began to feel frightened.

Katie managed to keep her voice low. "What do you mean? How do you think it happened?"

David leaned over her, bracing his hands on the back of the chair. "What I think is, you were supposed to be taking care of things. That's your job. You're the woman and that's your job."

"I did take care of things—"

"Apparently not!" he shouted. In his fury, spit sailed out of his mouth.

She gently raised her hand to wipe her face. "Apparently, David, it didn't work. But, I can show you my pill case. I can show you where I took a pill every day."

He pushed away from her then. "All you can show me is where you pushed a little pill out of the case. That's all you can show me. You can't prove anything to me, can you? Can you?"

She tried to hold back the tears, but she lost the battle and began to cry. He spun around and walked out of the room toward her bedroom, returning within moments with a large leather belt from her closet. Her eyes widened in horror as he drew his large arm back and she pleaded, "What are you going to do? David? What are you going to do?" And then she felt the sting of the first blow against her left shoulder. She crouched down, trying to protect herself, but it was of no use. By the time he was finished with her, her body bruised and broken, she had begun to bleed and had lost the baby. To make up for it and to entice her not to press charges, he supported her over the next two years while she had gone to school. But, she did not see him during that time. Not once. Not even when she graduated from college as a legal assistant. It wasn't until years later that he swooped into her life once more. . . .

Katie looked across the table at Marcy, who had never known the devastation and degradation of being beaten to the point of miscarriage. "No. No children."

"But you are married."

"Oh, yes. For about five years."

"Do you think you'll have children? I mean, it's never too late, you know."

The beating she had taken from David left her unable to conceive, something she had not known about until years later. She and Ben talked about adopting. They probably would one day. One day soon. If she could only get back to him. "We've talked about adopting. But tell me all about your children," she said, changing the subject.

Marcy positively beamed. "Well, there's Michael. He's sixteen. Very tall, like his dad. Very handsome. Also, like his dad. He's into baseball. Plays for a league here. Right now he's taking a summer school course in French, so when you meet him, don't be surprised if he tries to impress you with a little *parlez-vous Français*. Just try to pacify him."

Katie smiled. She'd pacify him all right. Ben had paid for two years of immersion French classes, which she graduated from with flying colors. To reward her, he had taken her to Paris for two glorious weeks of shopping and culture absorbing, as he called it.

"Why summer school? Did he fail last year?"

Marcy laughed. "Oh, no. Nowadays, kids go to summer school to take courses they don't want to have to take during the school year. You know, it lessens their workload. He should be back any minute actually," she noted, glancing up at the red-lacquered clock from K-Mart.

"And the others?" Katie inquired.

"Melissa is thirteen. She's still asleep. You remember how that is. Hormone city. She's a good kid, though. Very studious."

"Does she look like you?"

"Everyone says she does, but I don't see it. You never do, I think."

"You know," Katie began, shifting her weight in the chair, "I thought you were your mother this morning."

Marcy frowned playfully. "I don't see that either." Then she smiled. "More coffee?"

Katie looked into her half-empty mug. "Just warm it up," she answered, then added jokingly, "I don't think I have enough of a buzz yet. But if we keep this up, I'll never get to sleep tonight."

Marcy got up to get the coffeepot. "Tonight is a whole day away."

"Don't you have three children? Who is the third?"

Marcy poured the coffee and replaced the pot. "Mark. Mark is eleven, but we keep him tied up in the basement. . .you know, so that Ol' Man Cheevers can scare the dickens out of him. We just never did like the kid."

Katie gave her a shocked look. "What? Oh! I see you haven't lost your sense of humor!"

Marcy burst out laughing. "You got that right. Mark's out working with his father. He'll probably take over the farm one day, like Charlie took over for his dad. Right now, they're mainly working in tobacco and corn."

"What about Michael? Doesn't he want to work on the farm?"

"He's like a fish flopping around on hot cement." A smile formed on Katie's lips as she noted the way Marcy enunciated the last word as if it had two distinct syllables. "He hates it out there. He goes. And he works with his dad when he's forced to. But it's not his dream."

"Which is?" Katie heard the front door open and close, followed by the call of a young man in search of his mother.

"Mom? Mom, you here?"

"Michael?" Katie asked.

"Michael," Marcy confirmed, then called, "I'm back here, Son! In the kitchen!"

Heavy footsteps came down the hall. Katie turned to see a tall, lanky, blond-haired, brown-eyed young man of sixteen turn into the kitchen doorway. He was well dressed in clean jeans and a short-sleeved, multicolored sports shirt. "Mom, I—" He stopped as soon as he saw Katie sitting before him.

"Michael, this is Katie, my childhood friend. You remember me telling you about her." Marcy made the introduction. "Katie, my son, Michael."

Katie extended her hand as she prepared herself for the French words she knew would follow.

"*Bonjour, Madame. Comment allez-vous?*"

"*Bonjour, Monsieur. Je vais bien, et toi? On me dit que tu es en train d'apprendre le Français.*"

"*Oui. Vous parlez si bien, madame!*"

"*Et toi! Tu n'es pas en première année, j'imagine?*"

"*La seconde. Je veux bien enseigner—dans l'avenir.*"

"*C'est une grande ambition. Tu as bien choisi je pense.*"

"*Merci. Pardonez-moi, mais je dois aller faire les études.*"

"Let me know if I can be of any assistance to you," Katie said, returning to English.

"*Merci encore.* I will."

The two of them turned to Marcy, who had leaned back in her chair and folded her arms across her chest. "Now where did you learn to do that?" she asked Katie.

"College. I'll tell you about it later. For now, I have to go. I don't want to outstay my welcome, and I understand that my mother and your mother have gone to some farm to pick vegetables, so. . ." Katie stood, followed by Marcy.

"Oh, no! First you tell me what was said! I'm at a disadvantage here and as his mother I want to know," she teased.

"Your handsome son just informed me that he wants to be a French teacher when he grows up."

"That's it? All that and that's it?"

Katie looked at Michael and gave him a broad smile. "The rest is our little secret." She winked at the young man, who blushed appropriately.

Michael cleared his throat. "Mrs., um. . . ," he began, then looked at his mother for help in Katie's last name.

Katie intervened. "Just Katie, please." She looked at Marcy for permission to instruct her son. "That's okay with you, isn't it?"

"Oh, sure. But I'll expect Mark to call you Mrs. Webster or Miss Katie, at the very least."

Michael cleared his throat for the second time. "Okay, well. . . Katie, would you like to come and see one of my games sometime? I play baseball."

Katie felt flattered at the young man's attention. *Volontiers!* Then, to Marcy, "I told him I'd love to."

Marcy frowned playfully. "Mmmm Hmmm. . ."

Marcy walked her friend to the door and gave her a tight hug. "Please come back."

"I will. I promise. I'm just a couple of minutes away."

"But for so long. . ." Marcy's eyes misted over. "I want to know, Katie. But I won't beg you to tell me. Whenever you're ready."

Katie smiled. "I promise. One day, I'll fill you in. But for now. . ."

Marcy gave her a quick hug and then pushed her teasingly out the door. "For now, go home! Something tells me you'll be shelling peas the rest of the day!"

Katie laughed easily and started down the steps when she heard Marcy call her name. She turned slightly to see her friend standing in the open screened door.

"I almost forgot! Sunday the kids—Michael and Melissa—are singing at church. You'll be there, right?"

Church? Katie's eyebrows raised slightly as she pondered for a moment the prospect of attending a service in the church she had been raised and baptized in. Brooksboro United Methodist Church stood proudly at the end of Main Street just past the downtown district. Its brick structure was large, and its proud, white steeple beckoned its members to come and learn about God each and every Sunday morning. Katie remembered how her father always parked the family car on the west side of the building. Every week, parking in the same spot. It was as if by some unwritten rule, that one spot was solely his. And it was the same inside the church. Every week they sat in the same section on the same oak pew. Katie remembered how cool it felt against her skin when they arrived and how hard it had become an hour later. The same piece of wood, bringing both comfort and discomfort. How could that be?

81

She wondered if the carpet was still blood red, if the stained-glass windows, arched and pointed toward heaven, still exquisitely depicted the life of Christ. Did the smooth and polished, massive wooden cross still hang behind the pulpit, flat against the stark white wall, offering hope and forgiveness and, above all, mercy to everyone who put their faith in what it represented?

She speculated on how it would feel to walk through the wide, double doors; to see the older, socially prominent, backbone-of-the-community men and women dressed in their Sunday best; to smile at the little boys wearing shiny loafers and little princesses in Mary Janes. Did they wear those anymore? Was going to church something that was prepared for on Saturday night? Did mothers continue to lay out their children's clothes after Saturday's dinner? To roll Little Susie's damp hair just before bedtime? And if they slept on those rollers. . .or attempted to sleep on them. . .did they swear, as she had sworn, that they would never do this to their daughters?

"I hadn't really thought about it. I mean, it's been so long since I've been to church. . . ."

On those words, Marcy walked away from the screen, allowing it to slam against the door frame. She took a few steps toward Katie and placed her hands on her hips.

"You haven't been to church in a long time?" she asked, as if it were the unpardonable sin.

Katie shook her head no. She folded her hands across her abdomen and licked her lips. Sweat was beginning to pop out across her forehead. It was ten degrees of hot, she thought and then chuckled silently. The old saying had been a favorite of her father's. She hadn't heard it or thought it in years, possibly because there was nowhere else on this planet that felt as hot as the South in the summertime.

"You and your husband don't go?"

"Not really. I mean, we went for special things. . . ."

"What kind of special things? Christmas and Easter?"

"Yeah. Christmas and Easter. Anyway, I hadn't really thought about going. . . . I don't know what Mama wants to do. . .you know, with my being gone so long and all. . . ."

"I've never known Miss Carolyn to miss a Sunday!" Marcy said as she made her way to Katie and placed her hand on Katie's arm. "Listen. You and Miss Carolyn plan to come to church on Sunday. You be sure to tell her I said so and that Michael and Melissa are singing a duet. And, you tell her I said for y'all to plan to have Sunday dinner with us afterward, okay? Mama and Daddy'll be here, too. It'll be just like old home week!"

Katie smiled and nodded. "Okay. I'll tell her." She took two small steps toward the sidewalk, turned again, and added, "Your children can sing?"

"Beautifully."

"Do tell. Their mama could never carry a tune in a bucket," she playfully muttered, then sprinted toward her mother's home as Marcy called out, "I heard that! And, I'll see you Sunday!"

CHAPTER SIX

Carolyn was squatting in front of the leafy, green row of pea plants several rows over and a few feet down from her friend Roberta. The two women had busily snapped the long pods from their stems for more than two hours. When they had arrived, the sun had not yet burst through the haze of low-lying, light gray mist, and the warmth and humidity had been noticeable but tolerable. An hour later, the incandescent orb cut through the dull vapor with brilliant victory and was now blazing in the bright blue, cloudless sky. The ladies donned wide-brimmed straw hats to protect their skin and to keep the rising temperature at bay. Even so, they occasionally had to wipe sweat from their brows with the bandannas they kept tucked into their watchbands. The heat brought with it the small but pesky gnats, buzzing about them, alighting tenaciously on the sweat-induced stickiness of their faces and doggedly humming as they crawled with unabated perseverance in and out of their ears. When they became intolerable, the toiling women blew them away by forcing air from an extruded lower lip, a southern skill mastered from early childhood. They intermittently talked about the weather, Roberta's husband, Sam, and Marcy and her children. Carolyn mentioned the Ladies Sunday School Committee luncheon that was to be held in her home the following month and asked Roberta if she would help with it. Roberta told her that, of course, she would. For the most part, though, they picked the peas in silence, dutifully focusing on their monotonous task, punctuated by the steady snapping sound as pea pods were separated from the vine. It was as if the unremitting tedium of pea picking developed a life of its own, momentarily separating them from the predictability of their small-town existence.

Carolyn felt her tongue beginning to stick to the roof of her mouth. As she scooted down the row without breaking her squat, she glanced to the end to see how much farther she had to go. She ascertained about twelve feet and decided she could not wait that long to slake her thirst. She and Roberta had brought more than enough water in washed-out, gallon-sized milk jugs. After dropping another handful of pods into the half-filled basket, she knocked the dirt from her gloved hands and slowly straightened her body. Her joints ached and her muscles twitched. She would often say she was getting too old for this, but her mother, at age eighty-four, was still picking fresh vegetables on a weekly basis without complaining. But, Carolyn thought, her mother did every-thing without complaining. Katharine Mills, known to family and friends as Kate, was a fine example of fortitude, tenacity, grace, and charm. All these rolled into one tight, petite, unbending package. *One unbending, unyielding, controlling package,* she reiterated to herself, half-smirking inside at the addendum.

She pulled the bandanna from her watchband and wiped her face. It felt blistered from the inside out. *Goodness,* she thought as she sighed heavily, *it's hot!*

"I'm getting some water, Roberta," she called out as she began mak-ing her way out of the pea patch.

Roberta took all of two seconds to jump up. *Remarkable,* Carolyn thought. *How that woman has managed to stay so vital is beyond me.*

"I'm right behind you!" Roberta answered in her soft, sing-song voice. Carolyn thought it to be one of the most endearing, yet tooth-grinding, irksome things about her best friend. A woman her age should have the voice of a grandmother, not a teenager. She always seemed to have an abun-dant supply of effervescent energy, sounding chipper and unnaturally optimistic, even when there was no apparent reason for such effusion.

Wordlessly, they made their way to Sam's truck, which Roberta had driven to Mr. Jenkins's farm and parked in the shade of a large old oak tree. The water jugs were kept cold in Styrofoam ice chests in the bed of the old green Chevy pickup that Sam had purchased for hauling yard debris and for days such as these. It had served them well over the past twenty or more years.

When they reached the truck, they removed their gloves, then Roberta reached over the side and opened the ice chest, pulled out Carolyn's jug and handed it to her, then reached over for her own. Carolyn took the heavy, wet container, opened it, then brought its mouth to her parched lips. She gulped the cold water quickly, then wet her bandanna and wiped her face again. The coldness of the cloth brought an instant relief. She watched as Roberta did the same. Together, they replaced the caps and put the jugs back into the melting ice inside the ice chest. This ritual had been performed so many times before that by habit and in silent unison they turned and leaned against the side of the truck for a moment of rest.

Carolyn took a deep breath and exhaled. It was time to tell her friend the news. "Katharine came home," she announced unceremoniously.

Roberta had a tiny, pale, and freckled face that reminded Carolyn of a china doll. Her limpid, dark brown eyes had an impenetrable quality that lent an obviously mystical air to the otherwise carefree sparkle of her personality. Those brown eyes now fixed their gaze upon her friend as she swung her head around reflexively at this momentous news, betraying her immense astonishment. Roberta's rosebud lips formed a wide "O," and her amber-flecked brown eyes widened. "What did you just say?" she asked with rhetorical stupefaction.

Carolyn smiled in spite of it all. "I said that Katharine came home." There was no need to repeat herself a third time. Roberta was clearly as shocked as she had been. "I know, Roberta, I know. I was just as dumbfounded as you are. Only it was like a part of me was given back, because I had given up hoping long ago."

Roberta reached over and grabbed her friend, embracing her in a tight hug, then released her. "When did this happen? Why didn't you call me? Tell me everything! No! First, let's go sit down. Do you want to sit under that tree or in the back of the truck?"

"The back of the truck."

Roberta all but ran to the rear of the truck and released the tailgate for the two women to sit on. When they got comfortable, their legs dangling off the edge, Carolyn continued.

"I was cooking supper two days ago and I heard the doorbell ring. I went to answer it, not having any idea who it could be at that hour and no one calling me or anything to say they were coming over—"

"Not that anyone does around here," Roberta interjected.

"No, that's for sure. Anyway, I opened the door and there she was."

"What did she say? What does she look like? Where has she been?" Roberta brought her small hand up to her chest and pressed, panting for breath. "I just can't believe this. I mean, all these years of wondering and praying. . . ."

"You can't believe it! How do you think I feel?"

Roberta took her friend's hand in hers and squeezed. She had so often thought of how horrible it must be not to know where one's child is. She sympathized with her friend, but she could not empathize. Everything had been so hopeless for Carolyn during that first year. She had been so powerless to control the issue. She hired private investigators, but they had come up empty. They didn't have a clue as to where to begin looking. Katharine had left a four-word note that read: "I'm out of here." However, she had given no indication as to where she was going or for how long. Roberta had watched her friend panic, then grieve, then become bitter and hard. There had been a languishing and reluctant acceptance that at times seemed rather that she was in denial of her sorrowful portion. Finally, as if to dissipate her anguish, it was as if Carolyn never had a daughter. Roberta hadn't heard Carolyn say Katharine's name in years. Roberta could never fully enter the disheartening misery of Carolyn's world. No one could. This was Carolyn's own private, quiet desperation that she lived out with grief-stricken pangs from day to gloomy day.

"I don't think I can imagine how you feel."

"I've been thinking a lot about how it was at first. All the lies I told everyone."

"No one blames you for that, Carolyn."

"No. I know. And I don't give a rat's pajamas what people in this town think anyway, but—"

"Yes, you do. You know you do."

Carolyn gave her friend a hard look. "No. I don't."

Roberta shook her head slightly. "I don't mean to argue with you, Carolyn, but if you didn't care, you wouldn't have told all those lies. You weren't protecting Katharine. You were protecting yourself."

Carolyn shifted herself over six inches from Roberta, then looked again at her dearest, most honest, most infuriating friend. "I can't believe you are saying these things to me, Roberta Anderson. I mean, here I am. . .telling you that my daughter has come home after twenty-five years. . ."

Roberta gently shifted herself over the necessary six inches to her friend. "You are my best friend in the whole world, Carolyn Morgan. And I am yours. If I can't say this to you, who can? You may be able to fool everyone in town, not to mention your mother and father, but not me. Never have and never will."

There was a stone lying near Carolyn in the bed of the truck. She picked it up swiftly, then threw it out toward the field of peas. "Yes, I know. I know, I know, I know."

Roberta looked thoughtful. "I know that you know that I know, but I would never have brought all of this up unless Katie had returned. I don't believe in adding unnecessary sorrow when someone is already down." Roberta was picking her words carefully.

There was a pause, then she added, "So! How is it going? This homecoming?"

Carolyn felt her shoulders slump. "I don't know. One minute I'm so happy to see her I could kiss her and the next I'm angry for all the misery she put me through for so many years. Her mother! Her own mother! How could she?"

"You never said what happened before she left. Oh, I know you had some sort of argument, but Marcy and I had arguments over everything from leaving her shoes at the front door to more serious issues like curfew and whether or not she could date outside her religion or race. She never left home over them. What in the world could the two of you have argued about that could have led to all this?"

Carolyn grimaced. She hardly wanted to admit the truth. Even now, it was too painful. But this was Roberta, and as she said, she could never fool her. "Buddy Akins."

"Buddy Akins? Oh, Carolyn!" Roberta giggled slightly. "That's absurd!"

"What do you mean, absurd! She was going to marry him!"

"She wasn't going to marry him, Carolyn." Roberta's eyes were twinkling. All this time. . .she had thought it had been something more serious. . . .

"What makes you so sure?" Carolyn could feel her dander rising again.

"Because Marcy told me. Katie was going to college. She wasn't getting married to anyone!"

"College? She hadn't even applied to a college. Hadn't looked into scholarships! Gave absolutely no indication!"

"Katie was going through a rough time of it then, Carolyn. . .what with Stan's death. . . I don't think the child knew what she wanted to do until the last minute. She told Marcy that she would have to wait until winter quarter to get in, but she wanted to at least get started."

Carolyn was truly shocked. She had never known, never even suspected. "What was she going to study?"

"Marcy said something about Katie not knowing what she wanted to do, but being very sure that she wanted to go to school. In fact, if I'm not mistaken, it was Buddy who talked Katie into going to college."

"Buddy! What are you talking about, Roberta Anderson?" Carolyn's emotions were swinging like a pendulum: one moment angry and the next astonished and confused.

"Well, if you're going to get angry. . ."

"I'm not angry!" she retorted, then sighed deeply in an effort to calm herself. "All right. All right. Now, I'm no longer angry. And I'm certainly not angry with you. I'm angry with. . .oh, I don't know who! I guess I'm angry with Buddy Akins." Carolyn shivered slightly. "Ohhhhh, I can hardly say his name. I certainly don't go into that hardware store. That man! That horrible man!"

Roberta answered calmly, "And why would you be angry with Buddy? For encouraging your daughter to go to college?"

"No, of course not! Okay, then. Not Buddy. At least not about that. I suppose I'm angry with Katharine for not telling me."

"Did you give her a chance?" Roberta asked gently.

Carolyn swung her head around to face the woman who sat beside her and kindly held her hand. "Did I—?" The entire conversation was too much. Carolyn buried her face in her hands and moaned. Katharine had planned to go to school! Why hadn't she known? Why had everything been so difficult that last year? She remembered the day she had driven to the hardware store where Buddy Akins worked after school. She had been determined, almost frightening herself with the strength she found to challenge that ne'er-do-well. When she walked into the store, she had seen him standing near the rear, broom in hand, sweeping the floor. This was what her daughter desired beyond an education and the freedom it would offer her!

As soon as he saw her walking toward him, he stopped in his labor and gripped the broom handle tightly with both hands. He nervously licked his full lips—the Akins' trait—and blinked hard. The blue in his eyes had been piercing. He raised his chin in defiance, then lightly jerked his head, the white-blond hair tossing. He had been expecting this visit for the two years he had been seeing her daughter. He had known that one day it would come—this showdown—Carolyn had seen it in his eyes and in the way his nostrils pinched.

When she had made her way to him, he looked down at her and spoke her name with conviction. "Mrs. Morgan," he had said.

She had not wasted any time getting to her point. "I want you out of my daughter's life." She had dipped her hand into the side pocket of her slacks and brought out a thin, white envelope. "There is a five thousand dollar check in this envelope with a stipulation that if you sign it and cash it, you will not see my daughter again socially. If you do, my lawyer will see you in jail. I've already spoken to him about this, so believe me when I tell you I will not hesitate to put you there." It had not been true. She had not spoken to a lawyer, but she knew that five thousand dollars would go a long way where someone like Buddy Akins was concerned. "It's a lot of money. I suggest you think it over carefully." And with that she shoved the envelope into his shirt pocket, turned, and walked out, her shoulders and back ramrod straight.

The following morning the check cleared the bank, and her daughter was gone. When questioned as to Katharine's whereabouts, Buddy had claimed that he knew nothing. But when Carolyn had asked him about the check, he gave her a casual smile, then whispered, "Unless you want everyone in this town to know the truth, I wouldn't ask that question." He had turned and walked away, and she realized that her plan had backfired.

She shook her head free of the memory and when she composed herself said, "I was such a fool and yet I was so sure of myself. We were not communicating properly. But that doesn't change the fact that she left me for twenty-five years without so much as a phone call. I just don't think that's fair."

Roberta looked down at the dirt under their feet. That much was true. "Have you asked her why she didn't call? Where she's been?"

Carolyn looked down. "No."

"But, Carolyn, you've had two days!"

"I know," she answered resignedly. "I did ask her the first night. She was so adamant in her need not to speak of it right then. And. . .I don't know. . .she seems to be. . ." Carolyn's voice trailed off as her eyes skimmed the uniform rows of pea plants.

"Seems to be. . .what, Honey?"

"Seems to be hiding something. I think that. . .I can't say for sure, and I don't want you to repeat this. . . ."

"Of course not."

"I think she's in some sort of trouble. But I don't know what kind."

"Trouble in her marriage perhaps?"

"I thought that. But when she spoke of her husband, her eyes lit up. One sentence is all she gave me, and I knew that this man was everything to her."

"Hmmmm. . ."

"I want to talk to her, Roberta. It just seems that every time I attempt to speak, angry words spew out of my mouth." Carolyn shook her head in resignation.

"You'll have to work that out for yourself, Carolyn. Take your time. Maybe go to the library and get a book on forgiveness or something."

"Remember all the books I read in the beginning, Roberta? Every self-help book I could find."

Roberta nodded and smiled brightly. "You said that Stan would refer to them as 'brain candy.' "

Carolyn laughed lightly at the memory. "I read everything from Adler to the Proverbs in the Bible."

"Stan wouldn't think of those as brain candy."

"No. It's the one thing Stan and I would have agreed on in this situation. Stan loved to read his Bible, didn't he? Thought every problem in the world could be answered between its covers."

"Perhaps they can," Roberta answered softly.

Carolyn took her free hand and patted the hands the two friends held together. "Perhaps they can," Carolyn repeated.

The two women sat for a few moments, both gazing out over the endless, uniform rows of green pea plants that led to the horizon. The world was silent and the air was still around them. It was as if life was finally filled with that peace which went beyond comprehension. Slowly, and in unison, they began to swing their legs to and fro. They took deep and even breaths. They stared, but they did not speak. At this place in time, words were no longer necessary.

CHAPTER SEVEN

Katie returned from Marcy's to an empty house. She closed the front door, shutting her eyes as the sound of the latch echoed solemnly around the cavernous foyer. She didn't want to be here alone just now, only there was nowhere else to go. It was so quiet she immediately heard the grandfather clock ticking, and she found it faintly annoying. This house, for all its antebellum charm, had a way of overwhelming her with its musty lifelessness when it was vacant. Although going to the bank would have been a chance to get away, she had to wait for her mother's car. She hoped that borrowing it would not be too much of an imposition or cause for another scene.

She slowly climbed the stairs and went into her room to retrieve the check from behind the framed photograph, then placed the check into her purse. She took a few moments to step into the bathroom and reapply a touch of lipstick, ran a brush through her hair, and washed her hands. Stepping back into her bedroom, she grabbed her purse, then walked back down the stairs.

She hadn't been in the formal parlor since her return and decided that now was a good time to do so. Opening the French doors almost ritualistically, she ushered herself into the shrinelike chamber and shut the door with both hands behind her back as she gazed around her. The room was dark and warm. She looked at the large bay windows that faced the street and noticed that the shades were drawn. She walked over and pulled them open, allowing the sun's light to fill the room. Why was it so warm in here, she wondered, then looked around the room for an air vent. As she suspected, the two louvered floor vents were shut. Using the toe of her sandal against the levers, she opened them and felt an immediate rush of cool air as it hit her squarely in the face and billowed the silk of her culottes around her shapely thighs. She was reminded of Marilyn Monroe's famous pose from *The Seven-Year Itch*, and she laughed lightly, then turned.

Preserved with museum-like consistency, the room was exactly the way she remembered it from twenty-five years ago. Her great-grandmother's camelback, tapestry-upholstered sofa was still sitting directly in front of the unused fireplace. Dark blue wingback chairs faced each other from either side of the sofa. She had always admired the ornately carved mahogany end tables with matching Tiffany lamps atop them. However, now her trained eye could appreciate their value and beauty all the more. A large sofa table was placed against the foyer wall. A massive, antique curio cabinet filled with her great-grandmother's Imari china stood as a proud centerpiece on the opposite side of the room. In the corner between the fireplace and the bay windows was a baby grand piano positioned diagonally.

That piano. She stared at it for long moments, wondering whether to embrace it or to kick it. For ten, long, insufferable years, her mother had insisted that she take piano lessons. It meant thirty minutes of practice before school—thirty minutes she could have spent in bed—and an hour of practice after school—an hour she could have spent with her friends. Despite her lack of self-discipline at the time, or at least her unwillingness to practice without being goaded into doing so, she fortunately had a great proficiency for playing the piano. Her long, agile fingers would poise gracefully over the ebony and ivory keys, sweeping up and down them as classical pieces were executed with flawless precision. Her mother would love to sit on the sofa, her back to the piano, soaking in a spirited sonata or a dreamy nocturne. The acoustics in that room seemed to rivet one's attention, perhaps the only distraction being the tapping of Katie's foot on the sustaining pedal.

In her ninth year of instruction, she and her teacher had come to an impasse. Katie refused to play the pieces as they were written, but would rearrange the compositions into something a bit more modern and dramatic. Her teacher would scold her and earnestly implore her to play the music as it had been arranged, but she would not. She would take liberties with the form, often adding burlesque elements. She had refused to do what was expected of her with the defiant nonconformity that was becoming so typical of her blossoming personality. She sought after self-expression and independent interpretation within the measures of the timeless pieces. Katie had laughed scornfully when her teacher threatened to call her mother. In fact, Katie practically dared her, knowing that her father would stand behind her on this issue. He had not really encouraged her flagrant disregard for musical convention, but his amused delight at her new style of playing gave tacit approval to her unyielding attitude.

That evening, a stern-faced Carolyn Morgan had stood in the doorway of Katie's bedroom.

"I got a call from your piano teacher," she began, fists placed firmly on her narrow hips.

Fifteen-year-old Katie, sitting on her bed, her American Literature book spread out before her, responded nonchalantly. "So?"

"So? So? Is that all you have to say for yourself? So?"

Katie placed the bubble gum she had been chewing onto the front of her mouth and pushed against it with her tongue, forcing a bubble that popped loudly against her full lips. She giggled, then pulled the gum from her mouth and placed it back on her tongue. What did her mother want? An apology? Hadn't she been complaining about these lessons for years? "I guess."

Her mother turned then and called downstairs for Katie's father. "Stan? Stan, get up here! We have a problem." She turned and glared at her daughter. "A big problem!"

"Oh, Mother, really!" Katie huffed, slipping her hand under the back cover of the schoolbook and slamming it shut.

"Don't you 'Oh, Mother' me!" Carolyn snapped back. She turned again toward the hallway. "Stan!"

Moments later, Katie's father plodded dutifully up the stairs in his house shoes, eventually appearing at the doorway of Katie's bedroom. "What's going on in here?" he asked, removing his pipe from between his teeth.

"Your daughter has all but threatened her piano teacher," Carolyn reported.

"I didn't threaten!" Katie defended herself.

"What would you call it then?" Carolyn asked. "I tell you! I don't know what to do with you," she continued, not waiting for an answer.

Ever calm, her father rested his shoulder against the door facing. "What happened, Kitten?"

"I don't want to play the way she wants me to, Dad."

"Which is?"

"The old way. I want to add my own style and she won't let me."

"She's the teacher," Carolyn added. "Not you, Katharine. You should do it her way, but no. . .you have to do it your way. . . ."

"Hush a moment, Carolyn," Stan ordered.

Katie watched her mother square her shoulders. *How dare he,* was written all over her face. Katie looked down to keep from laughing.

There was a moment of silence in the room before her father continued. "Katie." Katie looked up and met his warm and loving eyes. "Do you want to continue taking lessons?"

This was it! Katie thought. The moment she had waited for! Finally, someone asking her what she wanted. "No, Sir. I don't." She watched her mother's shoulders slump as she turned and walked defeated out of the room.

Katie never took another lesson. Occasionally, she would sit and play one of the last pieces she had learned, but eventually the lid had been closed over the keyboard, never again to be opened.

Until today.

Ben had insisted she study piano again. She had been resistant at first, but with Ben's charming persistence, she eventually gave in.

"I don't want you to call someone I will be uncomfortable with, though. Not at first, okay?" she told him as they dined at The Hamilton Place's fine restaurant, Bonaparte's, sitting at their usual table near the fireplace. Softly orchestrated music floated about them. The exposed beam cathedral ceiling soared above their heads, where a colossal wrought iron chandelier was suspended with imposing dignity. The warm fireplace, strategically placed in the far right corner, crackled romantically over the muted tones of polite conversation. A single candle in the center of their exquisitely prepared table shed a warm glow over their faces as they leaned toward each other. Placed on each table, Waterford vases designed exclusively for The Hamilton Place, with its distinctive etched monogram, held a perfect pink rose that contrasted well with the rustic French decor of the dining room. Upon arriving at the restaurant, female guests were offered a rose to enhance the magical romance of their dining experience.

"If that's what you want," Ben responded equitably.

Katie used her fork to slice into the piece of apple pie that was before her. "I need these calories like a hole in my head."

Ben chuckled as he bit into a piece of his own dessert. "How about a swim later? You can work it off. Will that make you feel better?"

Katie dipped her head slightly as she grinned up at her husband. "You are priceless, Ben Webster! Most men would have said something like: 'Now, Honey. . .you know you don't have to worry about your weight.' But not you. You tease me with talk of a midnight swim."

"Would you like to stay here tonight or head out to the country?" As president of The Hamilton Place, it was necessary for Ben to keep a suite of rooms as a residence, but they kept a country estate for weekends and holidays. Compared to the suite where the managing director lived, the Websters' suite was modest. Double doors from the third floor hallway led to an unpretentious, but beautifully decorated foyer. Beyond it was an extensive sunken living room personally decorated by Ben to resemble an old English estate, complete with baby grand piano. There were two bedrooms, with private baths, both of which boasted whirlpool tubs. There was an updated efficiency kitchen and a formal dining room where she and Ben entertained on numerous occasions. Beyond one side of the living room were two sets of French doors that opened out to a garden terrace with a dark green cast aluminum patio set, perfect for breakfast, late afternoon teas, or early evening cocktails. Katie loved living there—just the two of them—but it was also the perfect place for entertaining friends or luminaries. Sometimes tea would run into cocktail hour and dinner, all with a stunning view of the city day or night. Whether alone or with company, this place was her retreat from the hustle and bustle of Manhattan. She also found that here she could escape the persistent flashes of memory that so frequently haunted her consciousness. It was like a sanctuary from her troublesome and murky past, which sporadically threatened to rear its ominous head.

"We can stay here. Whatever is easiest for you."

"I'm a little tired. Why don't we stay here for the evening? We can swim in the indoor pool."

With that they slid their chairs back and walked out of the restaurant, making their way to the front desk, where Ben picked up the key to their suite and informed the night manager of his decision to stay the night. Making their way to one of the elevators, they passed Jacqueline's, the hotel's ladies' boutique, which was actually run by businessman Bucky Caballero.

Ben stopped suddenly and swung around to look at the heavy paneled double doors that led into the shop. "You know. . .if I'm not mistaken. . ."

"And you rarely are," Katie said, slipping her arms around his waist and resting her chin against his broad chest so that she could look into his eyes. At six foot, six inches, he was one of the few men she had ever been able to do this with.

He chuckled as he took her chin between his thumb and forefinger and gave a little squeeze. "You're so right," he said between mockingly clenched teeth. "As I was saying. . .I believe the young lady who manages this shop for Caballero was at one time a music major." Ben swung his arm around Katie's shoulders as he led her toward the elevators. "She's a bit younger than you. I can ask her if she'd be interested. Would you like that?"

"That'd be fine."

"You're sure? I can get anyone you desire."

"No, no. Let's keep this simple, okay? Besides, I really don't need the pressure of a maestro."

"Then I think she'll be perfect."

Andrea Daniels, called Andi by her friends, had indeed been the perfect choice. Born of a black father and an Asian mother, Andi was nothing short of stunning. Her skin was honey brown, her dark eyes slightly slanting, her lips full and red, and her long, straight black hair framed her petite face. Like her father, she was tall and willowy. Like her mother, she was exotic and charming.

A week after Katie's conversation with Ben, Andi had driven her BMW to Ben and Katie's country estate for their first one-hour lesson. As Katie descended the staircase to meet the young woman whom the housekeeper, Maggie, was showing in, she noted the widening of the dark eyes as they took in the massive foyer of their home. Determined to put Andi at ease, Katie extended her arm in greeting and commented, "It's a little overwhelming, isn't it?"

The two young women laughed, and Andi replied, "It's like something out of a magazine. You must love living here."

Without answering, Katie motioned toward the living room and asked Maggie if she could serve them coffee, "please." It was like that between Katie and the plump, matronly, silver-haired housekeeper. Even though Katie was the employer and Maggie the employee, Katie never abused her position. In truth, Katie had never grown accustomed to her position within the household. And Maggie—dear sweet, loving Maggie—had been with "Master William" since childhood. Ben considered her as much a mother to him as Lois Webster, who had given him life. Had Maggie turned to Katie and, in her brisk British accent, said, "Miss Katie, I'm very busy at the moment," Katie would have seen Andi to the living room, then prepared and served the coffee herself. But Maggie gave a slight nod of her head and asked, "Would you like the cinnamon coffee today, Miss Katie?" Maggie knew it was Katie's favorite.

Katie turned to Andi. "Do you like flavored coffee, Andi?"

Andi smiled, showing even, pearly white teeth. "I adore it."

Katie turned back to Maggie, who had taken a few steps toward the hallway that led to the back of the house. "Yes, Maggie. Cinnamon coffee." She took a step toward the living room, then quickly turned again and added, "And, Maggie? Hazelnut cream, please."

Maggie nodded again and made her way toward the kitchen.

Katie and Andi spent the next two hours getting to know one another. While sitting comfortably on the leather camelback sofa and sipping the flavored coffee from Katie's favorite Old Virginia Roses coffee set, Andi told Katie about herself and how she had come to live in New York City.

"I grew up just outside of Chicago," she began. "Dad was a truck driver. I used to be so ashamed of that," she said, looking down to her cup and saucer. "He never made enough for me, but he kept us clothed and a roof over our heads. And I suppose I'm more grateful now than I was then. Maturity does that, doesn't it? Makes us more mindful of the sacrifices of our parents?"

Katie shifted uneasily. Memories of her mother and father swept through her like a torrential wave. She swallowed a sip of the warm coffee, as if doing so would wash down the half-forgotten memories. "How did you come to live in New York?" she asked, changing the subject.

Andi laughed lightly. "Two things I love more than life itself. One is fashion. I studied every fashion magazine I could get my hands on! And two, the piano. I was blessed with talent. I worked very hard. My senior year of high school, I was accepted at NYU."

"Did you graduate?" Katie asked incredulously. *If Andi had,* Katie thought, *why would she be working as a manager of a small ladies' boutique?*

"I know what you're thinking. . .why the boutique, right?"

Katie blushed and Andi went on. "All my life I've had a desire. . .a pull, really. . .to absorb culture. I couldn't afford much, but I window-shopped at the best stores and boutiques this city has to offer!"

Katie giggled. This was something they had in common, though she would not say so. To do so would give away too much of her past. . . and nothing could make her do that.

"Anyway, one day I decided to visit Samuel Jordan & Co.—Bucky's company was called that then. I figured I couldn't afford to live in homes that grand, but what was stopping me from looking at how the other half lived?" She took in the room around her. "As you live. As I walked in the door, the chimes sounded and he turned from where he was standing. . .he was overseeing the placement of a framed photograph of a magnificent piece of property. . .and the next thing I knew he was offering me an excellent job with an incredible salary while I was having dinner with him at Bonaparte's."

"I never truly understood why he has two such opposite businesses."

It seemed to Katie that Andi stiffened a bit, but then relaxed and smiled. "Diversification. Bucky loves beautiful homes and beautiful women. As a matter of fact, he jokes with me all the time about his two priorities, top real estate and leggy women! You can't imagine the impression you've made on him," she added lightly. Actually, Katie could. On the rare occasions that she had seen Bucky, she had felt his eyes on her. It made her uncomfortable, but she would never have said anything to Ben. Doing so would move him from protective to obsessively jealous, and she did not want to be the cause of conflict between the two businessmen who had dealings with each other. Andi continued, "I'm just happy that I have the opportunity to work among beautiful clothes and beautiful people." She gave a slow smile. "And eat at Bonaparte's whenever I so desire," she added with a wink.

Ever proud of her husband's business, Katie smiled and, leaving behind all thoughts of Bucky and why Andi would leave her studies for a job with him, asked, "Do you like Bonaparte's?"

Andi laughed. "I must confess this to you. . .although maybe I shouldn't. . . ."

Katie felt closer to Andi in this short period of time than she had to anyone since leaving Marcy in Brooksboro. It was wonderful to have a girlfriend, a chum, a comrade. "No, no! Tell!" Katie exclaimed.

Andi looked about as she placed her cup and saucer deliberately on the rococo-style coffee table. It was as if Andi were about to give away government secrets. "Okay. . .here goes! One Christmas, when I was broke, I asked all of my family to give me money for my gifts. During the New Year sales, I went to Saks and purchased a simple black dress. . . simple, mind you. . .that was regularly priced at $549.00, but was on sale for $197.00. Back then, I thought that was exorbitant! But I had enough money to buy it and enough left over for dinner the next evening. Naturally, I wore the dress. . . ."

"Naturally," Katie agreed, amused.

"And naturally the eyes of every man in the place nearly popped out of their heads!"

"I can imagine," Katie remarked. And she could.

"Well. . .this is the part you had better not tell. . .I did more than steal glances. . . . I also stole a sterling place setting and a white linen napkin with THP monogrammed in gold stitching in one of the corners."

Katie burst out laughing and Andi followed. "Don't tell Mr. Webster," she said, dabbing at the joyful tears that formed in her eyes. "He may want them back!"

Katie laughed all the harder. She felt like she was in high school again, and it was delightful. "I promise! I won't!" And she never had.

From that week on, Andi had either driven to Katie's country estate or Katie had come to The Hamilton Place for two-hour lessons. Andi was an excellent teacher and Katie a willing pupil, and, although they formed a warm friendship, they never saw each other socially.

Until the fund-raiser given by Bucky Caballero's company. . .

In her mother's formal parlor, Katie slowly opened the cover of the highly polished piano, then slid the padded leather stool from its place and sat down. Positioning her hands in the center of the keys, she took a deep breath, closed her eyes, and began to play Brahms' "Waltz in A-Flat." Her shoulders rose and fell, her head dipped and swayed as her eyes remained closed and her fingers danced over the ivories. As soon as she hit the final note, a faint clapping came from the doorway, and her eyes flew open to see her mother standing in the now-open doorway, wearing overalls, her hair plastered to her head with perspiration.

"I see you've come a long way from 'Love Is Blue,'" Carolyn commented, as she moved into the room toward her daughter.

Katie gave an amused smile. "I'd say so."

Carolyn stood beside the piano and leaned against it, resting her forearms on its surface. It brought a moment of surprise to Katie. The mother of her past would have never done that. "You'll leave a mark," she would have said. But this mother seemed perfectly at ease.

"When did you take up the piano again?"

"About a year ago," Katie answered, pulling the cover over the keys.

"Oh, no! Play something else for me. I always loved to hear you play."

"I remember that."

"Well. . .except for 'Love Is Blue.' You played that song into the ground!"

Katie laughed and her mother joined in. It felt good, this bantering. It felt like what Katie had always hoped for with her mother. "Can I play for you later? I really need to go to the bank and I was wondering if I could use your car?"

Carolyn straightened and shoved her hands deep into the side pockets of the overalls. "Katharine, we need to talk. . . ."

Katie quickly stood and replaced the stool. "Not now, Mama. We will, but not now."

"When then?"

Katie looked around uneasily. "Maybe tonight," she answered as she made her way toward the foyer.

"Katharine, are you in some sort of trouble?" Carolyn asked quickly from behind her.

Katie stopped short, took a quick breath, then spun around. Her eyes met her mother's and the lip-chewing began again. Carolyn took slow steps toward her, never breaking her eye contact. "You are, aren't you?"

Katie stopped chewing on her bottom lip and felt it quiver. She folded her arms across her abdomen as tears pushed their way to the surface of her eyes and she looked down, blinked hard, then looked back at her mother. "If I answer you. . .yes or no. . .will you let it go for now? Please?"

Carolyn took a moment to consider the proposition, then answered. "Yes."

"Promise?"

"Oh, Katharine, really!"

"Promise!"

"Yes, yes. I promise!"

Katie moistened her lips slowly, then nodded. "Yes. Yes, I'm in trouble. . .sort of. But it's not of my own making."

Carolyn brought her hand up to her chest and pressed lightly. "Oh, my. . .I knew it. . . ."

"Mama!" Katie exclaimed, then softened. "May I have the keys, please?"

CHAPTER EIGHT

Brandon Caballero, called Bucky by family and friends, sat behind his light oak desk in the suite of offices on the second floor of his Madison Avenue real estate firm, B. Caballero Properties, Inc. Like himself, the agency was a cut above. He accepted properties that began at five hudred thousand dollars—starter homes that he comically referred to as "two bedrooms and a closet"—and soared way beyond the five million dollar mark. With sales in the high seven figures, he was second only to Edward Lee Cave, Inc., in the number and value of upscale residential sales. He employed seventeen professional men and women, all of whom adored and respected him. He had seen to that personally. And, other than his sister and her husband, no one in the office knew of the illegal escort service he was operating under the guise of Jacqueline's Boutique. When it came to those employees, one could call them by whatever title they wished, including high-priced escorts, but in reality those men and women were prostitutes. And they were his.

B. Caballero, Inc.'s clientele were unceremoniously referred to as Rich/Park Avenue. Some worked in Manhattan, living in the city or posh outlying suburban areas during the week. They would then retreat to their lavish weekend properties in the Hamptons—properties that his firm had also listed, sometimes exclusively. Others were retired or international clients. Like Bucky, they could easily recognize the finer things in life, whether it be exorbitantly priced properties, auctioned artwork, or exquisite designer furnishings. His personal preference was for French art, his favorite piece being a fifteenth-century miniature from Jean Fouquet's *Les Heures d'Etienne Chevalier* portraying St. Bernard of Clairvaux preaching and resisting the temptations of the devil. A copy of the print hung on the wall behind his desk. Occasionally, he would swivel the large, black leather office chair around, tilt back, and stare at it, almost mesmerized by its antiquarian complexity. Today, as he sat with St. Bernard diligently watching over him, he tapped a fountain pen on a yellow legal pad that lay diagonally in the center of his tidy desk, notwithstanding the stacks of files atop it. From beyond the double oak doors leading to the secretary's work area, he could hear the determined click-clicking of his sister's high-heeled pumps against the peach-colored marble floor. *Mattie,* he thought, and the tapping of his pen ceased as he leaned back and closed his eyes.

Had life been different. . .he thought reflexively, obsessively. How would it have changed things? How would he and his sister have been affected? Perhaps they would not be the cynical, conniving, and controlling people they now were, he mused. Perhaps they would be honest in their business dealings. Perhaps Mattie would be a homemaker, president of a garden club, mother to a brood of happy children. She would have been a good mother. A loving mother, as their mother had been before her premature death.

Indeed, the turning point in their lives had been her death. Until then, the two of them, along with their brothers, had led relatively normal childhoods, much like the families around them. Their father had been a successful attorney and their mother a pediatrician in an era when few women held professional positions outside the home. The Caballeros lived well. Vacationed in enviable spots. Drove the best luxury automobiles. Entertained in a style that drove the community wild with excitement upon receiving an engraved invitation for such an event. It had been a picture-perfect life until Janice Caballero was diagnosed with brain cancer. Her death had been slow and painful. . .especially as seen through the eyes of twelve-year-old Bucky. His beloved mother would no longer cup his face in her soft hands, manicured nails lightly brushing his charmingly boyish rosy cheeks, and tell him what a "looker" he was.

"You're such a looker, my Bucky," she would tell him, almost whispering the words. "You'll break many a heart. Do you know that, Son?"

"Oh, Mama." He would blush, secretly loving the richness of her display of affection.

"Just remember your mama when all the pretty girls come around. Just remember who loved you first," she would tease, then reach down and kiss him soundly on both cheeks. "You'll be a handsome, handsome man. . .just like your papa. But you'll be even more handsome. The best looking Caballero yet."

And he was. Although not a tall man, he was well proportioned and, as his young receptionist put it, "buff." He had to ask someone at his health club what it meant. "It means you're lean and muscular, Mr. Caballero," one of the personal trainers informed him as he twisted a short white towel in his smooth, tanned hands. "A young chick told you that, huh? Way to go, Mr. Caballero!" he continued, then snapped the towel into the air with a burlesque flourish.

Bucky's thick black hair, at age fifty-one, had neither thinned nor turned gray. He wore it layered and combed straight back. His facial features were angular and chiseled and would be almost gaunt if not for his flashy good looks. His eyes were a misty shade of gray and his brows were heavy. When Bucky Caballero looked at something or someone, it was with an influential look of inspiring intensity that commanded immediate respect and demanded attention. Thanks to the health club's tanning salon, he sported a year-round tan. His nails were meticulously manicured. His tailored suits bore his monogram on the right inside coat pocket which peeped out coyly when he reached for his ostrich-skin billfold. He was a man's man, dynamic and successful in his far-flung businesses—both legal and illegal. The public loved him, especially so in the last six years. He had begun the annual fund-raising event sponsored by B. Caballero,

Inc., and he knew he had hit gold. Substantial amounts were raised at the star-studded charity functions he put together and directed with such passion. However, only 45 to 50 percent made its way to the charity's beneficiary. Maintaining a public image of legitimacy and even do-goodism was all part of his con game. It kept his ego afloat amid the buoyant currents and eddies of his exuberant life. The satisfaction he derived from putting one over on people had an obsessive quality about it.

As a child, there had been other hobbies. . .hobbies that helped him enormously as an entrepreneur. Early on in his childhood, he had become feverishly enamored of the luxurious lifestyles that only massive wealth could afford. He had also begun to study diverse cultures with inquisitive fascination. The East and the West, having such differing cultural norms concerning beauty and luxury and leisure, engrossed him to abstraction. He was often tantalized by what he felt was a lifestyle even more affluent than the one he knew, and he determined that he would one day attain it. As he matured, it became very clear to him what it was that people craved both interpersonally and materially. He knew that if he gave it to them, really laying it on thick if necessary, he could be taken into their trust. He knew how to use the persuasive intensity of his personality and heartbreaker good looks to full effect, and he knew the impact he had on people.

Only the finer things in life appealed to him, whether it was real estate, the decorative and fine arts, fashion, or literature. Everything had to be the best and he knew that if he gave enough people—moneyed people—what they wanted, he would also get what he wanted in return. "The triumph of moneyed interests," he would frequently mutter to himself, as if it were an obsessive religious incantation. He seemed to know intuitively the extent to which people, especially wealthy people, needed to feel significant. His present life attested to the fact that he understood very well how to make them feel exceedingly, and even obscenely, significant. His morbid interest in poring over nonfiction books about the Mafia had developed from a passing fancy to an almost fanatical fixation. "Everyone has some kind of hang-up; this happens to be mine," he would tell himself with glee whenever his daily life intruded upon his fantasies—or vice versa. He found himself becoming more and more awestruck by the origin of the secret organization, their terrorist strategies, their to-the-death loyalty to each other, and their ironic, tribalistic devotion to home and family. The blood oath secrecy seemed to resonate with his deep-seated need for family, a family that had been cruelly twisted and distorted when he entered adolescence.

His one other hobby—nay, his pride—was Mattie. His lovely Mattie, who had suffered more than all the others at the death of their mother. She had been a child of six at the time, with dark brown hair that fell in ringlets to her waist and large brown eyes that held sparkle and fire. Those eyes were cold now. Calculating. Bucky twitched involuntarily at the thought.

One could hardly blame Mattie, for she had no control over her life from the moment they lowered their mother's casket with its virginal white satin lining into the ground—with its ornate silver handles glinting orange in the early evening sun. The rich, black soil fell in heavy clumps atop its lustrous cherry finish as their father strategically planned his next marriage. It wasn't that their father had not loved their mother but rather that he was a man incapable of living alone or caring for the quartet of Caballero children by himself.

Within a matter of months, Mino Caballero married Germaine Muldinaro, a striking beauty with a vicious tongue, who ruled the children with unsparing sternness. Feeling or showing no affection for her stepchildren might have been enough to enrage the young Bucky with a smoldering resentment that was to fester and grow with each passing year. However, Germaine wielded her adult power over Mattie with even greater ruthlessness than with the boys. The fact that Mattie was a carbon copy of their beautiful mother seemed to fuel this cruel woman's bitterness all the more. The fact that Bucky so adored his mother made this habitual treatment of Mattie, her living embodiment, all the more unbearable. As Bucky matured into adolescence, he began to realize that Germaine viewed Mattie not merely as competition for

Mino's affections but also as an ever-present reminder of the woman she knew he would always adore and whose shoes she knew she could never fill. In her husband's presence, Germaine was the paragon of maternal love, but when he was not home, as was often the case, her black eyes were icy cold, her jaw set, and her words cruel.

Over the years, Bucky felt compelled to protect his sister all the more. They confided in each other their realization that Germaine was absolutely single-minded in her overarching quest to secure a place for herself socially and to spend as much of her husband's money as possible. With fashionable clothes and impeccable grooming, her glamorous and shapely outward appearance belied her unsympathetic loathsomeness on the inside. Bucky despised her, but no one hated her as much as Mattie.

After high school, Bucky was accepted at Cornell University, where he studied business for his undergraduate studies and finished up with his MBA at Columbia. He then obtained his certification from the NYU Real Estate Institute. Some of his friends had teased him that he "worked too hard at being overqualified" and that he "had too much icing on his cake." He would reply calmly that he always liked icing better than the cake and that it was better to be overqualified than unqualified. His goal was to work with the ultrarich, and they respected degrees and knowledge as much as the glamour and glitz they surrounded themselves with.

His time at school was divided between his books and his brotherly concern for his sister. He visited her often, and each time he thought she had become more like their stepmother than the time before. Her childlike innocence and endearing winsomeness were long gone. An oppressive demeanor that broke what little of his heart was left for such feelings had replaced her contagious laughter.

"I have but one soft place in my heart," Mattie had confessed to him during one of his visits. "And that is for my brothers. You can just forget the rest of the world. I refuse to let anyone get next to me, Bucky. I will leave this pit one day and I will rule my world. You'll see."

Bucky had managed to keep his emotions at bay until that fateful day in 1966. He had just accepted a job as vice president of marketing for a well-known, white glove, real estate broker in New York City. Samuel Jordan & Co. was owned by its namesake, a kind, older gentleman who was to become his mentor. Sammy, as he was affectionately called, had taken an instant liking to Bucky and spent a great deal of time training him in all phases of the New York real estate market. Sammy's investment of time paid off handsomely. Bucky's natural charisma and strong instincts for sales and marketing were to increase revenues by over 100 percent in the first twelve months of his tenure with Samuel Jordan & Co. Bucky took great pride in this new phase of his life. Renting a modest but clean ground-floor brownstone apartment in The Village, he began his adult working life with earnest ambition. He worked hard for Sammy, exchanging playtime for long hours at the office. He characteristically brought stacks of work home at night. He dated only once or twice a month and even then it was more of a ritual formality.

Women, to him, were a means to an end. Nothing more. There would never be anyone like his mother. Germaine had seen to that. Even Mattie, with so much splendid potential, could not measure up to their mother. Thanks to their stepmother, Mattie's potential had been effectively stifled.

Two years after his move to New York, Mattie graduated from high school, then came to the city for a summer of fun and frolic before entering college. Bucky, shrewd in business savvy, but soft toward his sister's plight, determined that he would use the time to reach his sister's unyielding heart. But she had no sooner unpacked her bags when the telephone shrilled. It was to be a harbinger of tidings that would make their lives even gloomier and destroy what should have been their inheritance, their birthright.

Mino Caballero was dead, killed in an automobile accident. The shock of losing his father paled for Bucky when—at the reading of his will—he discovered that his father's entire estate had been left to his stepmother. As soon as Mino's attractive, young attorney had spoken the last words, Germaine Caballero had stood proudly and looked down her nose at her husband's four offspring. Squaring her shoulders, she reached into her black leather clutch purse, brought out an embroidered linen handkerchief and announced, "Mattie, you have two weeks to vacate my home. If any of you have anything personal that belongs to you, I expect you to remove it immediately. However, I also expect you to clear with me everything that you claim to be yours." She then dabbed at the corners of her tight red-painted lips with the handkerchief, as though she had just swallowed a morsel of tasty meat.

Ten years of emotion seemed to rise like bile within Bucky. His eyes glazed over, his rock-hard muscles stiffened even more, and his heart turned stonier. He rose slowly from the wingback chair, then turned slightly to face the woman he hated with more passion than seemed humanly possible. "What about Mattie's college fund?"

The attorney cleared his throat discreetly. "That, of course, will be entirely up to Mrs. Caballero, since the fund was in your father's name and not your sister's."

"How could my father have been so stupid?" Jimmy, his oldest brother, stood and asked. Frank, their younger brother, sat quietly, the fingers of his hands woven together and thumbs twirling furiously around each other.

The attorney removed his fashionable glasses slowly and shook his head. "I only do what I am told to do."

Bucky looked over at his stepmother and noticed the seductive way her lashes lowered as she looked at the man behind the mahogany desk. He knew what she was up to, the despicable snake. "Wait a minute. My father hired you a couple of years after he married Germaine. I always wondered why he let old Mr. Jamerson go. They had been together for years and all of a sudden. . ." Bucky snapped his fingers and turned to Germaine. "It was you. The two of you. You've been having an affair, haven't you?"

"How dare you!" she shrieked at him. Frank's finger twiddling stopped, and Mattie rose to stand behind Bucky. "I loved your father!"

"You loved my father's money!" Bucky bellowed at her. "You're a no-good piece of trash, Germaine. And you know what happens to no-good pieces of trash? They end up in the trash can. That's where you'll end up. Where you belong. In a trash can!"

She smiled then, a slow, easy, catlike smile that imprinted itself on Bucky's brain, never to be removed. To his death, he would remember her look. The look of a victor. The look of someone who would not. . . could not. . .be stopped. At least not in this lifetime. "Well, then I guess we'll have something in common, won't we?" she asked rhetorically out of the corner of her mouth, her eyes shifting to Mattie.

Bucky lunged for her, but Frank jumped up quickly and grabbed him. Jimmy grabbed him from the other side. "Let her go!" they ordered, as Germaine flinched, then turned and walked out the door. Bucky freed himself of their grasp with a brisk twist of his shoulders, then turned and pointed at his stepmother's accomplice. "I'll get you," he said. "I'll get you if it's the last thing I do!"

Mattie had become his responsibility. Jimmy had joined the armed services and Frank was busy putting himself through medical school. Jimmy sent money when he could, but it wasn't often. He eventually made the air force his career, and the family rarely saw him. Frank graduated magna cum laude and went on to become a respected cardiologist. At a medical conference in Anaheim, California, he met the future Mrs. Frank Caballero and decided to settle in the area. In the end, that left Bucky and Mattie as the sole New York survivors of what had once been the promisingly large, highly respected Caballero family. Mattie studied business in school, then joined Bucky at Samuel Jordan & Co. as Sammy's new assistant. Bucky knew that Sammy had given her the job as a favor to him, and he was grateful. But it wasn't enough for what he wanted. . .what he needed. With his focus taken off supporting his little sister, he set his sights on creating his own financial empire. . .one that would eventually change the ladies' boutique business that his stepmother and her philandering attorney-husband had established in several four- and-five star hotels across the city.

Initially, Germaine's had been a raging success. But Germaine Caballero knew more about spending money than making it and eventually welcomed news of her near-bankruptcy rang joyously in Bucky's ears. Together, he and Mattie formed a dummy corporation and waited for Germaine's bankruptcy to be finalized. He sent his lawyer to the hearing and instructed him to make preparations for purchasing the remains of the business as soon as possible. In two months' time, Germaine and her husband were living with his relatives in a small community outside of Chicago, where she reportedly tried her hand at running a single boutique. Meanwhile, Germaine's logo was being replaced with Jacqueline's with its now-famous sketch of a well-rounded woman with accentuated hips.

Bucky rode the crest of that wave of satisfaction for a very long time indeed. "Vengeance is sweet, sayeth the Lord," he said, proposing a toast to Mattie with mock, high-sounding eloquence over a celebratory champagne dinner, just the two of them.

"I don't think God is behind this, you know. I sometimes wonder if He even knows we're here," she had replied with stoic resignation.

Bucky and Mattie were now the proud owners of a business they knew little about. They had a need for someone who could manage the business and an even greater need for the finances to run it. They brainstormed methodically until Bucky remembered stories of the exploits and business ventures of Chicago Black Hand gang member Big Jim Colosimo. Big Jim had taken a noncompetitive route to success, using high-class prostitution as the true moneymaker behind a legitimate business.

Bucky and his sister could have never imagined the revenue that could be generated from such a simple idea. They hired a woman named Victoria, shrewd in business and adept at handling the finer points of the high-class escort business. . .especially those that allowed their escorts to go one step further. Eventually, Victoria decided to marry one of their best customers, a local politician, elevating her socially and leaving her post with the Caballeros open. Bucky and

Mattie had deliberated over a suitable replacement until the afternoon a beautiful young woman named Andi walked into the realty office. She was obviously hungry for more than life was giving her at that point and willing to do anything to change that. She was an exotic beauty who was also smart and charismatic. . .three qualities she would need to run both Jacqueline's of The Hamilton Place and the escort service, where the private books were kept in a locked file in the back office of The Hamilton Place boutique.

Andi had been easy prey. Bucky had been overseeing the placement of a framed photograph of one of their Hampton properties when he heard the chimes of the front door. He instinctively turned and was instantly captivated by the woman's beauty. Making quick steps toward her, he asked with characteristic charm and enthusiasm, "May I help you?"

She blushed slightly as she swept her long, straight, inky black hair over one shoulder. He studied her for a nationality. The honey brown skin told him she was African. The exotic facial features told him she was Asian. "Yes. A friend told me that you displayed photographs of properties. I thought I might look around a bit."

She was lying. But she was fairly good at it. This woman didn't have enough money to make rent, much less purchase one of the property listings his agency advertised. But she was intriguing. "Why don't I show you around?"

"Thank you. I'd like that."

As they walked around the "gallery of homes," Bucky spoke to the starry-eyed young woman in soft, tantalizing tones. "What do you think of this little hideaway?" he asked teasingly. The "little" hideaway was a modern-styled brick mansion with spectacular views of New York's lush valleys and mountains. He heard Andi sigh and watched her tiny rosebud lips curl in a dreamy smile. "It's one of a kind, isn't it? Dramatic architecture. Barrel-vaulted entry, five bedrooms, four and a half baths, media room, studio, and a master suite that beckons one to enter and never, ever leave."

"Mmmmm," she moaned, with genuine longing.

"Not a bad price either," he continued to tease, pointing to the high seven figures printed in the right-hand corner of the glossy photo.

She turned her head slightly and gazed up at him with her dark, slanting eyes. "A little more house than I would be looking for," she said.

"Just what are you looking for, Miss—"

She turned fully to him. "Daniels. Andrea Daniels."

"Miss Daniels. I'm Brandon Caballero," he replied, extending his hand slowly.

"The B. Caballero? Mr. Caballero?" she asked in astonishment.

Apparently, his fine reputation had reached even the little people, he thought. He gave her his best infectious smile and she returned it. "That's correct. Didn't expect someone like me to show you around, did you?"

She blushed slightly. "No. No, I didn't."

He paused for effect. "You're very beautiful when you blush like that, Miss Daniels," he said, his voice low and titillating.

Andi blushed all the more, but continued to look him in the eye. He admired that quality in a woman. "Andi. My friends call me Andi. You can, too. That is, if you'd like."

Bucky raised his chin slightly and gazed down his sharp nose at her as if he were studying a rare and precious artifact. "I'd like to, yes. And I'll tell you what else I'd like. Let's put strolling about the photographs behind us and have dinner together this evening. Perhaps then you can tell me more what it is you are looking for in housing."

Andi's eyes danced in sheer pleasure while Bucky mentally checked off another conquest. He would have her eating at his table that evening, out of his hand after dinner, and in his employ by morning.

Later, he took her to Bonaparte's for a champagne dinner. She had worn an expensive black dress, which indicated she had style and class. She exuded it really. She was also charmingly effervescent and well able to keep up with all his lighthearted banter. Laughingly, she recounted another dining experience at Bonaparte's, during which she had stolen a place setting. This indicated she had questionable scruples and a certain risk-taking gutsiness. He liked that.

"What do you do, Andi?"

"Do?" she asked, perplexed.

"Yes. Do. For a living. You must do something to make money. That's a beautiful little frock you are wearing." And it was beautiful, although he could have done better by her. He had mildly insulted her, and he wondered if she would realize it. If not, she was perfect as a replacement for Victoria, who at one time had been properly groomed for the position for which she had been so well suited. Yes, Andi seemed to have the potential to perform intellectually. But if she was too smart or too sensitive, he would not be able to mold her into the woman he would need for her to become in order to please his customers, keep his books, and remain steadfast and silent about his slight indiscretions.

She did not acknowledge the oblique insult that brought an archaic smile to his lips. She lightly touched the satin material that tightly hugged her midriff as she whispered, "Saks Fifth Avenue."

Interesting, he thought. "Do tell."

She blushed coyly. . .prettily. He knew that she was his for the taking. "Christmas gift."

"Frankness. I like that."

She squared her shoulders and looked him directly in the eyes. "If it is worth my while."

Perfect, he mused. "You didn't answer my question."

"Question? Oh. Work. I'm a music major at NYU. To be honest with you, I work on campus for mere peanuts."

"Really? A woman of your intelligence and sophistication?" he baited.

"Thank you, Mr. Caballero," she said, beaming radiantly back at him.

"Bucky."

"Bucky," she whispered.

"Are you finished with dessert? I have something I want to show you."

He read her face as her eyes widened and her lips pursed together. He knew that she assumed he was going to "show her his bedroom etchings."

118

What he had in mind was much better than that. Having a woman was easy. Finding the right person to manage his business was not.

Moments later, he took her by the elbow and escorted her down a long, cherry-paneled hallway where the closed gift shops and salons of The Hamilton Place were located. When they stopped in front of the locked doors of Jacqueline's and he retrieved the key from his coat pocket, he heard her gasp involuntarily.

"Do you like beautiful clothes, Andi?" He spoke softly, whispering the caressing words near her ear.

She licked her bottom lip as she stared ahead. "I love beautiful clothes."

He opened the door, flipped on the light, and studied her face for the expected reaction. It shone with enthusiasm like a child's at Christmas. Bright. Filled with wonder and amazement. Then a look of confusion replaced it and she spoke quickly. "Do you want to buy me one of these dresses? Is that it? For a price?"

He looked her seductively in the eye. "And would you pay that price, Andi?"

She hesitated for a moment, never breaking eye contact, then whispered her answer, "Yes."

He chuckled lightly, then walked over and cupped her face in his hands. He kissed her gently. Once. Twice. Then whispered in her ear, "Don't worry, Puppet. It's not sex I want. I have a job for you."

She stepped back slightly. "A job? But what about my classes?"

"It will mean putting your studies on hold. But only for now. But you must understand that in exchange for that, I will pay you well. Very well." She gave him a perplexed look. He gently took her by the shoulders as he continued, "Andi, I can put you where you've always wanted to be. You will have the best, do you hear me? I'll put you in a beautiful apartment. Buy you beautiful clothes. Teach you everything you need to know to be socially acceptable. You'll have it all, Puppet. Just say yes. Just say, 'Bucky'. . . , come on. Repeat after me. . .'Bucky'. . ."

"Bucky. . ."

"I would love to manage Jacqueline's. . . ."

He watched her eyes widen and her lips part in a smile. "I would love to manage Jacqueline's. . . ."

"And make a lot of money. . ."

"And make a lot of money. . ."

"And wear beautiful clothes. . ."

"And wear beautiful clothes. . ."

"And be one of the beautiful people. . ."

"And be one of the beautiful people. . ."

"And live in an upscale apartment. . ."

"Yes. Oh, yes."

"Say it," he demanded.

"And live in an upscale apartment."

"Now seal it."

She wrapped her arms around him as if he were saving her from sinking to the bottom of the ocean and pressed her lips hungrily to his. The purchase was complete. She was his for life.

Two years after Andi had come to work for him, Bucky found himself sitting across the desk of another estate attorney, this time as the recipient of good news. Having no close relatives and thinking so highly of him, Sammy had left the controlling interest of the company to Bucky with him at the helm as president. The rest of his estate had been left to nieces and nephews. . .the ones he liked, anyway.

After what he thought was an appropriate amount of time, Bucky changed the name of the company to B. Caballero, Inc., and began to make a distinguished reputation for himself. When he had stumbled upon the idea of sponsoring an annual fund-raiser, he knew he had struck gold. Government officials, celebrities, and high society attended; they were as eager to have their names in the paper or on the eleven o'clock news as he was to reap the personal benefits. The sheen of his supposed charity would make him less a target of law enforcement probes. Add to that the numerous government officials who had availed themselves of Bucky's high-priced escorts. He felt he had built himself a fortress.

From his position, Bucky had more collective dirt on them than they could ever have on him. This year's AIDS Foundation gala had been his most prosperous ever.

Bucky heard a light tapping on his door and knew that it was Mattie. As was so typical of her, she never waited for him to call her in. She simply tapped and entered. He looked up to see his beautiful sister sweep into the room, her trim figure outlined in a light pink Coco Chanel suit, her long black hair secured in a tight chignon. She carried an air of great authority, which she clenched as tightly in her fist as the leather folder she was now holding in her left hand. Bucky noticed the bright sparkle of the gold and rubies from the wedding set that her husband, David Franscella, had given her. He had somehow convinced her to marry him in 1979 after they had dated briefly. Bucky knew that she did not love David—was incapable of loving any man romantically—but that for social purposes, he served her well. Bucky suspected that they had separate bedrooms, but had never asked. His sister was cold and she controlled her husband in the way that she controlled every fiber of her being, with an iron will.

Naturally, David benefited from the relationship. He lived in a fashionable New York City brownstone, hobnobbed with the elite, drove expensive cars, wore tailor-made suits, had a membership at the best health club, dined in the finest restaurants, and carried the clout of working for B. Caballero, Inc. What more could a man who had originally worked as one of their escorts possibly ask out of life? And truth be told, he served his purpose well as Bucky's personal assistant. He took care of the uncomfortable business—the things Bucky pretended were beneath him.

Bucky dropped his pen and gave his sister a polite smile. "What can I do for you, Mrs. Franscella?" he asked, teasingly.

"You can drop that Mrs. Franscella line for one thing," she answered curtly. "You can get me a drink for another." Mattie dropped into one of the leather wingback chairs in front of his desk and crossed her shapely legs, lightly tapping her foot adorned in leather pumps that perfectly matched the color of her suit.

Bucky rose dutifully and crossed to the wet bar. "Your pleasure, Madam? The usual?"

Mattie gave a cool look of reserve. "Make it a double."

Bucky reached for the bottle of vodka he kept reserved for his sister while observing her in the mirror behind the bar. "This early in the day, Mattie? What's got you all riled up?"

"Name it. Co-op board reviews, clueless appraisers, Mrs. Ashford Griffin. . ."

Bucky brought the prepared drink to his sister, the ice clinking pleasantly against the crystal, then rested against the front edge of his desk. "That old battle-ax giving you a hard time again?"

Mattie took a long swallow of her drink, then rested her head against the back of the chair and closed her eyes. "That woman is a thorn in my flesh. As demanding as she is, you'd think she was the only client we have. I've never known anyone so hard to please in all my life."

Bucky reached down and lightly brushed Mattie's soft cheek with his knuckles. "Save yourself, Pet?"

She opened her eyes and gave him a catlike smile. "I am not hard."

Bucky walked around the desk and returned to his chair. "Oh? And what would you call it, then?"

Mattie thought for a moment before answering. "Ruthless."

"Merciless."

"Don't be ridiculous. I can get along with people as well as anyone. . .as long as they don't get in my way."

Bucky chuckled, but it wasn't with a happy spirit. It was the same for him. He was the epitome of cordiality. . .unless someone got in his way. Someone. . .such as William Benjamin Webster.

Mattie read the changed look on his face. "What do you know about Mr. Webster?"

Bucky took a deep breath, then released it. He stood, reached for the gold cigarette case and matching lighter placed carelessly on the desk, and walked toward the large window that overlooked the city streets and massive skyscrapers. Removing a cigarette from the case and snapping it shut, he thoughtfully placed the cigarette between his lips with a slow, deliberate motion. With a quick flick of his thumb, the wick on the lighter blazed; and he held it to the cigarette, squinting against the smoke. "Nothing. Yet."

He inhaled on it deeply, then blew the gray smoke through tightly pursed lips. "David's out now. . .trying to find out something."

Mattie stood quickly and walked toward her brother with one arm resting across her middle and the other holding the glass close to the side of her face. When she was directly in front of him, their eyes locked, and he saw determination in the way she held her face and cocked one brow. "I won't lose everything I've worked for because of one man, Bucky. We've never had to kill anyone before, but I'm not above having it done now. I hope you and I understand each other on that. I hope we see this the same way."

Bucky met her gaze with the same authoritative look. "I don't want you worrying your pretty little head over it. I'll handle it, you hear me? I don't want you involved."

Mattie gave a sarcastic chuckle. "Involved? You're kidding me, right? I'm up to my eyeballs in this. We all are. And you and I both know that men like William B. Webster will never understand what we do or why we do it. They look down their noses and pretend they would never use the service we provide. A good service. The kind of place where men and women in our social circle and from international circles like ours can go and be assured of a quality escort when they need one. The fact that some decide to take it a step further than that. . . well. . .we can hardly be blamed for that now, can we?"

Bucky took another drag from his cigarette. "You're kidding yourself, Matt. We take a pretty high cut off those 'further steps.' And you know it. Our books are the proof of what we really do—and it's the major source of our revenue."

Mattie swung away from Bucky and walked toward the middle of the room. "Only Andi sees those books!"

Bucky was right behind her. He grabbed her by the arm and turned her to face him. "And we don't have one idea as to where Andi is, in case you have forgotten. She could be sitting across the desk from your friendly neighborhood FBI agent, for all we know!" he hissed through clenched teeth. The pressure of the past week was beginning to show. He immediately regretted losing his temper with Mattie. It wasn't her fault. Mattie straightened her shoulders and Bucky released her arm.

"Don't you know someone at the bureau? Someone who might have come into one of the Jacqueline's for something other than a blouse?"

"Yeah, I know someone. I've sent David to talk to him over a nice, gratis brunch."

"When do you expect him back?"

Bucky gave a quick look at his Piaget. It was almost one o'clock in the afternoon. "Any minute," he answered, then walked over to his desk and ground the cigarette into a crystal ashtray. Just then, the office door opened and David Franscella strolled in.

CHAPTER NINE

At a little after one o'clock on one Friday afternoon, William Benjamin Webster had walked toward the New York City location of The Hamilton Place. THP, as it was commonly called among the personnel, was a chain of five-star hotels located domestically in New York, Chicago, and Los Angeles, and internationally in Paris, Rome, Sydney, and London. Plans were underway for a prime location in Atlanta and soon thereafter in Geneva.

The Hamilton Place had been founded by his great-grandfather and was recognized as one of the finest, most elegant hotel chains in the world. Celebrities and dignitaries knew that this was the place to be, a place where they could be pampered without "obsequious simpering," as Ben put it. Adding a forceful, "Groveling. It means, no groveling when you have to interact with celebrities," when he was met with the inevitable bewildered frowns. The not-so-famous knew that this was the place to go if you wanted to see the "beautiful people" without being treated rudely. The corporate mission statement ensured that all guests were treated as VIPs: Patronizing attitudes were absolutely not tolerated at any level of management or staff. After all, a seeming "nobody" could be a head of state or a "big shot" could be just a "nobody." New employees at all levels were required to carry the mission statement with them at all times and read it every workday until it was committed to memory. Professionalism and adequate staff training were Ben's number one priorities.

He was called William by family and friends, Mr. Webster by hotel personnel, and Ben by the one person who mattered the most in his life. His wife, his world, his reason for living. . .Katie. He took a deep breath and released it as he adjusted the coat of his dark, understated Briani suit. It was the only thing about him that could be called understated. Handsome beyond words, Ben was tall, broad-shouldered, and naturally tanned. He wore his dark hair combed straight back. His eyes were dark brown, commanding and yet playful. His nose was straight and his full mouth had a deep cupid's bow in the center of the upper lip. His jaw was set resolutely square, and his chin was indented with the slightest hint of a dimple. His face reflected the bright ambition and enthusiasm that steadfastly burned within him and was unfailingly evident to all he came into contact with.

Ben's intelligence and wisdom were equal to his good looks and charm. As a child he had been sent to the best private academies, then received his college education at Cornell University, where he graduated in Hotel Management. He graduated in 1972 with a bachelor of science degree. He had immediately taken a position at THP-New York, where, at his father's insistence, he began training as a bellhop, eventually graduating to doorman, concierge, front desk manager, and day manager of the hotel. When Ben was twenty-eight, his father suffered a massive heart attack that left him a wheelchair-bound invalid, thrusting the young Ben forward, forcing him to take the reins as president and CEO of The Hamilton Place. His father and the executive board held their collective breath, waiting for Ben to make his first mistake. They nervously listened as he announced a decision to restore the hotels to their original opulence. He hired a top hotel interior designer, who decorated each of them with sophistication reminiscent of the Loire Valley chateaux. With its quiet, yet undisputed elegance, the chain had become more successful than his great-grandfather could have ever dreamed. Yet it had been the result of a hunch, backed up by the self-confidence, business training, and practical experience that told him this was the right thing to do.

Now, at forty-five, Ben was considered one of the most masterful and proficient businessmen of his generation. He was often interviewed on talk shows and by journalists. His face had graced the cover of a dozen magazines, including *Money, Hotel Business,* and *Travel & Leisure.* He was admired by his colleagues, respected by his employees, and loved and adored by his wife. His Katie.

It had been more than two days since he had seen her, yet it seemed a lifetime. Since he put her on the southbound Amtrak train at 7:05 P.M. on Tuesday, he had relived every moment of their six years together over and over. He recalled with vivid clarity the first time he had ever laid eyes on her. In the early nineties, his cousin Cynthia Ferguson had purchased stock and become a partner in the upscale law firm of Mosely, Carter, and Troup. Having been his personal attorney for years—as well as a dear friend—he naturally transferred his records to her new office. He called her one morning to ask her to join him for lunch later that day.

"I'd love it," she replied, and he could picture her removing the gold-framed glasses and tousling her short, red-gold hair as she wrinkled her nose playfully. "I need to get out of this office in a desperate way. I already have more work to do than I can possibly manage."

"I hope they've provided you with a proficient assistant."

"A real gem, William. Her name is Katie. She's sweet, she's bright—smart as a whip, really—and honestly the tallest, most beautiful woman I've ever seen."

Ben was mildly amused and his curiosity peaked. "Well, I can't wait to meet her then."

"What time are you picking me up, darling cousin?"

"I have a short appointment at eleven this morning. Can you get away around noon or a little after?"

"Noonish is fine-ish," she teased. Since childhood, they had made fun of the stilted, "jargonesque" language, as they called it, of their social equals.

"See you then, Cyn."

"Ta-Ta," she responded breezily.

A few minutes after noon, he arrived at the law firm and was escorted into Cynthia's office by her secretary, to find his cousin standing next to a woman nearly six feet tall. Her long, smooth chestnut hair glistened with a lovely, healthy sheen that he could not take his eyes off. Nor her delightful, laughing blue eyes. He was instantly attracted to her with a force he had never experienced in his life. Until this moment, he had been preoccupied with school or with expanding his family business. Until this moment, he had dated only the most elegant and beautiful society women of the elite circles he moved in. It had taken him many years to realize what it was about them that grated upon his sensibilities so. He found their lack of simplicity and purity of heart to be something he could not live with for long. Some of them had been downright superficial. *The glittering butterflies that only flutter in rarefied environments,* he often said to himself. Until this moment, he did not feel that he had truly lived.

"William," Cynthia greeted him with a kiss, then turned to Katie. "Katie, may I present my cousin, William Webster. William, this is my legal assistant, Katie Morgan."

Ben waited to see if she would extend her hand in greeting. When she did, he responded. Her handshake was firm. "Nice to meet you, Mr. Webster," she replied, her gaze impressively steady.

He had been intrigued by the lilt in her voice. "Do I detect a southern accent?" he asked her.

She smiled, a captivating smile, and answered, "Yes, Sir, you do."

"What part of the South are you from, Miss Morgan?" he asked, using her name, a technique he had long ago learned as a method of making those around him feel comfortable.

It seemed to him then that she stiffened slightly, then answered, "Georgia." She turned to Cynthia and quickly added, "Y'all enjoy your lunch. I'll have the information you need when you return." She looked at Ben again, extended her hand for a final handshake, and said, "It was nice to meet you, Mr. Webster." She then coolly turned around and walked out the door.

Ben gave his cousin an astonished look. "I think I was just dismissed," he noted with mock sarcasm.

Cynthia laughed with him. "Yes, 'Mr. Webster,' I think you were."

Ben tried to keep the conversation at lunch about family and mutual friends, but it somehow kept returning to Katie. How long has she been working for the firm? Where does she live? Is she seeing anyone? Exactly how tall do you think she is?

Cynthia smirked knowingly over her oriental chicken salad. "She's been with the firm since '85. Rumor has it that Mr. Mosely knew her and helped her get into school, but I don't have a clue as to where he knew her from or why he would help her. It's probably just a silly rumor. She certainly is gifted enough as a legal assistant, so whatever brought her into the business is fine with me. The staff loves her, although I don't think anyone knows a lot about her. She stays fairly quiet about her personal life, but I can tell you this: There are no framed photographs on her desk. And to answer your last question, she's five feet, eleven inches."

"How do you know that?" Ben asked through a half smile.

"I asked her," she replied matter-of-factly. "I see no need to wonder. If you have a question, just ask. And," she said, shaking her fork at him, "I'd advise the same for you."

"And what does that mean?" he asked, as he cut a piece of his filet mignon.

"It means, dear, lonely, shamefully available cousin, that if you want to see her socially, ask her out."

Ben had done exactly that. When he returned his cousin to her office, he stepped into the cubicle where Katie worked. She had been busily tapping away on the keyboard of her computer, a pencil wedged between her teeth and another one shoved behind her ear. She was somewhat startled when he approached, and the pencil fell nervously from her mouth to the floor. He found the moment strangely endearing.

"Oh! Mr. Webster. Did you enjoy your lunch, Sir?" she asked, reaching for the pencil without taking her eyes off him.

There was an office chair positioned flush against her desk and he motioned to it. "May I?"

Katie looked around momentarily, then nodded. "Certainly. Is there something I can do for you?"

Ben sat in the chair and shoved his hands into the pockets of his trench coat, wrapping it around his legs in the process. "Yes. You can agree to have dinner with me on Saturday evening. Provided you are not busy, of course."

There was an uncomfortable moment of silence before she answered, "No. . .no, I'm not busy. But I mean. . .what. . .what do you. . .why do you? . . ."

Ben laughed out loud, something he was not commonly known to do. This woman was already making an indelible mark on his life, he thought. "Is there some reason why I should *not* want to have dinner with you, Miss Morgan?"

Katie blushed. "No. No, I can't think of any. I'm just not accustomed to having men like you ask me out."

"What kind of men are you accustomed to having ask you out?"

Katie quickly looked down and in doing so dislodged the pencil behind her ear. It, too, fell to the floor, and she nervously reached for it while mumbling, "Pencils. You can never find one until you don't need one, then they're falling all over the place."

Ben laughed again and she straightened, slapping the pencil onto the desk. "Actually, Mr. Webster," she began honestly, "I'm not accustomed to having any men ask me out."

Ben thought she was kidding and told her so.

"No, Sir. I'm not. Not too many men want to ask the friendly neighborhood Amazon woman to dinner."

He leaned over slightly and replied softly, "Afraid you may attack them, are they?"

She laughed easily. "Yes, Mr. Webster, I suppose they are."

"I'll take my chances."

She playfully narrowed her eyes and mimicked, "He is boldly going where no man has gone before!"

He laughed again. "Okay, then," he said standing. "First things first. My name is William—not Mr. Webster. Second, I need your phone number so that I can call you later and get your address. Does that work for you, Katie? May I call you Katie?"

Katie stood. "Of course," she answered, then reached for one of her business cards and scribbled her phone number onto the back.

He took it, staring at it for a long moment. Katharine Morgan, Legal Assistant, it read under the arched Mosely, Carter, and Troup.

"They haven't added Miss Ferguson's name yet," she noted.

"So, I see. I'm surprised Cynthia hasn't raised quite a stink over it."

Katie smiled. "She has. The new cards should be in later this week, and the new signs will be painted by the end of the month."

"That's my girl!" he said teasingly. "Thank you, Katie. I'll call you tomorrow evening and we'll discuss where and when."

She simply smiled and nodded—another moment he saw as endearing.

On Saturday evening, he took her to Bonaparte's, where they sat at his personal table near the fireplace. She looked incredible in a short, A-lined, black velvet dress with scoop neckline. She accessorized simply with a single strand of pearls and matching pearl stud earrings. He recognized them as genuine and wondered how someone on her salary afforded them, but didn't ask. She immediately impressed him as having the full range of human complexity—solitary and yet totally connected, compellingly assertive, outspoken and charmingly brazen, and yet supremely compassionate. An unusual blend of deep South and urban sophistication. A paradox, a puzzlement, and an enigma that reached inside his hungry heart and fed him with delight.

Katie noticed the monogram stitched on the cuff of his crisp, white shirt and inquired, "What is your full name, William?"

He cleared his throat and straightened his shoulders. "William Benjamin Webster, at your service, Ma'am."

She giggled, then replied, "Hmmmm. . .you know, you don't look like a William to me. Anyone ever call you Bill?"

"Not to my face," he answered, playfully furrowing his brow.

"Will?"

He growled.

"Willy?"

"No."

"Billy?"

"Someone called me Billy once—," He grinned.

There was merriment in her eyes. "And then what happened?" she asked, reaching for her glass of wine.

He frowned as if sincere. "I had to kill him."

She nearly spilled her wine, she laughed so hard. "Okay, okay. . . ," she said in an attempt to calm herself, then looked around the room. "People are beginning to stare," she commented by talking out of the side of her mouth.

She thought that people were gazing at them because of their frolic. But he knew that they had been admiring the beautiful woman across from him all evening. It would have been impossible not to. "It's you they are compelled to stare at. Every woman in this room is wishing she looked like you, and every man regrets that he is not sitting where I am sitting at this moment."

She silently looked at him for a moment as if perplexed as how to comment. But then she smiled and said, "Ben."

"What?"

"Ben. You look like a Ben."

"And what does a 'Ben' look like?"

"Oh, I don't know," she answered, slowly sitting back in her chair, tucking a strand of the glimmering chestnut hair behind an ear. "Handsome. Powerful. Distinguished."

He gave her a half smile, then reached into his inside coat pocket for a cigar, removing it carefully from its leather cigar case. It was a smooth, full-bodied Davidoff, which he indulged in once or twice a week. He inspected the medium-gauge, six-inch, hand-rolled beauty, running its length up and down his nose as if to savor the subtleties of the aged tobacco. He snipped off the tip with a solid gold cutter. It was a rare treat he allowed himself, but it was truly exquisite to be treated with the company of one such as this long-legged beauty who sat across from him.

"Do you mind?" he asked.

"No. I enjoy the smell of a good cigar." She leaned toward him, took the candle from the table's centerpiece in her hand, and extended it so that he could light his cigar. *How perfect,* he thought. *How completely perfect.*

During the following year, between board meetings, long tired hours at the office, and business trips, Ben taught Katie about his world and his lifestyle. He brought out the best in her and she brought life to him. He doted on her, buying her beautiful clothes and jewelry. He taught her about art, wine, and the ballet. She challenged him in games of touch football, fed him fried chicken and homemade ice cream. He brought the best that life could offer into her world and she was the best that life offered in his. The hometown qualities and the cultured woman were completely one. Ralph Waldo Emerson had written that beauty without grace is the hook without the bait. He had surely meant it for Katie.

Best of all, she loved him.

Katie shared very little about her past with him. He knew that she was from Georgia, but when he asked her for specifics about her home or her family, she became vague, her eyes misting over and her gaze suddenly far away. He yearned for her to share with him but was willing to patiently wait. When they married a year later, she did not include anyone from her family on the guest list. She invited associates from the law firm. No one else.

It wasn't until their honeymoon that she opened up. "I ran away from home when I was eighteen years old," she began unexpectedly. He had taken her to Hawaii. They were standing on the balcony of their elaborate hotel suite, watching the sun slowly set in a fiery blaze of orange, fuchsia, and deep purple. The breeze from the lanky palms swept her hair away from her face, which shone in the luminescent glow of the fading sunlight. He noticed that she gripped the railing as if she were holding onto a lifeline.

"Pardon?"

She cleared her throat discreetly and repeated herself. "I ran away from home when I was eighteen." He noticed her swallowing deeply. "Twenty years ago I ran away from home," she reiterated.

"You're kidding me."

She never once stopped staring at the horizon. "That's how I got to New York. I ran away from home and ended up in New York."

"Why? How?" he asked quietly.

"I went to Atlanta first." There was a look of pain that flashed across her face. "And I met another runaway named Abby. She said she had a sister who lived in New York and she would let us live with her. So, we hitched to New York." She spoke as if she were separated emotionally from the situation.

Ben couldn't picture it. His wife? His beautiful Katie? Faded blue jeans and an unwashed T-shirt? Thumbing her way up the coast? "And then what happened?"

She gave a small grimace. "We arrived."

He did not respond for a moment. "And did you live with her sister?"

"For awhile. Then, we got our own place. Then, Alexi—Abby's sister—died."

"Died? How?"

"Drug overdose."

"Good heavens!" he nearly exploded.

And still she looked ahead. "And then Abby went to live with Alexi's boyfriend. Then the two of them were arrested. Abby went to jail and I haven't seen her since."

Ben stood quietly, trying to digest all that she had said. Finally, he commented, "Wait a minute. How did you get to the law firm?"

She turned then and looked into his eyes. He had seen something then that he never before witnessed: There was a combination of pain and remorse so deep that it went beyond suffering and guilt. It almost frightened him, but he wanted her to go on.

"I worked hard. I went to school. I got a job."

"And your family?"

"They still don't know where I am."

"What? Katie, are you telling me that for twenty years your mother and father have had no idea as to where you are?"

She looked back to the fading sunset. "My father's dead. He died when I was a junior in high school. He. . .he was. . .my best, best friend. . . ." And with that she began to cry.

He took her in his arms and allowed her to cry until there were no tears left. *Poor kid*, he thought. *What must she have gone through to cause her to leave her home, family, and friends for twenty years without contacting them?* "Katie," he said gently as he lifted her chin to look at him. "What happened to make you leave home?"

Using the tips of her fingers, she brushed away the remaining tears that lay on the apples of her cheeks. "It was so stupid. I realize that now, but it seemed so monstrous then."

"Age often has a way of bringing things into perspective."

"My mother. . .she's so. . .she was so. . .I don't know. . .controlling. When I was a little girl, I wanted to be just like her. It was as if she were a queen, someone to place on a throne and worship. I adored being with her. She was my rock. My buddy. We had our little rituals, you know? Every morning the same thing. And she had this garden. . .this English garden. . .the prettiest flowers you've ever seen. She spent hours there. Therapy, I guess. But she made me a part of it. She told me what each flower was and how it grew. Sunshine or shadow, warm weather or cool. . .that kind of thing. But then one day everything seemed to change. She. . .it was as if she became a dictator over my life. I had to take piano lessons, which I detested. And she knew how much I hated those lessons, but for nine long years she demanded that I do it. She would say, 'Katharine!'—she always called me Katharine. Never Katie, like everyone else. Except Daddy. He called me Kitten. She would say, 'Katharine, good little girls from good southern families always take piano lessons.' Suddenly everything was about what little girls in our social position could and could not do."

"What social position was that?"

Katie raised her eyebrows and made a face like that of a snob looking down her nose. "We were the Brooksboro Morgans."

He chuckled slightly. "And I suppose that was pretty important."

She sniffed. "To Mama it was. You see, she was a Mills. And a Mills. . .well. . .I don't know how to explain this. Ben, have you ever been to the South?"

"A few times. Atlanta mostly. I vacationed once in the North Carolina mountains. Does that count?"

"Not even close. Southern society is unlike anything you've ever come across. I mean, you think you know some uppity people? Well, the people I come from could stare your society down and make them feel like worms to be coiled around a fishing hook and sent flying into the murky waters as bait for the big fish."

Ben tried to picture his old friend Ashley Sylvia Trenton, the biggest snob he ever met, coiled around a fishhook. It brought an unexpected smile to his lips.

Katie continued. "Southern society has money, but it's old money. Houses have been passed down from one generation to the next. Bloodlines are important. Who one's parents are is very important. When a girl says to her parents that she has a date on Friday night, her mother's first question is, 'Who are his parents?' and her father's first question is, 'What does his father do for a living?' And. . .if you are of this class. . . well, it's not so much that it's spoken. It's just that it is. When a girl of this class turns sixteen, she's debuted. There are lavish balls and we wear white. Personally, I thought it was ridiculous, but Mama. . .well, Mama said, 'Katharine, you'll look back one day and be glad you did this. It tells everyone that you've been set apart.' But I didn't want to be set apart. I wanted to be like everyone else."

Ben touched the tip of her nose with his finger. "You seem fairly normal to me."

"Well, of course! You see southern people are a relaxed people, Ben. But they are also very. . .oh, what is the right word. . .cultured. But it's our culture, don't you see? You could never figure it out. We. . .we're just as comfortable in silk eating with Grandmother's silver, china, and crystal that we are praying we inherit, as we are in khakis and sports shirts eating off paper plates at a picnic!"

"And you don't think I could figure this out?"

She shook her head in a firm "no."

"So, let me see if I've got this right. You and your mother were at odds over social issues."

"More than just that. There was a boy. . . ."

"Ah!"

"Don't sound so smug. His name is Buddy. . . ."

"Buddy? Sounds like a true southern name."

"Very funny. His real name is Chad. But we called him Buddy. I think it was a family term of endearment. Anyway, Buddy and I met in a chemistry class. Naturally, I had known him all my life, but had never actually talked to him. And then we were paired up in chemistry. . .lab partners. . .and he was so different!"

"Different than the boys your mother wanted you to date?"

"Yes. He was cute and smart and so sure of himself in spite of his lack of social standing. Here I was, the social debutante butterfly, and there he was, with not two nickels to rub together to make a dime! And yet he was the most genuine person I had ever met! But my parents would never have understood. Or so I thought. So we hid our relationship. The kids at school knew about it, but no one told. I would sneak out of the house to see him and meet him down on the corner. I wished he could come up to the house like all the other guys I knew, but my mother would have had a fit! Then, one night Daddy saw Buddy and me out with a few friends. He asked me about it. I admitted our relationship and he agreed to keep my secret. No one understood Mama like Daddy!" She took a deep breath before continuing. "But then Daddy died. . . ."

"How?"

"Massive heart attack. He lived for a few days, though. Buddy would sneak up to the hospital to see me. We'd hide in the stairwells, and he would hold me while I cried."

She grew quiet for a moment and Ben sensed that she was reliving the memory. "Then what happened?" he whispered.

"Mama found out. It was horrible. More than I can talk about right now. And then I ran. I don't know where I thought I was going or what I thought I was doing. I just ran. I truly imagined I'd go back. But then. . ."

"Then?"

She looked him directly in the eye. "I ended up in Hell's Kitchen, Ben. I couldn't call my mother then. What would I tell her? 'Look at what your little debutante became, Mama?' It would have broken her heart. Staying away was easier than facing the truth. So I stayed away." She moved away, walking over to the other side of the balcony, and stood with her back to him.

He walked up behind her and placed his hands on her shoulders. "And in all that time no one has known where you are?"

She shook her head silently.

"Don't you think you should call your mother?"

She turned to face him. "And say what? 'By the way, I'm alive and well'?" she asked sarcastically. "Ben, I wanted you to know the truth, but it's my business. One day, I'll call. But not now. And I don't want to talk about it day after day. I've lived twenty years by myself and she's lived twenty years by herself. Maybe now. . .maybe now if I called it would be the wrong thing to do. Can we please just leave it at that for now? I just felt like I had to tell you the truth. So you wouldn't ask any questions about my past or my family. I just hope you can still love me."

"Of course, I still love you. I'm a little shocked, and it may take some time to digest what you've told me. But I still love you."

And he did. His love for Katie had grown every day. With the aid of an investigator, Ben had already learned of her past work experience. He had loved her anyway, and she had never known of his discovery. He felt it was best that way. When she was ready, she would tell him. Until then, he was content to wait.

Over the next few years, she spoiled him with her love and he made her life a fairy tale. He showered her with gifts. They traveled extensively. They attended and hosted lavish parties. Ever mindful of her hidden brilliance, he encouraged her to further her education. He sent her to school to study French, art and music appreciation, and literature. But it was when he encouraged her to take piano lessons that their idyllic life fell apart. . . .

CHAPTER TEN

Fifteen minutes after one o'clock on that same Friday afternoon, Katie had walked through the weathered, walnut double doors of the small Brooksboro bank. The bank customers included just about every farmer and merchant in the small town of Brooksboro, not to mention the fine, easy-going citizens of the quiet county. When she stepped into the coolness of the air-conditioned expanse of the main lobby, she was filled with a strong sense of familiarity. Very little had changed. It was as if she had entered another time capsule. Dark walnut paneling, the familiar high ceiling, with elaborate molding just beneath it, brought back a flood of childhood memories. Glossy walnut railing corralled the various departments such as New Loans, Accounts Payable, Money Markets & CDs, Remarketing, and New Accounts. A row of glass-front offices was at the back of the room. She recognized the bank's president, Mr. Hughes, as he sat behind his desk talking on the telephone. All these years, she mused, and he's still here. Older, but remaining. It brought an unexpected smile to her lips.

To the right of the room was the row of tellers, who sat high on their stools, professionally entering numbers into the computers that had not been a part of the banking process twenty-five years ago. They all seemed so young to Katie. And with an aura of confidence, they seemed so sure of themselves and the job they were doing.

"Is someone helping you?"

Katie jumped slightly at the sound of the deep southern accent and turned to see a lovely young woman, who sat nearby with a switchboard telephone system on her desk. Her hair was pushed away from her face by the telephone headset, bringing all the more attention to the large eyes that stared quizzically at Katie. Katie ascertained that she couldn't have been more than eighteen years of age. And yet here she was working at what Katie guessed was a full-time job.

"I'm here to open a new account," Katie told her.

"New Accounts are at the far left-hand side of the room, just before you get to the offices back there," she answered, motioning to the back of the lobby.

"Thank you," Katie whispered and began to make her way in that direction. She passed several men and women, casually dressed for their trip into town. A few wore business suits. At least four men who stood in the long teller lines were inappropriately dressed in overalls. But Katie suspected they were their best overalls. When she neared the New Accounts section, she saw that the clerk was helping another customer, so she took a seat in a nearby area, which held eight to ten dark-wood English bar chairs. Sitting there she noticed two young men dressed in old jeans, yellowed white undershirts, alligator skinned boots, and soiled baseball caps sitting across from her. For a moment she was reminded of the young men from Hell's Kitchen she had encountered and she frowned slightly, as if trying to push those memories back deeper into the dark recesses of her mind, a walled-off portion of her past. They nodded simultaneously as they greeted her with "Ma'am."

She smiled casually.

"Sure is a scorcher out there, ain't it?" one of them asked her politely.

She crossed her legs and slid farther back into the seat. "Yes. It certainly is."

"Must be nearly a hundred out there," he continued.

"Weather man said ninety-four," the other added, fixing his gaze on her legs. "My goodness, you got some long legs, don't 'cha?"

Katie tried to relax. She had grown up with people like this. They were harmless really. They were just trying to be nice. But it had been so long. . .

"That's what they tell me," she responded kindly. She then opened her purse and peered inside as if to end the conversation.

"I don't believe I know you," the first man said. "You new here?"

Katie looked up momentarily. "Not really. I used to live here. Many years ago." She looked back into her purse and hoped that the two men understood her body language.

"You know," the second man said to the first. "I was driving down on 95 the other day and I got off at exit 13. . . ."

Katie glanced up and watched the two men through her long lashes.

"Uh-huh," the first man said.

"And I went into that truck stop. . .you know, that new one down there?"

"Uh-huh."

"And did you know they got a free movie show in there?"

"Is that right?"

"So you know what I did?"

"Watched yourself a movie?"

"Watched myself a free movie," he reiterated to his friend. Katie looked down as her lips broke apart in a wide smile and a giggle escaped her. She glanced back up and saw the two men smiling at her. "Made ya smile," he said as he winked at her.

"Yes, you did," she admitted. Just then she heard the woman behind the New Accounts desk call out, "Next?"

"That would be you, Ma'am. We're just here with our sister."

Katie rose to her feet, aware of goggle-eyed leers as she strode away from the two men. She saw that the bank customer who had previously been sitting at the New Accounts desk was walking toward them. "Thank you," she replied, then made her way over to the desk as she brought out the cashier's check that Ben had given her days earlier.

"May I help—," the woman began, but broke her sentence off as Katie reached her. Katie looked first at the woman and then at her desk, where a nameplate read ANGELA E. MARTIN. "Katie? Katie Morgan?"

Katie looked back at the woman who stood before her, mouth slightly open in surprise. She looked familiar, and Katie tried to recall who she was, but was unsuccessful.

"I can't believe this," the woman continued. She walked over and gave Katie an awkward hug, leaving Katie feeling somewhat strange. Hugging any and everybody was not a normal custom in New York. "Please sit down. I just can't believe this. I have prayed and prayed. . ."

"I'm sorry. I'm at a disadvantage," Katie said earnestly. "I'm afraid. . ."

Katie stared at the woman, again searching for a clue. She was near Katie in age. She had shoulder-length, dark blond hair tied back at the nape of her neck with a large black bow. She was husky in build with full lips and sparkling hazel eyes that seemed filled to overflowing with goodness, mercy, and tenderness.

"Angela," the woman supplied. "Angela Evans. Why, I was practically your cousin!"

Katie sat back suddenly. Angela Evans. Her cousin? As Katie remembered it, she had been her nemesis and the true cause of what transpired between her and her mother the night she ran away.

Angela's mother, Lorian, had married Katie's great-uncle, George Williams, when the girls were freshmen in high school. In spite of the fact that Angela came from "the wrong side of the tracks," as her mother kept repeating, Katie had liked Angela right away. But Carolyn Morgan had not accepted Lorian as either a contemporary or as a family member. She viewed the woman as a gold digger.

"White trash," she remembered her mother saying to Roberta Anderson over afternoon coffee in the formal parlor. She and Marcy hid behind the swinging door that led to the dining room. They listened intently, struggling to stifle occasional giggles. "And the worse kind of white trash. . .the kind that thinks they aren't when they are. If that woman thinks for one second that I'm going to allow her into my circle, she's got another think coming." Roberta remained quiet while

Carolyn continued in her tirade. "And what in the world is Uncle George thinking? He's the laughingstock of the entire family, never mind the town. If Aunt Mary knew he'd married that two-bit floozy, she'd roll over in her grave. Just roll right over. And I'll tell you this much: Mama says she won't speak to her either although Daddy acts like everything is just peachy. Men! They always stick together. I can't stand this, I tell you! I just can't stand this!"

"I understand she is joining the church this weekend," Roberta finally commented.

"No! You don't—where did you hear that?"

"Mary Ann told me. Said it was on the reports she filed this past week." Mary Ann was the church secretary at the Brooksboro United Methodist Church. She took her vows of secrecy very seriously. . .she only told two or three of her closest friends the "news" from within the church office walls. "And you know Mary Ann," Roberta continued. "She doesn't repeat gossip, so you'd better get it right the first time."

"Well, I never! Using the church to further oneself is tantamount to blasphemy against the Holy Spirit! And you know what the Bible says about that!"

Lorian's every attempt at breaking into the exclusive social circle of Brooksboro ladies failed. Eventually the honey that dripped from her tongue turned to spewing acid. And her daughter, who in the beginning had been Katie's friend, became equally as bitter. She had adopted a "you owe me" attitude, which never sat well with any of the young people of Brooksboro. Angela became verbally cruel against Katie, making biting comments about her height. She had reduced Katie to tears on more than one occasion. Even more ruthless was Angela's boyfriend, Cail Fontaine, who made her life a living nightmare whenever their paths crossed. Katie wondered if Angela and Cail had married, though the inscription on the nameplate indicated that they were not.

Katie now gave her warmest, most courageous smile to her "old friend." "I'm sorry, Angela. I wouldn't have recognized you if you hadn't said something. I guess time has a way of making us forget the people we swore always to remember."

A look of sincere sadness crossed over Angela's face and she leaned over her desk so that she could speak more privately. "I can't imagine that you would ever want to remember me, Katie. Though I have certainly remembered you. Like I said, every night I have prayed. . ."

"Excuse me?"

"Katie? Can we talk honestly for a few minutes?"

Katie shifted uneasily on the cushioned vinyl of the chair she sat in. "I guess so."

"Look, Katie. When I asked God to please bring you into my path at least once more before this life was over, I told Him that if He did, I would promise to lay it all out on the line. And I know that the good Lord, in His infinite wisdom, cares just as much about this little thing as He does about the big things. This has been my giant to destroy, so here's the first stone in the sling—if you get my meaning. The Angela Evans you remember is not at all the Angela Martin I am today. Shortly after you left, I went off to college. . . . Mama insisted that George send me to a Bible college up in North Carolina, where I met the most wonderful man!" She reached for the ornate silver picture frame that sat on her desk, then extended it for Katie to view. The photograph showed a loving family: Angela, her husband wearing a minister's collar, and three young children: two boys and a girl.

"My goodness," Katie declared. She handed the photo back across the desk to the hand that awaited it. Angela took it, looked at it briefly, and smiled proudly.

"My husband is a pastor."

"Really?"

"Oh, I know what you're thinking, Katie. Angela Evans married to a minister of the gospel?"

"Oh, no. . .I. . ."

"No, please. That's what I would be thinking if I were you. Oh, Katie! When you ran away, I knew it was my fault and I felt. . .well, at first I felt just fine, almost proud of myself, to be honest with you. . .but then. . .when you didn't return. . .I felt. . ." Katie watched as tears formed in the corners of the woman's hazel eyes. "I was such a spoiled kid, Katie. And I thought Cail Fontaine was everything! When I found out that he had a crush on you. . ."

Katie looked down and whispered, "You went to your mother. . ."

"Who in turn went to yours. She told her everything about you and Buddy! I thought you'd just get busted by your mother and that would be that. I never dreamed it would lead to. . . Oh, Katie! Where have you been?"

Katie looked up, tears forming in her own eyes as she looked into the misty eyes of her old classmate. "New York." She nearly choked on the words. "I went to New York. I've been living there for twenty-five years." Perhaps she shouldn't tell her this piece of information, she thought, but the origin of her check would tell Angela that much. "So, you didn't marry Cail?"

"Lordy, no! And thank God for large favors! In a little tizzy I broke up with him, thinking he would beg my forgiveness and stop thinking of ways to attract you."

"Attract me? He was nothing but verbally cruel to me! How many 'tall jokes' can one person come up with?"

"Oh! That was just a front. You know how boys can't reveal how they really feel, so they just bluster their way through. He was so jealous of Buddy he couldn't see straight. But he wasn't about to spill the beans to your parents. He knew that would seal his fate for life! One thing is for certain: Every kid at ol' BHS was willing to keep your secret. . .yours and Buddy's. Have you seen Buddy since you've been back?"

Katie fell into an uneasy silence. Having a conversation with Angela about Buddy didn't feel right, no matter how much Angela had changed or how much time had passed. "No."

"Make you uncomfortable to talk about him?"

"A little. Do you ever see him?"

"Oh, all the time. He's in this bank near about every day. Making the deposits from the hardware store."

"He's still at that hardware store?"

"Went from floor sweeper to manager to owner. He bought it from Mr. Zeigler years ago."

Katie nodded. "And he's doing okay?"

"You know what they say around here, Katie. Fine as frog's hair."

Katie laughed, but a fresh supply of tears filled her eyes and Angela joined her. She reached for two tissues from the tissue box that sat at one corner of her desk. She extended one to Katie and then used one herself. "Aren't we a sight?" she exclaimed through slight chuckles.

"I'd say we are," Katie agreed as she dabbed at the corner of her eyes with the tissue.

"You know, your mother told everyone you went to Berkeley. She would leave town periodically on the pretense that she was visiting you. I suspect she fooled some, but she didn't fool everyone. Eventually, she gave up the charade. I felt so sorry for her. I've barely been able to look her in the eye for twenty-five years. And when my husband became the pastor of the church. . .well, you can imagine Miss Carolyn wouldn't step through the doors for our gospel sings for a good six months. But then. . .somehow she softened. She even smiled at me. I think that God has done a real work in her heart. I can't speak for her, of course, but I really think. . ."

Katie was shocked at the words she was hearing. "My mother told people I went to college?"

"Didn't you know?"

"No. No, I didn't know. My goodness. . ."

"Anyway, Katie. . .forgive me? Please?"

Katie was momentarily stunned by the request. "Sure. . .sure! I forgive you. Sure! Now, if I can just open this account. . . ," she said laughing.

Angela opened the bottom drawer on the right-hand side of her desk and pulled the appropriate forms for new accounts. "So, you're back in town?"

"For awhile," Katie responded honestly.

"Good! Okay, Morgan. Katharine, right?"

"Actually, it's Webster. Katharine Morgan Webster."

"You're married?" Angela's face seemed to light up at the announcement. "How wonderful! Is your husband here, too?"

"No, just me."

Angela's face fell. "Problems?" she whispered.

"No," Katie smiled. *Not the kind you think,* she thought. "Just some time for me and Mama. You know. . .twenty-five years. . ."

"Oh, sure. Sure. Okay, what kind of account do you wish to open?"

"Kind? I guess a regular checking."

"Okay. And how much will you be depositing?"

"I have a cashier's check here for a hundred thousand."

Angela's head shot up. "Excuse me?"

"Will that be a problem?"

"Oh, no. You will be depositing the entire check into this account?"

"No. I want to keep a thousand out in cash. Is that okay?"

"Typically, no. But I'll check with Mr. Hughes. Since your mother is a long-standing customer of this bank, I'm sure there will be no problem. He just loves bending the rules for his best customers. Now then, what bank is the check written from?"

"First National of New York," Katie supplied.

"May I see the check?" Angela requested, hand extended. Katie complied.

"Let me run this over to the tellers. I'll be right back," she said, standing. "Oh. I'll need a driver's license and another form of ID."

"Is a New York driver's license okay?"

"Yes, that's fine."

"I don't have any other identification," she told her.

Angela hesitated, then added, "That's okay. I think we can get around it. After all, it's not like you're a stranger!"

Angela left Katie alone with her thoughts. Katie's mother, saving face with stories of Katie going off to college. . .Buddy, owner of the hardware store. . .Angela, sorry for her actions twenty-five years ago. . .

The day before their graduation, Buddy called Katie at home.

"Katie? Can you come down to the store? I need to talk with you."

"What's wrong?" Katie sensed the urgency in his voice. Two years with a person and you grew to know each other fairly well.

"Just get down here. Your mother's not back yet, is she?"

"No. . .how did you know my mother was out?"

"Just come down here. I'll tell you when you get here."

Katie hung up the princess phone in her room and quickly slipped out of the house, hoping her mother would not walk through the front door as she made her way out. Minutes later she drove her red VW Beetle into the parking lot of the hardware store, pulled up the parking brake, and got out. The silver gravel sparkled in the hot light of the late May sun as it crunched under her white toe-thong sandals. She quickly made her way through the glass double doors where Buddy stood waiting for her. He grabbed her hand without so much as a hello and began to pull her past hand tools, rakes, hoes, and shovels to the back of the building where the manager's office was located.

"Mr. Zeigler said we could use this room for a few minutes. . .to talk, I mean."

Katie stepped back for a moment. "Well, what else would we be doing, Buddy Akins?"

Buddy blushed, the red tint crossing his cheeks and disappearing into the white blondness of his hair. He gave her a boyish grin. "Look here, Little Miss. I know we said that we would go our separate ways after graduation, but you're still my girl—for one more night anyway— and I still have the right to. . ." He looked around devilishly, as if to make certain no one could see or hear them. "Tickle you!" he exclaimed, grabbing for her waist, his fingers digging into the sensitive flesh.

"Buddy! No! No!" she giggled, doubled over in the pleasure-pain.

He released her, his face turning somber. "Enough play, Katie. We gotta talk."

She resumed her composure and tilted her head slightly. "Buddy. . . what's wrong?"

Buddy reached into the back pocket of his jeans and pulled out a folded piece of paper, then extended it to her. "This," he said.

She took the paper from him, opened it, and stared down in horror. It was a check from her mother, made payable to Buddy, in the amount of five thousand dollars.

"What in the world?"

"Your mother. Paying me off."

"Paying you off? She knows?"

"She thinks she knows. She thinks you and me are getting married, is what I'm thinking. There was a letter in the envelope, too. A letter saying that if I signed the check, I gave up all rights to you or would go to jail."

"What?"

Buddy looked at her sheepishly. "Can you beat that?"

Katie vacillated between anger and shock, settling on a eerie all-over numbness. "I don't know what to say."

"I'll tell you what to say. We're gonna go down to the bank and cash this check. . . ."

Katie looked up at him in surprise. "What?"

"Listen to me, Katie. You gotta get this right. You gotta. You deserve so much more than this little town can ever offer you. You and I both know that. You were meant for big things. Really big. I want you to have this money, you hear me? We'll cash the money and you do something for yourself. I don't care what. Put it away or use it for your education. Go on a cruise when you graduate from college. Shoot! Don't tell and I'll join you," he joked.

Katie laughed, but she didn't feel jolly. Her mind continued to race. "I'm going to send away for some applications to universities next week. I probably won't get in until the winter quarter, but it's something."

"Come on, Katie," Buddy said, pulling her toward the door. "Let's go to the bank. You can wait outside in my truck. . . . Just keep your head down so none of the old ladies in town will call your mama or anything."

Katie stopped short. "Oh, Buddy," she whispered, tears forming in her eyes. "I'm so sorry. You're the one who deserves so much better than this. I don't know why my mother. . .if she only knew you. . . ."

Buddy took a step forward and cupped the side of her face in the palm of his hand. "No chance of that, Katie. It's just as well. I'm gonna settle down here in this little hick town and one day I may even manage this hardware store. . .if I work hard enough. But you deserve to get out."

"All I ever really wanted was to graduate from high school, get married, and have some kids. I never really aspired much further than that. But I guess. . ."

"No guessing, Katie. You'll do just fine. And one day. . .you look back on your old beau, Chad "Buddy" Akins. . .and you remember me fondly, ya hear?"

Katie laughed lightly and Buddy wrapped his arms tightly around her. She rested her cheek against the muscles of his shoulder. "What was it we saw in that old movie that day in school. . .*Tea & Sympathy*, wasn't it called?"

"Mmmm," Buddy said. "I know. 'Years from now, when you speak of this—and you will—be kind.' "

Katie stepped back. "That's it."

He kissed her then, hard and sweet. It was good-bye. They both knew it and they savored it. From this moment on, nothing would ever be the same.

Sitting in the chair across from the New Accounts desk, Katie slowly licked her lips at the memory. It was as if she could still taste him on her tongue. For a moment, she could actually smell the stale, sweet scent of recently smoked Marlboros. She sighed deeply, then turned to see Angela making her way toward her.

"Got it," she said. "Mr. Hughes said no problem on the cash. If nothing else, he knows your mama is good for it. Just a few more things and you're set."

Katie nodded, temporarily unable to speak. She was glad to have cash money because she wanted to stop by Marcy's on her way home to ask her to join her on a trip to Savannah the following day. She wanted to do something special and the idea of shopping for clothes with her old pal made her smile.

Less than ten minutes later, after a tight squeeze from Angela and a tearful "see you later," Katie made her way toward the front doors of the bank. Walking slowly, she reached into her purse and pulled out Kevin's John Lennon sunglasses, then placed them carefully on her face. She paused to check her watch for the time, but found that she had not put it on that morning after her shower. She turned slightly to look around for a clock on the walls, but could not locate one. Spotting the young woman sitting at the desk with the switchboard, she moved gracefully to her and asked her for the time. The young woman looked down at her Timex, then with a smile, answered, "It's about ten after two."

"Thank you," Katie replied, then turned to the doors. As her hand reached out to push against the chrome bar, the door swung open from the outside. She stepped back slightly to allow the patron entrance. It was a man, tall and well built, his features shadowed by the halo of sunlight that penetrated from behind him. As he stepped into the artificial light of the lobby, his face came into view, and she momentarily studied him. He wore a plaid, cotton, short-sleeved shirt and black jeans, which were belted by a thick leather belt. His receding blond hair was practically shaved and his skin was deeply tanned. He smiled automatically at her with his full lips and she noted the twinkle in the piercing blue of his eyes. She gasped involuntarily, and his name formed on her tongue.

"Buddy."

CHAPTER ELEVEN

A light summer breeze blew gently through Ben's dark hair as he nodded to THP's head doorman, Miguel Jordan, standing proudly at his post in front of the impressive midtown hotel. Dressed in the regulation light gray, brass-buttoned uniform with head held high, Miguel often reminded Ben of a palace guard. A forty-year veteran with THP, Miguel had been discussing the particulars of a diplomat's imminent arrival with the senior Mr. Webster when THP's president suffered his massive heart attack. What a trooper Miguel had been, then and always. Miguel's physical proximity to his father during that crisis and his levelheaded management of the emergency endeared him all the more to Ben's affections. It was as if Miguel were a sort of moral anchor during that difficult transition as Ben took over the reigns of THP. After all, he had grown up with the man, who seemed like a permanent fixture, welcoming all, both great and small. Ben would often ask his advice on certain matters owing to his long experience.

Miguel had a flair for making people feel important in a wonderfully restrained sort of way, and this Ben drew from for himself and other employees. Ben had seen many businesses flounder and even fail because of the management's absurdly high-handed approach with their employees. He found their shortsightedness difficult to understand. Under Ben's presidency, management held a service-oriented attitude of respect toward and feedback-elicitation from employees. Arrogance was absolutely not tolerated. Ben wanted the workplace to feel like home for those who worked there. He knew the vital importance of low turnover, something many of his colleagues in the industry did not seem to grasp.

"Been to the club for lunch, Mr. Webster?" Miguel asked in his heavy Latin accent.

Ben often went to his private club, The Marco Polo, located inside the Waldorf-Astoria, for lunch. Today, however, he had taken a refreshing and much-needed stroll along Fifty-first Street, purchasing a hot dog from a street vendor. He needed the escape. . .the time to think. . . to plan. . .to reflect. . .

The unraveling of his near-perfect life had begun at the AIDS Foundation fund-raiser sponsored by B. Caballero, Inc., which had been held in the Grande Banquet Room of THP. The thousand-dollar-a-plate dinner was open to the public but attended only by New York City's social elite. Naturally, he had always been invited to the various fund-raisers sponsored by Bucky, but over the past several years had merely sent a donation. This year, however, he and Katie decided to attend.

As soon as he and Katie arrived, they were swept through the crowd of fashionably attired contributors. Soft music mingled with the hushed tone of conversations and the tinkling of ice in crystal cocktail glasses. The room glittered with shimmering pastel light as it reflected off exquisitely sequined gowns that clung dangerously to hourglass figures. At one point Paul Worth, the hotel developer in charge of Atlanta's THP, had stopped him. Katie stood dutifully by his side, listening to their business conversation. Moments later, he became aware of her light touch on the sleeve of his tuxedo.

"Excuse me, Darling. I see Andi over there. Do you mind if I go and speak to her?"

Ben looked in the direction Katie was indicating and saw the beautiful manager of Jacqueline's conversing with a distinguished older gentleman who appeared to be her date.

"Certainly, Sweetheart. Go ahead. I'll join you in a moment."

He watched his wife as she elegantly glided across the room toward her new friend. They exchanged greetings, followed by Andi introducing Katie to the man standing proudly by her side, cocktail glass in hand.

"Now, where were we?" Ben heard Paul ask, returning his attention to him.

Only a few minutes passed when Stephen Lewis, a senior member of the mayor's staff, approached him.

"William," he began in a voice that seemed to be half under his breath. "May I see you for a moment?" He looked about sheepishly before adding, "Alone?"

Ben looked uncomfortably at Paul who, sensing something was wrong, stated, "I'll call you tomorrow. We'll need to fly down to Atlanta on Monday night, so I'll give you the itinerary when I call. How's that?"

"Tomorrow's good. I'll be ready to go." The men shook hands and Paul stepped away, leaving Ben alone with Stephen. "What's the matter, Stephen? You look positively ill."

Stephen cleared his throat discreetly. "William. I understand that you are very protective of your wife. . . ."

The hairs stood up on the back of Ben's neck as he turned immediately to search the room for Katie. He spotted her quickly, still conversing with Andi and Andi's gentleman friend.

Turning back to Stephen, he answered, "Of course, I am. She seems all right to me."

Stephen stepped closer and lowered his voice to an almost inaudible murmur. "Then why is she being seen with a high-priced prostitute?"

Ben turned and looked toward his wife again. Again, he saw only Katie and Andi.

"I don't know what you're talking about, Stephen. That's Andi Daniels. She works at. . ."

"I know who she is, William." Stephen looked behind him, then back to Ben. "I can trust you, can't I?"

"You know you can, Stephen."

"I have a wife, William. Children and little grandchildren. Not to mention my career, and you and I both know the good I've done."

"What is it, Stephen?"

"Andi Daniels. I know her. I know her. Listen to me, William. I believe what other people do behind closed doors is their business. . . that goes for me, too. . .and I wouldn't want this to get out. . .the Mrs. and all. . .but I like you and I like your wife. I wouldn't want either of you to get hurt. And I've always been fond of your father and mother."

Ben stepped away from Stephen immediately and began to make his way toward Katie. A hundred questions raced through his mind. If Andi was a high-priced prostitute, then why was she working at Jacqueline's? Was Jacqueline's all it appeared to be? Was Bucky Caballero involved in this? And if so, how? He felt his pulse rate quicken as he reached Katie and Andi. The two women turned to him and smiled. Before either of them could speak, Ben abruptly grabbed Katie by the forearm and informed her that they needed to return to their suite.

"But. . . ," Katie protested.

"Don't argue with me, Katie. Not now," he whispered tersely in her ear. Then to Andi, he said, "You must excuse us. It's an emergency."

As he and Katie made their way out of the banquet hall, Katie half-stumbling in her pumps beside him, he turned to look at Andi—to see if he had left her suspecting anything. She was looking enquiringly at Bucky, who shot a quick glance toward him, then back at Andi. Ben was certain then that there was a connection between Jacqueline's and what he had just learned about its manager. By the time he and Katie reached their suite, he was incensed—almost furious—and wanted to return to the gala and face Bucky then and there. But he knew better. In this case, "Discretion was the better part of valor."

As soon as the door to their suite had been firmly closed, Katie turned to him and demanded an explanation. "Ben! What in the world? That was totally out of character for you. And Andi! What must she think?"

The enormity of the situation struck him, and he grabbed his wife and held her tightly to him. "Don't ask any questions, Katie. Not now. Not yet."

She pulled away from him. "Not now? Oh, Ben!"

"Listen to me, Sweetheart. Do you trust me? Do you?"

Katie looked into his eyes as she answered. "You know I do."

"Then trust me completely. Don't ask any questions now. I will tell you what I can when I know more. And don't speak to Andi. If she asks you about any of this, tell her that I was feeling ill and needed to retire. Can you do that, Katie?"

He read the confusion on her face and the concern in her eyes. "You know I can, Ben. I'll do anything for you."

The following day Ben contacted a childhood friend, Philip A. Silver, who was working at the New York City's division of the FBI.

"I need to talk with you, Phil. It's urgent. Can you meet me at The Marco Polo for lunch?"

"Sure, William. What's this all about?" Phil asked him.

"Let me talk with you there. I think I've uncovered illegal escort services originating out of my hotel."

There had been a moment of silence followed by Phil clearing his throat. "I'll talk with you at the club. Noon?"

"Noon is good."

The following morning, a few minutes before noon, Ben walked through the thick oak door ornamented with a winged Venetian lion, the symbol for the private club. He briskly made his way through the familiar small lounge, then into the bar area where Phil was sitting at a small table, sipping a steaming cup of coffee.

Ben joined him, ordered a Perrier with lime for himself, then spoke in hushed tones to his old friend.

"There's been some suspicion," Phil began after Ben told him of his discovery. "But what we knew. . .well, we didn't have anything to tie it to."

"You knew that an illegal escort service was inside my hotel and you didn't call me?" Ben asked.

Phil leaned over the small table, resting his forearms against the edge. "Look, William. If I tried to bust every illegal escort service in town, I'd never have time to see my kids. Besides, we don't move until we have something concrete. We need evidence. Actually, we need that certain link in the chain of evidence to bring down the house of cards that I suspect Mr. Caballero has been building for some time now. But I'll be honest with you. I was thinking drug importation. Couldn't find a thing on him, though. Until this minute, I didn't even know that he owned. . .what'd you say this place was called?"

"Jacqueline's."

Phil reached into the front pocket of his crisp white shirt and pulled out a pack of gum. He extended the open pack to Ben, who shook his head no. Slowly and deliberately he pulled a silver-wrapped stick of gum from the pack. He unwrapped it, letting the wrapper fall silently to the table. He folded the sweet-smelling gum down the middle, then folded it back down the middle again. Popping it into his mouth, he looked over Ben's shoulder and Ben knew that he was thinking. . .calculating. . .weighing the evidence. "Jacqueline's, huh?" he finally said. "Who'd suspect that?"

"I looked into it this morning. It's owned by a dummy corporation of which I suspect Bucky is a silent partner."

"Could be. . .could be. . . ," Phil said, all the while munching on the gum. "You may find that he's listed two of his employees. . .or two family members that you'd not tie to him. . .as the corporation's president and secretary. I'll do a little research on this when I get back into the office. In the meantime, take a little trip to the boutique and see if you come up with anything. Here's another thought. Many times these escort services advertise on the Internet. They may be using a catch phrase. . .something that you would pick out before we would. Check it out. If you find anything, let me know."

Ben left The Marco Polo and went directly to his office. He called Katie as soon as he slipped into the leather comfort of his chair to inform her that he would be spending a few hours working.

"Why didn't you just come up and tell me?" she asked. She sounded nasal.

"I knew that if I did, I'd never get out of there. You're too much a distraction," he teased. He didn't want her to hear any concern in his voice. He didn't want her to question what work he had to do. "You sound stuffed up. Are you coming down with a cold?"

Katie sniffed slightly. "A little summer cold, I think. Don't worry. I'll be fine. Maggie has me in bed and is fussing over me now."

"Hot tea and lemon?" Ben asked, remembering how Maggie fussed and fluttered over him like a mother hen whenever he had been ill.

"With honey," she teased back.

"I won't be long," he promised. "Stay in bed. I'll see you soon."

"I love you," she said.

"I love you," he answered, then placed the phone gently back on the receiver.

He swiveled the chair slightly so that he could better face the computer, which sat at an angle on the right side of his large desk. Within moments he made his way to the World Wide Web. Placing the cursor at the oblong box located next to the words NET FIND, he typed "Escort." Seconds later, he stared at the first ten of several million Ford Motor Company Web sites. Realizing his error, he went back to NET FIND and typed "New York Escort Services." Seconds later, he began reading the names of escort services located all across the state of New York. He shook his head. It would take him days to find anything connected to Jacqueline's. . .if he found anything at all.

He deleted the page and went back to NET FIND, this time zeroing in on the services located in New York City. Seconds later, he leaned back in the high-back chair, closed his eyes, and sighed deeply. He couldn't believe the number of services listed. *No wonder Phil had said the FBI and other law enforcement couldn't bust them all*, he thought. *There would not be time for anything else.*

Leaning forward, he cupped his hand over the computer mouse and began to scan down the page. It was going to be a long afternoon, he decided. Long and disturbing. He had no idea of the enormity of the market that had apparently infiltrated his business.

It took over two hours of reading advertisements before he found it. It was so obvious. Almost too obvious. He vigorously rubbed his eyes with his fingertips, then looked at the screen again. . .just to make certain. . . .

ANDREA'S ESCORT SERVICE

New York City's only four- and five-star hotel escort service.
Ultimate, sophisticated, upscale, sensual, private, and discriminating.
International men and women individually selected
To make your stay in the Big Apple
A tantalizing and memorable experience.

Below the ad was a phone number followed by hyperlinks that allowed one to read the ad in various other languages. "I can't believe this," Ben whispered. He copied the page and sent it to the computer's printer, then cleared the screen. Holding the printed page, warm from the printer, he dialed Phil's home phone number.

"Phil," he began. "I found it. And you were right. There're thousands of them."

"Are you sure?" Phil asked him. "Sure you have the one in the hotel?"

"I think so."

"Okay, here's what we'll do. Tell your secretary that you are expecting an old classmate tomorrow around eleven. Don't let on that I'm with the Bureau."

"Okay."

"I'll be there at eleven. In the meantime, William, don't do anything foolish. Just go along as if nothing is different. Got it?"

"Got it," Ben answered. "I'll see you at eleven."

As soon as he ended the call, he dialed Paul Worth's pager number. He replaced the receiver, stood, and stretched. His muscles ached. He was more tired than he realized. He walked over to the large set of windows that overlooked the New York City skyline and fleetingly wondered how many buildings within his vision were housing illegal escort services. He shook his head slowly. It didn't matter, really. All that mattered to him was the one being operated out of the very building his family had prided itself in. He would do whatever it took to bring Bucky Caballero down.

The phone rang and he moved quickly to answer it. "William Webster."

"William. Paul. You called?"

"Look, Paul. I can't leave tomorrow evening. What's the latest that we can fly to Atlanta?"

There was a momentary pause. "We have the meeting with the board on Wednesday morning. We'd have to leave no later than Tuesday night. Unless you want to catch a red eye?"

Ben thought quickly. Tuesday night would give him two days. It might be enough.

"Tuesday night is fine. Have your secretary call my secretary, okay?"

"No problem. William? Is everything okay?"

"Oh, sure. Sure. Katie's a bit under the weather and I want to stay with her," he said, using Katie's summer cold as an excuse.

"Tell her that I said to get well soon."

"I'll do it," Ben replied, then ended the phone call.

When he arrived at their suite, he found Katie in far worse condition than he thought she would be. She was sleeping; her hair was damp from the slight fever her body was trying to rid itself of. He leaned over the bed, gave her forehead a light kiss, and whispered, "I'm home, Baby." She stirred slightly. "No, no," he continued. "Go back to sleep." She nodded, never once opening her eyes. Within seconds, her breathing became deep and even.

"I called the doctor," Maggie informed him when he had slipped quietly out of the room and closed the door gently behind him.

"And?"

"Summer colds are going around. He said it won't last long, but to be safe he called the pharmacy and sent up an antibiotic. I gave her a little toddy my grandmother used to make."

"Mmmmmm. I remember those toddies. She'll sleep through the night if nothing else."

Katie awoke with a sore throat, slight fever, and muscle aches. Ben ordered her to stay in bed, then left her in Maggie's tender care.

When he arrived at his office, Ben treated the morning like a typical Monday. He performed his duties as if nothing had occurred on Saturday evening. On one occasion, he passed Andi in one of the first-floor hallways. She stopped short, but he nodded to her and greeted her as he usually would.

"Good morning, Andi."

She appeared guarded. "Good morning, Mr. Webster. How is Katie? I'm so sorry that the two of you had to leave in haste Saturday evening."

She's fishing, Ben thought. "We were, too. I realized I was expecting a phone call. It was just as well. Katie came down with a terrible cold and has been in bed ever since."

"Oh, no." Andi seemed only half-satisfied with his answer. "Please tell her I hope she gets well soon."

Ben looked deep into the chocolate brown eyes. He didn't blink and neither did she. "I'll do that. In fact, later today I may step into the boutique to buy her a little something."

Andi arched one of her perfectly shaped eyebrows and gave a half smile. "That would be wonderful, Mr. Webster. I'll see you there."

At eleven o'clock, Phil arrived at Ben's office as expected.

"I saw Andi today," Ben informed him.

"Do you think she's suspicious?"

"I'm afraid so. I told her I would come into the shop today to buy Katie a little something."

"Good idea. Why don't you do that now? Try to get the layout of the place. . .how business is done. Look for a separate phone line. My guess is that you'll find another phone under the counter or in the back office."

"My security manager has a key. If I don't find anything today, we can go in after hours."

"When do they close?"

"Six o'clock."

"I'll be back at six. No telling what we'll find."

But they found nothing. If Andi had not called Ben the following day, they would still have nothing.

CHAPTER TWELVE

"Mr. Webster?" Miguel asked, jarring Ben back to the present and the head doorman who stood before him with a quizzical look on his face.

"I'm sorry, Miguel. I suppose I got lost in a train of thought. You asked me a question, didn't you?"

Miguel chuckled, the brass buttons running down the length of his jacket moving silently with the rise and fall of his slender chest. "Yes, Sir. I asked if you went to your club today."

"Not today, Miguel. Hot dog vendor."

Miguel again chuckled lightly, then became serious. "I left a message for you with your assistant. When you have the time, let me know what you want me to do."

"About?"

"Princess Anne will be arriving in two weeks. We received a call today that she and her staff will be staying here."

Ben furrowed his brow, flexed his jaw, and looked around. He was proud to have the princess stay at his hotel, but right now. . .with Katie in hiding. . .her life in possible danger. . .

"I'll talk with Vickey when I get upstairs. Thank you, Miguel."

"Yes, sir, Mr. Webster."

Ben slipped into the half-exposed leaf of the oak and glass revolving door, gripped the brass handle, and pushed his way through. As he stepped

164

onto the pale green marble floor of the elegant and expensively decorated lobby of his hotel, he smiled. It never once failed to excite him with its sophistication. When he renovated it years before, he instructed the decorator to use muted tones on the sofas, chairs, draperies, and flooring. On the cream-colored walls were large Baroque beveled mirrors and bright murals depicting open vineyards and English gardens. Massive chandeliers bedecked with extensively tiered droplets of crystal were suspended from the high ceiling with imposing grandeur, the light reflecting off the marble-topped antique furnishings, bone china accent pieces, marble and bronze statues, gilded columns, and the peach-colored marble front desk.

As always, he listened intently to the sounds of business. His concierge, Juan Ramierez, was calling for a limousine for one of their prestigious guests. He recognized the man immediately as George Cameron, one of the state's top elected officials, so he walked toward him, hand extended.

"Enjoying your stay, George?" Ben asked. It seemed to Ben that Juan flexed uncomfortably beside him.

"Very much so. Thank you."

"Let me know if there's anything I can do for you," Ben commented as he continued toward the centrally located elevators. Passing the front desk, he observed several guests speaking to the front desk personnel, and he checked to make certain that they were making adequate eye contact. He was pleased to note that they were. He heard the front desk manager speaking in a monotone voice into one of the in-house phones as he glanced at his gold wristwatch. "It's now one ten in the afternoon," he was informing someone as he looked up and saw Ben walking toward him. "Yes," he continued. "I need you to send someone up to room 813. Apparently, the guests have left, but did not bother to bring down the key. Thank you." He swiftly replaced the phone onto the receiver and professionally added, "Good afternoon, Mr. Webster. I trust you had a pleasant lunch."

"Very pleasant," Ben replied, which was far from the truth. He missed his wife and was heavy laden with worry about her safety. His safety never once crossed his mind.

He passed the opened office door for the director of security, Roger Morris, and stopped, hoping to have the opportunity to speak with him. An elderly, fashionably dressed woman sat primly in one of the small chairs opposite Roger, who rested his forearms on his desk and listened intently as she lightly fingered the diamond broach that sparkled off her jacket's lapel.

"I'm just not certain," she was saying as Ben stepped quietly into the room. Roger looked up briefly and acknowledged him with a slight nod of his head. "Should I or shouldn't I leave it in the vault this evening while my husband and I are at dinner?"

"Mrs. Jennings, if you are not wearing the broach, then I highly advise you to leave it in the vault. You wouldn't want something that beautiful to be stolen, now would you?"

"Noooo," she answered thoughtfully. "But what if I decided that I want to wear it later in the evening?"

"There is always someone here to accommodate you, Mrs. Jennings. And may I inquire as to whether or not you have other valuables in your room?"

"Oh, yes!" she exclaimed. "I have my pearls, of course. And several rings that I am not wearing at the moment," she answered, stroking her hands lightly. "And my sapphire necklace that Howard gave me—I'll wear it this evening. A truly beautiful piece!"

"I'm sure that it is, Mrs. Jennings. Why don't you allow me to call someone to meet you back at your room, and we'll take care of all this for you?"

"That would be lovely. Thank you, Mr. Morris." Mrs. Jennings stood and, turning, saw Ben standing behind her. "Oh! Goodness, young man, you nearly scared me to death."

Ben smiled gently and said, "Good afternoon, Mrs. Jennings. How are you doing this afternoon?"

"Do I know you?" she asked aristocratically.

"Mrs. Jennings," Roger began, having stood from his chair. "This is

Mr. Webster, the president of The Hamilton Place."

"Oh, hello, Mr. Webster," she replied, extending her hand. He took it in his and gave it a warm shake. "You have such a nice place," she said. "Such a nice, nice place." She opened the clutch purse she retrieved from her lap as she stood and continued, "Now, let me see. . .where did I put that plastic thing?"

Ben smiled again as he peered over the top of her head and spotted her room key lying in the small black satin pocket of the purse. "I believe what you are looking for is in the little inside pocket."

"Oh, yes, indeed!" she exclaimed. "Well, then, let me return to my room. Mr. Morris, you will have someone meet me there?"

"They'll be there before you are," he assured her.

The two men watched the woman as she left the room. Roger picked up the phone's hand piece and punched four numbers on the pad. "Brian, meet Mrs. Jennings at room 488. She has some jewelry that needs to be placed in the vault. She's on her way now. Thank you, Brian."

Roger hung up the phone, then looked up at Ben. "Mr. Webster, what can I do for you?"

Ben quietly closed the door before answering. Roger had been the only person other than Phil whom he had entrusted with his suspicions about the hotel boutique. "Anything happening in Jacqueline's?"

"No, Sir. Not since Andi left. I haven't seen Mr. Caballero either. Have you thought about calling him?"

"Calling him?"

"Yes, Sir. Or perhaps having the day manager call him. You know, to ask him why the store hasn't opened. It seems to me that it would cause less suspicion if you didn't seem to know what was going on."

"I hadn't thought of that. Okay, as soon as I get back to my office, I'll have James give him a call. I'm surprised he hasn't been upstairs to ask me about it anyway."

"Me, too, Sir. You'll let me know, won't you?"

"Of course," Ben answered. "Thank you, Roger."

"Thank you, Sir. Your trust means a lot to me."

"Of course," Ben answered, then opened the door and left the room.

It was necessary for him to pass Jacqueline's on his way to the elevators. The door was tightly shut and locked and the lights out. Two female guests were standing in front of the door, verbally observing the sign that gave the shop's hours. "It says ten to six," one said to the other. Ben considered commenting, then decided against it. *Let someone else answer their questions,* he thought.

Approaching the elevators, he pressed the up arrow button and watched its light come on. He crossed his arms and waited patiently, interrupted in his thoughts by the voice of his general manager, James Harrington, who was speaking on his cell phone.

"Have you checked the laundry cart? Lost and found? Nothing, huh. Okay, let me know."

Ben gave him a puzzled look. "James," he said in greeting.

"Mr. Webster. Lady in 413 says housekeeping stole her daughter's favorite stuffed dog."

"Did you have Dennis look into it?" he asked as the elevator doors opened. Several guests exited as the elevator attendant held the door back with his gloved hand. Ben and James stepped in.

"Your office, Sir?" the young attendant asked Ben.

"Yes, thank you. James?"

"Six," he answered.

"Yes, Sir," the attendant answered and pressed the appropriate buttons on the wall pad.

James continued in the previous conversation with his boss. "The woman who cleaned, Maria Alvarez, doesn't speak English very well. She just looks perplexed and keeps saying, 'No take doggie. Maria no take doggie.' I believe her. She doesn't seem the type to—" The cell phone in James's hand rang. "Excuse me. . .James Harrington. Yes. Okay, good job." He looked at Ben with a grin as he folded the cell phone. "That was head of housekeeping. Lady in 413 just called down to apologize. The dog was under a pile of clothes draped over a chair."

Ben threw back his head and laughed. "You gotta love this job!" he said. James and the attendant laughed with him. "Look. . .James. . .if you have a minute, I need to speak with you about something in my office."

"Let me take care of something. . .won't take me five minutes. . .and I'll be right with you."

"Sounds good. Thank you," Ben answered as the elevator came to a stop and the attendant announced, "Your floor, Mr. Webster."

As soon as Ben stepped into the quiet of his office, his assistant, Vickey, was on his heels. She held a legal pad in one hand and a pen in another.

"I was beginning to wonder," she said, a breath of air escaping her lungs. It was not uncommon for Vickey to be this way. She took her job as Ben's assistant very seriously, sometimes, Ben thought, more seriously than he.

"I took a walk and got a hot dog," he told her as he stepped behind his desk and sat in his chair. "Not so good for the heart, but great for the spirit."

Vickey gave him a smile, although it was only a small one. At forty years of age, she was like a sister to Ben. She had been his father's assistant, though young, fresh, and slightly terrified when she began her career. By the time Ben had taken over, she was quite sure of herself and more familiar with the job of running a hotel than he was. She guided him gently through those first difficult months, stood firmly beside him in his decision making and vehemently supported him when the board squawked at his decision to bring the decorative changes to the old hotels.

Ben marveled at Vickey's ability to balance career and family. She had been married to her college sweetheart for over fifteen years. Together, they had a thirteen-year-old daughter, Chelsea, and an eleven-year-old son named Benjamin in honor of his godfather. They called him Benji. It was not uncommon for the children to accompany Ben and Katie out to the country on weekends. Sometimes they brought their friends and Ben would barbecue on the grill while Katie played games with them in the pool. For Chelsea's twelfth birthday, Katie treated the birthday girl and four of her best friends to a makeover at the hotel's salon, followed by a shopping spree at The Gap. When they were completely worn out from trying on clothes amid girlish giggles and the balance on his charge card was significantly higher, she piled them into a chauffeur-driven limousine. Sparkling grape juice was poured into crystal wine glasses as she ordered the driver to take them to their estate. Pizza was ordered and Ben was treated to a fashion show, each young lady parading around the living room while upbeat pop music pounded through the speakers of his sound system. He couldn't remember a more fun evening or a time when his wife's face seemed to glow as happily.

"Katie," he whispered later in the evening when his head rested on the pillow beside hers.

"Mmmm?"

"You deserve children." He felt her stiffen and turned his head slightly to look at her. He didn't know who caused her miscarriage, but he was very much aware of the circumstances around the unfortunate incident. "I don't mean to bring up a painful memory, but I was watching you this evening with those girls."

He saw her smile in the moonlight that shone across her beautiful face like a gentle alabaster caress. Her eyes remained closed. "It was fun, wasn't it?"

"You were made to be a mother. Everything about you. . ."

She frowned slightly as her brows drew together. "I can't even be a good daughter. What makes you think I could ever be a good mother?"

Ben propped himself up on an elbow and stared down at her. She opened her eyes to look at him. "That would only take a phone call to fix."

She groaned. "Let's not go there. Anyway. . .I can't have children. You know that."

"Would you consider adoption?" he asked and her face lit up.

"Really?"

"Sure. Why not?"

She was quiet for a moment, then responded. "I'd like that. But not just yet. But I'd like that."

He had known what she was thinking without going a step farther.

At some point, she would correct the horrible wrong that occurred between her and her mother so many years ago. Then she and Ben could consider adopting a child of their own. But for now. . .

"Princess Anne is coming," Vickey informed him looking down at the legal pad.

"So I've heard." She gave him a perplexed look. "Miguel," he clarified with a half smile.

"Oh. She'll be here in two weeks. We'll put her in the presidential suite."

"Make sure the British flag is hung out front. I noticed it was gone this afternoon."

"According to Miguel, it took a beating in last week's storm."

"Have you put in an order for another one?"

"Of course," Vickey responded, her eyebrows arched in mock horror. *How dare he think she was not on top of her job?* they seemed to say.

He chuckled. "Will it be here in time?"

"They said that it would."

"Okay, good. If not. . .don't put the battered one back. I'd rather have no flag than a battered one."

Vickey jotted notes on the pad as she nodded. "I'll see to it. Also," she continued, "you have a meeting with the Executive Committee this afternoon at four o'clock. You don't want to forget it. I have your notes from Atlanta typed and ready to present."

He smiled. The trip to Atlanta held a twofold purpose. Andi had called him late Tuesday morning with a request that he meet her at a designated spot in Central Park. He found her clutching a large manila folder to her chest. Without speaking, she handed it to him. It wasn't necessary for him to open it. He knew it was the information he needed.

"What is this costing you?" he asked her.

"I don't know exactly. But I'll have to leave New York as soon as possible."

"Where will you go?"

Tears formed in her dark eyes. "I don't know that either. I just know I can't do this anymore. You and Katie. . .you're good people. My parents raised me better than all this. . .I just got caught up. . . ."

Ben thought for a moment before he spoke. "I have an idea. Can you be ready to leave tonight?"

"For?"

"Paul Worth and I are flying to Atlanta to meet with officials and contractors in the morning. I want you to leave with us. From Atlanta. . . well, we'll cross that bridge when we get to it. Can you be ready?"

"I can be ready," she answered him quietly.

Presently, his mind began to race. He would speak with James shortly, then continue in his research against Bucky Caballero. He gave Phil a call earlier in the day, but he had not returned the call. They needed to get together. . .even more than he needed to meet with the Executive Committee. He frowned.

"William?" Vickey interrupted his thoughts. He looked up to find her questioning stare. "How's Katie's. . .mother, was it?"

He cleared his throat discreetly. "Yes. Mother. She's fine, thank you. Katie will spend just a bit more time with her and then will be home."

"I'm sure you miss her."

"More than you can imagine," he answered softly.

"Why don't you surprise her with a visit, then?"

"A visit? I. . .um. . .no. There's really not enough time for a visit."

"An unexpected gift?" Vickey suggested.

"That's not a bad idea. I'll have to think about. . ." Ben was interrupted by a tapping on the door. Vickey walked briskly to it and allowed James entrance.

"Thank you, Vickey," Ben said, politely dismissing her. "Hold my calls, please." She nodded at him. Before the door closed tightly behind her, he added, "And I will let you know about that gift."

As soon as James was comfortably seated in one of the leather chairs across from Ben's desk, Ben began to question him on his knowledge concerning the boutique.

"What's going on with Jacqueline's?" he began innocently. "I've noticed it has not been open the last couple of days."

James answered him. "I called Caballero on it. Said he would get back to me, but he hasn't. However," he continued, shifting his weight, crossing his left ankle over his right knee and tugging at the ironed pleat in the center of his pants leg, "Juan Ramierez stopped me just a few days ago. Apparently, he and Andi are friends. He tells me that Andi has been down with the flu and that Mr. Caballero allows only her to work the shop. Pretty foolish if you ask me, but that's his business. But I'll tell you this: If that shop doesn't open pretty soon, we need to call Caballero again. I've had a few inquiries on it. A hotel such as THP needs a nice ladies' boutique for its clientele. I'm sure you agree."

Ben nodded in distraction. His mind was racing with the distorted facts that James just relayed to him. Juan and Andi friends? Andi down with the flu? Ben knew the truth about Andi—only he and Phil knew the truth about Andi—and it had nothing to do with the flu. How did Juan Ramierez play in this game? Or did he play at all?

"Did you say that Juan and Andi are friends?"

James laughed lightly. "Can you beat that? I wouldn't figure someone like her with someone like him."

Ben leaned his elbows on the desk, brought his hands together, and laced the fingers. "Exactly what did he say to you?"

"Juan?"

"Yes. Juan."

James shrugged his shoulders. "Let me think about this. . .okay. . .I remember. . .he said, 'Oh, Mr. Harrington,' James mimicked the young concierge, using a thick Hispanic accent for emphasis, 'If you are looking for Andi Daniels from the boutique, she has the flu and won't be in for awhile.' I asked him how he knew that and he said, 'She and I are good friends, if you know what I mean by that.' And then he winked at me and clicked-clicked out of the side of his mouth. Gave me shivers. I mean, just think about it. That gorgeous woman and Juan." James laughed out loud and Ben joined him, though he found little humor in the moment. "Not that Juan's a bad fellow," James said finally. "It's just. . .well, you know. . ."

"Yes, I know."

James leaned forward and rested his elbows on his knees. "What's this about, William? Since when are you so interested in the boutique?"

Ben thought quickly, searching for a viable explanation. "I heard two ladies outside the doors of the boutique earlier. I thought perhaps the shop was closing down and just wanted to stay apprised of the situation."

James stood and Ben stood with him, extending his hand in gratitude for the valuable information that James had unwittingly given him. "Thank you, James. I'll see you this afternoon at the meeting."

James returned the handshake. "Four o'clock."

Ben nodded and watched as James turned and walked out of the room. He sat heavily in his chair. He was beginning to know too much. Far more than he anticipated in the beginning. It was making him weary and he rubbed his forehead vigorously. He missed his wife, too. He wished he could talk with her. Or at the very least let her know what was going on. He laid his head back against the cool leather of his desk chair, closed his eyes, and rested for a few moments. Soothing music played softly from the sound system overhead, blocking out the sounds of the outside world. Within moments he was asleep. . . . Though it was a light sleep, it was much needed.

He awoke a half hour later, totally refreshed and in full knowledge of his next move. He reached for his desk phone and dialed Phil's direct line number. They hadn't spoken since Tuesday afternoon when Ben called to tell him of the latest addition to his file against Caballero. Ben felt it was most imperative that they speak now. He suspected Juan Ramierez was the link between The Hamilton Place's guests and Bucky Caballero's secret business.

The phone rang five times before he heard a woman's voice on the other end.

"Agent Silver's desk."

"Agent Silver, please."

"Agent Silver has been called out of town on an emergency," the voice informed him.

"What? When will he be back?"

"We're not certain, Sir. Is there someone else who can help you?"

Ben felt his mind reeling from the news. "What? No. No. Tell him to call. . .never mind. Never mind." He ended the call by placing the pad of his index finger on the button. He held it there while he thought about what to do next, then dialed Vickey's extension. She answered on the second ring.

"Vickey," he said quickly. "About that gift."

He sensed her smile on the other end of the line. "I knew I could talk you into it."

"Call around to a few bookstores. See if any of them have a copy of Ben Jonson's *Volpone*."

"V-o-l-p-o-n-e?"

"That's it. Hardback, okay?"

"Sure. Ben Jonson's *Volpone*. Anything else?"

"No. That's it. When you find it, have it delivered as soon as possible."

"I can handle it."

"I've always known that," he responded gently, then added, "and one other thing. Call down to personnel and have them send up Juan Ramierez's file. Actually, have them send up the files of everyone in that department. All the concierge employees."

There was a moment of silence on the other end. "Yes, Sir. I'll take care of it."

CHAPTER THIRTEEN

David Franscella pushed the door shut as he walked into his brother-in-law's office. He was a tall man, muscular and well built. He wore his hair long, securing it in a fashionable ponytail at the nape of his neck. Mattie disapproved, which gave him all the more reason to wear it that way. He ran one of his tanned hands along the top of his head as he surveyed his wife and Bucky, who were standing in front of Bucky's desk. Mattie was nursing a vodka as she often did when under stress. David noticed the fine lines that formed around Bucky's mouth, and he could feel the tension in the air.

"Did I miss something?" he asked, using humor to elevate himself over Bucky and Mattie, albeit for only a moment. They wanted the information that he possessed, and that put him in an interesting position. They'd have it in a matter of minutes, but it was his and his alone for the present. Grinning, he strolled over to his wife and planted a perfunctory kiss on the rosy glow of her high cheekbone. "Darling," he greeted her.

She moved away from him slightly and sighed deeply. He disgusted her. He knew that much. But she needed him, too, though she would never admit to it. She needed his charms at social functions, his strong and able body for running her errands, his masculine presence to make her feel as if she were a woman with a heart not made of granite. It was, of course, but there were moments when he could convince her it wasn't.

"Learn anything?" she asked curtly.

"Oh, yeah. Plenty," he answered as he made his way over to the bar. "Get anyone anything?" he toyed. "Mattie? A refill?"

She came at him like a cat on the prowl. "Stop it, David! What do you know? Where is Andi? And more importantly, what does William Webster know?"

David took his time as he prepared a scotch and water. Completing the task, he sipped his drink, then turned and faced his family as he leaned against the edge of the bar. "My source says there's been some buzzing around the bureau about illegal escort services. Even more about escort services being run out of hotels. He said he hasn't heard any particular names being spilled, but he'll keep his ears open. He's to call me as soon as he knows anything. Also got him to run a little check while we were out. An Andrea Marie Daniels flew to Atlanta on Tuesday evening. Also on the plane was one William B. Webster. Webster returned the following day, but without Andi. After that she could have gone anywhere. But I know this much: She didn't fly. There's no record of her boarding a connecting flight."

Mattie looked at Bucky. "She could have taken the train."

"Or rented a car," Bucky added. "Or, for that matter, changed her identity. But why? Why would she just jump ship like this? I've given her everything, haven't I?" He walked behind his desk and sat heavily in his chair, moving like a man determined. *They are not going to take all this away from me,* he thought. *They are not!*

Mattie looked at her brother and gave a sarcastic smile. "Everything but yourself, dear brother. That woman would have walked over coals for you if you'd asked. She loved you. You never saw that, but I did."

Bucky looked away. "I saw it," he answered. "But I could get more out of her as an employee than as a lover."

Mattie walked over to the desk and set her empty glass on top of it as she looked down into her brother's eyes. "Have you checked her apartment?"

"Yesterday. The closet is basically empty. Toiletries gone. A few odds and ends missing."

"What about the wall safe?"

"Still has Andrea's records in it." Bucky owned the apartment that Andi lived in, and he had decided to leave the extra set of records hidden there. "Not that they couldn't have been copied."

"Tell me, when was the last time you saw Andi?"

"Tuesday, I think. Yeah, it was Tuesday. The day I asked her to. . ."

"To what?" Mattie asked, suspiciously. David moved slightly from his position at the bar.

"To be nice to Juan."

"Juan Ramierez?" David asked incredulously. "The concierge from The Hamilton Place? That little weasel?" David asked.

Bucky stood in anger and pointed a finger at his brother-in-law. "For your information, that 'little weasel,' as you call him, keeps an eye on things for me at THP. He's my connection between some of the guests and Andrea's. And he's the one who called to tell me that Andi didn't open up the shop on Wednesday. He's been blindly in love with her since the day I sent him over there to apply for the concierge job. I've told her in the past to be nice to him, but she just flicks him off like lint on her best suit jacket," he said, demonstrating the latter action. "So, okay. I told her to be nice to him. Told her that Juan came to me informing me of Webster nosing around. Next thing I know, she's disappeared!"

There was momentary silence in the room.

"Isn't it a little strange that someone from the hotel has not called?" Mattie noted.

"Someone did. I acted innocent enough, then called Juan and had him inform this guy, James Harrington, that Andi had the flu and wouldn't be back for awhile."

"The flu? In the middle of summer?"

"Never mind that! We've got to do something about Webster," Bucky growled. "He's ripping my life to shreds. What's his Achilles' heel? He's got to have one. Everyone does."

Mattie chuckled. Lightly at first, a gentle peal of laughter that rang out in the large office. Then she stopped short. "Katie," she purred.

David took a step forward. "What did you say?"

Mattie turned to look at her husband. She blinked slowly. "Katie. His wife. You've seen her. That tall woman. Perhaps we can get something on her."

David turned uneasily and looked out the window.

Bucky picked up the action immediately. "Do you know her? David? Do you know her?"

David swung back to face Mattie. He wanted this moment. A chance to stare down his cold wife and make her wonder. . .wonder about who might have warmed his bed when she refused to do so. . . wonder about just how far he would go to defy her. "Yeah. I know her. Known her for years." He watched Mattie's chin rise defiantly. She was daring him, stupid woman. "She used to work as an exotic dancer at a little club called Private Dancer, then moved to a more upscale joint called West End Men's Club."

"Why haven't you said this before?" Bucky asked him.

David shrugged his shoulders. "Nobody's concern before. What she did before she met Webster is her business."

"And just how well did you know her?" Mattie asked him, her eyes narrowing to thin wicked slits.

He gave her a grin. "That's my business."

She moved quickly, making her way to him and slapping him soundly across the face before he even had time to take a breath. "How dare you!" she shrieked. She raised her hand to slap him again, but he caught it at the wrist and held it in midair.

"Stop it!" Bucky ordered. "Kill each other later. Now we have to think. Here's the perfect item to hold over Webster's head. He shuts up or we spread it all over society that his beautiful little butterfly used to earn her way as a stripper. God only knows what else she's done. That's it!" He slapped his hands together. "We got him!"

David dropped Mattie's hand and moved away from her and toward Bucky. "Not quite," he said softly.

"Meaning?" Bucky asked.

"I did some further checking. Katie Morgan Webster also left the hotel with her husband Tuesday evening. He returned, but she didn't."

Bucky spun around, picked up the telephone, and dialed Juan's pager number. They stood in a silent watch, waiting for the return call that came minutes later. Mattie and David stood quietly listening as Bucky spoke, then replaced the receiver.

"Juan says he hasn't seen her," he said finally, then cupped his face in his hands and rubbed his eyes with his fingertips. "Word is she's gone to visit a sick family member."

Mattie sneered at her husband. "Well, you're the great source on Katie What's-Her-Name Webster. Where's her family?"

David looked upward for a moment, stretching his neck to the left, then to the right as he searched his memory for the answer. He looked back suddenly at Bucky. "Some little town in Georgia," he said, supplying the answer. "But she never told me exactly where."

Bucky approached David with his index finger extended from a balled fist and poked him in the chest. "Find her," he said through clenched teeth.

David looked surprised. "What do you want me to do? Go to every little redneck, backwoods town in Georgia?"

"Do I have to tell you everything? Start with paper trails. Then old records. Look up every Morgan from Georgia since 1920, for all I care. But unless the idea of a prison sentence appeals to you, find her!"

"And then what?" David asked.

Bucky raised his eyebrows slightly. "Get two or three of your little gooneys together, get yourselves down to 'Little Podunk,' and take care of her," he reiterated, enunciating each word slowly and forcefully. "If Webster has sent her down there, it's because she knows something," he speculated. "So you take care of her."

CHAPTER FOURTEEN

The reflection of the sun made it impossible to recognize the woman speaking to him. "Buddy," she said again.

Buddy Akins took another two steps into the lobby of the bank, allowing the glass door to close behind him. The coolness of the air-conditioning wrapped pleasantly around him, and he instinctively shrugged his shoulders. He squinted his eyes as he looked at the woman who stood before him. She was quite beautiful; any fool could see that. But with her eyes shielded by the round sunglasses she wore, he couldn't seem to make out who she was. As the owner of the town's only hardware store, he thought he pretty much knew everybody. Occasionally, however, someone he was not familiar with would call out to him on the streets of Brooksboro or Savannah. He would always resort to a safe, "Hey, there. How's it going?" "Great," they would respond. Or: "Can't complain. And you?" And he would reply, "Kickin'. Kickin'."

He decided to use the same approach with this woman. "Hey, there. How's it going?"

"Buddy!" she exclaimed, like a mother scolding her young child. He felt uneasy. He looked over to Jennifer, the switchboard operator, and raised his eyebrows.

"I'm sorry," he said, looking back at her. "I'm at a loss here."

She reached up toward the sunglasses that shielded her eyes and kept her identity from him, slowly peeling them away from her face. "It's me," she said in a near whisper. "Katie."

Buddy's mouth fell open and he cupped it with his hand as he two-stepped backward. "Goodness sakes!" he exclaimed. "Katie. Katie. Dear God!" And with that he threw his arms around her and gave her a tight squeeze. She laughed at the suddenness of it, nearly stumbling when he released her. "Where are you. . .what have you. . .Katie!" And he started to laugh.

She laughed with him, then looked around the room. A few of the faces turned their way in puzzlement, making her blush lightly. Buddy knew this wasn't the place to talk. . .or there *would* be talk. . . .

"Wait a minute. I gotta pick up some new deposit slips, but it'll only take a minute. You got somewhere to be? Do you have a minute?"

She laughed again. It sounded like pure, sweet magic to him. It had been too many years of wondering. . .not knowing. . .fearing the worst and knowing the part he played if anything terrible had happened to her. "I'll wait outside the doors," she spoke in a quiet voice.

He watched her slip out the door, then darted over to one of the tellers, Janice Teal, an older woman who had been alive longer than dirt and would die for a piece of good gossip. "Buddy Akins," she innocently greeted him. "How are you today?" There was a wicked twinkle in her eye and a lilt in her voice. He grimaced. If he knew Miss Janice. . .and he did. . .she'd be on the phone with his wife as soon as he walked out the door.

"Miss Janice. I'm just fine. It's a little too hot out there today, though. I came by to get some deposit slips. My order hasn't come in yet, and I sure could use them."

"Business must be good, Buddy."

"Yes, Ma'am," Buddy affirmed.

Miss Janice opened one of the drawers beside her and pulled out a short stack of blank deposit slips. Buddy nervously looked toward the glass doors. Standing close to the old parking meters that were no longer in use was a woman he had long since given up ever seeing again. He occasionally would try to picture her in his mind. . .the way she would look at this stage and that stage of her life, but he hadn't even come close to this. She had an aura about her, seeming to have overcome her insecurities concerning her height. She stood erect and proud, her backbone straight and her shoulders back. He watched as she raked her fingers through her hair and it glistened in the hot June sunlight. Her obviously expensive blue silk culottes whispered across her form like pajamas. She seemed totally unaware of how beautiful she was. It was as if charm and grace and class met in perfect symmetry. And though Miss Janice, who sat across from him punching his account number into the coding machine, would undoubtedly argue with him, he didn't view Katie now in a sensual way, but as a breath of fresh air. He actually felt himself breathing easier since he saw her—no more than five minutes ago—and realized for the first time that a part of him had held its breath for twenty-five years. Twenty-five years and one month to be exact. Every May twenty-sixth that rolled around. . .he thought of her, reliving every moment that elapsed in the days before she disappeared.

"Friend of yours?" he heard Miss Janice inquire.

He turned his head to look at the silver-haired, sharp-featured woman. She was what some people would call handsome, but in an austere, almost brutal kind of way. She wore her makeup attractively, was always impeccably coifed, and turned herself out in the smartest outfits that always seemed to be overly accessorized. Her chin was raised a few degrees too high and her nose was a bit too pointed. She socialized with the likes of Katie's mother (who would be the second person she would call after he left the bank) and Miss Roberta, and she drove a brand-new, leased Lincoln Town Car, which she exchanged every two years for the newest model.

"Miss Janice, I think you know who that is," he said, giving her his best grin in hopes of melting her. He got along well with the people in Brooksboro. As a youth he had been considered a ne'er-do-well. Now, in his forties, he was a loyal husband, a good father, Cub Scout leader, supporter of the BHS Band Boosters, past president of the PTA at Brooksboro Elementary, vice president of the Baptist Men's Breakfast Club, and owner of the much-needed hardware store. He knew that he had gained a solid reputation with the good citizens of Brooksboro, but it was one he had worked hard for.

"If I didn't know better," she said through tight lips, "I'd say that was Carolyn Morgan's girl." She slipped the neat stack of deposit slips into an envelope, which she placed on the counter between them and slid toward him.

He took them off the counter and winked at her. "I'd say you're correct in that assumption, Miss Janice. Looks like Katie Morgan has found her way back to Brooksboro."

"Lord, Lord," she sighed. "I thought that girl had met with some sort of misfortune and left this good earth."

"Me, too, Miss Janice. Me, too."

He walked out of the bank and into the heat where Katie stood waiting for him. For a moment they just stared at each other, twenty-five years disappearing in the haze and the humidity that enshrouded them, until Katie smiled and said, "Hi."

He returned the smile. "Hi, yourself. Listen. . .within about three seconds every busybody in town is going to swoop down on us. Carroll's Drugstore has a coffee shop in it now. You want to go there and have a cup of coffee with me? We can talk, and it's a lot cooler," he suggested with a laugh. He took a step in the general direction of the well-established drugstore.

She began to walk beside him. "I guess it beats a poke in the eye, but what will make us safer in Carroll's Drugs than we are out here on the street? Won't our having a cup of coffee be a red flag?"

"Well, to be honest with you. . .the only person I'm really worried about is my wife and she works there, so. . ."

Katie laughed. "So, let's just bring this little surprise meeting out in the open and dare anyone to say anything."

He blushed a bit. "Something like that. Anyway, Sarah. . .my wife. . .

she knows all about you. . .about everything that happened. She's probably one of the few who knows everything. . .the check and all that mess."

Katie looked down as they continued down the sidewalk toward the drugstore. They began to walk under the storefront awnings and the shade made the heat a bit more bearable. "Yes. The check. Ever think what would have happened if you had kept that money?"

"Nah," he drawled honestly. "I was more worried about what happened because I hadn't kept that money." They stopped in front of the single glass door that led to the drugstore and looked knowingly at each other. "Come on," he said, then pushed the door open.

They no sooner stepped into the store than they were met by a tall, pretty woman with pale blond hair, much like Buddy's. It was straight and silky, cascading around her trim waistline. Her unadorned skin looked like priceless porcelain. A smile was forming on her rosebud lips as she greeted her husband with a light kiss. "Miss Janice beat you to it," she said mischievously. He glanced over to Katie, who seemed confused. "You must be Katie," Sarah said, extending her hand.

Buddy watched as two of the most important women in his life greeted one another. "Yes," Katie said. "You're Sarah?"

"I sure hope so. Y'all come on back and let me get you some coffee."

They made their way past the card section and the displays of bric-a-brac. Buddy nodded at Jim Carroll, the pharmacist, who had taken over from his daddy, Jim, Sr. Jim nodded in response. In the back of the store was a newly renovated area that had been decorated with ice cream parlor tables and chairs. A short bar ran along a part of the length of the back wall where coffee sat brewing. There weren't any other customers in the shop, so he and Katie had their pick of tables. She chose the one sitting in the center and wisely sat with her back to the front door.

Sarah placed her hand on Buddy's shoulder as she spoke to Katie. "I know how he likes his coffee. What about you? We have regular, decaf, and today we have Hazelnut."

"Yeah," Buddy grumbled. "They've started brewing all those un-American flavors these days."

Katie grinned at him, then said, "Hazelnut. Cream and sugar, please."

"Sure thing," Sarah answered, gave his shoulder a light squeeze, then turned to fill their orders.

Buddy set his elbows on the table and leaned forward. "Katie, where have you been?"

She smiled broadly. "I have certainly heard that question enough in the past two or three days. New York."

"City or state?"

"City and state. I live in the city during the week and in the country on weekends, holidays, things like that."

"Oh? A rich girl, huh?"

Sarah returned with a tray holding their cups of coffee, a creamer filled with Half-n-Half and a matching sugar bowl. "Did I hear you say New York City?"

Katie looked up at her and smiled. "Yes."

"I've been there a few times. I had grandparents that lived in Albany, and we would go into the city occasionally."

"Oh," Katie replied with a nod as she began to prepare her coffee.

"Well, I'll leave you two alone," she said.

"You don't have to," Katie insisted.

Sarah looked at her husband, then back to Katie. "No. I think you two need to talk alone. It's okay. I'm not a jealous wife or anything like that." She walked away from the table and toward the front of the store.

Katie followed her for a moment, then turned back to Buddy. "She's terrific, Buddy."

Buddy smiled. "She's the best," he said. "Sarah's family moved to Brooksboro shortly after you left. She was a senior at BHS. Pretty depressed about having to move during her last year and all that. Her daddy is Mr. Zeigler's first cousin, so she came into the store pretty regular. Anyway, she's a real fun girl, and she actually asked me out on our first date. I guess that was about six months after you left. . .not that it mattered. . .you and I. . . ," he trailed off.

"So you went out?"

186

She gave him an easy out and he breathed a sigh of relief. "Yeah. Dated the rest of that year and got married just as soon as they shoved that diploma in her hands. A year later we had our daughter and two years after that our son."

"I'm glad for you. You're happy then."

"I've been real happy, Katie. But now that happiness is. . .you know . . .complete, I guess you could say. I've wondered. . .and worried. . ."

"I'm okay."

He looked at the set of large rings that encircled her ring finger. "You're married." It was said more as a statement than a question.

"Yes."

"That's it?" he laughed. "Just 'yes'?"

"What more do you want?" she laughed with him.

"Either you've turned into a real Yankee, or for some other reason you are not being very enthusiastic. Kids?"

"No. No children."

"No kids? Really?"

She tilted her head slightly and smiled. "Really. But my life is full."

"Tell me about it."

She sat silent for a moment, staring first into his eyes, then around the room. "My goodness. Things sure have changed," she observed.

He wasn't going to let her escape so easily. "Husband with you?"

She turned back and looked directly into his eyes. "No. And no we are not having problems. I just decided that it was time to come home and see Mama."

As she declared her last line, she twitched slightly and Buddy knew instantly that there was more to it than that. "After twenty-five years? Your mama thinking you were dead, making up stories like you wouldn't believe. . ."

Katie grimaced. "I've heard about those stories. I am truly sorry for all that. But at the time. . .there wasn't any other way."

He sat quietly for a moment, periodically sipping the hot coffee and observing her as she drank hers. After a few moments, he spoke quietly.

"I don't believe you, Katie. What are you running from?"

Surprise washed over her face. "What. . .what do you mean?"

"I mean, what are you running from? You've always run, Katie. I remember one time you telling me about the kids teasing you about your height. . .remember? Playing in the garden? And you told me you took some sort of refuge in that honeysuckle bush. But when the kids started calling for you, you ran. Ran to your mama."

"You still remember that, Buddy?"

"I remember everything, Katie. Every detail."

She smiled, but shook her head. "Well, I wasn't. . ."

"Then there was that time you and Marcy stood in front of Old Man Cheevers's house. You thought you saw his eyes staring down at you. . . ."

"I did see his eyes!" she exclaimed.

"That's not the point, Katie! The point is that you ran! You ran! And when you and I were dating, you ran from facing your parents with the truth of the matter. When I gave you that money. . . I loved you with all my heart! I just wanted you to have what your mother was trying to steal from you. I confess. It was my own revenge. I thought you would just put the money away and we'd take that little vacation like we joked about. . .that cruise. . . But then you were gone. . . ."

"We had a fight," she interrupted.

"What?"

"We had a fight. That night. Mama and me. She was waiting for me when I got home, both barrels filled and the gun cocked. She nearly tore my head off. And my words were just as cruel. She even hit me," she whispered, lightly touching her cheek with her fingertips. "Right across the face. She had never done that before. And I told her how much I hated her—which wasn't true, but right then it was my only defense—and she kept telling me what my responsibilities were. I was a Morgan. A Brooksboro Morgan. And her people were Millses. She said it like that made them just shy of God and His angels. And then she said. . ." Katie trailed off as tears filled her eyes and she looked down. A tear slipped down her cheek and dropped into her cup of coffee, forming a tiny ripple that moved across the surface.

"I didn't mean to make you cry," he said softly. Buddy looked up to see if his wife was nearby. She was straightening paper products, but looking his way. He reached over and placed his tanned and rough hand on Katie's soft arm while pleading with his eyes to his wife for her to join them. She understood the hint and began to walk their way, picking up a box of tissues from one of the shelves.

"Here ya go, Katie," she said softly, placing the box in front of Katie. Katie gently tore into it, pulled one of the white folded tissues from inside, and began dabbing tenderly at her eyes and cheeks.

Sarah sat in one of the empty chairs between Buddy and Katie as Buddy said, "What'd she say, Katie?"

"If your father were here, she said, if your father were here. . .and I said that Daddy knew. And that he had supported me. She looked. . . strange. I've never seen her so angry. Or disconnected from me. A hardness came into her eyes and she muttered, 'You killed him. Sure as I'm standing here, you killed him. He couldn't stand knowing how you were throwing away your life and it killed him.' Then she turned and walked away. And I slammed the door behind her—we were in my room—and I just looked around the room for a moment. I remember feeling lightheaded. And like I was going to be sick or have a stroke or something. Physically sick. The next clear memory I have, I was on a bus headed for Atlanta."

"I thought you said New York," Buddy interjected.

"I ended up in New York. A few weeks later. I met a girl in Atlanta—Abby—and she and I went up there together. We lived with her sister. We got an apartment together. We even worked together for a long time."

"Waitress?" Sarah asked, innocently.

"Something like that," she said as she took the coffee cup in shaking hands and brought it up to her trembling lips.

Buddy nodded slightly, and Katie could tell that he understood, even if his wife did not. He took a deep breath before continuing. "What are you running from now, Katie?"

When she hesitated, he plunged in. "Look, this little town has changed a lot since you were gone. So have you. But I still care about you. I don't want you to keep running. And this town may not be the refuge you think it is. So please tell me. What's wrong?"

She didn't answer at first. She was busy calculating her answer, but he waited, giving her the time to put her thoughts together. Finally, she squared her shoulders, raised her chin, and smiled. "Nothing. I'm just here to see Mama."

He started to respond, but she shook her head slightly. "Don't, Buddy. I appreciate your concern. And I realize that you feel somewhat responsible for what happened to me. But you're not. I chose my life's pattern. And in the end. . ." She lightly touched the rings on her left hand. "In the end, I did all right." Buddy watched as she slowly stood and looked down upon him and his wife. "I really must be going. Really. I'm okay, but Mama is bound to know that by now I've seen you, and I must go home and face the music. How much do I owe for the coffee?"

Sarah shook her head. "It's on me. A welcome home."

Katie smiled. "Thanks, Sarah. You, too, Buddy. I'll be in touch."

As she turned to walk away, Sarah commented, "Anytime, Katie. Anytime."

It was an open invitation from a special kind of lady and Katie knew it. Most women in her place would have exposed their claws, but Sarah Akins had not. Buddy was luckier than he realized. She wished she could tell them just how lucky.

Buddy and Sarah watched as Katie walked away. Before she left the store, Buddy called out to her, and she paused. "Whatever it is, Katie," he said evenly, "we'll be here. Just don't keep running."

Katie nodded, took a deep breath, and pushed her way back into the hot air of the afternoon.

Carolyn was standing in the foyer when Katie walked in the front door.

Her hands were planted firmly on her hips, her lips were pulled tight, and her eyes were narrowed. *She knows,* Katie thought. *She knows and she is ready to do battle.* Even the way she stood with her feet braced a foot apart from each other said she was prepared for offense.

Katie turned to close the door quietly behind her, then moved to face her mother. "Mama," she greeted her. "I see you've heard."

Carolyn moved to fold her arms across her abdomen. "Me and everybody else in town, I'd say. I wouldn't be—"

Katie walked past her mother and began to ascend the stairs, her mother no more than two steps behind her.

"Where do you think you're running off to?" Carolyn accused.

Katie stopped. *You always ran, Katie. You ran. . .you ran. . .* Katie swung around to face her mother. "I'm not running anywhere, Mama. I'm going upstairs to call Marcy to see if she wants to go to Savannah with me tomorrow. And above that, I just don't want to talk to you about this right now."

"Well, you're going to talk to me about this. I have a reputation to uphold in this community and whether you care about your own or not, I still have to live with these people. You can just run off willy-nilly to New York City and stay gone for twenty-five years. Never mind what your mama is going through. Never mind what the people of Brooksboro are saying. Or your grandparents. . ."

"Nana Kate. I forgot about Nana Kate. Is she okay?"

"She's as ornery as she ever was!"

"She's not ornery!"

"Don't change the subject with me, Katharine Morgan!"

Katie took the two steps down to her mother. "Webster. I'm Katie Webster. Katie. Not Katharine! Katie! Katie Webster!" Katie could feel the quivering in her voice and she silently willed herself not to cry.

"Which brings me to another point. What do you think your husband would think about you being seen walking around town with another man—that man—no more than two days after your arrival?"

Bring the shadows of your past into the light. . . .

"Ben wouldn't read something vile into it, I can tell you that much. Ben trusts me. Always trusted me. Even when I wouldn't tell him—" Katie stopped short.

"Wouldn't tell him what?"

Katie took quick breaths. Her lips were tightly shut. Her eyes seemed to glaze over in a wash of lamentable memories. "I can't," she whispered.

Carolyn seemed moved by her daughter's appearance. "Can't what?" There was a new tenderness in her voice.

"I can't, Mama. I just can't."

"Yes, you can. You can tell me, Katharine. What is it? What is it you can't say?" Katie started back up the stairs, but Carolyn stopped her with a touch to her arm. "Something you did when you got to New York? What did you do? What did you do, Katharine? How did you take care of yourself?"

Katie turned again to face her mother, gently pulling her arm away from her mother's touch. Her eyes were hooded and her lips drooped sadly at the corners. She shook her head slowly as she whispered, "Don't, Mama. Don't ask questions with answers you don't want to hear."

She heard the quick intake of her mother's breath as she turned and slowly made her way up the stairs to her old bedroom, the sound of gentle crying fading behind her.

CHAPTER FIFTEEN

Katie took in the room around her. The fireplace, which by this time usually roared with a boisterous, crackling fire, was empty of all but the ashes from the night before. The heavy, William Morris tapestry drapes were pulled tightly together, shutting out all but a trace of attenuated light. Standing in a filigree silver candelabrum, a solitary ivory tapered candle flickered atop the Renaissance Revival bedroom desk near French doors that led to the rose gardens, pool, and tennis court. Its light illuminated an oil painting of an ornate goblet and a loaf of bread that Ben had purchased during their first trip to Paris together. She walked slowly toward the only light in the room, becoming increasingly aware of the stillness inside her home.

Where is Ben? *she thought.*

She jerked open the French doors as a bolt of lightning and crash of thunder broke the dark sky apart. Rain began to pelt the brick verandah. She felt the light mist of dampness on her face, then slammed the doors shut.

Running out of the living room and through the foyer, she began calling for the housekeeper, "Maggie? Maggie, are you here?" As she gripped the banister at the base of the staircase, she felt tightness in her chest. The room became darker. She reached over to the light switch to her right and flipped it, but the room remained dark. Looking upward toward the lights, she flipped the switch up and down a few more times as if to make sure.

She ran up the stairs and walked quickly down the hallway toward her bedroom. Her heart pounded in her chest, keeping time with the rolling thunder beyond the safety of the walls around her. She passed a guest bedroom and noticed the closed door. That was unusual. Ben had a rule about the doors being kept open. Katie was certain it had been open when she left for the city earlier in the day. Perhaps Maggie had closed it. If Maggie cleaned in there today, why would she have closed the door? Grappling with these details at all only added to the free-floating turmoil that was escalating within her.

Inching her hand toward the doorknob, she felt a tremor race up her spine. Something was wrong in this house. Where was Ben? Where was Maggie? In all the years she lived here, one or the other met her when she walked through the front door. But. . .not today. No roaring fire to welcome her. No lights burning invitingly. Her eyes narrowed and her breathing became erratic, rasping deep in her throat. The cadence of the rain pounding harder against the house added to the intensity of her feelings. Her ears began to clog and her throat to constrict. Something was wrong in this house. . .something was wrong. . .something was. . . She had to know. She had to. . .

Katie opened the door slowly as she inched her way forward. The thumping of loud music reverberated in her ears, and her eyes widened as she stood in the open doorway. She shook her head back and forth, no. . .no. . . . It couldn't be. It wasn't possible. How could the old club, Private Dancer, be in her home?

As if by an unknown source, she was pulled in. The cages—those horrible cages that displayed the dancers like seductive prisoners—hung from the ceiling in the four corners of the room. Three of them were occupied. The one she always danced in was empty and, as if beckoning to her, the door suddenly swung open for her entrance. And then, the next thing she knew, she was mystically inside and the cage's door slammed shut.

She grabbed hold of the bars, pressing her face against the cold, sticky metal. "Let me out! Somebody help me! Somebody, please. . ." Wild-eyed she stared out at the room of mostly male patrons and dancers who writhed and shimmied to Donna Summer's "Love to Love You, Baby" pulsating from the speakers. No one seemed aware that she was trapped in the cage. She fell to her knees and felt the spike of her shoe heels dig into the flesh of her upper thighs. Remembering that she had worn dress flats for her shopping trip, she jerked around to look at her feet. Adorning them were sparkling, gold leather spiked shoes favored by exotic dancers. Becoming aware of her attire, she ran her hands over the short gold leather skirt and gold bustier. Lightning swift, she scooted to the back of the cage, pushing herself along with the spiked heels of the shoes.

"Oh, no. . . Oh, no. . ."

"Hey, you!" she heard someone yell. "You! You up there sitting in the cage like she ain't got no work to do!"

Katie leaned over and looked below. It was Leo! Leo knew she was trapped, and he had come to help her. "Leo! Leo! Get me out. Please, get me out!"

Leo pulled the fat stogie from between his clenched teeth. "Wadda ya mean, get you out? I'll get you out when your shift is over. Now, dance! I ain't payin' ya to sit up there like a scared rabbit!"

Katie pulled herself up onto her knees and grabbed the bars. "No, Leo! Listen to me! I don't work here anymore, remember?" Katie pressed the palm of her hand to her forehead. "What am I saying?" she asked herself. "This is my home!" Then to Leo, "Leo, this is my home!"

Leo stuck the cigar back into his mouth. "Yeah, well it might as well be my home, as much time as I'm spending here with you no-goods!" Katie's eyes followed him as he turned and walked away, then rested upon a lone man sitting at a table near the center of the room. He looked vaguely familiar, but she couldn't quite place him. He saw her, too, and a slow smile broke across his face. He was a handsome man, with devilish brown eyes that danced with flecks of gold. There were deep dimples in his cheeks, dimples that made her gasp with her own desire. Such a handsome man! Where had she met him before?

He shifted his weight in the chair and leaned his elbows on the table, giving her a wink.

"Help me," she mouthed to him. "Help me, please!"

He started to move. She shifted slightly in anticipation of his releasing her from captivity, but instead he reached into the pocket of his leather jacket and pulled out a wad of cash. He held it up toward her. . .teasing her with it. Did he want a private dance? She shook her head. She didn't do that kind of thing anymore. But then he began to count each individual bill, and she saw that it was three one thousand–dollar bills.

Then she knew where she had seen him before. It was in Atlanta, after she had run away from home with the money her mother had given Buddy. She had taken a bus to the state capital, checked into a four-star hotel, where she spent several days ordering room service and shopping at the upscale malls across the street. She had been quite proud of herself. Proud and clumsy. While browsing in a bookstore, she spotted him behind the front counter. Their eyes met. He gave her a dimpled grin. She remembered the way she tenderly nibbled at her bottom lip and lowered her thick lashes. She slipped away momentarily and walked toward the periodicals. Grabbing a Cosmopolitan from the shelf, she slinked up to the counter and naively pulled out her stash of bills for the purchase.

"Live around here?" he asked her.

She leaned onto the counter. "I'm staying at the hotel across the street," she answered.

He leaned onto the counter from the other side. "Really? With anybody?"

"Just little ole me." She had never been so brazen in her whole life. But she was an adult now. On her own. No Mama to tell her what to do and whom to see.

"Got dinner plans?" he asked. " 'Cause I get off around six and I could take you to dinner. That is, if you don't have other plans. I imagine a pretty little girl like you. . ."

"Oh, no!" she interjected quickly. "I have no plans."

"Pick you up at seven, then?"

"I'll be waiting," she said breathily and then started to move away.

"Hey, Honey," he called out and she nearly melted at the endearment. "You gonna tell me your room number or you gonna make me guess?"

She blushed. How silly of her. "Three-o-one."

He winked at her. "Three-o-one it is then."

If she had been older, wiser perhaps, she would have realized that he never asked for her name. Something was wrong when a man didn't ask your name before he asked you out to dinner. She didn't know it then. But later that night, with her money and her chastity snatched from her with a strange sort of professionalism, she had learned her lesson. She thought about calling her mother, but what would she have said? "Hello, Mama. I'm out five thousand dollars. Two thousand I spent on a hotel room and shopping at the mall, but the other three thousand was stolen by a man who also took my virginity. . . . Rape? No, it couldn't be rape, Mama. You see, I let him in my room, Mama. And he said all kinds of sweet things, Mama. . . . No, Mama. It's my fault. All my fault. I'm bad. I'm bad, bad, bad!"

"Katie? Katie is that you?" Katie heard a familiar voice bringing her back. She peered through the bars and saw Abby. Dear, sweet, not-too-smart Abby. She looked the same as the last time she had seen her. Her auburn hair was dirty and hung straight to her shoulders. She was wearing frayed cutoff jeans and a white blouse she tied in a knot at her midriff. Her eyes were glassy from drug use and she held a marijuana cigarette between the thumb and index finger of her right hand.

"Abby! Abby! Get me out of here. I don't belong here, Abby!"

Abby's face turned cynical. "Yeah, well, neither does anybody else! Why would I help you, Katie Morgan? When they took me and M.D. off to prison, did you come and git me out? Huh? Did ya?"

Katie began to cry. No, she hadn't. She and Abby had moved into their own apartment shortly after Katie started working at Private Dancer. For three years, they had stripped and partied. As time went on, Katie began to "manage" her drug addiction, while Abby's increased to the point of causing friction between the two of them. Then Alexi died of a drug overdose. She expected Abby to go straight because of her sister's death, but instead she moved in with M.D. Katie had been horrified that Abby would move in with a man she had always sworn to hate. A few months later, Abby and M.D. were arrested in a major drug bust. Abby called Katie and asked her *to bail her out, but she declined. Katie never saw her again.*

"No," Katie cried honestly to her old friend. "But I can help you now, Abby. I'm married to a rich man, Abby. I can help you now!"

Abby turned on her heel and called out, "Bye-bye, Katie. Bye-bye."

Katie started to call after her, but suddenly felt the jerking of the cage as it lowered to the club floor. When it came to rest, the door opened and Katie looked up to find one of the older dancers there. At thirty-one, Kristen had been a seasoned dancer. She had taken Katie and Abby under her wing, taught them the ropes, and protected them from Leo's advances and the physical and verbal abuses from the other dancers. In 1979, an angry customer had killed Kristen. Katie had been rocked by the brutality of it. Once again she picked up the phone to call her mother, to beg for forgiveness. Once again she talked herself out of it. What could she possibly say at this time that would make her mother understand her situation? "Hello, Mama. This is Katie. . . your daughter. The one who left four years ago. . . Mama, I want to come home. I'm tired of this life, you see, and I. . . What kind of life? I'm a stripper, Mama. And a druggie. I'm a stripper and a druggie. I'm bad. Bad, bad, bad!"

Katie stood slowly in the cage, terrified at seeing her dead friend standing in front of her.

"Come on, Honey," Kristen said, her voice echoing as the music played on. "Ain't got all night. My turn in the cage." *Katie walked past her slowly, afraid that Kristen would touch her and cause her own untimely death. But Kristen smiled a crooked smile, showing her uneven teeth. Her flaming red hair fell in tight waves to her shoulders.* "I know, Honey," *she said.* "You're thinking I'm dead."

Katie nodded slowly.

"I'm dead, all right. And so are you."

Katie whispered, "Noooo."

"Yes, you are, Honey. The day you set foot in this place, you was as good as dead."

"No!" *Katie screamed and began to run for the door. As she reached it, a hulk of a man stepped from the shadows, barring her way. David Franscella! She brought her hands up to her lips to stifle the scream as she swallowed the panic and bile that rose to her throat.*

"Katie," *he whispered slowly.* "What are you doing here?"

"I'm leaving," *she said quickly, suddenly very sure of herself.* "If you'll just move away from the door, please."

His eyes turned menacing. "What do you want to do that for? Your shift over?"

"I don't work here, anymore. You know I don't. I'm married! I'm Mrs. William Benjamin Webster!"

David began to laugh. A low laugh that seemed to rise from the core of his black heart. As he did, the music stopped, and Katie heard the laughter of all the patrons in the room. It began softly at first, then rose to a crescendo. She swung around to face them. They barked with laughter. Louder! Louder! And then she heard a distinct, baritone laugh that caused the hair on the back of her neck to prickle. She swung around to seek out its origin.

It was coming from behind David Franscella.

"Who is it?" *she asked him.* "Who is laughing at me?"

A shadowy figure stepped from behind the massive form of her former lover. Bucky Caballero. She took a step back as he pulled a gold, monogrammed cigarette case from his dinner jacket pocket. Never taking his eyes off her, he opened the case, took a cigarette from it, tapped it a few times, and placed it gingerly between his lips.

"Your husband know you're here, Mrs. Webster?" *he asked as David turned to light the cigarette.*

"I don't think he knows she ever worked here," *David answered for her.* "Does he, Katie?"

Katie began to cry. "No. No. He can't find out. He would never forgive me. Please, let me out. He can't know. . . . Mama can't know. . . . I'm bad! I'm so very bad!"

"Katie?" *Katie swung around at the sound of Ben's clear, strong voice, a voice that held safety and power. She knew she should be thrilled for him to help her out of the room, but instead she wrapped her arms around her chest in an effort to hide her immodest attire.*

She looked up at David with large pleading eyes. "Help me. Ben mustn't see me like this, David. You have to help me. You have to. If I ever meant anything to you. . ."

But David only snickered as he looked down his straight nose at her. "Why should I help you, Katie Morgan? What did you ever do for me, huh?"

"Katie?" Ben's voice rang out again, and again Katie looked about wild-eyed. In the far right corner she could see his six-foot, six-inch frame pushing through the massive crowd of people.

"David," she pleaded, turning back to him. "Please! You don't understand!"

She heard the drawing of Bucky's cigarette and smelled the gray smoke as he blew it through his thin, drawn lips. "What is it William Shakespeare wrote in Hamlet? 'The very substance of the ambitious is merely the shadow of a dream.' Who is the more ambitious here, Mrs. Webster? Your husband? Or me? I can answer that for you. The answer is: me. Ah, but your husband is making my life a little tough right now, Mrs. Webster," he said, his voice low and commanding. She turned slowly and looked at him with sad eyes and he continued, "I'm afraid we cannot help you. And you see, Mrs. Webster. . .we are very much in control."

CHAPTER SIXTEEN

"Do you remember the seventh-grade chorus?" Marcy asked Katie the following day. Riding in Marcy's white Ford Explorer down Highway 21 toward Savannah, they began to reminisce about old times. When they were out of Brooksboro city limits, Marcy slipped in a "Creedence Clearwater Revival" CD. CCR had practically been a staple during their teen years. They would meet their friends at a local parking lot where everyone piled into the back of Billy Turner's old pickup truck. Entertainment for the evening often consisted of driving down dirt roads at breakneck speeds with CCR blaring on the truck's eight-track tape player. The close-knit group of friends would throw back their heads, hair billowing in the breeze, and sing at the top of their lungs. Today, Marcy and Katie sang loud and off-key with John Fogerty as he belted out "Down on the Corner."

"What?" Katie couldn't hear Marcy over the noise of the music.

Marcy reached over and turned down the volume, then repeated, "Do you remember the seventh-grade chorus?"

Katie frowned slightly. She knew where this was going. "Yeah, yeah," she said, nodding.

"Remember when we were practicing for that—what was it—?"

"Spring Fling."

"Yeah! Yeah! The Spring Fling. And we were singing 'Aquarius,' weren't we?"

"You just love this story, don't you?" Katie grimaced as she looked out her window to the stretch of farmland beside her. "Look at all those bales of hay."

"Don't change the subject! Anyway, as I recall. . ."

"And I'm sure you do. . . ."

Marcy gave Katie a teasingly firm look. "As I recall, you stood just behind me on the risers." Katie began to chuckle in spite of herself. "And when the song was over, I turned to you and said. . ."

The two friends quoted together, " 'Would you mind not singing so loud in my ear?' " They broke off in a fit of laughter.

"It was the single most hurtful moment of my life," Katie informed her.

"Oh, posh!"

"No, I'm serious. I was emotionally ruined that day!" But the laughter in her voice told a different story. "I'm surprised I haven't had to have therapy over this, Marcy. I mean, there I was singing my little heart out and you insinuate that I sing too loud and off-key."

"You do sing loud and off-key."

"See there? Still you hurt me!"

"You got over it."

"Hey, Marcy? What ever happened to Billy Turner?"

"Billy? Oh my, I don't even know. I guess he got married and has a house full of kids."

"You don't see him anymore?" Katie asked, looking ahead. An approaching car flashed its headlights as they went by, warning them of a surveillance law enforcement officer ahead.

"Thank you, buddy," Marcy said to the passing motorist, raising her hand slightly in a friendly hello.

Katie smiled as Marcy applied her foot lightly to the brakes. "I had forgotten about that."

"About what?"

"The way southerners wave to passing motorists whether they know each other or not. In New York, if you did that, you'd be taking your life into your own hands. Anyway. . .Billy Turner? Do you ever see him?"

"See him? Noooo. . .I guess I haven't seen Billy in a long time." She leaned forward slightly and looked left to right. "Do you see a cop car anywhere around here? I don't."

Katie peered out the window to the lush landscape that stretched out on either side of the road. Farmland, dotted with horses and other livestock, occasionally gave way to swamps, with large cypress trees that emerged and reflected on the still, black water below. The flat, pale, scalelike foliage had always reminded Katie of death somehow. In spite of this, she felt eerily at peace whenever passing similar scenes such as this. It seemed as if the tree, appearing dead, was quiescent in the surrounding calmness of the dark water. And yet, amidst apparent death was abundant life.

"Katie, are you looking for cops or what?" Katie heard Marcy say to her. She straightened and blinked several times before answering, "Oh, yeah. Yeah. I don't see one either. . .oh, yeah I do. Just behind those trees on the left."

"Quick!" Marcy exclaimed gleefully. "Close your eyes! Maybe he won't see us!"

The women laughed heartily as they continued down the highway.

Half an hour into the trip, with "America's Greatest Hits" having replaced CCR, Marcy discreetly cleared her throat and shifted slightly in her seat. "Hey, Katie. I heard you saw Buddy yesterday."

Katie read nervousness in Marcy's voice. "Now, wherever did you hear that?"

"Well, to be honest with you, Theresa Simmons."

"Who in the world is Theresa Simmons?"

"You don't know her. But she and her husband are good friends with Buddy and Sarah. Oh. I heard you met Sarah."

Katie smiled. "She's such a nice person, isn't she?"

"I always liked her. Anyway, how did it go? I mean, being with Buddy again?"

Katie flipped the sun visor down in search of a mirror. Finding one, she reached into her purse and pulled out a tube of lipstick and began to apply it. "It went fine. What is there to say? I bumped into him on the way out of the bank. He didn't recognize me at first, but when I pulled my shades off, he did. He looks really good, don't you think?"

"I guess so."

"And naturally every busybody in the bank was looking at us like we had just hatched an egg right there on the floor. I stepped outside while Buddy did his banking, then he came out and suggested we go to the drugstore, which we did. . . ."

"Sarah works there."

"Yes, I know. And then we just talked."

"Theresa said you were crying."

Katie all but jumped in her seat. "How did she. . . Oh, for crying out loud! Can't a person do anything in this little town without some-one else knowing about it?"

Marcy laughed. "Oh, please! You can't sneeze without someone three blocks down saying, 'God bless you.'"

"I had forgotten all this, I really had." The frustration was clear in her voice. "What else did this Theresa person tell you?"

"That's it. Well, except that you practically ran out of the store."

"I did not run."

"But did you cry?"

"It was nothing. We were just going over old stuff."

"Like the night you ran away?"

Katie was silent for a moment before answering. "Yeah. Like that night."

"I won't bug you about it. Don't worry." Marcy applied her brakes as they approached a red traffic signal. "We're almost there. Where do you want to go? Do you know?"

Katie blinked her eyes several times to clear the tears that had begun to gather there. "The best shopping mall or plaza."

"Got it." There was a space of silence as they sat at the light. When it changed and they began to move again, Marcy added, "Katie?"

"Hmmm?"

"What's it like? Living in New York City?"

Katie thought for a moment before answering. "It's everything you have imagined and more. It's Broadway and off-Broadway. Strolling in Central Park on crisp, spring afternoons, and nights at the opera or the ballet. It's afternoons leisurely spent in some of the best museums in the world. It's three-course lunches for the price of the year."

"Excuse me?"

Katie laughed. "It started off as a promotional thing during a Republican convention. The restaurateurs wanted the delegates to try some of the better restaurants, so they offered a three-course lunch—appetizer, main course, and dessert—for a cost of whatever the year was. For example, in 1993 the price for the meal was $19.93 and in 1994, it was $19.94 and so on and so on."

"Drinks come with that, or are you just supposed to choke on all that delicious food?"

"Drinks, tax, and tips are extra," Katie answered, using a professional announcer's voice.

"Sounds wonderful. New York, I mean. The meal, too, but especially the city."

"It can be. It can also be your worst enemy."

"Was it ever yours?"

"My worse enemy? Oh, yeah. The first few years. The first few years were hard."

"Then why didn't you come home?" Marcy asked, turning the car into a shopping mall's parking. "I'm sorry. I said I wasn't going to do that."

Katie was silent as Marcy searched for a parking space, then swung into the first available one. "It just kills me," she began. "People who will drive around for ten minutes looking for a closer spot than the first one they see. By the time they find one, I'm already in the mall and have made my first purchase."

Katie smiled as Marcy put the car in park, then turned the key and yanked it out of the ignition switch.

"Marcy," Katie said with a deep sigh. "Sometimes there are no answers to certain questions. Or, the answers are not easily understood. . . ."

Marcy turned to look at her. "You don't have to tell me anything, Katie. Really."

"It's just that. . .I want to. . .I really do. . . . But what happened to me is not easily explained. How can I make you understand what it's like to sink into a pit so low you can't see daylight? And yet you know that with just one phone call, it can all be over. You can be out of the darkness. But you just can't get yourself to make that phone call. Because being exposed is almost as painful as being in the confused and shadowy blur you call your life. You don't even think about day to day. You think about minute to minute. Because in a flash, all that which is real to you can become lost and that which was fantasy becomes absolute."

Marcy stared at her as if she were meditating on what she heard, then shook her head slightly and said, "I don't understand a word you just said. I look at you right now and I see a totally beautiful woman who looks like she doesn't have a care in the world. But when you talk like this and I look into your eyes—eyes that I have known so well—I see something I cannot explain or understand. It's like you've seen the lowest places and the highest places. And you never got an in-between. And quite frankly, Katie, all I've ever known was the in-between."

Katie gave her a brief smile. "Lucky you."

"Can you tell me? Just one low place? Or maybe just one high place?"

Katie smiled. "The highest place has been my husband. Ben—my husband—is like a brilliant light that's been turned on in a gray room. But when he shines. . .oh. . .the gray becomes white, beautiful white. The room is a beautiful place to behold." Katie bit her bottom lip as she smiled. "Yeah, that's the high place. It doesn't get much better than Ben."

"Then why didn't he come with you? Is something wrong?"

Katie lowered her eyes, then looked back up to Marcy. "Not the way you think. But I can't. . .I can't. . ." Katie shook her head.

"Enough of this," Marcy said authoritatively. "This is supposed to be our fun day. Let's get going. I need a new pair of jeans in the worst way. And last year's bathing suit was actually the same one I've had for two years. Charlie is talking about going to Tybee Beach for vacation, and I'll be darned if I'm going to wear that old thing again this year."

The mall interior was abuzz with activity. Mostly teenagers, Katie thought. Their raucous chat and the upbeat music from the shops mixed awkwardly with the individual shops' music and the mall's piped-in Muzak. Mothers strolled their crying, fidgeting infants and toddlers while teenage lovers wrapped their arms around each other and clumsily shuffled down the open corridors. It had been years since Katie had been exposed to the hubbub of a mall. Her shopping had been done in the most exclusive shops in New York City.

Marcy seemed to come alive. In the first large department store that they shopped in, she flitted from one rack of petite clothes to the other. "Does this look like me?" she'd ask, holding a blouse, dress, or pair of slacks up to her small frame. Whether Katie nodded or gave a disapproving, "Nooooo," Marcy would replace the item. "I don't need it anyway. I need jeans and I need a new bathing suit."

"There're jeans over there," Katie said, pointing to the far wall where jeans were neatly folded and stacked in individual cubicles.

Marcy looked in the general direction, then back to Katie. "Why aren't you looking at anything?"

Katie leaned against a nearby mirrored column and crossed her long legs at the ankles. "Because unless someone chops my legs off at the knees, I will never be able to wear a petite anything!"

Marcy laughed. "You've certainly changed your attitude about your height in the last twenty-five years. Oh! Look at this cute little tee!" She whipped a fuchsia T-shirt from the tightly packed rack of clothes. "Cute, huh?"

It was. "It would look great with black jeans. Do you ever wear black jeans? Or even white jeans. White jeans and. . . Look at this. . .here's a black tee like the fuchsia one. You should get these. These and the jeans."

Marcy chewed on her bottom lip for a moment. "Charlie will just shoot me, but they really are cute. And I could really use them."

Katie took her friend by the hand and pulled her toward the back wall. "Never mind Charlie. This is my treat."

Marcy stopped short. "What? No! I don't expect you to do this!"

Katie smiled as she took Marcy's hand and again began to walk toward the display of jeans. "Look, Marcy. This day is on me. I owe it to you for all the crud I put you through."

"You don't owe me anything, Katie. We're friends. We always have been and we always will be."

Katie mentally sized Marcy, then pulled a black pair and a white pair of size five jeans from the shelves. "Five, right?"

Marcy playfully snatched them from Katie's hands. "I was a three until Mark was born. Then I just spread all over."

"Oh, please," Katie teased.

"Katie, this is great, but I really can't. . . ."

"Marcy! Listen to me. I can afford it, okay? I can afford this and anything else your heart desires, so don't worry about it. Let me do this!"

Marcy stilled. "What do you mean by that?"

Katie smiled. "Between me and you?"

"I've always been the soul of discretion."

"I deposited a hundred thousand dollars yesterday at the bank. And, yes, it's my money. So please. Let me buy this for you. And lunch. And. . ." Katie looked around and spotted the fragrance counter. "And your favorite perfume. And we'll go and have a makeover. How's that?"

Marcy appeared stupefied. "That's wonderful," she muttered.

"There ought to be a place around here that has the full treatment. Hair, nails, facial. The whole deal. We'll even get our eyebrows waxed."

Marcy burst out laughing. "You're teasing me."

Katie placed her hands firmly on Marcy's shoulders and guided her toward the dressing room. "No, I'm not, so hurry up. I need new clothes, too, and you're wasting time. Now get!"

Marcy did not reply. She simply stumbled into the dressing area and mumbled to the attendant, "Four items."

"Room six," the young woman said, handing Marcy a plastic marker with the number four on it.

Lunch consisted of soup and salad at Ruby Tuesday's. The two friends talked endlessly about the morning's purchases. Marcy finally agreed to allow Katie to purchase the jeans and tees, as well as a bathing suit, a negligee, cologne and bath gel, and a pair of white sneakers. While Marcy was trying the shoes on, Katie slipped over to the jewelry counter and purchased a pair of cultured pearl stud earrings, which she slipped into Marcy's shopping bag. Nothing dressed up jeans and tees like simple pearl stud earrings, Katie decided.

Katie purchased for herself a dress, two pairs of jeans, and several casual tops. She found a variety of short sets to her liking as well as workout clothing for her morning runs. While searching the jewelry counter for the earrings, she had seen an intricately woven silver and gold chain that she bought for her mother. *A peace offering*, she thought hopefully.

After lunch, Marcy and Katie moved on to a salon located on the first floor of the shopping mall. As they approached the front black-marble desk, a young woman greeted them. "May we help you?" she asked courteously.

"Do you accept walk-ins?" Katie asked, shifting the shopping bags from one hand to another.

"For everything except perms," she answered. "We need to make an appointment for that."

"That's not a problem," Katie informed her. "We don't want perms. We just need a shampoo, cut, and style as well as a manicure and pedicure. Do you do facials?"

"We certainly do!" The woman beamed.

"That, too."

Marcy was in awe at how self-confident Katie had become. A real woman of the world who knew how to assert herself in a charming and upbeat way. It was quite evident that she was in her element here, and yet all that wealth bestowed upon her had not spoiled the essence of her character. At heart, she was basically the same country girl she grew up with, despite her sophisticated veneer.

Katie and Marcy spent the next two hours being pampered in a fashion that Katie was certainly accustomed to, but Marcy found terribly exciting. She fairly shouted, "This is so much fun!" several times, much to the delight of the employees and management.

As the hairdresser was giving Marcy a trim, she commented, "You have a little gray here and there. Wouldn't you like for me to do a color?"

"Oh, no. . . ," Marcy answered quickly.

Katie straightened in the padded chair beside her where her hairdresser was trimming her dark chestnut hair. "Yes, Marcy! Do it!"

"Do we have time?" she asked, glancing at her thin-banded Timex.

"We have nothing but time!" Katie exclaimed. "Do it! You'll look great! You need to add a little warmth to the color. With all this and the negligee, Charlie will think he's married another woman!"

Marcy laughed freely. "Okay! You talked me into it!"

Half an hour later, Marcy's hair was covered in goop and Katie's makeover was complete. As Katie paid at the front counter, she inquired, "Is there a store where I can buy gourmet coffee?"

"Oh, sure," the young woman answered. "Just go back upstairs and toward the food court. I won't even have to tell you which store. Your nose will guide you! It's absolute heaven."

Katie laughed. "I know. Is there anything better than a good cup of coffee?"

"You must love coffee as much as I do."

Katie raised her eyebrows teasingly. "It's my passion."

While moving through the thinning crowd and following her nose toward the coffee shop, Katie thought how pleasant the day had been. She and Marcy had long had this coming. As teenagers, they had come here for a day of shopping, but it had never been anything like this. Back then, it had been to purchase one item, like a prom dress. Or a bathing suit. New outfit for a special date or school clothes. But today had been gay and carefree. And for once she had not thought of New York or Bucky Caballero. Nor had she seen Andi's beguiling face in her mind's eye.

But she had not stopped thinking about Ben. With every purchase she thought of him. *Ben would like this,* she would say to herself. While observing the people around her she would think, *Ben would find this amusing.* Or, *Ben would frown on that.* Her whole existence was Ben. She loved him with a passion she did not think possible. Perhaps because he was just so wonderful. Or, better still, because in spite of everything he knew about her, he loved her. He would give her the world on a silver platter if she asked. But all she wanted was him. To feel his arms around her. To hear him say her name. *Katie.*

She closed her eyes briefly, then began to look among the storefronts for the coffee shop. It was then that she spotted him. A tall, handsome man, broad shouldered, with long hair secured in a ponytail at the nape of his neck walking toward her. Was it. . .could it be. . . David Franscella?

Katie did not wait to find out. She quickly turned and began walking away. She wasn't quite sure where she was going, but she knew that she had to get away from this man. She didn't want to return to the salon for fear of endangering Marcy and the others. She felt her heart begin to race. With wild eyes she looked back and saw that the man was still moving toward her. His face was not clear, they were at least thirty yards apart, but it looked like David. She would be willing to bet it was him.

She stopped for a moment, just long enough to get her bearings. A large department store was at the end of the corridor. She decided that going there would be her best bet. She could easily get lost in the maze of clothes racks. Or find her way into the ladies' rest room. Surely, he would not follow her there.

She picked up her pace as she moved forward. She felt tears stinging her eyes. Ben. She wanted Ben. Without him, she wasn't sure what to do. If she managed to get away from David, what then? What if he caught her? What would he do to her? Was Ben okay? Was Ben in trouble?

She walked through the wide opening of the store, turned left, weaving through various displays of ladies' fashions. A saleslady ahead of her smiled warmly and greeted, "May I help you find something today?"

Katie looked behind her hurriedly, then back at the lady. "Rest room?" she asked, panting.

The sales lady gave her a courteous, but astonished stare. "Certainly. Go through the men's department. It's between men's and sportswear."

"Thank you," Katie said breathlessly, then moved toward the men's department. She glanced behind her once more, but saw no one. Perhaps she had eluded him. Perhaps it wasn't even David. She slipped around a circular rack of men's shorts and looked in the direction of the front door. From here she could see if he came in, but he would not be able to see her. If necessary she could slip into one of the empty dressing rooms behind her. She grasped the rack's cold chrome rod and tried to steady her breathing. A sigh escaped her lips and she felt a trickle of perspiration slip down the side of her face.

She continued to look toward the main entrance. Still, no David. Maybe she was safe now. Maybe she always had been. Perhaps she was the victim of an overactive imagination. Perhaps. . .

A strong hand clasped her shoulder in a vise grip. Katie whirled around and screamed.

CHAPTER SEVENTEEN

"Whoa!" A male salesclerk said, jumping back slightly. He glanced around the store to make certain that Katie's scream had not alarmed security.

Katie stared at the young man standing directly in front of her with several hangers of Ralph Lauren Polo shirts hooked on the finger of his left hand. "Ma'am?" he asked, as she slumped against the clothes rack, then brought her hand up to her chest and silently willed her heartbeat to return to normal. "Hey, are you okay?"

Katie glanced over her shoulder toward the entrance of the store, then back at him. "I'm sorry. I thought you were someone else."

He studied her before commenting. "Will you be okay?"

"Yes. Yes, thank you." Katie stepped away from the men's department and pretended to shop the nearby cosmetic counter where no one seemed to be working. She waited long enough to assure herself that, if David Franscella were in the mall, he was long gone. Then she returned to the salon where Marcy was having her hair blown dry and styled.

"What do you think of the color?" the hair stylist asked.

"It looks wonderful," Katie answered. Her voice quavered slightly, and she hoped her friend didn't notice.

"Where's your coffee?" Marcy asked.

Katie looked down at her hands, which still trembled.

"I um. . .I decided to wait for you."

Marcy frowned. "Uh-huh." She glanced at the stylist. "Are we about done here?"

The whir of the blow dryer stopped and the stylist returned it to her station's table. "There we go! Is this what you hoped for?"

"It's perfect," Marcy commented, slipping out of the seat but hardly looking in the mirror. She grabbed Katie's hand. "What's wrong?" she whispered.

"Nothing," Katie whispered back. "Nothing."

"Uh-huh. Let's go get that coffee then and we'll just see about that."

It was on their way to the food court that Katie saw the man she had thought was David Franscella. Relief hit her like a wave as she witnessed the "twin" with a little girl gathered up in his arms and a lovely woman, apparently his wife, walking beside him. "Daddy," the little girl was saying, "Mommy and I saw the Barbie dolls!" To which the man replied, "Did you find one that you want Daddy to buy for you, Princess?" The little girl nodded excitedly.

Not exactly the killer-type, Katie surmised with a smile.

Marcy left her at a small table in the center of the food court while she purchased two cups of coffee. When she returned, a smile spread across her face as she placed the tray on the table and said, "I splurged and bought two slices of pound cake. Hope you like pound cake."

"I adore it. So do my thighs."

In silence, they prepared their coffee with the cream and sugar packets Marcy had thrown on the tray, then took the first bites of cake. Marcy took a tentative sip of coffee. "Hot," she observed. "Be careful with yours."

"Thanks."

"Okay, Katie. Here's the deal: I wasn't going to say anything about this—"

"About what?" Katie set the Styrofoam cup on the table.

"Not too long ago I was doing some research about mob crime in New York City for my column."

"Your point?"

"Katie, we may not have seen each other in twenty-five years, but you are still my best friend. Something has frightened you—and I don't just mean this afternoon."

"What makes you think that something has frightened me?"

"I study people. It's a skill I guess you could say. It makes for great writing."

Katie raked her newly styled hair with her fingernails. "Oh, yeah."

"Katie, are you in some kind of trouble? Are you involved with the mob in some sort of way?" Marcy leaned closer to Katie and whispered, "Is Ben a mob lord?"

"Ben? No!" Katie actually laughed.

Marcy turned red-faced and sat back. "I'm sorry. This just doesn't make sense to me. You disappear one night into thin air. No one seems to know where you've gone and the one person who just might know isn't saying a word. Not even to me, your best friend."

"I'm sorry."

"No. No more sorries. For twenty-five years. . .no word from you. And then, boom! You just drop back into town to reconcile with your mother. Uh-uh. I don't think so. Something is rotten in Denmark." Marcy reached over and took Katie's hand. "Katie. Talk to me. You can trust me; you know that you can. What are you running from?"

"First, you're so sure I'm frightened and now you think I'm running. What makes you think I am running?"

"Intuition. It comes with becoming a mother."

Katie took a sip of her coffee. Her head was beginning to throb and the muscles of her neck were tensing. She felt as though she were about to burst. She had kept this inside for too long. Not just the issues of Bucky Caballero, but the last twenty-five years. The man in the bookstore in Atlanta, Abby, Private Dancer, Leo. The ghosts of her memories were haunting her in her dreams, spilling over into reality. She wanted to be free of them, the secrets and the fears. Thinking that the father of the little girl who happily anticipated her new Barbie doll had been David Franscella was the final straw. She couldn't do this anymore. She couldn't pretend that the last twenty-five years were someone else's nightmare or fantasy. They had taken more than half of her life. Right or wrong, saint or sinner, she simply had to face up to what she had done. Redemption began with Ben, but absolution was sitting here in front of her. It could happen now. God knew she had to trust someone. "I have to trust someone," she whispered across the table.

"Katie, Katie. It's me. Marcy. Your friend." She spread her palm across her chest.

"But you're too close to my mother. My mother isn't ready for this. . . any of this. She thought. . .would think that. . ."

Marcy gave a gentle smile. "I'm your friend."

Katie closed her eyes and counted to ten, then opened them. "I need you to swear—"

"I swear."

"Okay. Okay. Where to start?"

"How about with your husband."

"My husband isn't a mob lord. He owns The Hamilton Place," she began, having taken a deep breath.

"The hotel chain?" Marcy's eyes widened.

"Yes."

"All of them?" Marcy asked, leaning over the table.

"Yes."

"I'm impressed."

Katie smiled. "You'd be even more impressed if you knew the man of character my husband is. You would never imagine that he is as powerful in business as he is. Or as wealthy. He is very unpretentious."

"So with all this I can safely assume Ben is not who you are running from."

"No, although that would be a very good assumption. Inside several four- and five-star hotels in the New York City area are ladies' boutiques called Jacqueline's. Very exclusive lines of clothing. THP has one. They are owned by a man named Bucky Caballero through a dummy corporation."

"How do you know this?" Marcy asked, leaning back in the wrought iron chair.

"My husband is gathering information on him for the FBI."

"Why? What's so bad about a man owning a ladies' boutique?"

"That's just it. It's more than just a boutique. It's a front for a high-class escort service."

"Ah, I've read about that. You're talking prostitution."

"Yes."

She nodded slowly for a moment, then asked, "Your husband—Ben—tell you this?"

"Not exactly."

"Explain please."

"Bucky Caballero is also the owner of B. Caballero, Inc., a real estate brokerage. He owns it with his sister, Mattie Franscella. Her husband is David Franscella."

"Should I know that name?"

"No. But it will be important later. I never knew Mr. Caballero or his sister very well because I wasn't interested in being a social butterfly. My interests lay solely in loving Ben and furthering my education. Bucky and Mattie have been known for their charitable donations in past years. Every year they hold a dinner for one charity or another. Ben and I hadn't attended before, but this year we thought we should. This year they threw a fund-raising gala event for the AIDS Foundation."

"Commendable."

"It would be, if they were donating all the money to the foundation. But records indicate they profit from their galas."

"That's not so unusual, Katie. I've done an article on that. It's shameful, but common."

"That may be, but I think that Bucky's reasoning for the galas is neither raising money for the foundation nor for himself. I think it places him in the good graces of the public officials who attend. Public officials who are also patrons of the escort service."

"I'm beginning to follow you. As patrons they aren't so likely to turn him in. And as a pillar of the community, he's not a likely suspect."

"Exactly." Katie nodded. "Somehow, Ben found out what's going on."

"How?"

Katie took a deep breath. "This is so complicated."

"I'll try to keep up," she said with a smile.

"The manager of the boutique is a woman named Andi. Apparently, she is also the manager of the escort service."

"Like the madam?"

Katie frowned. "You could say that. Andi used to be a music major at a local university. Ben wanted me to take piano lessons and suggested that I take them from her."

"Before he knew about the escort service."

"Certainly!"

"Sorry. Go on."

"Andi and I are close; we became friends of sorts. At the last gala, she and I were talking when one of her old 'clients' went to Ben and told him the truth about Jacqueline's."

"Oh, wow. And Ben told you?"

"Not really. He called a friend of his with the FBI. Together, they began to investigate. In the meantime, I came down with a cold and was stuck in bed drinking Maggie's tea."

"Maggie?"

"Our housekeeper. She's wonderful! She's been with Ben since he was a child."

"I see. Okay. You had a cold. . .and apparently a housekeeper." Katie could hear both the anxiousness and the teasing sarcasm in Marcy's voice.

"On Monday—last Monday—I went a little stir crazy and decided I would go into Ben's study in hopes of finding a good book to read. I searched the shelves, found a book, then went to the chair behind Ben's desk. I noticed that one of the drawers had not been shut all the way. I don't know why I did it, but I opened it and began to flip through the different files. I shouldn't have, but I did. That's when I found a file labeled 'Bucky Caballero.' I opened it and found the information that Ben had gathered. There wasn't much to know then. . . . Ben had only been working on it for a couple of days. . .but I did find out about the dummy corporation. Bucky and his sister are making a fortune in the escort service business. They're even featured on the Internet."

"And all that slimy business is going on right there in Ben's hotel."

"Exactly."

Marcy was silent. Katie could see that she was mentally cataloging everything that she had said. "And so Ben has sent you back here. . . now. . .to what? Hide? Or is there something else? Some other turn of the screw? You weren't one of those escorts were you? When you first left here?"

Katie took a nervous sip of her cold coffee. "No, not exactly." She looked Marcy straight in the eyes. "I did, however, work as an exotic dancer."

"Oh, Katie," Marcy exhaled deeply as she spoke.

"Are you sure you want to know this?"

Marcy studied the question for a minute before answering. "Yes. Talk to me."

"After I got to New York and became a dancer, I had a nasty drug habit and was living a not-so-wonderful life. There's no need in getting into all that now; it would only serve to make us both very sad. Later, I went to college, where I studied to be a legal assistant. Got a job at a top law firm. . ."

"How did you manage that?"

"To be honest with you, the senior partner had been a regular at the club where I was working. By this time, I was dancing at an upscale men's club. Mr. Mosely, the senior partner, was an older gentleman. Grand-fatherly." She smiled at the fond memory. "I was always nice to him. Talked to him on my breaks. And he would tell me that I really ought to get out of the business. He told me that I was smart and could do any-thing I wanted. During time, I had been seeing someone. . . ." She trailed off.

"Someone?"

"David Franscella."

Marcy leaned back in her chair again. "Goodness! You were seeing the brother-in-law of the man who is running an escort service out of your husband's hotel? Small world, huh?"

"Very. But I didn't know about his wife. And I didn't even know Ben. I felt that David was involved in some sort of nasty business, but I didn't know what. Then. . .one day. . .David became very angry with me."

"About what?"

"I was. . .I had become. . .I was pregnant."

"You have a child? You told me you didn't."

"I don't. David was very upset. . .my being pregnant would conflict with his life with Mattie, obviously. . .and he began to beat me."

Marcy placed her hands over her face as her elbows came up to rest on the table. "Oh, Katie." She removed her hands, and Katie saw the tears that had formed in her eyes.

Katie took a deep breath and pressed on. "To make up for it, David began paying for my education. I graduated, much to Mr. Mosely's delight, and he had a job waiting for me. Started me off at the very bottom, too. But he allowed me to work my way up and, in the process, to reclaim my dignity."

"Why didn't you call home then?"

Katie looked down. "By that time, I didn't feel worthy enough to call."

"Were you still with David?"

"Noooo."

"And that's when you met Ben."

"Yes. But he never knew about my days as a dancer. My biggest fear was. . .is. . .that Ben will discover the truth. Funny thing is that the truth was waiting to be discovered, but it wasn't about me."

"Ben sent you back, didn't he?"

"Yes. On my own, I might never have returned. I hope that doesn't hurt to hear."

"It does, but I'll get over it."

"Ben doesn't want anyone to know where I am. . .to know the truth about what we know. . .or anyone here to know who I am."

Marcy nodded. "Ben's right. If you tell him you've told me, be sure to tell him I won't say a word."

"I won't be talking to him."

"What do you mean?"

"He won't call until this is over. That was the agreement."

"Oh, Katie."

"I know. I miss him terribly."

Marcy sat quietly for a moment. "What frightened you earlier? When you returned to the salon, you were shaking and white."

"I thought I had seen David Franscella. David is the one person who knows I am from Georgia. The one person who can track me down. So, thinking I had seen him, I tried to get lost in the crowd. But it turned out that the man I thought was David wasn't after all."

"Did David know that you were from Brooksboro or just Georgia?"

"Just Georgia. I never told anyone that I was from Brooksboro. Except Ben, of course."

"So you're still safe?"

"I think so."

"Katie, whatever happened to Andi?"

"On Tuesday morning, Andi called Ben and asked him to meet her in Central Park. When he did, she gave him an envelope with copies of Andrea's records."

"Andrea's being. . ."

"The name that the escort service goes by."

"I see."

"I left late that afternoon. Ben had a scheduled flight to Atlanta for later that evening. He had a business meeting there the next day. He told me that he was going to take Andi with him. He and the FBI made arrangements to supply her with a new identity upon her arrival. From Atlanta she would go somewhere else. I don't know where."

"I see. Is there anything else?"

"No. That's just about it. Marcy, you can't tell anyone this. Not even Charlie."

"Of course not."

"Thanks. It feels good to know I'm not alone down here."

"You never were." The two friends stared at each other for long moments. "Ready to go home? Back to Brooksboro?"

"Yes. Yes, I think I am."

CHAPTER EIGHTEEN

At precisely noon on Sunday, the members and visitors of the Brooksboro United Methodist Church walked out of the large, white double doors and spilled down the numerous brick steps leading to the sidewalk below. Clusters of men and women congregated, speaking casually, an occasional bark of laughter erupting. Children ran to the cars owned by their parents, innocently calling out to each other.

Katie stepped out of the cool vestibule and into the blinding sunlight as the pastor, draped in a black clerical robe, extended his hand to her in greeting.

"Good morning," he said to her. Then to her mother, "Miss Carolyn. How are you today?"

"I'm fine, Brother Bob. Just fine. This is my daughter, Katharine. She's visiting from New York."

Brother Bob gave Katie a friendly, but astonished glance. "Really? So you're Katharine."

"Katie," she said softly. "Please call me Katie. I'm afraid my mother has never adapted to my nickname."

"That's because it's not your name," Carolyn argued halfheartedly. "I named you Katharine. If I had wanted to name you Katie, I would have named you Katie. But that's beside the point, isn't it, Brother Bob?"

Brother Bob, a small-framed, slightly balding man with twinkling

223

eyes and a smooth, handsome face, merely beamed. "I understand how you both feel," he said diplomatically. "As you can suppose, my real name is Robert. Mother and Dad have always called me Robert and everyone else in my life called me Bob. I tell everyone I really don't care. Call me what you want to call me, as long as you call me to supper!"

Katie laughed out loud, deciding then and there that she really liked Brother Bob. Carolyn smiled, but did not laugh. She did, however, comment, "Sorry. Just wanted to introduce my daughter to the preacher."

Katie felt a sense of warmth at the comment. Her mother wanted to introduce her. It was almost a way of saying, "I'm proud to introduce. . ."

Marcy and her family were waiting for Katie and her mother when they descended the steps. The five of them, standing alongside Roberta and Sam, who greeted her lovingly when she entered the sanctuary of the church, made a cheery Norman Rockwell picture.

"Melissa," Katie spoke to her best friend's daughter. "I can't begin to tell you how much you look like your mother. I feel as if I should be running off with you to talk about Saturday night dates."

Melissa gave Katie a mischievous grin. "So that's what my mother used to do after church! To hear her tell it, she remained inside the church for prayer at least a half an hour after everyone else had left."

Marcy gave her daughter a frown. "I have never said that. Katie, don't encourage her."

Everyone laughed.

"I enjoyed hearing the two of you sing," Katie continued, now looking at Michael, who appeared starstruck by his mother's friend.

"Did you really? I mean, thank you, of course," Michael replied with a blush.

"The harmony was incredible. It reminded me of The Carpenters."

"The carpenters?" Mark asked, astonished. "You mean like Mr. Lewis?"

With the exception of Katie, who did not know Mr. Lewis, the members of the small group laughed again. Marcy saw Katie's confusion and supplied, "Frank Lewis. We went to school with him. He's a contractor.

Builds all the new houses around here."

Katie understood Mark's confusion and she smiled at the adorable, freckle-faced child. "No, Mark. You see The Carpenters were a singing duo back when your mother and I were young. They were a brother and sister team, just like Michael and Melissa. They sang beautifully together!"

Michael placed a hand on the top of his young brother's head. Mark scrunched his nose as he looked up in adoration at Michael, who commented, "You know, Sport. Remember that song that Melissa and I sang at the talent show?"

Michael and Melissa began to sing a capella, "I need to find a place to hide away. Far from the shadows of my mind. . ."

Marcy gave Katie an uneasy look, but Katie noted the implications in the words. She folded her arms across her abdomen and looked toward the business district of their little hometown. Marcy could sense Katie's deep thoughts and determined that she would not see her friend become maudlin today. "What say we all go home and get something good to eat?" Marcy announced.

Katie returned from her reverie. "Mmmm. What are we having?"

The group turned and began to walk toward their cars. Michael made a deliberate move so that he walked beside Katie. She smiled knowingly. "Marcy? How about if Michael rides with Mama and me? He and I can work on his French." She gave Michael a quick glance. He was beaming with appreciation.

"Can I, Mom? Dad?"

Charlie, who Katie was beginning to believe was a man of few words but of much action, nodded. "Go on ahead, Son. We'll meet you at the house." Katie looked deeply into his eyes as he spoke. Charlie was very well aware of his son's crush, but was equally aware that Katie had it under control and would treat Michael's emotions with tenderness.

"We'll go home first," Carolyn announced, "to change our clothes. We'll meet you there shortly. I'll bring the peanut butter pie."

"My goodness!" Katie exclaimed, regarding the well-set formal dining room table, which seemed to buckle under the weight of filled serving dishes. She had arrived only moments before, having been to her mother's home, where she changed out of the silk dress that she had worn to church. She now wore a more comfortable, short denim dress and sneakers, which she would later wear to Michael's ball game. "Do you eat like this all the time? I'd be as big as the side of a barn!"

Marcy slipped up behind her, carrying a linen-covered bread basket that was rounded out by piping hot, homemade biscuits. Katie took a deep breath, basking in the heavenly aroma. "Do you realize how southern you are beginning to sound? I'd say you're just about one of us again."

Katie laughed easily. "I guess I am," she observed. "But I'll be honest with you. I always was. As soon as I spoke, someone would ask me if I was from the South."

"Do I detect a southern accent?"

"Yes, Sir. You do."

Katie closed her eyes at the memory. *Oh, Ben. How I miss you. . . . Please end this madness soon. . . .*

"Katie?" Marcy asked, concern clearly registered in the tone of her voice.

Katie opened her eyes. Everyone gathered around the table was staring at her. "I'm sorry," she apologized. "I was thinking about my husband. The day we met, when we were introduced, he commented about my accent." Katie gave a short laugh. "I was actually quite intimidated by him that day!"

Charlie pulled back the armchair from the head of the table and everyone followed suit, sitting on the plush, hunter green seats of the large Queen Anne dining set. "Were you ever terrified of me, Marce?" he asked his wife, who sat at the opposite end of the table.

Marcy smiled broadly. "Absolutely every morning when you get out of bed. In fact, I hardly recognize you." Their children laughed merrily. Charlie bowed his head. The family and guests did the same as Charlie discreetly cleared his throat.

"Heavenly Father, for what we are about to receive, we thank You. Pardon our sins, dear Lord, and grant us Your peace."

"Amen," they said together. Marcy reached for the serving dish of fresh snap beans before her and began passing each item around the table.

"Why were you afraid of your husband, Katie?" Sam asked her.

Katie smiled as she took the plate of sweet potatoes and began to serve herself. "Not exactly afraid," she corrected. "Intimidated. My husband is. . ." She momentarily stalled. How much of this should she tell? she asked herself. How was she to phrase the answer to Sam's question without revealing who Ben was.

"Is?" Melissa asked. All eyes were on Katie, whose eyes knowingly met Marcy's.

"An important and influential businessman."

"Oooh!" Melissa exclaimed. "I'll bet he's handsome, isn't he?"

Katie smiled. "Yes, he is. Very handsome. He's tall. . . ."

"He'd have to be," Mark declared innocently and everyone laughed. Katie laughed too.

"Very tall, actually. Dark. Handsome. But even if he were an ogre, he'd still be the love of my life." Katie turned to look at her mother, who was sitting next to her. Carolyn was listening intently. This was the most she had heard her daughter speak about her son-in-law.

"What does your husband do?" Charlie asked.

Katie took a deep breath and looked at Marcy again. "He manages a hotel." She found that telling the white lie was fairly simple.

"In New York City?" Charlie asked.

"Sam and I honeymooned in New York City," Roberta supplied, freeing Katie from having to answer.

"Really?" Katie asked. "I guess I didn't know that."

"Naturally, that was a long time ago. Biggest place I had ever been in. Then and now. I couldn't imagine living there."

"I could," Michael said. "Do you live in an apartment, Katie? Penthouse?"

Katie shook her head no. She had just placed a forkful of squash into her mouth and was enjoying the taste. "No. We live in the hotel. We have our own suite."

"Wow!" Melissa said. "I am, like, so envious! You must live a fairy tale life!"

Katie looked down at the simple yet lovely china place setting before her. She knew that a look of sadness crossed her face, and she did not want it to be detected. Then again, perhaps Melissa needed to learn certain realities of life. "I love my husband very much," she whispered. "And we have a wonderful life." She looked up and locked eyes with the pretty teenage girl who sat directly across from her. "But do not confuse life with fairy tales. If a life is filled with light from the sun, then it only stands to reason that the same sun would also cast a shadow."

Melissa gave a quizzical look. She did not fully understand.

" 'But such is human life,' " Michael quoted. " 'Here today and gone tomorrow. A dream, a shadow, a ripple on the water. . . .' "

Katie responded, "Mark Twain." *Play the game with me, Ben. . . .*

"That quote was included in a San Francisco letter," Carolyn interjected.

Katie looked at her mother in astonishment. "That's right. How did you know that?"

Carolyn shrugged her shoulders. "My dream was to teach literature, you know."

"No, I didn't know. Mama, I can't believe this! Why didn't you become a teacher?"

"I married your father."

"So? Teachers can't be married?"

"Not according to my mother. Being Mrs. Stanley Morgan was acceptable. Being a high school lit teacher was not."

Nor was being Mrs. Buddy Akins, Katie thought. She locked eyes with her mother's, eyes that seemed to portray the same thought. There was momentary silence in the room.

In an effort to change the subject, Marcy asked, "Tell us how you met your husband, Katie."

Katie blinked, then looked to Marcy. She smiled sweetly, as if to say thank you. "I met Ben when I was working for a law firm in New York. I was legal assistant to his cousin Cynthia. One day he came to our offices to take her to lunch. I happened to be in her office going over some papers and naturally she introduced us. When they returned from lunch, he stopped at my cubicle and asked me out for dinner later that week. As I said, he was very tall and quite good-looking and I knew he was a well-respected businessman. I couldn't imagine why he would want to take me to dinner. . . ."

"I couldn't imagine that he wouldn't," Michael muttered, then blushed and added, "Sorry. Didn't mean to butt in."

Katie smiled warmly at him. "Well, I was a bundle of nerves. I kept dropping my pencil. I stammered and stuttered. I'm surprised he didn't cancel the invitation!"

Carolyn glanced at her daughter. Clearly, she wanted to know more, but her gaze was intense. Katie squirmed, then sat up straighter.

"That's enough about me," Katie exclaimed happily. "I'm ready for some peanut butter pie! How about you, Mark?" she asked the lad, who had eaten all the roast beef and potatoes on his plate, but little of the vegetables.

"Yum! Yum!" he cheered.

Marcy slid back in her chair. "Melissa, clear the table please. Michael and Mark, you two can help. Charlie, would you help me in the kitchen?"

Within moments Marcy's clan had cleared the table, leaving Katie with Roberta, Sam, and her mother.

"How did you enjoy the service this morning?" Sam asked Katie.

Katie smiled warmly. "I enjoyed it immensely. I hate to admit it's been awhile since I've attended a service for the sheer purpose of it being a Sunday morning."

"What's the world coming to," Sam asked, "when God's children don't attend services on Sundays?"

"Sam, hush," Roberta scolded. Turning her eyes to Katie, she added, "Why not, Dear?"

Katie glanced guiltily over at her mother. "I don't know, really. I suppose once you get out of the habit of going. . ."

"And you were out of the habit?"

"I'm afraid so."

"Well, what's past is past. What did you think of this morning's service?"

Katie picked up her dessert spoon and began to fondle it. "It made me think. When Michael and Melissa sang 'Amazing Grace'. . .well, I've never been so moved." Katie recalled the singing of the beloved hymn. She had closed her eyes, allowing the words to wash over her. "Amazing grace, how sweet the sound, that saved a wretch like me. . . ."

Can you save me, Lord? she had prayed silently. *I am the most wretched of sinners. Can you possibly love me enough to restore my soul?*

"My grandchildren have beautiful voices," Sam commented as the Waters family returned to the room, bearing pie and coffee. Katie started, cleared her throat, and decided the answer would have to come another day.

The two teams on the baseball field were already warming up when Katie and Marcy arrived to watch the game. Roberta, Sam, and Carolyn had driven to the ballpark together. The trio brought along folding lawn chairs so that they would not have to endure the agony of sitting on the bleachers. They positioned them along the right side of the bleachers, near the fence, which assured them of a good view of the game. Charlie had driven Michael, Melissa, and Mark in his truck an hour earlier so that Michael would arrive in time for practice. Katie spotted him and his two youngest children standing near the concession booth in obvious debate over drink selections.

Marcy spoke to her parents as they passed. "Katie and I will sit up on the bleachers with Charlie and the kids."

"All right," Roberta answered.

"And Mama? Try not to make such a spectacle of yourself," Marcy added with a pat to her mother's shoulder.

Roberta gave a humph, clapped her hands together, and shouted, "Look alive out there! Look alive!"

Katie and Marcy laughed as they made their way up the narrow bleachers. Sitting, Katie adjusted the short skirt of her denim dress in an effort to protect herself from the hot aluminum. "I should have worn jeans," she said. She glanced over at Marcy, who was wearing the black jeans and fuchsia tee Katie bought her the day before. "You look great in those, by the way."

Marcy grinned, running the palms of her hands down her thighs. "Thanks. My best friend bought them for me." She batted her eyelashes playfully at Katie, who laughed. Marcy turned her attention to the young men on the field. "I think it's better that you wore the dress," she added with a playful grin. "You're not used to these hot summers anymore. You'd probably sweat to death." Marcy's eyes never left her son as he threw practice balls to his teammates.

Katie scanned the crowd for signs of people that she might know. Amazingly, she recognized no one. Her eyes rested on Michael's team coach. "Marcy?" Katie dropped her head toward her shoulder as she looked at her friend.

"Hmmm?"

"Am I wrong, or is that Cail Fontaine down there?"

Marcy looked at her friend and grinned. "Nope! That's him all right, the cad!"

Katie returned the smile. "Why do you call him that?"

"Are you kidding? He's the biggest flirt this side of the Mississippi," she said in a hushed voice.

"He used to be the biggest jerk this side of the Mississippi."

Marcy nodded in agreement as she said, "Oh, yeah. He used to tease you about your legs, didn't he?"

"Mercilessly."

"He was just jealous of Buddy. He liked you, ya know."

Katie's mouth twitched. "I know. I didn't know until the other day, though. Angela told me. Seems that set off the chain of events twenty-five years ago," she said emphatically.

"How do you mean?"

"Like you said, Cail was jealous of Buddy. Angela was jealous of me. When Angela discovered how Cail felt about me, she broke up with him, thinking he would change his mind. He didn't. She took our secret—Buddy's and mine—to her mother. . . ."

"Ugh. Lorian never did know how to keep her mouth closed. She ran straight to your mother, right?"

"Yeah."

"What did she say?"

"I don't know, really. Exactly. Parts of it came out in our argument the night I left. It's been so long, I can't recall it all. I don't think I ever really put it together until the other day when I saw Angela."

Marcy gave Katie a quick pat on the leg. "I didn't know any of this. I knew that Cail liked you, but I didn't know the rest."

Katie looked at Cail out on the field. He hadn't changed a bit. He was every bit as good-looking as he had been in school. Maybe even more so. She watched as he picked up a ball from the red dirt and threw it to the third baseman. "Hustle, Hustle," he called out.

"When did you find out that he liked me?" Katie inquired.

"Right after you left. Right after graduation. I ran into him uptown and he asked me if I knew where you had gone. I told him no. That no one did. But that I hoped to hear from you. Of course, I never did, but anyway, he said that he never knew what you saw in Buddy. That he'd just been waiting for you two to break up so he could ask you out. The whole 'long legs' thing was his 'guy way' of flirting, I guess."

Katie set her mouth firmly. "Well, it wasn't flirting to me. It was rotten teasing."

Marcy looked down at the long, firm, tanned legs next to her. "He wouldn't be teasing you now. . . ," she said mischievously.

Katie's eyes narrowed. "What do you mean, Marcy Waters?"

Marcy gave a quick look to the field, then back at Katie. "Wanna have some fun?"

Katie smiled. "I might. What do you have in mind?"

Marcy pulled off her large sunglasses and extended them to Katie. "Here. Trade."

Katie removed the John Lennon sunglasses from her face, replacing them with Marcy's large, inexpensive ones. Marcy, in turn, slipped Katie's onto her face. "Hey, these are nice," she commented, looking first one way and then another. "Where'd you get these? Around here?"

Katie thought of Kevin and smiled. "Never mind my sunglasses. What are you thinking of?"

"In a few minutes, Michael will walk over toward the dugout for a drink. When he does, walk down these bleachers—ever so slowly, mind you—then walk over to the fence there and call him over. Tell him to play along. He'll do it, don't worry. He loves a good joke, especially at Coach Fontaine's expense. Then, trust me, Cail Fontaine will waste no time running over to see who the new 'skirt' is." Marcy smirked. "In my shades, with your new look, he'll never recognize you. Make him sweat, Katie. Really make him sweat. Then come back and sit down. Tell Michael not to tell him who you are until you're safe at your seat here. Game?"

Katie thought about the prospect for a moment, then gave a delighted smile to her friend. "Game." She looked back at the field. "Did he ever marry?"

"Oh, sure. Didn't everybody? Jana Robbins. But they divorced after five years."

"What happened?"

"The flirting. The affairs. She got tired of being the brunt of all the jokes around here. Anyway, she got married again to. . ." Marcy paused as she looked back out to the field. "Wait a sec. They're coming to the dugout. Now, girl. Go."

Katie stood and squared her shoulders. Taking one bleacher row at a time, she slowly made her way to the ground, then walked over to the chain-link fence near the dugout. Upon reaching it, she laced her fingers through the openings and called out, "Hey, Michael. Come here a sec, will ya?"

Michael looked over his shoulder at his coach, who immediately looked to see where the unfamiliar female voice had come from as he dropped practice balls into a five-gallon bucket. He spotted Katie and watched as young Michael Waters ambled over to the beautiful, tall woman with the incredible, long legs. His curiosity peaked, he quickly picked up the bucket by its handle, and took it into the dugout. That done, he made his way over to where the object of his desire was hurriedly speaking in hushed tones to his first baseman. As soon as he arrived, Michael stepped back.

"Coach," Michael said, acknowledging him as he turned and walked toward the dugout with an undetected grin on his face.

Katie took in a deep breath and gave a beguiling smile to Cail.

"Well, hello," he returned.

"Hello," she said matter-of-factly.

"I'm Coach Fontaine. I don't believe we've met."

She raised her chin ever so slightly. "I'm a friend of Michael's mother."

Cail looked toward the bleachers, spotted Marcy, and gave a slight nod in her direction. She, in turn, waggled her fingers to say hello. This was more fun than she'd had in years.

"New in town?" he asked, looking back at Katie.

"You could say that."

"I did say that." He flashed a grin, then reached up and adjusted the ball cap low on his forehead. Studying her for a moment, he tilted his head to one side. "Hey, don't I know you? Haven't we met somewhere before?"

Katie turned her face slightly and felt a light breeze blow her hair across her cheeks. She reached up, tucked the chestnut strands behind her ears, then looked back at her former adversary. "Oh, come on now. You can do better than that."

He chuckled and she added, "Been coaching the team for long?" Out of the corner of her eye, she spotted Michael's face as he peered around the corner of the dugout. If she looked at him, she would lose it, so she took a step backward and folded her arms across her abdomen.

"About fifteen years. My second wife and I split up and I took up coaching to—you know—fill the lonely hours." He gave a faux coy glance to the ground and coolly shifted his weight to one foot as the cleated shoe of the other toed the grass near the base of the fence.

"Poor baby." She faked a pout.

"Maybe later you'd like to help me fill some of the other lonely hours." He gave her his best smile. "A man can only coach for so long, you know."

Katie began to walk beside the fence; her fingers strummed the chain links as she made her way back to the bleachers. He walked along beside her, peering at her through the diamond-shaped links that separated them. "I don't think so," she said, stopping in front of where she and Marcy were sitting.

"Why not?" he asked.

"Just don't."

"Give me one good reason," he called out. "Just one and I won't ask again, I swear."

Katie looked back at Marcy, who was about to burst from the glee of it all, then back at Cail. Turning back to Cail, she pulled off the oversized sunglasses as she pursed her lips.

"Sometimes," she said in a whispered voice, "revenge really is sweet."

His eyes widened and he took a step backward. "Katie Morgan," he drawled.

She gave him her best smile. "Katie Webster," she replied.

"Well, I suppose I asked for that one," he admitted honestly. "Life sure can be funny sometimes." Katie gave him a smile, warm and friendly, a smile that said, "I forgive you, Cail Fontaine."

He returned the smile with a tip of his hat and a nod of his head. "So what are you doing back in town? We all thought you had dropped off the face of the earth."

"No, no. I'm just back visiting Mama." Katie turned slightly and looked over to where her mother was sitting, deep in conversation with Roberta. "How are you doing these days, Cail?"

"I'm running the Village Motel out there on the highway. It's slow, but steady. The hotel/motel business can be a killer sometimes."

Don't I know it, Katie thought. *And in more ways than one.* She only smiled in return.

Cail ran his fingers across the brim of his hat in a quick, fluid motion. "I gotta get with the boys here. Y'all come to see us if you can now."

"Thank you. It was good seeing you again."

"Good seeing you, too. Enjoy the game." He watched her as she turned and made her way back up the bleachers to where Marcy, who had been joined by Charlie, Melissa, and Mark, was waiting for her.

Bucky Caballero answered the private telephone line in his home office as he always did. "Yeah."

"Bucky. This is David."

"Yeah."

"I found her."

CHAPTER NINETEEN

"How long will you be gone?" Carolyn asked her daughter.

Katie, dressed for her morning run, stood before her mother in the garden where Carolyn was meticulously weeding one of the beds. "Not long. Half an hour. Forty-five minutes at the most. Are you going anywhere or will you be home when I get back?"

"I'll be here. I think I'm going to can some pickles this afternoon. Want to help?"

"Do you already have the cucumbers?"

"No. I'll have to go out to the market to get them. You can go with me if you'd like. I'll bet it's been years since you've been to a real farmer's market."

Katie smiled. There seemed to be a genuine warmth coming from her mother this morning. A peace between them. A bond she had not felt since she was a child. "I'd like that. We'll go get the ingredients, then come back and can. Yes, I'd like that."

Carolyn retrieved her trowel lying at her right knee and began to aggressively shovel around a tenacious dandelion. "Good," she said tersely. "These weeds!"

Katie smiled and said goodbye, retreating through the back door of the house. Carolyn took hold of the base of the dandelion and pulled until she was able to take it out by its roots. Once done she sat back on

237

her heels and slung the unwanted weed into the five-gallon bucket behind her.

Weeds. They reminded her of Monica Carpenter Bell's testimony, which she had given to the United Methodist Ladies Circle. Monica had been a classmate of Katie's and high school sweetheart to Bobby Weaver, who had died tragically in a car accident the summer before their senior year of high school. Monica went on to graduate from high school, then college, where she majored in biology with a minor in horticulture. If for no other reason, this endeared her to Carolyn.

Monica eventually married the county extension agent, Joseph Bell. They had a daughter, Ashley. Monica taught biology at BHS. She was a frequent speaker in the area on various topics: agriculture, horticulture, motivation, death, and was a frequent guest of the UMLC. Carolyn enjoyed her displays of flora and fauna, but had been particularly moved by the personal spiritual testimony she had given several years before.

"When we are in our teenage years," Monica had begun in her soft, deeply southern accent, "we believe we are invincible. We believe that we are immortal and that nothing—not even God—can touch us. We believe that life is to be lived for the moment and that soon enough we will become responsible adults. So why rush it?" The question brought a chuckle from the small, intimate group of eleven women. "My junior year of high school was such a year. I was president of the 4-H Club. I was the only female member of the Future Farmers of America. I was secretary-treasurer of the Beta Club. Cheerleader. Honor roll student. And girlfriend to a sweet young man named Bobby Weaver, whom all the world adored. Especially me. He was perfect. Nice-looking. Came from a good family. Good student when he wanted to be. Football star. Funny as all get-out! Smart in all ways but one. He drove his car too fast.

"Now, in those days we thought it was cool to drive a car too fast. Speeding down endlessly straight country roads, dirt and dust billowing like smoke behind us. What was the harm? We were young, right? We were living in the now. As I said, we were invincible!

"But one rainy, summer's afternoon, Bobby failed to beat the odds. You remember. This whole town remembers. The school closed. The funeral home was packed with mourners. The funeral itself was worthy of a prince.

"I remember how I cried. Oh, I cried and cried. Clutching the rim of the satin-lined coffin, falling to my knees crying, 'Get up, Bobby! For the love of God, get up!'

"But, of course, he didn't. He just lay there, looking every bit as good-looking as he had on the night of our last date.

"I suppose I was too much of a sight, because the next thing I knew my daddy came up behind me—you ladies know my daddy. Big man. If my daddy comes up behind you and places his hands on your shoulders, well. . .you're immediately aware of it!" The group chuckled again.

" 'Come on, Monica,' Daddy said to me. 'Daddy wants to tell you a story.' Then he led me back to this little room behind the viewing room where Bobby was laid out.

"I will never forget what my daddy said to me next. Mainly because it was what led me to know the Lord on a personal level. He said, 'Did I ever tell you the story about the elderly woman whose children and grandchildren were all coming home for a festive dinner?' I shook my head no as I blew my nose into his clean, white handkerchief. Men used to carry them around in those days. You remember, don't you, ladies?" The ladies nodded in unison.

"Then my daddy told me this story: 'Once upon a time, in a beautiful city, there lived an elderly woman. She lived all alone. Her sons and her daughters moved far away, and she had not seen them in a long, long time. Then, one day, one of her sons called her and told her that he and all his siblings were coming to see her. They were bringing their wives and husbands, their children, and grandchildren. Oh! The woman was so happy! She went through every room of her home and cleaned until it was spotless. She pulled her finest china, crystal, and silver from the old china cabinet. She washed or polished each piece by hand, careful not to break anything, careful that everything was perfect. She went to her mother's old cedar chest, and finding her mother's white linen, removed it, oh, so gently. She washed it, starched it, and ironed it until it was at its crispest. Then she took it to her dining room table and placed it over the dark, polished wood of the tabletop. Next came the place settings. Then the crystal. Finally the silver. Everything was perfect.

" 'The woman went to her kitchen and began to prepare the favorite dishes of her children and grandchildren. And when the grand dinner was prepared, she went to her bath. She freshened up. Powdered herself. Applied light touches of makeup so that she would look her prettiest. She slipped on her best dress. Oh, she was so excited!

" 'Her family would be arriving any moment. She went into the dining room to make certain that everything was as it should be. But no! Something was missing! *What is it?* she asked herself. And then she knew. She had not gone out to her garden to pick flowers for the centerpiece. She wanted a lovely, colorful centerpiece that would show her family how happy she was that they were coming home for this festive meal.

" 'So, she went out to her flower garden. Because she had been so busy with her preparations over the past several days, she had neglected her garden. There were weeds scattered among the beautiful, colorful flowers.

" 'What do you think she picked?' my father asked me. 'The flowers or the weeds?'

"I answered between sniffles, 'The flowers. Not the weeds.'

" 'That's right,' he assured me. 'And our heavenly Father does the same. His children are all coming home one day. There will be a great feast. And in the centerpiece will be the beautiful flowers that He chose from His garden.'

"I hugged my father until I thought he would burst! Yes, yes! Bobby was a flower. All our loved ones are flowers. Flowers in the centerpiece. And I knew then that I wanted to be one of God's children and that I would follow Him forever."

The story had left Carolyn in an unusual public display of tears. She rarely showed her emotions in such a way. Her mother had taught her that it was most unladylike and "not befitting a person of her social position." However, in this instance, the tender allegory had moved all the ladies in her circle to tears. For once, Carolyn was not alone in her grief.

She quietly thought of Stan. Her precious, dependable Stan. He had been tall, extremely handsome, endearingly funny, wise, levelheaded when it came to business and raising their daughter, a good provider, and highly respected and loved by all who knew him. She had grown to love him more than she ever expressed openly; and this was the deepest regret of her life. She should have told him more often that she loved him, admired him, needed him, and wanted nothing more than to grow old with him.

She had met Stan when they attended the University of Georgia together. She had hoped to get her four-year degree, then return to Mills, Georgia, a small town named for her father's family. Stan—Stanley Morris Morgan—was a senior majoring in accounting when she had begun classes at the university. They had met in October at a Fall Festival dance and were immediately attracted. By Thanksgiving they were dating exclusively, though she refrained from telling her mother or father about him. She knew that her mother's lifelong dream was to have her daughters—Carolyn and her sister, Irene—marry well, have children, and live fairy-tale lives.

During Christmas she told Irene about Stan. . .how handsome, smart, and funny he was. . .that she thought she just might be in love, but that she was afraid to tell their mother. . . .

"Why?" Irene asked her. "You'd make her day, not to mention the fact that you'd be giving her the best Christmas present she could ever ask for. A son-in-law who aspires to work in a CPA firm. Glory! Maybe then she'd let me off the hook a little. Do you know how many times she's asked me about the men at my campus? 'See anyone you like, Irene?' Or, sometimes she gets downright dirty with it. Do you know she actually asked me the other day what I am doing that is keeping the men away from me!" Irene, older by two years, dressed in a pink sweater, dark gray wool skirt with a wide black belt, and by far the prettier of the two Mills girls, sat cross-legged in the center of the soft, fringed pink chenille bedspread of their four-poster bed. Carolyn was sitting at the vanity, its mirror framed with postcard-sized photographs of their favorite movie stars. The base of the vanity was skirted in the same material as the white, crisscross Priscilla curtains that hung in the large bay window. Carolyn, already dressed for bed, was putting her dark brown hair in neat and even rows of pin curls. She held several bobby pins between her pursed lips, refraining her from speaking, so she gave a simple nod of her head. Yes, she could easily imagine that their mother, Kate Mills, would say such a thing.

"It's not like I don't want to date. It's just that I'm waiting on the right one to ask me out." The way she had said "right one" caused Carolyn to look directly at her sister in the reflection of the mirror. Having finished one of the pin curls, she removed the remaining bobby pins from her mouth and turned to face Irene.

"Do you have your eyes on someone, Irene? Are you waiting. . .just waiting for him to ask you out?"

Irene fell back against the row of hand-embroidered pillows that their mother had lovingly made and placed at the head of their bed. Pulling one from behind her, she wrapped it in her arms, close to her breast. "Oh, yes!"

Carolyn jumped up from her seat and joined her sister on the bed. The box spring mattress creaked as the bed rocked gently from the impact of Carolyn's less than graceful arrival. "Who is he? What's he like? What's his name?"

Irene sat up, jumped off the bed, and nearly sprinted to the closed door of the room. Opening it slightly, she peered out, first to the left and then to the right. Having satisfied her curiosity, she quietly closed the door and rejoined Carolyn. "Shhh," she scolded. "Mother has ears like radar! If she thinks I have an interest in someone, she'll be up here measuring me for my wedding dress before I even have my first date with him!"

Carolyn nodded eagerly. "Tell me, Irene!"

"His name is Calvin. Calvin Singletary. He's totally dreamy and. . .if you breathe a word of this I will personally kill you. . . ."

"Your secret is safe if mine is!"

"Cross your heart and hope to die?"

"Stick a needle in my eye! Now, tell!"

"Air force career man."

Carolyn fell back on the bed laughing. "Mama is going to have a fit!"

And Mama did. Her one consolation had been that Calvin made the military his career. Her heartbreak had been that he and Irene, having lived all over the world, eventually settled in Kansas, where Irene said they had been their happiest.

Carolyn, however, was left behind to make Mama happy. Happy and proud. When Carolyn finally told her parents about Stan, it was only because he had asked her to accompany him to Brooksboro to meet his parents during spring break. Her mother had been delirious with joy. Her daughter was dating someone of social importance. He came from a long line of prominent southerners. He was going to be somebody!

Two years later, Stan's career was firmly in place. Irene was married and living overseas with Calvin. Kate was dropping subtle hints of marriage to Stan and Carolyn much the same way that American planes had dropped bombs in Japan. Stan had certainly been excited at the idea. He had already purchased a small starter home and a diamond ring. When Carolyn suggested that they wait until she established herself as a teacher of American literature, he looked disappointed, but seemed to understand.

Kate Mills, however, did not.

"This is a once in a lifetime offer, Carolyn. You're going to throw away a fine man like Stanley Morgan to teach high schoolers? I think not."

"Mama, it's hardly your decision."

"Someone has to make the decisions for you. You certainly aren't thinking for yourself."

"I am thinking for myself. And I will marry Stan. Just not right away. I want to establish myself as a teacher first. Then we will get married."

"Why bother? Why bother to teach? Why not just get married? You certainly won't want to teach after you get married."

"Why wouldn't I want to teach? What do you think I've been knocking myself out for these past few years?"

"Now, Carolyn you listen to me. Having a college education was your father's idea. And I suppose it can't hurt you. But a young woman of your caliber is expected to marry a man like Stanley. Marry and have children. You can't raise children properly if you're in the classroom teaching everybody else's children."

Carolyn stood, picked up the bucket of weeds, carrying it to the large trash can on the left side of the house, shaking her head of the memories. She had done as her mother expected. She had married Stan. And yes, she had loved him. Oh, how she still loved him. But it always seemed as if she had been the sacrificial lamb.

She didn't regret it, though. She had been proud to be his wife. She had been thrilled to be Katharine's mother, even when her own mother insisted on instructing her in every aspect of raising her own child. Nevertheless, she and Katharine had been close—very close—until Katharine reached puberty. Then, it was as if a brick wall had slammed down between them, leaving one unable to reach the other. Looking back, she could neither blame it on herself nor her daughter. It just seemed to have naturally occurred and to have happened overnight.

"You cut the onions, I'll cut the cucumbers," Carolyn instructed her daughter as she stood at the kitchen sink, washing enough cucumbers to fill six quart-sized jars. She placed all the ingredients for the pickles—salt, vinegar, sugar, celery seed, and mustard seed—to the left of the double-sided sink and a small bag of medium-sized white onions to the right.

Katie quietly retrieved a cutting board from the drawer where her mother stored it and a sharp vegetable cutting knife from the knife rack next to the stove. Carolyn watched her, smiling. "Have you ever put up pickles, Katharine?"

Katie grinned. "Not since my junior year in high school. Remember my home ec project?"

Carolyn laughed. "I've never seen such a mess in all my life. But you wanted to do it on your own. Wouldn't let me help you."

Katie pulled an onion out of the bag and began to slice the thick skin, pulling it away from the bulb. "I was willful, wasn't I? Mrs. McKay ended up giving me a C. She should have given me an F, but she said that at least I tried!"

"Do you cook a lot now?" There was a tinge of reserve in Carolyn's question. She was not certain as to where the line of privacy began and ended with her daughter.

Undaunted, Katie answered with a shake of her head. "Not really. Occasionally I'll whip up a little something if it's Maggie's day off."

"Maggie?"

Katie stiffened slightly. Was she saying too much? "Our housekeeper. How many onions do we need?" she asked, obviously changing the subject.

"Six." Carolyn turned the water off and began to slice the cucumbers with a knife she laid beside her earlier.

Katie pulled five onions from the bag and set the bag away from her.

"Why do you need a housekeeper? It's just the two of you, right?"

Katie stepped away from the sink and walked over to a cabinet where her mother kept mixing bowls. "I'm going to put all these in a bowl, then wash them together. You know, instead of one at a time."

Carolyn understood. Katharine did not wish to discuss her life in New York further. Three days ago Katharine promised that they would talk about the trouble her daughter seemed to be in. But when she returned from the bank, they had the terrible argument about Buddy Akins. After that it had not seemed appropriate to bring it up.

"Do you know what I was thinking about today?" Carolyn asked cheerfully.

Katie, ready for a fresh topic, answered, "No. What?"

"I was thinking about the day that your aunt Irene and I were telling each other about our new fellows. Irene, of course, was telling me about Calvin and I was telling her about your father. We sat in the middle of our bed giggling like children, scared to death that Mama would overhear."

Katie smiled. Her mother rarely gave a glimpse into her life as a child. "Why didn't you want Nana Kate to overhear?"

"Are you kidding me? She would have called a minister to set up wedding dates before we could have left the room! Irene hadn't even had a date with Calvin yet. She had seen him at a few dances. . .talked to him briefly a few times. That was it."

"What about you and Daddy?" Katie stopped peeling the onions and rested her hip against the counter.

Carolyn glanced out the window. A nostalgic look of happiness swept over her face. Her lips curled in a Mona Lisa smile and she raised her chin slightly. "Daddy and I had been seeing each other since the Fall Festival dance. But I didn't want Mama to know."

"Did you and Daddy go to a lot of dances?"

Carolyn nodded her head lightly. "Oh, yes. In those days, we had football games. After the game, the home team would host a dance. Everybody attended. Suddenly, the students you swore to pulverize on the field an hour before were your new friends. Those dances were a lot of fun."

"Did Daddy play football?"

"No. Although he could have! He was so big and strong. He enjoyed the game, but never wanted to play it. Baseball. He was on the baseball team. But you have to remember that he was a senior my first year of school."

"I didn't know that."

Carolyn looked at her daughter in astonishment. "Didn't you?"

"No. You never really talked—"

The conversation was cut short by the ringing of the doorbell. Both women turned around, then Carolyn reached for a dishtowel and said, "Now I wonder who in the world that could be."

CHAPTER TWENTY

Katie and her mother stood shoulder to shoulder, staring at the kitchen door leading to the family room. The doorbell rang a second time.

"You're not expecting anyone?" Katie asked. The question she was asking herself was much more alarming. Could someone from Bucky's office have found her?

"Since when does someone from the South call first?" Carolyn asked, almost amusingly. She moved toward the door.

"I'll get it," Katie said hurriedly, placing her hand on her mother's shoulder.

"Don't be silly, Katharine. I'll get it. You've been spending too much time listening to an old woman talk history and not slicing onions. Get busy and I'll see who this is. Probably Roberta."

Katie watched her mother leave the room. The fading sound of her soft footsteps kept time with the thump-thump-thump of her own heartbeat. Taking a step back, her hip brushed against the countertop. She jumped, clasped her hands together. Beyond the kitchen window the Moroccan Broom stood guard against the north wall of the property. The daisies stretched their stems and playfully opened their petals wide to the summer sun. The tea roses stood proud and regal, as if they merely tolerated being in the garden with what seemed to be beneath them. In the center of the garden, the old honeysuckle bush beckoned to her the reprieve of feasting on its succulent sweetness. If she went to it, if only for a moment, she could be a child again, safely sampling honeysuckle while the other children searched for her.

She felt the pressure of the death grip she had on her hands. Looking away from the window, she relaxed momentarily. Her eyes rested on the countertop. The knife she had been using lay forgotten near the bowl of onions and discarded onion skins. She reached for it, grasping it tightly in her fist. She watched her knuckles turn white and listened as her mother opened the front door.

"Well, hello, Jim." She could hear her mother's greeting only faintly.

There was a mumbling from the other side of the door. Katie let out a pent-up breath and wondered who Jim was.

"Well, my goodness. Wonder who."

Katie took a tentative step forward. She heard more mumbling from the other side of the door, then her mother's faint laughter.

"My daughter, Katharine," her mother informed the man.

What was this about? Katie asked herself, then moved quickly toward the kitchen door and into the family room. Before she realized what she was doing, she was walking down the hallway with the vegetable knife secured firmly in her tight fist. Her mother stood in the open doorway with her back to Katie. Standing just beyond her was a young postal worker, a man who appeared to be in his twenties. He wore the standard postal shorts and shirt, black socks, and polished black shoes. His cap was tipped back on his head and his dark black hair glistened from perspiration. His mailbag was slung across one of his shoulders. When he saw her, he smiled broadly.

"This your daughter, Mrs. Morgan?"

Carolyn turned quickly and Katie noticed that she held a small parcel in her hand along with the various envelopes of her daily mail.

Katie stopped short and her mother smiled. "Yes." Turning back to Jim, she said, "Jim, this is my daughter, Katharine. She's visiting me from New York City." Then, turning back to Katie, she said, "Katharine, this is my mailman, Jim."

Jim extended his hand to shake hers, so Katie took the necessary steps to meet him. When she extended her hand for the introductory greeting, Jim stepped back suddenly.

"Mrs. Morgan, does your daughter always carry a little knife like that?" he asked, alarmed.

Carolyn and Katie looked down at Katie's hand where, indeed, Katie still carried the little knife. The two women laughed together. As Katie shifted the knife to her left hand, she said, "I'm sorry, Jim. I was slicing onions." She extended her right hand again and Jim took it firmly in his.

"Nice to meet 'cha, Katharine."

"Thank you. Nice to meet you, too."

"I brought you a package there," he informed her, nodding toward the parcel in her mother's hand.

"For me?" Katie asked, somewhat shocked. Who would be sending her a package?

"No return address, but it's postmarked New York City. Your mother was just telling me that you live there."

Katie leaned toward her mother to get a closer look at the package. "Yes. I live in the city." With the various envelopes splayed across the top of the box, she could not tell whom it was from.

"Visiting long?" Jim asked her.

Katie turned back to him and smiled. "I'm not certain how long I will be here, Jim. But I am enjoying my stay with Mama very much."

Jim took a step back as if he was preparing to leave. "You got a nice mama, Katharine. She's always been sweet to me."

"Oh, Jim," Carolyn said suddenly. "Don't you want a glass of iced tea?"

"Some of your sweet tea?" he asked, a broad grin spreading across his face.

"Is there any other kind?" she asked. "Don't go anywhere. I'll be right back with a tumbler full."

Carolyn hurriedly made her way down the hall, carrying with her the package and envelopes. Katie watched her retreat, then turned back to Jim, who was mopping his brow with a bandanna.

"It's a hot one," he commented.

"Yes."

"The package was addressed to Katie. Do you go by Katie?"

"Yes. I'm afraid Mama is the only one who calls me Katharine."

He squinted one eye shut as if he were assessing her. "Mind if I ask you a question?"

She tilted her head slightly and grinned. "How tall am I?"

He laughed. "You get asked that a lot, huh?"

Katie turned at the sound of her mother's re-entry into the hallway. "Now, Jim," she was instructing. "You keep this with you and enjoy it. When you bring my mail tomorrow, just leave it at the door." Carolyn handed Jim a large, light blue Tupperware tumbler. Jim accepted it. He took a big swallow of the cold sweet tea and said, "You see, Katie. Your mama sure is a nice one."

Katie merely smiled. This was a side of her mother she was not accustomed to seeing. But she liked what she saw.

"We'll see you soon," Carolyn said pleasantly, slowly closing the door. Katie turned and nearly sprinted down the hall toward the kitchen. Finding the package on the table, she grabbed for it, spilling the contents on top of it.

Carolyn was directly behind her.

"What is it? Do you know who it's from?" Apparently, her mother was as anxious about the package as she was, Katie thought.

Katie looked down at the package, running her hand tenderly over the handwritten address. "Ben," she whispered. "It's from Ben."

"Your husband? There's no return address. Why didn't he put a return address?"

Katie simply shook her head. She didn't know. She didn't care. She was just overwhelmed by the fact that he had sent her anything at all. She placed her palm against the brown packaging, closed her eyes, and inhaled deeply. Ben had written her name and address in his own pen. He had touched this paper. He had sent her something—and it didn't matter what—that he had chosen expressly for her.

"Aren't you going to open it?" Carolyn asked.

Katie opened her eyes. She had dropped the vegetable knife on the table when she had come into the room. She retrieved it, then flipped the small box over, and began to slice at the packaging tape. She was careful not to tear the paper where Ben had written her name: Mrs. Katie Webster. She fleetingly wondered why he had not written Mrs. William B. Webster or Mrs. Ben Webster. She found it somewhat disturbing that he had not written his name anywhere on the outside cover.

The brown packaging paper fell away from the small cardboard box inside. It, too, was sealed with packaging tape.

"Are you sure he wanted you to get this?" Carolyn asked. There seemed to be a nervousness in her voice, as if by viewing her daughter's mail she would get a glimpse at or a clue about her present lifestyle in New York.

Katie laughed lightly. She sliced at the tape with the knife and the box gave a faint pop. Gingerly opening it, she found lavender tissue paper folded over the contents. She lay the box on the table, then peeled back the tissue. Carefully concealed within its folds was a hardback edition of Ben Jonson's *Volpone*.

"*Volpone*," Katie whispered.

"One of my favorite of Ben Jonson's works."

Katie looked at her mother. "You are familiar with Ben Jonson's work?"

Carolyn gave her an exasperated look. "I told you yesterday that I wanted to be an American literature teacher."

"You only said literature. You didn't specify American lit. Besides, Ben Jonson was British."

"I know that, Katharine. Don't be impertinent. Do you think I read only American works of literature?"

Katie looked back at the book. "I'm sorry, Mama. I didn't mean anything by that."

Carolyn didn't seem affected by their ill-spoken words. "Why did your husband send you a book, do you think?"

Katie shook her head. She still had not removed the book from the box. "I don't know. He and I play this game. Ben encourages me to learn. He sent me back to school for various studies, literature being one of them. He sometimes quotes something famous and I tell him who said it."

"Like yesterday. When Michael quoted Mark Twain."

"Yes."

"Why don't you open the book? See if your husband inscribed in it. Perhaps it's a first edition."

Ben wouldn't have it any other way, Katie thought. She removed the book carefully. It was old; the dark brown cover was faded. She ran her fingertips lightly over the gold-embossed lettering of the title, then lifted the cover slowly. On the first blank page Ben had written:

Drink to me only with thine eyes,
And I will pledge with mine;
Or leave a kiss but in the cup,
And I'll not look for wine.

The third line was oddly underlined. Katie gave it a curious look. Other than the occasional inscription, Ben never wrote in or dog-eared a book. Especially a piece of literature such as this. Even more strange was his choice in underlining: Or leave a kiss but in the cup. . .

"That's strange," Katie commented without thinking of her mother standing beside her.

"What's strange?"

Katie closed the book suddenly. "Nothing."

Carolyn's lips drew firm and she placed her hands on her hips. "Don't do this, Katharine."

Katie quickly placed the book back inside the box, neatly folding the tissue back over it. "Don't do what?"

"You know what. The other day, back in the formal parlor, you said you would tell me the truth."

"I promised you that we would talk."

"I assumed that what you would tell me would be the truth. What is the point of talking if it's not going to include the truth."

Katie threw her hands up as she exclaimed, "All right! What is it? What exactly do you want to know?"

Carolyn pressed her lips together tightly before answering. "I want to know what kind of trouble you are in."

"Why?"

"Why? Why? How can you ask me that? You're my child! If you are in trouble, I want to know it! If you are in need, it is my God-given right to meet that need!"

The words hit Katie straight on, took hold of her heart, and squeezed. Suddenly, she was eighteen again, faced with her own inadequacies, iniquities, and poor choices. She had been so afraid that her mother would turn her back on her, she had run. Buddy had been right. She was a runner. For years she had run until there was nowhere else to go. No one that she could truly turn to. Even her accomplishments had come on the shirttails of fear, deception, and wrongdoings. Perhaps if she had not been so accustomed to flight, she would have insisted on staying with Ben and fighting the evil that lurked within the walls of Jacqueline's. Then and only then could she have returned to her mother as a whole person. Ben had been her savior, but she had been afraid to be totally honest with him. In a sense, she had run from telling the truth. Until she released it all, she was merely spinning in her own tracks. She was no longer sliding into the mire or falling into the shadows. But she wasn't basking in the light either.

"Would you, Mama?" Katie said, barely audible.

"Would I what?"

"Meet that need?"

Carolyn seemed almost demure for a moment. This was the moment that she, too, had waited for. She didn't want to twist the opportunity into another "everyone loses" war.

"Yes, if I could."

Katie pulled one of the chairs out from the table and sat. Carolyn did the same, then grabbed her daughter's hand. "Where did you go, Katharine?"

Katie took a deep breath. "At first to Atlanta. Then to New York."

"Why? Why did you do that? How could you do that to me?"

Katie shook her head. Tears formed in the corners of her eyes, then silently slipped down her cheeks. "I don't know, Mama. Something inside of me snapped that night. I honestly don't remember anything from just after our argument until I was halfway to Atlanta. Then I guess I just went insane. I lost the money. . . ."

"That I gave to Buddy?"

There was a fleeting moment of tension before Katie answered. "Yes. Why did you have to do that, Mama? Why pay him off like that?"

"I wasn't thinking clearly. If your father had been here, he could have handled it better. That Lorian Evans. . .coming over here. . .saying all kinds of vile things about my daughter and Buddy Akins." Carolyn spewed the name as if it were a curse word.

"See? There you go! Why do you have to say his name like that?" Katie's voice elevated slightly.

"Because! Because I can't stand what he did to you!"

Katie snatched her hand away from her mother's. "What did he do to me, Mama? What do you think he did that was so terrible that you had to kick him in the gut by offering him money like that? Buddy is a man of pride. Of principle. He always was and he still is!"

"He stole your virtue for one thing!"

Katie stood so quickly the chair toppled behind her. "What! Have you lost your mind?"

"Lorian told me! She told me everything! Everyone at BHS knew that the two of you would slip out of school. . .that you left our home in the middle of the night! And for what? To be with him, that's what!"

Katie's hands flew to her mouth in horror. She stared at her mother for what seemed an eternity before she declared, "I never did anything with Buddy that I would be ashamed of! Never! He wasn't like that!"

The color bled out of Carolyn's face and she covered it with her hands. "Oh, no. Oh, no. Oh, no," she said, shaking her head back and forth.

Katie took a deep breath, retrieved the chair from the floor, and sat down again. Much calmer she stated, "Mama. . .Mama, look at me."

Carolyn slid her hands down her face. She looked tired and worn. Her eyes were lifeless and watery. Katie knew that she, too, was on the brink of tears. "Don't cry, Mama. Let's just get through this. It's time, don't you think?"

"Yes."

"Didn't you know better than to believe Lorian Evans about anything?"

"God forgive me, Katharine. My hatred for Buddy Akins was stronger than my good sense. I should have known better. I should have asked you, rather than attacked you that night. The things I said. . . about your father. . ."

Katie looked down. "It's okay."

Carolyn took her daughter's hand into her own again. "No, it's not okay. It's important that you listen to me now. The saddest thing I've ever seen in my life was you kneeling by your father's hospital bed, begging him to get up, begging him to live."

"The saddest thing I've ever seen was a young woman in New York drinking a cola for dinner so that she could afford to feed her children a hot dog."

Carolyn shook her head quietly before whispering, "My sweet Lord. What you must have seen. . .because of me. . ."

"No, Mama. Because of me."

"Why do you say that?"

"Because I could have called. I almost did so many times. But I was so ashamed of what I had done. What I had become. . ."

Carolyn took a deep breath and let out a heavy sigh. "You are alive; that's all I care about. So often I wondered—I feared—but I would shake my head and say, 'No, no, no. I won't think about Katharine being dead.' I'd say, 'If I don't think about it, then it won't be true.' I looked, you know. I hired investigators, but they lost your trail in Atlanta. You could have gone anywhere, they said, from there. I couldn't let people know about the investigators—other than Roberta and Sam. I told everyone else that you had gone on a vacation, that with Stan being dead only a year and a half I felt that, with high school over, you needed the break. Everyone in town knew how close you and your father had been. Everyone knew the devastation his death had caused in your life."

"Mama—"

"And like an old, prideful fool, I wondered if everyone knew about Buddy Akins as well. Even now the bitterness and anger I thought I buried long ago courses like acid through my veins." Carolyn shuddered. "It scares me what I'm capable of."

"We are all capable of so much more than we realize."

"Do you know what a liar I am?"

"Mama, you are not a liar."

"Oh, yes, I am. The first four years everyone thought you had gone to Berkeley because that's what I told them. Sometimes, I would leave town on the pretense of going to California for a visit and would return weeks later, tanned and just bursting with stories." Silent tears spilled down her cheeks with the memory. "Oh, God! The yarns I spun. Lying to everyone but Roberta, Sam, and Marcy. Lying to my mother and father. Worse still, lying to myself."

"I know all about that, too, Mama."

"The fifth year was the worst," Carolyn continued, as though she had not heard her daughter. "It seemed that wherever I went, someone asked me where you were; what were you doing; when were you coming home? By the sixth year, the questions stopped." Carolyn choked on the lump that had formed in her throat. "In my heart, I knew that this small, gossipy town of Brooksboro knew my secret. My heartache."

Katie began to weep with her mother. Carolyn patted her hand.

"But the people were kind. They eventually avoided speaking of you altogether. Katharine, tell me now. How could I have been a better mother?"

Katie shook her head. "You couldn't have, Mama. You and I were both doing the best we knew how."

"Sometimes, you know, you have to do what you think is right in the eyes of God and man. Ultimately, children make their own choices despite their parent's best efforts."

"And a child's choices can be pretty bad. The things children do in an effort to grow up are the things parents are probably better off not knowing about. Don't look at me like that, Mama. It wasn't all you. It was me, too. It wasn't all you."

"You don't have to tell me anymore. I don't need to know. It wasn't your fault, Katharine. It was mine. I hadn't been there for you—truly been there for you—since you turned thirteen."

"Why is that, Mama?"

"I don't know, Sweetheart. I really don't know. I thought about it all today. The way things had been with my mother. . ."

"Yesterday you said that you wanted to be a teacher but that your mother didn't approve of you being married and teaching. Why not?"

"I don't know. I suppose you'd have to ask her that one. My mother had a strict set of rules that she thought young southern ladies were supposed to live by. . . ."

"And you didn't?" Katie teased.

Carolyn smiled back at her daughter. "The apple doesn't fall far from the tree."

"Nana Kate wanted you to get married. All you wanted to do was teach. You wanted me to go to college, but I would have been just as happy to be married and have a house full of kids."

"Then why didn't you? Roberta said you were planning to go to college."

"Truth? Buddy encouraged me to go to school. He said I was better than anything around here and that I should go to school and get my education."

Carolyn playfully rolled her eyes. "Buddy and I agreed on something. Who would have guessed?"

Katie and her mother laughed, then became sober. "Katharine, I need to ask you another question."

"Okay."

"As a mother, it is my right."

Katie seemed to draw back. "No, no, nothing such as that. Katharine, yesterday you mentioned you hadn't been to church in awhile. Tell me, where do you stand with God?"

Tears welled up in Katie's eyes, spilling over the corners. "I don't know, Mama. I can't believe God could love me, not after everything I've seen and done."

Carolyn took her daughter's hand and patted it. "That's not true, Katharine. God loves His children no matter what."

"Does He?"

"Katharine, I'm not saying I'm perfect. God knows I'm not. Look at all the damage I've done in our lives. But I know God loves me. I'm not really sure what I would have done had I not had my faith these past twenty-five years. If He can love me through all that, I know He can love you no matter what you've done."

Katie sat silent for a moment. "That's easy for you to say; you don't know the sordid details of my past. I mean, you probably have a general idea, but if you knew the whole truth, I wonder if you'd be so quick to say that God loves me."

"It doesn't matter what I know. Doesn't God know the whole truth about you?"

Carolyn sat quietly for a moment, leaving Katie alone with her thoughts. Yes, He knew everything. He knew about the night in Atlanta when all sense of self-worth was stripped from her as a virtual stranger forced from her the very thing she had kept sacred for Buddy. He had seen her lying in that roach-infested apartment in Hell's Kitchen, eyes glazed over from too much alcohol and drugs. He knew Abby. . .about the endless, sweaty nights of exotic dancing. . .no. . .stripping. . . .

"Call it what it is, Katie," she whispered to herself.

"What?" Katie looked up at her mother's face. "Mama, how can

God love me when He knows everything I've done?"

"I don't pretend to know the mind of God," Carolyn said firmly. "Best I can do is explain the heart of a parent. And I'm telling you this, Katharine; there's nothing you could do to make me stop loving you. Oh, I know I didn't show it too well, but I did love you."

"That's why you planted the petunias every winter."

Carolyn smiled weakly. "They were pansies, but that's right. I never stopped loving you, no matter what you did."

Katie closed her eyes. Had God loved her when David Franscella was beating her? Perhaps. What was it the Bible said?

"Mama, what is it the Bible says about good things happening to something or another, even when you're bad?"

"It says God can take anything bad in your life and make it into something good if you'll allow Him."

Katie nodded. Yes, the beating had been terrible. But it had led to her attending college, which led to work as Cynthia's assistant, which led to. . .Ben.

"I think I'm beginning to understand."

"A southern woman's faith is one of her most prized possessions, Katharine."

Katie sighed deeply. "Mama? Why didn't you ever call me Katie?"

Carolyn smiled broadly, then brought her daughter's hand to her lips and kissed it. "Because calling you Katie was my mother's idea. She was running everything else in my life. I at least was going to control that."

Katie laughed freely. She reached over and gave her mother an awkward hug, then pulled back. It was time. Grasping her mother's face between her hands, she said, "My name is Katharine Elizabeth Morgan Webster. My husband is William Benjamin Webster, owner of world-renown The Hamilton Place hotel chain. We recently discovered an illegal prostitution ring being operated out of New York's THP. Ben sent me here to keep me safe while he works with the FBI. That's the whole truth, Mama. Or at least that's everything you need to know."

She had confessed to her mother now. Maybe confessing to God wouldn't be so difficult.

Carolyn reached up and placed her hands over Katie's. "My little darling. You are safe with me. You are."

Katie stood and Carolyn stood with her. They reached for each other simultaneously, holding each other tightly, as fresh, cleansing tears rose up from their souls and poured down their faces. Minutes later, Katie wiped her face with her fingertips. "I'm going to go upstairs and freshen up. Then we'll finish those pickles, okay?"

Carolyn nodded. "I'll be here waiting for you."

Katie moved away slowly, then turned, and started to walk out of the door. On impulse, she stopped and turned. "I love you, Mama," she said quickly.

"I love you, too," she replied, then added, "Katie."

"How you gentlemen doin' this evenin'?" Cail Fontaine, sitting behind the registration counter of his small motel, greeted the three strangers that sauntered in the glass double doors.

They were big men, all of them, and clearly not from the area. They wore expensive sports shirts; the armbands stretched almost painfully across their biceps. The outlines of well-developed pectorals were easily detected beneath the comfortable cotton material. Their waistlines were trim and belted with thin, black leather belts. The muscles in their upper thighs bulged beneath the denim of their faded jeans. In spite of the fact that the sun had set a good half hour earlier, they wore dark shades, concealing their eyes. They all wore their hair long. The two on the end had pulled their hair back, securing it at the nape of their necks.

The one in the middle had not. "We need a room," he said. A scar near his mouth moved with each word.

"One room for each of you or would you like a room together?"

"Do you have two rooms adjoining?"

"I certainly do," Cail answered as cheerfully as he could. He felt himself begin to sweat profusely. These men made him nervous, though he wasn't entirely sure why. "Rooms eleven and twelve. Both have two double beds." Cail picked up the sign-in clipboard from his desk and set it on top of the counter for the men to sign. "If I can just get your names and addresses."

He watched as each man signed his name, leaving the address portion of the cards blank.

"No homes, huh?" he asked nervously. "Well, that's not really important anyway. Will that be cash or credit card?"

The man in the middle reached into his front pocket and pulled out a wad of cash secured by a silver money clip. He snapped out a hundred-dollar bill. Slapping it onto the counter, he asked, "Will that cover it?"

"Oh, yes, Sir. Yes, Sir. Here's your keys. Y'all just call down to the office if you need anything."

"We won't," he said calmly.

Cail watched as the men walked out of the doors, then stopped. The man in the middle stepped back into the lobby and raised his chin slightly. "Maybe you can help me. How do I get to Main Street from here?"

In the early morning hours, there was little activity in the small, private reception area of the private airport. No more than nine people were inside. One of them was the pilot for the single engine Piper Navajo that was being readied beyond the glass doors. Three people—a woman and two men—stood shoulder to shoulder at the doors, watching the preparation. After a time the taller of the men turned to the others and spoke quietly.

"You'll call me when you arrive in Canada?" he asked.

The woman, dark-haired and sharply dressed, turned an agitated face to the man. "We told you that we would, didn't we?"

"I'm double checking," the man replied firmly, though he seemed acutely unsure of the situation.

The shorter man stood silently listening to the minor bickering he had long ago grown accustomed to. He felt a hand on his shoulder and he turned.

"Mr. Caballero, just to check in with you. . .we have a four-mile visibility and a one-thousand-foot ceiling, so we won't have to file a flight plan. We will also be able to fly below radar coverage and without the transponder on. We are set to land at the private airstrip that you requested, so Customs will not have to be notified. Everything is set," the pilot informed him.

Bucky Caballero nodded, then turned to his sister and her husband. He placed his hand against the small of her back as he addressed his brother-in-law. "Lie low. As soon as you hear from the men in Georgia and locate the file, call me. When we have the file, it'll be safe for Matt and me to return. They'll have nothing on us. Especially now that. . ."

"Let's get going," Mattie interrupted. "We've already been through this." She reached up as if to give him a kiss, but stopped short. Instead, she turned, then pushed the chrome bar of the glass door.

The two men watched her as she walked away. Bucky Caballero extended his hand to David Franscella, who responded in kind. "Don't blame her, David. She can't help how she is."

"I know. I didn't marry her because we loved each other. You know that."

Bucky frowned. "Take care of things," he instructed. "And above all, don't let me down."

CHAPTER TWENTY-ONE

Katie awoke to the pitter-patter of rain falling against her window. She rolled onto her back, mesmerized by the blurring, snakelike trails of rain slithering over the panes as she gazed absently through the window. Bleary-eyed, her mind beclouded with too long a sleep, she stretched and smiled, remembering the previous day. She and her mother had finally made amends. Her mother called her Katie. They understood each other in a way that few mothers and daughters ever could.

Ben would be so pleased.

The very thought of his name brought a furrow to her brow. They had been apart for a week and she was weary of being without him. She wanted to talk with him. . .needed to be with him. More than all else, she had to know if he was all right.

She glanced over at the princess phone by her bed, toying with the idea of calling him. Were they truly in so much danger that a two-minute phone call would threaten their safety?

She shook her head no. Ben said that he would call when it was safe, but not until then. She trusted him with her life when she married him, she must trust him now. He was the wisest man she had ever known. She could count on him. He must be able to count on her as well.

She swung her long legs from under the covers and over the side of the bed as they glistened in the dim, morning light. Glancing back at the window, she realized she wouldn't be able to jog this morning. She knew plenty of people who would jog in the rain, but she wasn't one of them. That's what gyms were for, she thought with a smile. . .rainy days. . . .

She dressed quickly, made the bed, then went downstairs for her morning cup of much-adored coffee. When she walked into the family room, she saw her mother standing in front of the television, watching *Good Morning, America.* Katie smiled at her mother, who was apparently oblivious to her presence.

"Morning, Mama," Katie sang, then walked into the kitchen where a half pot of coffee brewed in the coffee maker. She took a mug out of the cabinet, prepared her coffee, and took a hefty sip as she peered through the kitchen window at the dreariness of the rain-drenched garden.

She heard Carolyn's footsteps behind her. Turning, she was immediately aware of the horror-stricken look upon her mother's face.

"Mama? What's wrong?"

A moment later her coffee mug slipped from her hand, falling to the floor, breaking into large, unmendable fragments.

Jean-Louis Boudreaux was saying good-bye to the patrons of his Paris brasserie in his usual friendly manner. *Café Citón,* located near *Place de l'Opera* and *Église de la Madeleine,* was a favorite dining establishment of tourists and local businessmen and women. This time of year the terrace, surrounded by an ornate wrought iron fence, was a favorite area for most. Patrons enjoyed viewing the sights and sounds of Paris while sipping hot coffee or conversing easily with others over a cold Orangina. At the suggestion of its concierge, guests of *L'Endroit de Hamilton,* a nearby hotel, often came for breakfast or their afternoon coffee. Now, a little after two o'clock in the afternoon, most of Jean-Louis's customers were returning to work, shopping, or browsing in a leisurely fashion.

"Au revoir," Jean-Louis called out in his raspy voice and with a nod of his slightly balding head as he stood near the entrance of the old establishment. *"Au plaisir de vous revoir, Monsieur.* Come again soon. Come again."

Christian Patrick, his headwaiter, approached him cautiously from the back. Jean-Louis did not like to be disturbed with seemingly insignificant matters while greeting or saying good-bye to his guests. Nonetheless, he turned to Christian and noticed that he was wringing a small towel with his small, slender hands.

"*Oui bien sur!*" he said impatiently. "What is it, Christian?"

"I am sorry to disturb you, *Monsieur*. But one of our guests. . ." Christian's words trailed off as he turned to look at a small table for two in the back of the cafe.

"The American? Our little sweetheart from *L'Endroit de Hamilton*? What is wrong?"

"I don't know," Christian answered, wringing the towel all the more. "She came in a few moments ago, ordered her coffee, and began reading her American newspaper. Then. . .the next thing I know. . ."

Jean-Louis stepped away from his headwaiter. "Stay here. I will take care of it."

"*Oui, Monsieur.*"

Jean-Louis approached the beautiful American woman who sat alone at the back of his establishment. Her head was bowed as if in prayer. Recently employed at *L'Endroit de Hamilton,* she had been a regular diner at *Café Citón* for a little over a week. She had instantly mesmerized Jean-Louis and his employees. She was an aloof, exotic beauty who had given no other information about herself than her first name.

"*Mon petite?*" Jean-Louis asked gently. "Little one?"

The tiny head moved slowly, revealing the beautiful Asian eyes, where fresh tears were welling up. Jean-Louis stood helpless as the tears gradually escaped, then trailed down the soft brown face.

Marcy Waters stood on the front porch of her home, waving good-bye to her rain-soaked children as they boarded the school bus. Mark, always the last to get on in the mornings and the first to get off in the afternoons, turned on the bus's steps and blew a farewell kiss to his mother. Marcy returned the gesture, then turned and walked back into the quiet of her home. Charlie had left hours ago, but she supposed he would soon return because of the rain.

She made her way into the kitchen, where she prepared her coffee. The kitchen table held the remains of the children's morning meal of Cheerios and toast with homemade preserves. Marcy gathered the dishes and set them in the sink. She brushed the crumbs of toast from her hands as she reached for a coffee mug. She simultaneously poured coffee and slipped two pieces of bread into the toaster. By the time she added milk and sugar to the hot beverage, her toast had popped up. She generously slapped a spoonful of preserves on each piece, placed them on a dessert plate, then retreated to the family room.

Michael had left the television on the news—something she fussed at him about to no avail. She hated the news. Her breakfast usually consisted of two pieces of toast and a cup of coffee over a rerun of *Leave It to Beaver*. Marcy was convinced that if she watched the show enough, and if Charlie would buy her a single strand of pearls, she would become as good a mother as June Cleaver.

As she reached for the remote lying on the oak coffee table, she caught the tail end of a report out of New York. Generally, she would not have been interested, but something she had heard in the background caught her attention and she froze as the story unfolded.

". . .Mr. Webster, owner of the illustrious hotel chain, The Hamilton Place, is believed dead in the explosion. We are now going live to New York, where our correspondent has been standing outside of the hotel waiting for a news release from the FBI agents assigned to the case. Greg?"

The scene on the television screen changed. A young man, dressed in a suit and firmly grasping a network microphone in his hand, began to speak. "Behind me is New York's The Hamilton Place, where William Benjamin Webster resided with his wife, whose whereabouts are yet to be determined. FBI agents are uncertain as to whether or not Mrs. Webster was with Mr. Webster at the time of the car bombing. We have heard unsubstantiated reports. . ."

The young man pressed his earpiece with his fingertips, turned suddenly, and then looked back at the camera. "Excuse me. The agents are about to speak."

The camera zoomed in on one female and two male FBI agents who stepped up to a cluster of microphones. The man in the middle cleared his throat before speaking. The bottom of the screen displayed his identity: Philip A. Silver, FBI Special Agent.

"Ladies and gentlemen, at this time we are able to give you only a short statement. We request that you keep your questions brief. We will give further updates as time permits."

Marcy noticed a dewy-eyed sheen to the man's eyes. She stood slowly, as if by standing she would be able to hear and comprehend him better.

"As you know, last evening about six o'clock, William Benjamin Webster was apparently killed in the explosion of his vehicle outside his estate in the Hamptons. His wife, Katharine, is not believed to have been with him at the time, and we are now trying to locate her. According to Mr. Webster's assistant, she has been visiting her mother in another state. We believe that we have located her and will be bringing her back to New York later today."

A voice called out from the crowd. "You say 'apparently killed.' Why's that?"

"Because of the nature of the explosion, there's no body."

Another voice called out, "Do you believe this to be homicide? And if so, do you believe Mrs. Webster to be in danger? Or is she a suspect?"

"No comment at this time."

"Agent Silver? Have you placed an APB on Mrs. Webster?"

Marcy did not wait to hear the answer. She ran out the door and down the street in the pouring rain.

Marcy, standing at the sink of Katie's bathroom, was wetting another cloth for Katie's head. Carolyn was slowly making her way down the stairs to prepare something light for her daughter to eat. She thought it was important that Katie keep up her strength. They had known for a half hour that Ben had been killed—or apparently killed—in the explosion of his automobile. Katie crumpled to the floor when she heard the tragic news. Within moments Marcy was running through the front door, screaming their names. It had taken both Marcy and Carolyn to lift Katie and help her up the stairs. She now lay quietly on her bed, lifelessly staring at the ceiling, clutching Ben Jonson's *Volpone* to her breast. She had not uttered a single word. Even when Carolyn told her Monica's story of the old woman's floral centerpiece.

When Marcy stepped over to the bed and placed the cloth over Katie's forehead, Katie stirred slightly.

"I don't believe it," she whispered. "It's not true. It's a lie. You don't know Ben. He wouldn't leave me like this."

Marcy was quiet for a moment before sitting beside her friend and placing an arm over her. "Listen, Katie. . .I know this isn't the best thing to say right now, but the FBI is looking for you."

"What?" she asked breathlessly. "Where did you hear that?"

"The news. This morning."

"I don't know what to do, Marcy. Without Ben. . .I don't know what to do."

Marcy stroked Katie's hair, pushing it away from her forehead. "Shhh. We're gonna get through this. We are."

Katie closed her eyes against the soothing touch of Marcy's fingertips.

"Katie, I have an idea."

Katie's eyes remained shut. Carolyn stood near the door but took a step toward the bed.

"Charlie and I have a condo at the beach. You and your mother can take off for a few days. . .go over. . .no one would know to look for you there."

Katie's eyes opened slowly and she shook her head no. "I'm not running anymore."

"What do you mean?"

"I mean, I'm not running anymore. If the FBI needs me—if they know where I am—so be it. I'm not running anymore."

"Katharine. . ."

Katie sat up slightly and looked at her mother. "No, Mama. I've been running for too long."

Carolyn nodded. "I understand."

"Do you?"

"Yes. Yes, I do."

Katie allowed her head to slip back to the pillow. For several moments she stared at the ceiling, then closed her eyes again. Carolyn continued to stand in place, watching her daughter, as Marcy resumed stroking her friend's hair. When Katie's breathing became steady and even, Marcy quietly stood and walked past Carolyn toward the door. As her hand touched the doorknob, she heard Katie stir behind her. The two women turned to look at the sleeping form on the bed. Katie took a deep breath, exhaled, and whispered, "Caballero."

Carolyn and Marcy tiptoed down the stairs. It was almost two o'clock in the afternoon. Earlier they had persuaded Katie to eat a small bowl of vegetable soup and drink a cup of hot tea, which Carolyn laced with a mild sedative. It was not enough to harm her child, but enough to calm her and allow her to sleep peacefully. Within a half hour, Katie was sound asleep, the book from Ben still wrapped in her arms.

"What do you think she meant when she said 'Caballero'?" Carolyn asked. "Have you ever heard her say that name before?"

Marcy answered with silence.

Carolyn stopped halfway down the stairs. "Marcy, do you know what's going on here?"

Marcy stopped a few steps below the woman who had been like a mother to her. "Miss Carolyn, do *you* know what's going on here?"

Carolyn looked down briefly, then returned her eyes to Marcy's. "Katharine is my child. There are things I cannot elaborate here. You're a mother; please understand." Carolyn swallowed hard. "She is my child."

Marcy's nod was barely visible. "I understand. I think you and I both know enough to know enough to keep silent."

Carolyn nodded as she began to go down the stairs again.

"I need to call Charlie," Marcy whispered, just as the older woman passed her.

"He's not home on a day like this?" Carolyn asked her as they walked into the kitchen. She was carrying a tray with the dishes Katie had eaten from. She set it down on the counter and began to make a pot of fresh coffee.

"He wasn't when I left. Oh my, if he has come home, he won't know what to think. Let me try to get him at home. If he's not there, I'll try to get him on his cell phone."

Marcy walked over to the telephone that hung on a nearby wall. She dialed her home number, reached her answering machine, and left a message for anyone who might hear it first. She then called Charlie's cell phone. He answered on the second ring.

"Hi, Sweetie," she said mildly.

"Where have you been?" he asked. "I've been calling all day."

"But obviously not worried enough to come home," she observed. "So, I'm not overly concerned that you were overly worried."

"What?"

"Never mind. I need for you to listen to me for a minute. The fact of the matter is, Katie is in some sort of trouble."

"What kind of trouble?"

Marcy briefly looked over at Carolyn, who began to run water in the sink for the dishes to soak in. "Remember Katie saying that her husband manages a hotel? Well, he does more than just manage it. He owns a whole chain of them. The Hamilton Place. Something horrible has happened and Katie is. . .well, she's not just here to visit her mother. She's hiding, Charlie."

"What makes you say that?"

"Katie told me." With that, Carolyn turned and looked at her. Marcy closed her eyes against the sorrow of a mother's eyes. "And the news. This morning, on national television, the news was about Katie's husband, Ben. His real name is William Benjamin Webster and he was apparently killed last night. The news indicated that someone may be after Katie as well."

"You're kidding. Are you okay?"

"Me? Me? For crying out loud, Charlie. I'm fine! But Ben Webster was blown to bits in a car bombing."

"Why?"

"I don't think I should talk about that over the phone. I'll have to tell you later. . .in person. . . ."

"I don't get it. Did the bombing take place in New York?"

Marcy started to answer, but then heard someone on the other end of the phone speaking in the background. "Who is that?" she asked.

"Wait a minute, Hon," Charlie was saying. Again, she heard a voice in the background. Then Charlie returned, "Listen to this. I'm having Coke and peanuts with Cail at The Village Restaurant. He just told me that three men, real mean-looking characters, came into the motel last night. This morning, when he came over here to get his breakfast, he noticed that they were driving a car with a New York license plate."

"Could they be FBI agents?" Marcy asked. Carolyn moved over to stand next to her. She looked anxious.

"I don't think so. Cail? Could they be FBI?" There was a pause. "Cail says he doesn't think so. Honey, if the FBI thinks that someone is after Katie. . .these men could be them. Cail said they asked about where Main Street is."

Marcy heard Cail speaking in the background again. Charlie added, "Cail says as far as he knows, they haven't left the room all day except to come over here and get something to eat."

"What are we going to do?"

"I don't know. But I tell you what. These men aren't locals. And they don't know our ways. I'm going to give Buddy a call. Between the three of us, we'll show them a little 'good ole boy' hospitality."

"Charlie, you be careful!"

"Don't worry, Sweetheart. We've got this much under control. In the meantime, you need to think about what to do with Katie and Miss Carolyn."

"I tried to talk Katie into taking her mother to the condo."

"And?"

"She said no. She says she's not running anymore."

"Today's a fine time for her to finally grow up. Tell her she's not running. Tell her she's doing what makes sense. 'Cause my thinking is that they aren't safe as long as they are in that house."

A little before three o'clock the doorbell rang. Carolyn and Marcy were drinking coffee and eating a bowl of soup in the kitchen. Katie remained upstairs, asleep. Startled, Carolyn jumped from her seat at the table. Marcy reached out and grabbed her by the arm. "Should we answer it?"

The doorbell rang again. "If we don't, whoever it is will wake Katie. I'll go. You stay by the phone. If I scream, call Sheriff Carlisle."

Marcy took her position by the telephone. Carolyn left the room and walked down the hall toward the front door. Through the glass pane she could see a man and woman standing with their backs to the door. It was as if they were checking behind them, and Carolyn instinctively knew that they were the FBI agents she had seen on the television earlier that morning. Glancing up the staircase before she answered the door, she listened for a sign that her daughter had awoken, but heard nothing.

She opened the door quietly. "Yes?" she asked guardedly.

The man and woman swung around to face her. He was tall and well built. She was small, but seemed sturdy and solid. His hair was dark, well groomed, with a sprinkle of salt at the temples. Her hair was auburn, twisted at the back of her head. He was distinctly handsome. She was equally as attractive. He wore a dark blue suit, white shirt, and plain tie. She wore black slacks, gray blouse, and a black jacket. Simultaneously, they reached into the pockets of their jackets, retrieved small leather credential cases, and flipped them open.

"Mrs. Morgan?" the man asked. It wasn't a question, really. He knew who she was.

"Yes."

"Mrs. Stanley Morgan?"

"Yes."

"Ma'am, we're with the FBI. I'm Special Agent Silver. This is my partner, Special Agent Richards."

"Yes."

"May we come inside and ask you a few questions?"

Carolyn silently stepped back and allowed them entrance. They closed their credential cases, slipped them back into their pockets, then walked into the foyer. Instinctively they took note of their surroundings.

"You have a beautiful home," the woman said to Carolyn.

"Thank you." She quietly motioned to the opened French doors leading to the morning room. The two agents moved past her, walking into the room cautiously. Again they looked about them, taking in the details. "May I get you something to drink? Some iced tea, perhaps?" She heard Marcy's light footsteps behind her. The agents swung around quickly. Without so much as a glance behind her, Carolyn explained, "This is my friend, Mrs. Waters. We were having lunch. Marcy, my guests are with the FBI." She felt Marcy stiffen.

The agents visibly relaxed. "I'm sorry to have disturbed you. Mrs. Waters, would you mind getting some iced tea for my partner and myself?" It wasn't a request for a drink. It was a request for privacy.

"Not at all." Marcy turned and went to do as requested.

When she left, Carolyn moved over to a chair. She sat, indicating with a regal sweep of her hand that the agents do the same. They moved to the sofa.

"Mrs. Morgan," Agent Silver began. "Do you know why we are here?"

"I think so. You are looking for my daughter."

"Yes."

There was momentary silence.

"Well," he asked. "Is she here?"

"She's asleep. I ask that you not disturb her."

"I'm awake," Katie said from the doorway. She had crept down the stairs so quietly that no one had been aware of her standing near them.

The agents stood. Carolyn folded her hands in her lap, bowed her head, and began to pray silently.

"Katie Webster?" Agent Silver asked.

"Yes." Katie stood still for a moment, then moved toward the sofa, extending her hand in greeting. Both agents shook her hand as they introduced themselves.

"You are William Webster's wife?" Agent Silver asked her.

"You are a friend of my husband."

Phil squinted his eyes at her. "How do you know that? Did William tell you that?"

Katie moved toward the chair where her mother sat with her head still bowed. She sat on the armrest and placed her hand on her mother's back in a comforting gesture.

"Yes."

"When did you last speak with your husband, Mrs. Webster?"

"A week ago," she answered stoically. "Let me save you some time. I know a great deal about Bucky Caballero and Jacqueline's." Carolyn's head snapped to attention.

"How do you know?" Agent Richards asked.

"I found the file that my husband was working on. I saw some of the evidence that he had gathered on Caballero."

"Do you know where that file is?" Agent Silver asked as he reached into his shirt pocket and brought out a pack of Juicy Fruit gum.

Katie silently shook her head.

"Any idea?" he asked, removing the silver wrapping.

Katie watched as he folded the gum, then again before popping it into his mouth.

"No," she answered.

The agents looked at each other briefly, then turned back to Katie and her mother. "Mrs. Webster. . ."

"Katie. Please, call me Katie."

"Katie. You are aware of what happened yesterday?"

"Yes, but I don't believe it."

Phil grimaced. "I understand. I scarcely believe it myself."

"I thought you were working with Ben."

"Ben?"

"I call my husband Ben."

Phil smiled faintly, apparently at the idea that William's wife considered the FBI to be working with her husband rather than vice versa. "I was called out of town. I was never concerned that it would go this far."

"Apparently," Katie said quietly. "Could this be a ruse?"

"If it is, your husband planned it on his own."

"Then it could be?" she whispered hopefully.

Again, the agents looked to each other, then back to Katie. "Mrs. . . Katie. I must inform you that there is every indication that Caballero or someone affiliated with him will next target you. . . ."

Carolyn looked up at her daughter sharply. "No!" she hissed.

Katie rubbed her mother's back, but her eyes never left the agents. "It's okay, Mama."

"We want you to return with us to New York. This evening. We will leave here, drive to Savannah, and catch a flight to New York. We can be there by late this evening. We can then go out to your estate in the country."

"Estate in the country?" Carolyn asked. "What estate?"

Katie took her mother's hand and patted it. "It's okay, Mama. I'll tell you later."

Phil cleared his throat before continuing. "I believe your husband went to the country this weekend to hide the file he was compiling. I also believe that he had obtained some vital information while I was away."

"What makes you think he found something you don't know about?"

"He tried to call me. That, and gut instinct."

"Have you questioned Bucky Caballero?"

"Mr. Caballero, his sister, and her husband have conveniently disappeared."

Katie stood. "Of course. You will have to excuse me. I will need to pack a few things."

"No!" Carolyn said, standing.

Marcy returned to the room, carrying a tray of glasses filled with iced tea. She froze in the doorway, not certain whether she should enter.

"Marcy," Katie said evenly. "I want Mama to go to your house."

Marcy, clutching the tray tightly, struggled with the idea of telling the agents about the men at the hotel. "Katie? I need to tell you. . ."

"Marcy?" Carolyn interrupted, giving her head a slight shake. Marcy understood the gesture and pressed her lips tightly together. "May I stay with your family?"

"Yes. Of course, you may." She walked into the room and extended the tray to Agent Silver and Agent Richards.

Katie moved toward the door. "I'll be right back. Then we can leave."

"Mrs. Webster. . .Katie. . . ," Agent Richards called out. Katie turned. "Are you afraid to fly?"

Katie gave her a quizzical look. "No. Why do you ask?"

"Our records indicate that you took a train down here."

Katie smiled sweetly. "That was Ben's idea. No one would expect the wife of William Benjamin Webster to be on a train."

Phil Silver nodded in agreement.

CHAPTER TWENTY-TWO

Katie collected her toiletries in her bathroom, then walked into the bedroom, where her suitcase was lying open-faced on the bed. She had already packed her clothes; each piece was folded neatly in two stacks. As she placed the items in her hands next to the clothes, she heard the bedroom door open. Turning, she saw Marcy standing there.

"I thought you might need some help," Marcy said as she closed the door.

Katie shook her head. "I have it. Thanks. But I do need to talk to you about something."

Marcy walked over to Katie. "I need to talk to you, too. Listen, Katie. I talked with Charlie a little while ago. Cail Fontaine told him that three men from New York arrived last night at his motel. Three not-so-nice men."

Katie looked at her friend. "You think they might be the men after me?"

"Yes. I do."

"Did you tell them?" she asked, indicating the FBI agents with a tilt of her head.

"No. I started to, but Miss Carolyn warned me off."

"I see."

"Katie? What can I do?"

Katie leaned over her bed, closed her suitcase, and secured it. Straightening, she looked toward the door. "For now, stand at the door and make certain that no one comes up those stairs."

Marcy walked to the door. "What are you going to do? Make a break for it?"

Katie gave a sad chuckle. "You read too many spy novels."

Marcy frowned. "Then what are you going to do?"

"First, I'm going to ask you for a favor."

"Anything."

"Will you go with me to New York? Do you think Charlie will let you?"

"Don't worry about Charlie. Yes, you know I'll go."

"Good. Good. I'm going to need you with me. . .to help me. . .to figure all this out. Somehow I've got to find that file."

"The one that Ben was compiling on Caballero?"

"Yes. The FBI believes that Ben had learned something more. The file from Andi. . .the records from Andrea's. . .all that was in the file. Ben had it when I left."

"Why doesn't the FBI have that file? Why would it have stayed with Ben?"

"I don't know. I haven't had time to think. . .I haven't had time to ask. . . ." Her voice was rising.

Marcy took a small step toward her. "It's okay. It's okay. You can find out later. What's the other thing you're going to do?"

"Call Ben's lawyer. Who also happens to be his cousin."

"The one you were working for when you first met him?"

Katie nodded. "She and Ben are more than just cousins, they're also friends. They even attended the same private academies and were classmates at Cornell. When Ben and I married, Cynthia served as maid of honor."

Katie picked up the handpiece of the princess phone and began to dial a number she retrieved from her purse. A moment later she said, "Cynthia?"

"Katie? Katie, is that you?"

"Yes."

"Where are you? I'm coming to get you."

"Wait! I'm in Georgia. And you don't have to come and get me. The FBI is here to take me home."

"Silver?"

"Yes. And his partner. Agent Richards."

"I know them."

"Will I be okay?"

"Yes. You're in the best of hands. But I don't want you to talk to them anymore than you already have without my being there, okay?"

"Will you meet me at the airport, Cyn?"

"Why don't I just meet you at the hotel?"

"I think we are going straight out to the house."

"Then I'll meet you out there. When is your flight?"

"I don't know. But as soon as we get on the plane, I'll call you."

"Katie. . .I'm sorry. . .about William. . .the whole family is. . ."

"No, Cyn. No. I don't believe it. Not for a second. I don't believe it."

"Katie, I knew him almost as well as anyone could and I—"

"Cynthia?" Katie interrupted.

"Yes?"

"When was the last time you heard from him?"

"Sunday evening. He called and told me what was going on. He was in the country at the time. . .he and Maggie."

"Is Maggie all right?"

"On the outside, she's as sturdy as always. Privately, she's a wreck. It'll be good for you to get back."

"And Ben's parents?"

"Not so good."

Katie frowned. "You tell them, Cyn. You tell them I don't believe it, okay?"

"Katie—"

"Thanks. I'll see you tonight."

Cynthia exhaled a breath of defeat. "I'll wait for your call."

Katie said good-bye and disconnected the line, then turned to Marcy. "We'll be leaving soon. I want you to take Mama home with you, call Charlie, and talk to him about your going with me, throw some things together, and come back down here. And the quicker you can do it, the better."

Marcy walked over to the door, then turned back to face Katie. "Give me a half hour. Can you do that?" She jerked her head toward the downstairs. "Can they do that?"

"I won't give them a choice. I'm calling the shots now."

Buddy Akins was standing behind his hardware store, clipboard and pen in hand, supervising the receiving of a truck delivery from Akron, Ohio, when Cail and Charlie approached him. He stuck the pen behind his right ear and tucked the clipboard under his arm as he called out to them.

"Hey, boys!"

"Buddy," they said together.

"What's bringing you fellas out here on such a dreary day?"

The two men stopped in front of him and looked up.

"Rain finally let up, thank the good Lord," Charlie commented. "My day's shot though. Have to make up for it later in the week."

"It's supposed to rain tomorrow, too," Buddy observed, then turned to one of the young men who was unloading from the back of the truck. "Y'all just put that in the storeroom, Gene. Take this and check the items off for me," he ordered, extending the clipboard.

The tall, lanky black man reached down from the back of the truck. "You got it, Buddy."

Buddy then turned to his friends. "What's up?"

Cail looked around nervously before answering. "Can we go inside and talk for a minute?"

Buddy's brows furrowed. "Sure. We can go into my office if you'd like."

The three men made their way into the back of the store, through the storeroom, and down a short, wide hallway that led to Buddy's office. Once inside, Buddy asked if anyone wanted a soda.

Both men declined.

"Sit down, then," Buddy offered. Charlie and Cail sat in the vinyl-covered office chairs. Buddy perched on the edge of his desk. "What's going on? You two look like there's trouble."

"Big trouble," Cail answered. "And it came right to my motel last night."

"Okay. . ."

Charlie leaned over, cracked his knuckles, and then rested his elbows on his knees. "Buddy, it's about Katie."

Buddy stood. "What about Katie? Katie's in trouble?"

"Looks like it. Marcy called a little while ago. You didn't see the news this morning, did you?"

"No. I leave the house at seven most mornings. Why?"

Charlie went on to explain the details that Marcy had given him earlier. Cail finished the story with his previous night's experience.

"We gotta do something, boys," Buddy said, moving to the back of his desk. He started to reach for the telephone.

"If you are calling Katie, don't bother. She's on her way to New York with the FBI," Charlie informed him.

"What about her mother?"

"She's at my house," said Charlie. "What I suspect is these three guys from New York will be paying Miss Carolyn's home a visit right after sundown."

Cail nodded beside him and Buddy commented, "The FBI know about those men?"

"I don't think so."

"So, what are we gonna do about it?" Buddy asked. "Call Sheriff Carlisle?"

"Let's not get that know-it-all involved quite yet, okay?" Cail said. "I say we get our rifles, load up, and pay Miss Carolyn's a visit."

"You still got that Remington Eight-Seventy?" Charlie asked.

"Clean and ready," Cail affirmed. "What about you?"

Charlie leaned back in his chair and crossed his ankles. "My Two-Seventy Winchester could stand a little action. Buddy?"

"I purchased a B-A-R just the other day. Got it right here in this closet." He moved toward the closet in the back of his office and brought out a leather-encased Browning Automatic Rifle. "Nice, huh?" he asked, opening the case and exposing the rifle.

Charlie and Cail stood and walked over to the desk. Charlie whistled. Cail carefully took the rifle from the case. A smile broke across his face and his eyes danced merrily. "What's say we welcome New York to Georgia with this little Howdy-Do?"

CHAPTER TWENTY-THREE

"Ladies and gentlemen, we at Delta Airlines want to thank you for flying with us today. . . ."

Katie opened her eyes. She and Marcy were occupying seats 6-A and B on an L-1011 bound for New York's La Guardia Airport. Agents Silver and Richards, who had not seemed overly pleased about Marcy accompanying Katie, were across the aisle sipping on sodas that had been offered to them earlier. Marcy, who chose the window seat, was sipping on a cup of coffee as she observed life outside the plane.

Katie had rejected the flight attendant's offer of a beverage. Instead, she clutched Ben Jonson's *Volpone* tightly to her breast, closed her eyes, and reflected on what might have happened to her husband.

Until she saw a body, she wouldn't believe he was dead. He was too smart and wise to allow that to happen. He knew that without him, she would be lost. . .life would be meaningless. . .she would be forever alone because no one could ever take his place.

She tried to imagine going home without Ben there to meet her. She fantasized about his miraculous appearance when she stepped into their house in the Hamptons. . .or at their suite in THP. Perhaps his assistant, Vickey, was hiding him. . . . Katie had an idea. . . .

"Excuse me. Agent Richards?" Katie leaned slightly into the aisle.

The book dropped to her lap. Agent Richards occupied the aisle seat across from her.

The attractive, almost handsome, woman turned to look at her. "Yes, Katie?"

"Earlier you said that we would go to the Hamptons to look for the file. Why not our home at the hotel? Or Ben's office?"

Agent Richards gave Katie a sympathetic smile. "We are hoping that the file is at your country home. Your hotel rooms and your husband's office were trashed over the weekend. Your husband's secretary found the office in disarray Monday morning. After the. . .incident. . .in the country. . .police went into your hotel suite and found it much the same way. The house in the country wasn't touched because police were able to block it off and secure it almost immediately after. . ."

"My home has been. . ."

Phil leaned over his partner. "Katie. We will have to ask you to accompany us back to the hotel to ascertain if anything was taken. But we can do that later. However, I must warn you that they did a rather thorough job."

Katie leaned back in her seat and squeezed her eyes shut. She tried to picture her beautiful home with seat cushions turned over, spilling onto the floor. She envisioned pictures hanging crooked on the walls, drawers opened, Ben's home office desk turned upside down. . . . She opened her eyes suddenly.

"Excuse me, again," she said, leaning over.

Both agents looked her way.

"My husband kept the file in his office desk. Did I tell you that already?"

Phil shifted slightly before answering. "You told us you didn't know the whereabouts of the file."

"I don't know where the file is. I do know where it was."

"Where in his office desk?" Agent Richards asked.

"In the bottom right-hand drawer."

The agents looked at each other, speaking silently with their eyes.

Agent Richards turned back to Katie. "If your husband kept the file there, it's gone."

Katie leaned back in her seat again, nauseous at the thought of someone. . .anyone. . .going through Ben's files. She felt Marcy's hand on her arm.

"You all right?" she asked.

She nodded, then shook her head. "I need a soda or something. I feel like I'm going to be sick."

"Take a deep breath and exhale slowly," she instructed as she pushed the call button on the armrest of her seat. Within seconds a handsome young steward stood over them.

"Yes, Ma'am?"

"My friend is not feeling well. A ginger ale, please. And crush the ice."

Katie kept her eyes closed until she heard the young man return. "Here you are," he said soothingly. Katie accepted the drink with a faint smile.

"Sip it slowly," Marcy said. "That's right. Take your time."

"Is she all right?" Agent Richards inquired from across the aisle.

Marcy nodded. "Just a bit queasy." She then spoke directly into Katie's ear. "What's wrong?"

Katie turned to face her. "Did you hear what they said?" she asked in a whisper.

She nodded. "The hotel suite. . .the office. . ."

"I can't bear the thought of someone going through Ben's personal belongings. Or his business files. You don't know Ben. He's so private."

"Tell me more about him."

She smiled and slightly raised her shoulders. "Handsome. Kind. Giving. Loving. Tender. He's six-foot-six. . .did I tell you that?"

Marcy shook her head. "That helps, huh?"

She nodded as tears formed in her eyes. Marcy was afraid that if the dam holding back the tears ever burst, she would neither be consolable nor would she be of any assistance to the FBI. "Take a sip of your drink," she said gently.

"He's smart. Wise. . ."

"Katie? Think about this: If he's wise, would he have gone to the country without that file?"

Understanding shone in her eyes. She quickly turned back to the agents. "Ben wouldn't have left the file there. He would have kept it with him."

Again, Phil leaned over his partner. "Katie, we can save all this for later if you'd like. We have a lot of questions to ask you, but I would rather not do it now. Is that okay?"

She nodded, leaned back in her seat, and took another sip of her drink.

Marcy patted her arm. "What's this?" she asked, pointing to the book. "You've been clutching this nearly all day." She retrieved the book from Katie's lap. "Ben Jonson's *Volpone*. May I?"

Katie nodded. "Ben sent it to me."

"When?"

"I got it yesterday."

Marcy studied the cover of the book for a moment. "That means he must have sent it. . .say. . .Friday?"

Katie nodded.

"You like Ben Jonson?" she asked her.

"Yes. Very much."

"You know, some people think that he actually wrote for Shakespeare."

"I know. Shakespeare was one of his students."

"I was helping Matthew with a project one time and read all about it. The character of Volpone was referred to as The Fox. Why was that do you suppose?"

"Jonson gave his characters the names of animals in order to show their likeness to the animals for which they were named."

"So, Volpone was named The Fox because. . ."

"Because he was sly?. . .devious?. . .greedy?"

"Especially greedy! Look here at the opening of act one. . . ." Marcy opened the book. Katie chose not to look, but rather to keep her eyes on her friend. It had been years since she had seen her in a studious role and it fascinated her. Somehow, though, motherhood had taken her from student to teacher, and Katie liked being with her old friend in this role. " 'Good morning to the day; and next to my gold!' " Marcy read. "You see Volpone is worshiping monetary wealth. Then, here: 'Open the shrine, that I may see my saint'—" Marcy stopped short.

Katie blinked. "What is it?" she asked, looking down to the open book where Marcy's finger pointed to the text.

"Someone underlined this."

Katie leaned over as if to get a better look. "That's strange. . . ."

"Why do you say that?"

"Look," she said flipping back to the cover page. "Ben never marks a book. Never dog-ears. . . But he inscribed this one and underlined. . . well, look. . . ."

Katie took the book from Marcy and read aloud. " 'Drink to me only with thine eyes, and I will pledge with mine; or leave a kiss but in the cup, and I'll not look for wine.' You see," Katie pointed out. "The third line is underlined as well. It struck me as rather strange yesterday when I received it. Ben wouldn't do things like this. Unless. . ."

"Unless what?"

"Unless he didn't do it and it came like this. Perhaps a previous owner. . ."

"Or. . .perhaps Ben is trying to tell you something."

Katie looked at her fellow traveler, whose eyes twinkled and danced. "What?"

"Look, I know you think I read too many spy novels, but just hear me out. When I write my column, it comes after a lot of reading current events and news briefs, etc. If this were a novel, and I was writing the story, my hero—Ben—would send a message to the heroine—you—that would be understood by only her. Now think. Why would Ben send you a book of a seventeenth-century writer?"

Katie raked her top teeth over her bottom lip before she spoke. "Ben and I play a game. He quotes lines from literature and I tell him who said it."

"Sounds like fun," she lightly teased. "Sometimes Charlie takes me fishing."

Katie smiled. "Ben and I both adore good literature."

Marcy leaned closer to her. "Then don't you see? This makes perfect sense! He would communicate to you through a piece of literature! A great piece of literature."

"Is everything okay over there?" Marcy and Katie jumped at the question from Phil.

Before Katie could answer, Marcy replied, "We're talking literature. Nothing of any interest unless you happen to like the works of Jonson, Shakespeare, Bacon. . ."

Agent Richards smirked. "I could never understand a word of it, personally. Do you really like that sort of thing?"

Katie smiled. "I adore it."

Marcy touched her arm and Katie returned her attention to her friend. "Shouldn't we say something to them?" Marcy whispered.

"Not yet. Ben sent this to me. Not them. He knows Silver, so why wouldn't he send it to Silver?"

"I don't know. . . ."

"I'll tell you why. Because Ben wants this in my hands. All I have to do is figure out what those two lines mean to him." Katie looked at the lines again, flipping from one page to the other. Finally, she answered, "Nothing."

Marcy took the book from her hands and began to fan the pages.

"What are you doing?"

"I'm looking for any other lines that may be underlined. . .wait! Here's one."

Katie took the book and read, "The blazing star of Italy!"

"Mean anything?"

Katie shook her head. "Nothing."

"Anything Italian in the house?"

"There're a lot of things. . .Italian Renaissance paintings, furniture. . . oh, wait. . .I think I know. . ."

Marcy shifted nervously. "What, Katie?"

"We went to Rome last year and Ben bought cuff links at this flea market. . .pewter stars. . ." She whispered the last words.

"Where does he keep them?"

"In a box inside his jewelry case."

"In your bedroom?"

"In his dressing room off from the bath."

"Keep looking," Marcy said, indicating the book.

Katie fanned the pages back again until she found additional underlining. She read, "Rook go with you, raven!"

They looked at each other for a moment before Marcy asked, "Do you have a chess set?"

"Yes, a very lovely one. We purchased it in Germany."

"Keep looking. . . ."

Katie fanned the pages again. "And your ladies sport and pleasure."

"Well?" she asked her.

"Do you think he means me? My sport and pleasure?"

"Could be. What do you play?"

"When we're in the country I play golf and tennis."

"Do you keep your clubs, racquets, yellow fuzzy balls there?"

"Yes."

"Keep looking. I think we're getting somewhere."

Katie fanned the pages again until she reached the first page again. "I'm back at the beginning."

"So, then what do we have?"

"My golf clubs or my tennis racquet, the chess set, the cuff links. . ."

"Open the shrine. . . . Katie, are there any wall safes in the house? Secret compartments?"

"Not that I know of."

"But there could be."

"Sure, there could be."

"Then all we have to do is figure out what 'Or leave a kiss but in the cup' means."

Katie pressed her lips together and searched her memory, but nothing about the line was even remotely familiar. She shook her head. "Nothing."

Marcy relaxed in the seat beside her. "Maybe it'll come to you when we get there."

Katie took another sip of her drink. "Yeah, maybe. In the meantime, I think we should keep this between us, okay?"

Marcy glanced at the two agents sitting across the aisle. Agent Richards was lazily flipping through a magazine while Phil gazed out of the window to the earth below. Marcy looked at Katie. "Okay."

At precisely nine-thirty that evening, three men left the small but comfortable motel located on the outskirts of Brooksboro. They moved quietly to the automobile parked directly in front of their rooms. They glanced about in apprehension of seeing another guest of the motel or patron of the restaurant next door. But the neon lights had gone out half an hour before and all the employees had gone home.

A full moon illuminated the blue-black, starless sky. Two of the men looked toward the motel office. The drapes were drawn and the lights unexpectedly out. The other man glanced at the neon motel sign, blinking NO VACANCY into the near darkness. He looked up and down the gravel driveway. There were only two cars other than theirs parked in front of the motel. He shrugged his shoulders in bewilderment but said nothing.

Silently they slipped into the car, gently closing the doors. The engine started quietly and the car rolled smoothly out of the parking lot and onto the narrow two-lane highway. It moved toward the sleepy, still town without incident. It stopped at the only traffic light at the north end of town directly in front of Brooksboro United Methodist Church. They read the marquee out front: Thou Shalt Not Kill. Each of them snickered.

The light turned green and the car slowly cruised past storefront windows that seemed to be watching the dark sedan glide through town toward South Main Street. The men had staked out the area in the early morning hours of that day so they knew the side street nearest the large, white frame house. As they approached it, they turned right, killing the lights, then the engine.

The car doors clicked open. The men stepped out, then carefully shut the doors. They adjusted the waistbands of their tight jeans, felt for the revolvers resting at the small of their backs.

The house was the fourth on the right. Single file, the three men slipped behind the first house. Within minutes they were behind the stone wall surrounding the Morgan home. The men bent slightly and moved quickly, searching for the gate. They found it at the far corner, old, weathered, and wooden.

The acknowledged leader gave the gate a light push. It was locked from the inside with a basic slip lock. The man grinned, then rammed it with his shoulder. The old lock gave way and the gate swung open. The men moved inside the yard.

A brick walkway leading to the back of the house provided an easy approach. At the back door the man in front tested the lock. He turned to the men behind him and smiled. It wasn't locked.

Idiots, he thought. *Small-town idiots.*

He stepped over the threshold followed by his companions. The third man left the door slightly ajar for an easy exit. They stopped for a moment, just long enough to get their bearings and take in their surroundings. All the lights in the house were out. There were no televisions or radios blaring. The men naturally assumed that, as all Bible-belters, the lady and her mother were already in their beds asleep. The first man retrieved his gun, a .38 Smith & Wesson, and the other two followed.

They moved out of the family room and down a hallway. None of the rooms downstairs appeared to be occupied. They stood at the bottom of the stairs and looked up. With a jerk of his head, the first man indicated they should move upstairs.

Slowly, carefully, they took each step until they reached the second-floor landing. Effortlessly, they stepped down the hall and into each room. But they found nothing.

The men, now standing in a back bedroom, shrugged.

"They got movies here?" one asked, stupefied.

"I don't think so," said another. "Maybe they went out to dinner."

They replaced their guns. "Let's go back to the yard," the leader said. "We'll wait for them there."

Less cautiously, they walked to the top of the staircase, then down the stairs. Heavy-footed, they went down the hallway and into the family room, where they stopped short. The back door was now shut, locked, and bolted. They stared at it as if waiting for it to magically open. They shifted nervously.

The sound came from behind them, and they quickly turned to see three men, well lit by the moonlight streaming through the windows, each with a rifle pointed their way. One of them, the center one—tall and blond—sniffed before he spoke.

"Welcome to Georgia, boys."

CHAPTER TWENTY-FOUR

"Maggie, oh, Maggie," Katie said breathlessly as she drew the older woman close to her.

Maggie patted Katie heartily on the back. "Little darling," she replied, then choked on a sob that rose to her throat and formed a knot there.

Katie stepped back, clutching the woman's plump hands in her own, and looked around the foyer of her country home. Everything was as she left it a few weeks ago, though now it seemed as if it had been years. She glanced up the staircase, hoping to see her husband coming toward her in his dashing, jaunty fashion. She momentarily pictured him, adjusting the cuff of his shirt sleeves, unaware of his overwhelming good looks and the aura of his presence.

"Good heavenly day," she heard from behind and turned to see Marcy with her mouth slightly opened, her eyes dazed by the wealth and splendor around her. She dropped her small luggage at her feet.

"Please come in," Katie whispered, aware now of the others in the room. She squeezed Maggie's hands, brought them to her lips, and kissed them lovingly before softly explaining, "Maggie, this is a friend of mine, Mrs. Waters. I'm going to put her in the guest room nearest to mine. I'm sure you know everyone else."

Maggie nodded.

"Agents Silver and Richards will stay with us this evening as well. Maggie, has Cynthia arrived yet?"

"She's in the library making a phone call. She should be out any moment."

As if on cue, the heels of Cynthia's shoes could be heard tapping down the marbled hallway. "Katie?"

Katie moved from around those who were gathered in the foyer and into the arms of her husband's cousin.

"Are you all right?" Cynthia asked her, pulling her away.

Katie nodded. "Has anyone heard anything?"

"No. But Caballero and his sister seem to have disappeared," she whispered.

"I know," Katie mouthed back.

"I just got off the phone with Dick Sanders, who operates a small airport just outside of the city. He said Bucky and Mattie were on the plane."

"No one else?"

Cynthia shook her head.

"Is something going on we need to be aware of?" Cynthia and Katie turned to the voice of Agent Silver.

Cynthia stepped toward him with her hand extended in greeting. "Hello, Phil. It's been a long time."

Phil took her hand. "Cynthia."

"Katie," Cynthia said lightly, "why don't I show everyone into the living room? Perhaps you could help Maggie take the luggage upstairs and then prepare some hot tea for us?"

Katie startled, then added, "Thank you, Cyn."

"As soon as I get everyone settled in, I'll be in to help you."

Katie noted Phil and Agent Richards's exchange of glances. Phil opened his mouth to say something, but was interrupted by Cynthia's "This way, everyone." Marcy, Phil, and Agent Richards followed her into the living room while Maggie retrieved Katie's suitcase from where it had been deposited beside the doorway. Katie grabbed Marcy's suitcase and started upstairs with Maggie on her heels.

"I want to talk with you, Maggie," Katie said quietly as they made their way up the staircase. "I want to know everything that happened."

"It's been awful, Miss Katie. Those agents moving about as if they own the place! The tacky yellow police tape around the property. I can scarcely go to the privy without one of them asking my intent!"

As they approached the open door of the first guest room, Katie stopped and peered inside. She half expected to see Private Dancer within its four walls. Instead, a single lamp gave shadowy illumination to the simple yet tasteful guest room. "We'll give this room to Agent Richards," Katie said quickly as she moved away from the doorway.

"How long do you think they'll be here, cluttering about the house?" Maggie sounded indignant.

Katie gave a sympathetic smile. "I know you don't like this, Maggie. . .having strangers mussing up the house, but I suppose it's necessary. We'll put Agent Silver in the room across from Agent Richards and. . ." The two women approached the guest room nearest the master suite. As they walked in, Katie continued, "Mrs. Waters in here."

This guest room, as all bedrooms in the house, had a small, table-top lamp that burned until bedtime. Katie had often basked in the simple joy of slowly walking down the hallway arm-in-arm with her husband as they made their way toward their bedroom, stopping at each doorway to turn off the lights. As it had been with the porch rockers of her youth, it was as if the events of the day were slipping into the shadows of yesterday as they walked toward the single light in their bedroom, their special place. It was truly the most warm and invitingly romantic room in the house. Tonight, it would be cold and unreceptive. Katie closed her eyes at the thought.

The two women continued toward the master bedroom in silence. As they approached it, Katie's footsteps faltered until she stopped completely. "I don't think I can go in there," she whispered, tears stinging her eyes. She buried her face in her slender hands and shook her head.

"Now, now, Miss Katie. You can do this. Master William. . .your

Ben. . .wouldn't want this, now would he?"

Katie shook her head again.

"After the shock of the first moment, it won't be so bad."

Together the two women walked into the room. Katie visibly blanched and she reached to Maggie for support. The older woman dropped the suitcase to her feet, took the hand of her mistress, and walked her over to the overstuffed loveseat nearby. Together they sat, clutching their hands.

"Tell me what happened," Katie requested, her eyes still closed.

"Master William said to me on Friday, 'Maggie, you and I are going to the country for a few days.' I said, 'Without Miss Katie?' and he said, 'I suspect so. It won't be the same, will it, Maggie?' he said. And I said, 'Indeed, not.' But here we came, first thing Saturday after breakfast. Master William stayed on the phone a bit, ran an errand or two, though I can't say where he went. . . ."

"He didn't say?" Katie's eyes opened and she watched the housekeeper intently during her account of the previous weekend.

"I've already told those nosy detectives down there that he didn't say a word to me. Not that he ever did. Master William doesn't need anyone's permission to leave the house. You know that."

Katie smiled. "Then what?"

"Nothing, really. On Sunday afternoon he says to me, 'We'll go home tomorrow afternoon, Maggie.' I thought that a bit strange, going home on a Monday afternoon, but that's his business, not mine. On Monday morning, he gets up, has his breakfast, and says, 'I'm running an errand. I'll be back in a flash. We'll head for the city this afternoon.' I remember saying to him, 'Master William, when do you think Miss Katie will be home? I'm missing her terribly.'" Katie patted the woman's hand. "And he said, 'Before you know it, Maggie.' He walked out the door. . .but first he. . ."

"He what, Maggie?"

"He gave a little kiss on my cheek here," she said, resting her palm against her cheek. "It was almost as if he knew."

"I knew it! I don't believe he's dead, Maggie. I think this is a ruse. I don't completely understand it or why he hasn't called me. But it's like something inside of me says, 'Don't cry, Katie. It's not true.' I would know if Ben were dead. And I don't know it. I don't feel it."

"Bless your heart," Maggie said. "I hope that you are right."

"What happened next, Maggie?"

"About an hour or two later the police were here, banging on the door like heathens!"

Katie smiled again. "I suspect we need to get back downstairs to the kitchen. Something tells me Cynthia has a piece of news for me."

Cynthia was already running water for the tea. While Maggie finished the task, Cynthia pulled Katie into a small room that served as a pantry.

"You asked if anyone else was on that plane," Cynthia began. "You're talking about David Franscella."

Katie blushed. "Yes. He's Mattie's husband."

Cynthia straightened. "Katie, I don't know how to say this exactly, except to come right out and say it. William talked to me the morning of the explosion."

"I thought you said he talked to you the night before."

"He did. The nature of our conversation on that last morning is private, and I didn't want to discuss it with you on the phone. Just in case."

"In case what?"

"Katie." Cynthia licked her lips and pressed them together. "William knew about your past."

Katie felt the blood rushing out of her face, through her body, and out of her feet. "What are you saying? What are you talking about?"

"He knew about Private Dancer and West End."

"Oh!" Katie threw the palms of her hands over her face and stumbled back. "No," she whispered. "No."

Cynthia placed both hands on the shoulders of her cousin's widow. "Katie, he's known all along, he told me."

"He never told me."

"He wanted you to tell him. He didn't care, Katie. He loved you that much."

Katie straightened. "He knew about David, didn't he?"

"Not until just this past week. He had hired an investigator years ago and found out about your past work experience. This week, while looking into the Caballeros, he rehired the investigator. That's when he learned about David."

"I'm so sorry." Katie began to cry.

Cynthia gave her a little shake. "We don't have time for that right now. You are the wife of William Webster. For his sake and for the sake of my family, I need to protect this information."

Katie nodded.

"Have you said anything to the agents—"

"No."

"Good. Let's keep it that way. Let me handle them from now on, okay?"

"Okay."

"I'll go back into the living room before they become suspicious. You help Maggie with the tea. Until I can get this straightened out, the less contact they have with you right now, the better."

"My main concern is for my client," Cynthia was saying to Phil and Agent Richards when Katie and Maggie returned with the tea service.

"Your client is not under any suspicion," Phil replied from his seat on the sofa. Agent Richards was sitting in a nearby chair, as was Cynthia. Marcy was standing near the French doors leading out to the veranda, observing the painting Ben purchased during their first trip to Paris together.

Maggie set the silver tray in the center of the coffee table. Katie sat on the sofa near Phil so that she could pour the hot tea for everyone. "Do you think I need legal protection, Cyn?"

Cynthia looked at Phil before answering. "That depends. Does she?"

Phil straightened and reached for the delicate cup and saucer that was being extended to him. He looked Katie directly in the eyes before answering. "No. I do not think she needs legal protection. But," he continued, looking back to Cynthia, "as her attorney, I am sure that you will want to be present when we question her tomorrow morning."

Katie handed a cup and saucer to Maggie for Agent Richards. "Tomorrow morning? Not tonight?"

Agent Richards answered as she accepted her tea. "Katie, surely you are exhausted. Our questions can wait until morning."

"But I have some questions," Katie insisted.

"Katie. . . ," Cynthia interrupted, almost pleading with her not to start anything so late in the evening.

"No," Katie insisted. "I have a lot of questions. Believe me, a lot. I won't ask them all now. But I have been wondering why my husband had the file and the FBI did not. Why, after he obtained the information from Andi, didn't he just hand it over?"

"Your husband received the information on Tuesday," Phil began. "He and Andi left that evening for Atlanta, where our agents greeted her. She then became a protected witness."

"Meaning?" Katie poured another cup of tea for Marcy and handed it to Maggie.

"Meaning wild horses can't get me to tell you where she is."

"I see. Again, the file?"

"William had meetings in Atlanta and did not return until Wednesday evening. He called me on Thursday morning, but I was away from my desk. On Friday he called again, but by this time I had been called out of town on an emergency. As I said to you earlier, I didn't think this was so serious. I told William when he first came to me with this that if we ran down every illegal escort service in this city, we would never have time to see our kids."

Katie nodded. "I understand. You also said that you think that Ben learned something else?"

Phil took a sip of his tea. "Mmmmm. Call it gut instinct. And I think he hid that file somewhere. He wouldn't have just left it at the hotel. My senses tell me it's in this house. We haven't tried to locate it. We wanted to wait until you arrived. You have a clearer feel for your own home."

Maggie muttered something unintelligible under her breath and walked out of the room. Katie smiled after her. "I'm afraid that the very idea of anyone going through her clean house is enough to raise her blood pressure."

Everyone smiled briefly at Katie's attempt to lighten the mood. Cynthia shifted in her seat. "Do you have any other questions you feel must be answered now, Katie? Or can they wait until the morning? I, for one, am very tired."

Katie shook her head. "I will have Maggie show everyone to their rooms. Phil, Agent Richards. . ."

Agent Richards stood. "Please. Everyone here is on a first name basis with the exception of me. Call me Sabrina."

Katie continued, "If you need anything during the night, Maggie's room is directly beside the kitchen."

When everyone but Katie and Marcy had left the room, Katie walked over to where she was standing. "What in the world are you so interested in over here?"

"This is a beautiful painting."

"It's *The Bread and the Wine*. Ben bought it in Paris."

"Does Ben ever buy anything in this country?"

Katie didn't answer.

"It is beautiful though."

"I spoke with Maggie upstairs," Katie said, changing the subject. "I'm more convinced than ever that you are right about the book. I'm also certain that Ben is not dead. I don't understand why he hasn't called me, but I trust that he knows what he's doing," she said firmly.

Marcy walked over to a nearby table and set her cup and saucer down. She returned to where Katie stood, placed her hands on Katie's arms, and gently said, "Katie, you have to be prepared for the possibility that that's not true. You know that, don't you?"

Katie's eyes brimmed with tears. She nodded. "Yes. But I prefer to think positively."

Marcy smiled at her. "Nothing wrong with that. If, in fact, he is alive, he would want you working on the clues he sent you in the book."

"I've thought about that, too. Meet me in my room in one hour. By that time I will have checked Ben's jewelry case."

"Why don't we get a few hours of sleep? You've got to be exhausted. . . . I know I am."

Katie frowned. "I guess so. Be at my door at four o'clock. There is a back staircase that leads to the kitchen. We'll come back downstairs to check the chess set and my golf clubs and racquet case. I still don't know about the other. . .'leave a kiss but in the cup'. . .though."

"Don't you?" Marcy asked, cocking an eyebrow.

"No, I don't," she replied firmly.

Marcy's eyes widened as she pointed to something behind her. Katie turned slowly.

And there it was.

The loaf of bread.

The cup of wine.

CHAPTER TWENTY-FIVE

An hour later Marcy lightly tapped on Katie's bedroom door. She opened it swiftly, whispering for her to come in, not wanting to take any chances that they would be heard.

Marcy paused a moment to take in the room around her. It was soft and feminine, like the woman who slept there, yet comfortable and bold as her husband had been. Or, perhaps, still was.

"Did you get any sleep?"

"I rested a bit. You?"

"No, not really. I keep thinking about the clues in the book. Did you find the cuff links?" she asked.

Katie extended a fist, then slowly opened her fingers to reveal two star-shaped cuff links and a key.

"A key," Marcy replied anxiously. She felt almost giddy with anticipation as to what this night would reveal to them, that she somehow had been knocked on the head and woken up in a Charlie Chan movie.

"I'm thinking that we will find a key in each of the locations."

"Then where to next?" Marcy asked.

"My tennis and golf equipment are kept in the pool house. The chess set is in Ben's office."

Marcy thought a moment, then nodded. "You decide. You know this house better than I do. Besides, there wasn't a single map in my room," she teased.

Katie smiled sweetly. "I say we go to the office first. It's near the back of the house on the first floor. From there, we slip out the kitchen door to the pool house. There's a cobblestone walkway that leads from the pool back to the verandah. We can come back that way, which leads us to the painting."

"I suspect that behind that painting is a wall safe. If I had been certain that no one would walk in on us earlier, I would have checked. But at least for now we have this much to begin with."

Katie walked over to a chest of drawers. "I have two small flashlights here," she commented. "Let me get them."

She retrieved the flashlights and returned to where Marcy was standing.

"What about an alarm? I'm sure a house like this is set with at least one."

"Don't worry. When we leave out the back door, I'll turn it off."

"And a key to get back in?"

"We'll just keep the door unlocked. We'll only be out for a little while."

"Then I guess we're set. Ready?"

Katie smiled slightly. "Ready."

The two friends stepped out into the hallway. Katie pulled the bedroom door to, but chose not to close it. Silently, she pointed for Marcy to follow her down a small hall to the right leading to a narrow staircase. They tiptoed down it quietly and into the dark kitchen. A trace of moonlight crept through the window, affording them just enough light to walk to a doorway leading to another hallway. Katie motioned for Marcy to remain quiet and to continue to follow her. Together, they made their way down the hall and into the large, masculine office where Ben spent so many quiet moments over the years. It had been his favorite room in the house; it had been completely his.

Katie flipped her flashlight on. The ray of light cut through the darkness and rested on an exquisite, large, and heavy chess set atop a round corner table flanked by two Louis XIV chairs.

"There it is," Katie whispered.

"Wow," Marcy commented. "That's some chess set."

They moved reverently toward it, as if by just being in this room they intruded on holy ground. "It is gorgeous, isn't it?" Katie replied when they stood beside it.

"Do you play? Or do you and your husband just collect massive table games?"

Katie shook her head. "It is one of a kind, but yes, we play. It's a lovely way to spend an evening." She closed her eyes momentarily and when they reopened, a memory seemed to linger within them. "Not that I ever won, of course." She smiled.

Marcy looked back to the set. The board was cut from black and white marble; the opposing pieces were cut from deep green and deep amber marble. The crowns resting upon the heads of the kings and queens were set with what appeared to be diamonds, rubies, and sapphires.

She reached out and carefully laid a fingertip against one of them. "Are these real?"

Katie nodded.

"Why don't you have these in a vault somewhere?"

Katie shook her head. "Ben always said that there is no point in having beautiful things unless you enjoy them."

Marcy's brow arched and she shook her head. "I cannot even begin to imagine living with all this. Come on, then. Check the rooks. You take the amber and I'll take the green."

Katie lifted one of the rooks, fully expecting something to be underneath, but found nothing. The second rook failed to provide what they were searching for as well. Marcy, too, came up empty. They looked at each other and shrugged.

"Any ideas?" Marcy whispered.

Katie pressed her lips together and shook her head.

"Nothing?"

"No."

Marcy looked around the room. Sitting in front of the wide, floor-to-ceiling, multipaned window was a massive, ornate cherry desk. An orderly desk set was positioned in the center, a globe on its left corner, and several books on travel on the right. Against the left wall was a plush, brushed leather sofa. An old, but well-maintained trunk served as a coffee table. A porcelain bowl filled with glass apples graced its center. Across the room stood a nineteenth-century breakfront filled with collectable pieces of porcelain, silver, and rare miniature books. There were narrow bookcases filled with books on either side of the windows. Marcy walked toward them, flipped on her flashlight, and began to read the highbrow titles. She felt Katie join her.

"Ben is an avid reader."

"So it seems," she whispered back. It was then that the light from her flashlight rested on a large coffee table book lying flat on one of the shelves. *Playing the Rook,* Marcy read. She extended her flashlight behind her and Katie took it, carefully keeping the light focused on the book. Katie watched intently as Marcy slid it off the shelf, opened, and fanned the pages to reveal a small key nestled between them.

"Well, look-a-here," Marcy said, a grin spread across her face.

"That makes two," Katie said. "This one is much smaller than the last."

"I noticed that. But I'm not going to worry about it now. Let's get going to the pool house."

They slipped into the pool house without consequence. Marcy noted immediately that, like everything else on the estate, it was large, elaborate, and tastefully decorated. Katie, guided by the beam of light from her flashlight, walked to a double, louver-door closet, opened it, and pulled a tennis racquet from a low shelf.

Marcy shone the beam of light from her flashlight toward Katie so that she could see without having to hold onto hers. Katie's face was bright and anxious in the light.

"Thanks," she said quietly. She set her flashlight at her feet. She

. began to unzip the leather case protecting the racquet as she continued, "My guess is that Ben would have placed another key here. The golf clubs are too cumbersome and difficult to go through, so. . ." She trailed off as she felt the soft interior of the case. "Nothing." She frowned.

In her attempts she pointed the handle of the racquet upward. Something bright and shiny at the base of the handle reflected in the light. "Katie!" Marcy exclaimed, stepping closer. "Look!"

Katie turned the handle toward her and smiled. "Bingo!"

Marcy pulled the tiny key from the base of the handle. "Looks like it's being held there by Silly Putty."

Katie turned the handle to her, then lightly touched the sticky surface. "Only a mother would say that," she whispered lightly.

Marcy continued, "That makes three clues, three keys. All we need now is a lead pipe, a candlestick, and Professor Plum in the library!"

Katie smiled. "The last two keys are so tiny."

"Lockbox keys, I'm thinking."

Katie nodded as she replaced the racquet in its case.

"Ready to see what's behind door number three?" Marcy asked her.

Again she nodded. But she did not speak.

Back in the house, Marcy quietly lifted the heavy painting from its hook while Katie held the flashlight. As expected, a lock-and-key safe was behind it. Marcy set the painting carefully at her feet, propping it against the wall, then reached into her pocket and brought out the largest of the three keys. It slipped easily into the keyhole. She turned it, heard the lock click, then pulled the safe's small handle. Katie gasped behind her. She was anxious; Marcy understood that. Her shaking hands caused the beam of light to dance around the vault's interior.

Within the short, wide interior of the safe was a lockbox. Marcy pulled it out, estimating its measurements to be fifteen by fifteen. It was heavy enough to indicate that another lockbox would be found inside. She reached inside the pockets of her slacks and retrieved one of the two keys. She tried it in the lock, but it didn't fit. She placed the key between her lips, again reached into her pocket, and brought out the last key, hoping against hope that it would fit.

It did.

"Hurry," Katie whispered as she opened it.

Together, they peered into the box to find another lockbox. Marcy walked over to a nearby table, Katie on her heels. She gently placed the box on top of the table, removed the key from between her lips, and slipped it into the keyhole, all the while praying for a perfect fit.

It was.

Marcy opened the lockbox slowly. Reverently. Whatever they found inside just might change Katie's life and she didn't want to rush the moment.

Katie felt differently. "Hurry," she said again.

Within the security of the metal box was a manila envelope. Across the top, in Ben's neat handwriting, was the name: Caballero.

"Oh, my goodness," Katie whispered, long and sweet.

Marcy pulled the envelope out, tucked it under her arm, and whispered back, "Let's get this stuff back into the safe before we go any further. We can go back upstairs to look through this file."

"Should I wake Cynthia?"

Marcy shook her head. "I want you to do me a favor, Katie. You know how much I love research. Let me go through this file, okay? I want to make some notes. I may never get this chance again. . . . Once they get hold of it, I'll never know what was there originally and what was taken out. When the news gets out, you'll need a reporter who knows the truth. I'm a reporter, or nearly one. Please?"

Katie nodded in agreement. "Okay. But in the morning we give it to Cynthia."

"Agreed."

CHAPTER TWENTY-SIX

Exhausted, Phil Silver walked into the guest room to which he had been assigned. He took his cell phone over to the bed with him, called his wife to say goodnight, then laid it on the bedside table. He fell immediately to sleep, a sleep so deep it seemed dreamless.

It was as if only seconds passed when he heard the intrusive ringing of the cell phone beside him. Wearily he sat up, turned on the bedside lamp, and reached for the slim, black phone.

"Hello," he answered huskily.

"Agent Silver, this is Dispatch. We have a call for you from Sheriff Carlisle in Brooksboro, Georgia, Sir."

Phil ran the thumb and index finger of his left hand over his eyes. "Yeah, yeah. Patch him through." Five long seconds went by before he heard the voice on the other end of the line.

"Agent Silvers?" A strong, masculine southern accent asked.

"Silver," Phil corrected. "Agent Silver." *Why is it that southerners love to add syllables where none exist and pluralize nouns and names?* he asked himself. He was usually a tolerant man, but as groggy and tired as he was right now, poor language skills grated on his nerves. "What can I do for you?"

"This is Sheriff Carlisle here from Brooksboro." Phil flexed his jaw muscles. Even during an emergency couldn't these people speed things up just a little?

"Yes, Sir," he said, sighing deeply. "Is something wrong down there?"

The man on the other end chuckled. Phil pictured the slightly over-weight, graying, mustachioed man he had met briefly upon his arrival in Brooksboro. "Well, I guess it's all according to how you look at it."

"Meaning?"

"I just got a call from Charlie Waters. I believe his wife is there with you in New York."

"Yeah?"

"Seems he's got some bad boys tied up in his barn you gentlemen up there might be interested in. 'Escaped Yankees,' they told me. We're a mite interested in sending them right back where they came from!"

"Is that so?" A smile started to form on his lips despite himself. He couldn't imagine what this had to do with him.

"Three strapping young fellows. Say they work for one Bucky Caballero," Sheriff Carlisle said, and he chuckled again.

Phil's eyes shot open. *"What?"*

CHAPTER TWENTY-SEVEN

Inside Katie's bedroom, Marcy sat in a comfortable, overstuffed chair. Her feet, crossed at the ankles, were propped on the matching ottoman. Her watch told her it was nearly five forty-five in the morning. For the past half hour she had been carefully examining the contents of the manila envelope she and Katie had found in the downstairs wall safe. Katie had long since fallen asleep on the nearby sofa, her head resting comfortably on a soft, round pillow, her body drawn up in a fetal position.

Marcy stole a quick glance at her. Poor soul, she thought. She endured quite a day. . .quite a night. . .quite a life. But at this moment it would have been difficult for anyone to read her pain. Her face was relaxed in peaceful slumber, her lips slightly parted, her glossy hair lying across her cheek like a child's gentle touch. At that moment, Marcy felt that she alone understood who the real Katie was. Perhaps even more than her beloved Ben. After all, she had known her forever and, in spite of their separation, the moment she had seen her old friend jogging up the sidewalk, the connection between the two of them had rebonded. Marcy shook her head slowly. She would never let her go again. Never again.

Katie had tried to stay awake and help Marcy with the notes she was scribbling on a steno pad, but no sooner had they pulled the contents from the envelope than she curled up on the sofa, closed her eyes, and, with a final yawn, surrendered to the much-needed sleep. Marcy, however, true to her old investigative desires, remained alert, noting Andrea's detailed records, enormous cash flow, impressive client list, and carefully constructed escort profiles. She found old records on David Franscella, who was, at one time, a male escort and was now married to Mattie Caballero. Marcy frowned, recalling the day that Katie believed she had seen him in Savannah. That was only a few days ago, but at this moment it felt a lifetime ago. Continuing on, she skimmed over the THP employee records of Juan Ramierez and wondered what he had to do with Bucky Caballero or Andrea's.

Perhaps, she pondered, the young concierge was the link between THP, Andrea's, and Caballero. It made perfect sense. Guests of the hotel, looking for an "escort," would ask the concierge, who would direct them to Jacqueline's beautiful manager, Andi. Being the concierge also placed him in a perfect position to watch over Caballero's investments: Jacqueline's and Andi Daniels.

Near the back of the copies was a small envelope with Katie's name neatly penned across the center. Marcy momentarily entertained the thought of waking Katie, but quickly decided against it. She was finally resting, and whatever her husband left for her would be better received after a little sleep. Folding it, Marcy placed it in the pocket of her slacks.

Marcy yawned and realized that she, too, was exhausted. She replaced the papers in the envelope, slipped them under the cushion beneath her for safekeeping, stretched languidly, closed her eyes, and, just before falling asleep, thought, *Note to self: Talk to Charlie about my going to work as an investigative reporter.*

A moment later a sound in the room awoke her. She groggily assumed that Katie was leaving the sofa for the bed. She blinked hard, opening her eyes just long enough to see a large fist coming toward her temple.

Katie jerked herself upright to see the shadowy figure of David Franscella standing over Marcy's slumping form. She gasped, trying to catch her breath to scream. Before she could, David bounded over to her and wrapped a gloved hand around her mouth.

"Shut up!" he hissed through clenched teeth. He jerked his hand tighter around her jaw and mouth. She felt momentarily sickened by the sweet pungency of the leather glove. It felt hot and wet against the tenderness of her flesh. "Where is it?" he demanded.

She struggled against him. He wrapped his free arm around her torso and held her firmly against him. "Don't make me hurt you, Katie. I'll do it. You know I'll do it."

She relaxed as best she could despite her apprehension. Fear gripped her fiercely. She remembered, almost relived, the pain of his savage physical abuse. He had beaten her, violently killing their child in the brutality and uproar of his untamed rampage. He had left her bloodied, bruised, and unable to conceive another child. Ben's child. Because of him. . .because of Bucky Caballero. . .she would never know the joy of carrying Ben's baby, of pushing life from her body and into the world, or of seeing her husband, her beloved Ben, cradle the tiny form in his strong arms.

She struggled again, forcing her elbow into the firm flesh of his abdomen. Unfazed by her comparatively feeble attempts, he gripped her all the more strongly. She kicked her feet, attempting to knock something. . .anything. . .to the floor and hopefully wake Phil or Sabrina.

David wrapped one of his legs around both of hers. "That's it!" he spoke tersely. "I'll snap your body in two like a pencil if you keep this up!"

Again she relaxed and he spoke against her face, his breath hot against her ear. "Now, then. Take me downstairs to your husband's office. I'll give you five minutes to find that file. You make one sound. . .one little peep. . .and I'll blow your head off. You hear me? Yours, your little friend's over there, and that old lady downstairs."

Katie cut wild eyes over at him. Had he hurt Maggie?

"You understand me?"

She nodded. She wasn't sure what she was going to do, but if she could get him downstairs, she could at least buy time.

"Then let's go," he ordered, jerking her toward the door.

Marcy wrapped her hands around her head and moaned. It felt as if a thousand explosives had gone off inside. She blinked a few times, trying to shake the cobwebs from her memory. Opening her eyes, she looked around the luxuriously decorated bedroom and tried to recall exactly where she was. She straightened herself in the chair, looked over to the sofa still bearing the imprint of a recumbent form on the one-piece down pillow.

"Katie!" she screamed and bolted for the door.

"What?" Phil Silver asked again. "No, don't repeat yourself, please. But tell me again, who took them to a barn?. . . I see. . . Waters, did you say?. . . All right, I'll get somebody down there first thing in the morning. What time is it anyway?. . . Is it already morning?. . . Okay, I'll call someone in a few hours. In the meantime. . .well, I'm assuming you'll put them in jail." It was more a question than a direct statement.

Sheriff Carlisle chuckled again. "I suppose by law I have to."

"I'll call you first thing in the morning. . .in the real morning," Phil replied, shaking his head at the absurdity of three men tied up in a barn.

He no sooner replaced the phone on the bedside table and lay back against the pillow when he heard Marcy's voice from down the hallway.

"Katie!" she was screaming.

Phil leapt from his bed, reached for the gun that was never more than a few feet from him, and ran toward the door. Opening it, he found his partner making her way into the hallway, a wild, dazed look on her face. They nearly ran head-on with Marcy, who was heading for the stairs.

Phil grabbed her by the shoulders. "What is it?" he demanded.

"Someone's got Katie! Someone's got. . ."

The gunshot reverberated throughout the house. The three turned toward the stairs and began running, taking the steps two at a time.

"Stay back," Phil ordered Marcy.

"Yeah, right," Marcy said sarcastically.

They stopped when they heard another gunshot, then ran in the direction of its origin, Ben's study. Skidding to a stop at the door, the two agents swung into the room, their guns held ready.

"Katie," Marcy breathed heavily at what they found inside the room.

Katie, bruised and clutching the side of Ben's desk from her position on the floor, was sobbing quietly. David Franscella lay sprawled across the floor, deep red bloodstains spreading across the front of his shirt. His lifeless eyes were open and fixed. Maggie stood firmly near the door with her feet braced apart, her arms limp at her side, and a gun clutched tightly in her hand.

EPILOGUE

"I can't believe I slept through the whole thing," Cynthia said from the doorway of the kitchen, her hands planted firmly on her hips.

"I still can't believe that two people I thought were intelligent pulled something like this," Phil Silver said from his position at the table. Katie sat below him, sipping from the hot cup of tea that Maggie set before her just moments before. She tasted the faint flavor of whiskey and smiled. *Dear Maggie,* she thought tenderly, *always believing in her toddies!*

Katie looked up at the man who gave her a somewhat authoritative stare. "We had no idea that David was going to break in like that," she whispered. "I left the door unlocked when we went out to the pool house. That must be how he got in."

"That's hardly the point, Katie. Concealing substantive information from law enforcement is a crime. I could get both of you on this one." He looked over at the brave woman's lawyer, who frowned, then to the housekeeper, who'd kept herself busy since the ambulance had been called some forty-five minutes earlier.

Maggie turned to him and shook her finger in his direction. "Now, you listen here! You'll do no such thing!" she exclaimed with righteous indignation.

Phil shook his head. "No, of course, I won't. For no other reason than out of respect for her husband."

Marcy walked in just then with Sabrina Richards behind her, clutching the manila envelope to her chest. "Am I going to need a lawyer?" She grinned at Cynthia. She joined Katie at the table, placed her hands on her shoulders, and gave a gentle squeeze. "You know, things like this never happen in Brooksboro. This is the biggest adventure of my life."

"You'd be surprised at what happens in Brooksboro," Phil said. "I got a phone call this morning that I followed up on a little while ago. Pray tell, you are the wife of Charlie Waters, correct?"

Marcy's smile fell. "Yes. What's happened to my husband?"

"Nothing. It's just that he and two of his friends have rounded up three men who went to Mrs. Morgan's home last night."

"Mama?" Katie moved in her seat.

"Your mother is fine. It's the three men you should be worried about."

Katie exhaled slowly.

Sabrina spoke from the door. "The ambulance is ready to leave, Phil. You may want to talk with one of the attendants."

Phil excused himself, but not before pointing to Katie and Marcy and ordering, "You two stay put. We need to talk."

Sabrina followed him down the hall.

Cynthia stepped toward the table. "Are you okay, Katie?"

Katie nodded. "Thank you, Cyn. I'm fine."

"I'm going out there to talk to Phil and Sabrina, then. Don't say anything to anyone unless I'm in this room though. Both of you."

Marcy raised her eyebrows. "Got it."

Maggie wiped her hands on a dishtowel. "You be a good lass and drink up on that hot tea."

Katie smiled lovingly at her. "Thanks, Maggie." She felt hot tears in her eyes.

"I'm going to see how much damage that no-account did to my carpet," she muttered. "But if you need me, you call me."

"I will."

She walked out of the kitchen, leaving Katie and Marcy alone. Marcy moved to the opposite side of the table. They locked eyes. At this moment, words were hardly necessary, but Marcy spoke anyway. "So that was David Franscella?"

"Yes."

"Where do you think Maggie learned to shoot like that?"

"I never knew she even kept a gun."

"Good thing for you she did."

Katie shuddered. "Ben never liked guns in the house. Ben is Maggie's employer, but she wiped his nose when he was a boy. In a way, she's more mother than housekeeper. So I guess if she wanted a gun. . ."

"She'd fit right in back home, huh?" Marcy moved to sit in a chair. "Katie, they still don't know where Caballero and his sister are. They suspect out of the country."

"They'll find them," Katie said with certainty.

"I suspect you're right on that one. Especially with the information that's in that envelope."

"What did you learn? Anything new?"

"I know the layout of the whole operation. The real patsy is going to be Juan Ramierez."

"The concierge?"

Marcy nodded. "He was not only an employee of the hotel, he was also an employee of Caballero. You see, visitors and guests would come to Juan to. . .you know. . .ask about certain services. Like escort services."

"Prostitution," Katie interjected.

"Exactly. Juan would send them to Andi at Jacqueline's, also owned by Caballero. The boutique business was doing okay for a boutique, but not bringing in the kind of money that Caballero wanted. Even with the kind of money he was making at his real estate company. So he ran an escort service out of it. He's not the first one to think of this. It happens all the time. And there's no telling how long he's been doing it. The records that Andi supplied will tell all that."

"And if Stephen Lewis hadn't told Ben. . ."

"It could have gone on forever. Apparently the escort service was a favorite among the local politicians. You should see some of the names and titles on that client list!"

Katie sighed deeply. "I think I'd rather not. No wonder keeping the service running was so important and profitable to Bucky."

Marcy nodded in agreement. "What's next, Katie?"

She shook her head, looking away. "I don't know, exactly."

"Will you stay here or go home?"

Katie looked back at Marcy and smiled. "Home?"

"Brooksboro, Katie. Is Brooksboro your home? Or here?"

She ran her fingertip lightly around the rim of the teacup before answering. "Brooksboro is so dear to me," she began in earnest. "But it's not my home anymore. I don't truly fit in with the people. Not even Mama."

"But things are better between you and your mother."

"I haven't had time to tell you about that, but yes, thank you. Much better. She and I talked for a long time the other day. It's as if she found my heart and I found hers. . .and. . ."

"And?"

"And God's."

Marcy nodded her head in understanding. "So, what'll you do?"

"I think I'll stay here for awhile and see what happens." She picked up the cup and saucer, stood, and carried it over to the kitchen sink.

Marcy stood, but remained by the table. "Be careful, Katie." It was all she knew to say.

Katie turned to face her friend. "I will. It's just that. . .I don't believe my husband is dead and I want to stay here and wait for him to return."

"I understand."

She smiled, resting her hip against the counter. "Thank you, Marcy," she whispered.

Marcy walked over and took her friend by the hand. "No," she said. "Thank you."

Katie smiled. "For what?"

"For coming home," she said firmly, then added with a whisper, "for surviving. Just promise me that no matter where you call home, you and I will stay in contact from now on."

"I promise," Katie said, squeezing Marcy's hand. "Now, let's go see what's going on out there. You may need it for the article I'm sure you're going to write."

Marcy grinned, took her hand, and linked it through her arm and began walking toward the door. Suddenly she stopped short. "Wait a sec!" she said, slapping her hand over the pocket of her slacks.

Katie turned. "What is it?"

"I forgot this," she said, displaying a folded white envelope.

Katie took it and unfolded it. "It's from Ben," she whispered.

Walking back to the table, she opened the envelope, pulled out a single sheet of paper, and began to read. Marcy watched her intently, heard her gasp. When Katie swayed slightly, Marcy moved quickly to catch her.

"Sit here," she said, pulling a chair over.

Katie complied. The paper floated down to her feet.

Marcy retrieved it and handed it back to her friend.

Katie shook her head. Her eyes were misty and dazed. "Read it," she whispered.

Marcy turned the paper toward herself and read.

Do not stand at my grave and weep.
I am not there. I am not asleep.
Do not stand at my grave and cry.
I am not there.
I did not die.

THE AUTHORS

Eva Marie Everson is the author of *True Love: Engaging Stories of Real-Life Proposals* (Promise Press, August 2000). She is also the coauthor of *Pinches of Salt, Prisms of Light*. Eva Marie and her husband have three children and live in Florida.

G. W. Francis Chadwick writes a financial trading advice column which is syndicated worldwide, teaches seminars for experienced investors, and specializes in stock trading systems and strategies. He makes his home in Atlanta, Georgia with two dogs, Blaaze and Cephus.